FAR FROM HOME

It's 1940 and Staff Nurse Polly Brown is far from home... She has been granted a posting at Cliffehaven Memorial Hospital on the south coast to be near her badly-injured husband, Adam. But her decision has meant that she has had to part with her beloved five-year-old daughter, Alice, who is travelling to safety in Canada. Polly's heart is torn in two as she says goodbye to Alice. But as she confronts the fact that Adam may not survive his injuries, a telegram arrives. The boat Alice was on has been torpedoed by a German U-boat...

FAR FROM HOME

FAR FROM HOME

by

Ellie Dean

Magna Large Print Books
Long Preston, North Yorkshire,
BD23 4ND, England.

British Library Cataloguing in Publication Data.

Dean, Ellie
   Far from home.

   A catalogue record of this book is
   available from the British Library

   ISBN   978-0-7505-3692-9

First published in Great Britain in 2012 by Arrow Books

Copyright © Ellie Dean 2012

Cover illustration © Samantha Groom

Ellie Dean has asserted her right under the Copyright, Designs and Patents Act, 1988 to be identified as the author of this work

Published in Large Print 2013 by arrangement with Random House Group Ltd.

Magna Large Print is an imprint of Library Magna Books Ltd.

Printed and bound in Great Britain by
T.J. (International) Ltd., Cornwall, PL28 8RW

Jean Partridge, and Daireen McKinley.
Two inspirational women.
RIP

Chapter One

September, 1940

Polly hadn't meant to fall asleep, but the anxiety and fear that had plagued her for weeks had finally caught up with her, and she'd succumbed. She opened her eyes, attuned not to the usual Herefordshire dawn chorus of birds, but to the steady, soft breathing of the sleeping child in her arms. Loath to wake her little daughter, Polly gently drew her closer, inhaling the sweet baby smell of her as she kissed the fair curls that lay in disarray on the pillow. Alice was only five and in all of Polly's twenty-three years she had never known such anguish, for this would be their last few precious hours together.

The knowledge that it could be many months, perhaps even years, before she would see her again brought hot tears rolling down Polly's cheeks. Yet she didn't wipe them away, for they were her only release from the heartache – the only visible proof she could allow herself in these quiet, still moments before she had to face the day.

Her lips fluttered on the peachy curve of her daughter's cheek, over the tiny brows and smooth forehead and into the sweet hollow of her neck where the very essence of her child could be breathed in and held like a precious

11

perfume. It was a scent Polly silently vowed she would carry with her until they could be together again.

Alice squirmed against her, her thumb seeking her mouth as she rolled away from Polly's gentle embrace and snuggled under the blankets.

To Polly it was as if her daughter was already distancing herself; already preparing, albeit unknowingly, for the long journey ahead that would take her far from her mother's arms to another country. Polly smoothed the tangled mass of her own hair away from her face, eyes closed, the tears soaking the pillow as she silently gave vent to the torment that had beset her ever since her darling husband, Adam, had been wounded in France.

Fate had been cruel as the shadows of war had lengthened and the threat of invasion grew with every passing day. Adam's injuries had brought him back to Cliffehaven Memorial Hospital on the south coast, far from Herefordshire, and now, directly in the flight path of the ever-increasing enemy bombing raids on London. Her anxious attempts to get more information about his condition had been constantly thwarted by the matron at Cliffehaven, but it was clear he was not well enough to come home and be nursed in Hereford County Hospital, where she worked.

Fearing he might die before she could see him, Polly had secured a Staff Nurse post at the Cliffehaven Memorial to be with him, but soon realised Alice would not be safe there. With her mother, sister and nephews leaving for Uncle

Peter's farm in Canada, she'd had no choice but to agree to Alice going with them. But it was a bitter dilemma, and she was still torn with doubts that she was doing the right thing.

Aware that she could no longer contain her emotions, and not wanting to disturb Alice and frighten her, she eased the blanket over the tiny shoulders, touched the glossy curls and left the bed. Dragging the shabby dressing gown over her thin nightdress, she swiftly left the bedroom and hurried down the freezing landing to the even icier bathroom. With the door firmly locked behind her, she sank to the floor and surrendered to her anguish.

'Polly? Polly, let me in.' The commanding voice was accompanied by a rap on the door. 'Come on. Don't make this harder for yourself than it already is.'

Her sister's voice cut through the fog of despair, and she stumbled to her feet. Smearing away the tears, she dragged her thick, curly hair into a rough knot on the top of her head, pinning it in place with the combs she kept in her dressing-gown pocket. 'I'm all right, Megan, really,' she sniffed. 'Just give me a minute, will you?'

'Only if you promise not to stay in there too long,' her sister replied. 'Wallowing in self-pity won't do you any good, you know.'

'Go away, Meg. You'll wake Alice, and I need some time to myself.' Polly wasn't usually so sharp with her older sister, but there were times when she didn't appreciate Megan's rather bossy manner – and this was one of them.

'Get on with it then,' Megan said crossly. 'I

13

need to get the boys washed and ready, and it's not fair you hogging the bathroom half the morning.'

Polly sniffed back the last of her tears as she listened to her sister's footsteps retreat along the landing and down the stairs. Megan was only two years the elder and meant well, and her abruptness had certainly forced Polly to take control of her emotions, but then Megan wasn't about to be parted from their mother, or her children.

Determined not to give in to the debilitating fear that she was about to lose everything she held dear, Polly lit the gas boiler and hurried through her morning ritual. She'd discovered long ago that calm could be restored with the familiar and mundane, and she welcomed it now.

Having washed and cleaned her teeth, she wiped the condensation from the mirror and unpinned her hair. It spilled over her shoulders and round her face in an autumnal tangle of gold and russet curls which sparked in the early sunlight pouring through the bathroom window. Adam called it her crowning glory, and had made her promise never to cut it, no matter how much Matron disapproved. At the thought of her husband, her resolve faltered, but she determinedly steeled herself against more tears. Megan was right. They achieved very little.

Her wide grey eyes stared back at her from beneath winged eyebrows and dark lashes, the sunlight emphasising the paleness of her skin and the shadows and hollows that told of sleepless nights and tortured thoughts. She looked away from her reflection as she brushed her hair and

14

twisted it into thick rolls on either side of her face, tying it back at the nape with a strip of ribbon. There was no need to pin it into the usual neat bun, for she wasn't working on the wards today, and wouldn't be nursing again until she arrived at the Cliffehaven Memorial.

Polly shoved the contents of the bathroom cabinet into her sponge bag, resolutely refusing to think of Adam's injuries and what she might find at the end of that long journey to the south coast. Today she must concentrate on Alice, keep her emotions under control, and make sure their parting caused the child as little trauma as possible.

Hurrying into the bedroom, she found Alice was still asleep, so she dressed swiftly in skirt, blouse, cardigan and sensible shoes and then finished her packing. Placing her two suitcases on the landing with her gas-mask box and overcoat, she returned to the bedroom and took a moment to instil the memories of the little house she wouldn't see again until after the war.

Polly had received the signed tenancy agreement two weeks before and the family from London would be moving in the next day. She'd stored away all the precious things she and Adam had collected over their six years of marriage, and locked them in a trunk in the attic. But the memories lingered so strongly she could almost hear Adam's tread on the stairs, his voice softly calling her – and feel his arms round her as he told her he loved her. They had been childhood sweethearts – their first kiss shared during harvest when they were barely fourteen – their last as

15

he'd prepared to board the troop train which had taken him to France.

She let her gaze wander over the bed where Alice had been conceived, to the sturdy furniture they'd had such fun finding in junk shops, the rag rugs she'd made and the pretty curtains she'd hung at the window. With a deep sigh, she tore her thoughts from the past and, after a long, lingering look of love, gently drew Alice from her sleep.

Polly and Adam had scrimped and saved to buy this little terraced house on the edge of Hereford, close to the hospital and the garage, where Adam worked as a mechanic before the war. They'd added a bathroom and inside lavatory, which they considered the height of luxury, and lovingly tended the pocket-handkerchief square of garden at the back. They'd shared their joy in Alice and been happy here, although Polly freely admitted it had none of the charm of Blackthorn Farm, which had been her family home for two generations. But she and Adam were the first in their families to actually own a house, and that made it very special. Polly prayed that the people from London would take good care of it.

Alice looked sweet in the little smocked dress which had puff sleeves and a broad sash at the waist. With white socks and sandals, and matching ribbons in her hair, it was as if she was dressed for a party. But Alice had strong views on what she wanted to wear, even though she was only five, and Polly was happy to indulge her today. Adding a cardigan to ward off the chill of

16

this early September morning, Polly helped her carefully negotiate the narrow stairs down to the kitchen which suddenly seemed cramped with so many people milling round.

Megan was still in her dressing gown as she busily stirred the porridge at the small range. Their mother, Enid, cradled a cup of tea as she smoked her first cigarette of the day and leant against the stone sink watching her twin grand-sons career round with their paper planes. Sam and Will were seven, with identical freckles across their snub noses, the same shock of bright red hair, and lusty voices. Dressed in their school uniforms, their long socks were already half-mast, the ties and shirt collars askew.

'About time too,' said Megan, who seemed un-able to emerge from her recent bad mood. She put the bowls of porridge on the table and swept her auburn hair from her forehead with the back of her hand. 'Sit down,' she ordered the boys, 'and stop making that awful racket. The last thing I need today is one of my headaches.'

'They're just letting off steam,' said Enid. 'Why don't you go and get ready in peace? Pol and I will keep an eye on things here.' Her grey eyes and faded auburn hair seemed to accentuate the paleness of her skin and the recent sorrow that had lined and aged her gentle face.

Megan took off the apron she'd tied round her thickening waist and threw it on to the back of a chair. Without another word, she left the kitchen and stomped upstairs.

'There are times,' said Polly, 'that I wish I'd never asked Meg to move in with me. She's not

17

exactly been the most pleasant company lately.'

Enid crushed the cigarette, out and drained the last of her tea before reaching for Polly's hand. 'Give your sister a bit of leeway, love. It can't be easy for her having to move out of her home in Birmingham to stay here especially with Tom fighting abroad and this baby on the way.'

'It's not easy for me either,' Polly replied softly. Tears threatened again as her mother squeezed her fingers. 'I can't do this, Mum. I can't let Alice go.'

All three children were wide-eyed with curiosity as Polly's tears began to fall. Enid rounded the table, fed Alice the last of her porridge, wiped her face clean and helped her down. 'Run along and play with Sam and Will in the other room, there's a good girl.'

She shooed them out of the kitchen and closed the door firmly. 'We've been through this umpteen times, Polly. There's no point in wavering now. We're leaving, and that's an end to it.'

'But I can't let her go. I don't want any of you to go. It's too dangerous.'

'Nonsense. The government wouldn't have organised the Children's Overseas Reception Board if they thought we were in any danger.' Enid sat next to her and took her hands again. 'The convoys have been leaving on a regular basis for Canada, South Africa, even Australia and New Zealand, and every one of them has been escorted by the Royal Navy and got through unscathed. There are to be nineteen ships in our convoy. It will be no different for us.'

'But the war has escalated. The supply convoys

are being bombed in the Channel; there are raids on London and all the important docks and factories. They've even started targeting the farms to ruin the harvest. How can you *possibly* be certain they won't attack a convoy crossing the Atlantic?'

'I can't guarantee anything,' Enid replied softly, 'but it surely won't be more dangerous than living right on the coast and in the direct flight path to London?' She pushed back her chair and reached for the packet of Woodbines which rarely left her side. 'Adam needs you, Polly, probably more than Alice at the moment, and your nursing skills have never been so important.' She lit a cigarette and blew a stream of smoke to the ceiling, clearly frustrated by this endless argument which had gone round in circles for weeks.

'I know all that,' Polly said with a tremulous sigh, 'but having to choose between my husband and child is impossible.'

Enid was staring out of the window at the suburban street and the line of houses opposite, her small, neat figure ramrod straight in her lightweight two-piece suit. 'Sometimes we don't get the luxury of choice at all,' she murmured. 'If your father hadn't had that fatal heart attack we'd still be living on the farm, out of harm's way, doing our bit for the war effort. As it is, Blackthorn Farm has new tenants and Megan and I are about to leave everything we've ever known to ensure the safety of our little family. You could come too – your nursing skills would be welcome – but your place is with your husband now – his needs must come first.'

Polly dipped her chin and toyed with the teaspoon, her unsteady hand making it rattle in the saucer. She'd heard all the arguments before, had gone over and over them in her head until she thought she'd go mad – and although she knew her mother's advice couldn't be faulted, she simply couldn't bear the thought of parting with Alice. 'What if Alice gets sick or has an accident and I'm not there? I'd never forgive myself if anything happened to her – or to any of you for that matter.'

'What if you abandon Adam and he dies without ever seeing you again?' Enid turned from the window, hands on hips, expression stern. 'I'm sorry to be so abrupt, Polly, but I've had enough of this. You've made your choice, the arrangements are in place. Alice is coming with me, and you're going to Cliffehaven to be with Adam.' She stubbed out the cigarette with vigour and grabbed the discarded apron. 'And if you start crying again,' she said tremulously, 'it will start me off. So I'd be obliged if you'd pull yourself together and help me with this blasted washing-up.'

Polly resolutely fought her tears and reached for the tea towel. Her mother was right, she admitted silently. Whether it broke her heart or not, she had to accept the fact that Alice and the rest of her family would be leaving within hours for Liverpool and the ship that would take them to Canada and a new life.

The shouts of the porters, the raised voices and the great exhalations of steam from the engines echoed in the vast concourse and resounded off the huge glass and steel roof as Enid found a porter to stow their luggage on a trolley and guide them to the correct platform.

The station was a hub for travelling to all points of the country, and now it was busier than ever with troop trains and arriving evacuees. Kitbags, suitcases and trolleys loaded with luggage and wooden cages housing live chickens only served to hamper the pedestrians.

It was market day, and the confusion was increased when a flock of sheep strayed on to the concourse from the street. To shouts of encouragement from the amused onlookers, the red-faced shepherd and bewildered sheepdog tried to round them up. The unwanted help of several over-eager Australian soldiers merely made things worse, and it was some time before the poor shepherd managed to round up his flock and get it safely back outside.

The children thought this was great fun, and it took all Megan's determination to stop the boys from joining in the fray.

'Look, Mummy,' piped Alice, jumping up and down in delight. 'That one's come back.' She giggled as the ewe hurtled on to the concourse and barged through a knot of chattering women who scattered with cries of alarm as they tried to keep their balance, and their dignity.

Polly could see the humour in the situation, but her smile was fixed, her face muscles already aching from the effort. She watched as a brawny Australian made a grab for the animal and successfully hauled it up and carried it outside to shouts of 'Good on yer, mate,' from his comrades.

21

From everything she'd heard about the Anzac troops' antics, she was surprised the ewe hadn't been smuggled into a kitbag and taken off to be prepared for a clandestine feast.

'Now the fun's over, we'd better get to your train. It's due to leave in ten minutes.' The middle-aged porter grasped the handle of his trolley and they followed meekly in his wake.

'Are you coming on the train, Mummy?' Alice looked up at her, blue eyes wide and suddenly uncertain.

'Not this time,' she murmured, clutching the small hand. 'Mummy's got to go and see Daddy. But Grandma and Aunt Meg will look after you until I get back.'

Alice's bottom lip began to tremble, and to forestall tears, which would only make her feel worse, Polly lifted her up and settled her on her hip. 'Look at the trains,' she said brightly, determined to distract her. 'Isn't it exciting? And see how the steam's coming out of that funnel! Shall we go and watch the man stoking the fire?'

'Don't want to.' Alice buried her head in Polly's shoulder.

'That's all right,' she soothed. 'And anyway, it's better we find you a lovely seat on your very own train, isn't it?'

Alice didn't reply, but buried her face deeper into Polly's neck. Polly kept walking, every step taking her closer to the platform at the far end of the concourse, every breath more shallow as her heart clenched and her chest tightened. She wanted this moment to be over – but then she wished it could last forever. It was as if she was in a dream, a terrible dream that she longed to wake from.

With Alice heavy in her arms, she swiftly bought a platform ticket and followed the others through the barrier. Her steps slowed as Megan and Enid identified their luggage from the pile on the porter's trolley and orchestrated its placement in the guard's van.

Alice clung more tightly to her neck. 'I want you to come with me,' she muttered. 'Don't wanna go with Grandma.'

Polly kissed her cheek and set her on her feet. She straightened the child's overcoat, tugging at the velvet collars and making sure the buttons were all done up against the chill sweeping along the platform. 'Grandma will be really sad if you don't go with her,' she said softly, not quite able to meet those wide blue eyes. 'And what about Sam and Will? Surely you don't want to miss all the fun they'll be having, do you?'

Alice thought about this for a moment and finally shook her head, making the curls bounce.

'Good girl,' Polly managed, fighting back her tears, desperately trying to keep her voice light and unwavering. 'Now, let me say bye-bye to everyone, and then we'll find you a lovely seat on this great big train. When you're settled, Auntie Megan has a special treat for you.'

The child's face brightened. 'What is it?'

'You'll find out in a minute.' Polly wanted to scoop her up and hold her, breathe in her scent, feel that sturdy little warm body against her own for one last time. But if she did, she knew she would find it even harder to let her go. She turned to the twins instead and, much to Meg's annoyance, ruffled their hair. 'Be good,' she said with mock sternness. 'And remember to send me a postcard now and again.'

The boys nodded bashfully and hastily clambered aboard the train, jostling to get to the window seat first.

'I'm sorry I was sharp this morning,' said Megan as she drew Polly into her arms. 'But this isn't easy for me either. I'll take care of Alice, don't fret.'

Polly nodded, unable to speak for the tearful lump that was growing in her throat. She clung to her sister, regretting the sharp words and small resentments that had coloured their relationship over the years. She loved her, would miss her horribly.

'Take care, Meg,' she managed finally, as she handed over the three bags of farthing chews.

Meg's eyes were bright with tears as she gave her one last hug and took Alice's small hand. 'I'll write,' she said hoarsely.

Polly watched helplessly as Megan gathered up Alice and took her on to the train. Blinking rapidly, she fought the tears as Alice perched on the seat and immediately began to open her bag of sweets. It seemed her child was quite content, unaware of the importance of this heartbreaking moment.

The guard blew his whistle, and the doors began to slam like a salvo of rifle shots along the length of the train. Polly crushed Enid to her. 'There are so many things I wanted to say to you, Mum, but now the time has come, I can't think straight. But I love you, Mum, and I'm going to miss you terribly.'

'I love you too, Polly. That's all that needs to be said.' Enid withdrew gently from Polly's fierce embrace. 'Stay safe, darling, and give my love to Adam when you see him. Your Uncle Peter will look after all of us, so don't fret, and, as soon as we arrive, I'll write you a long letter.'

'Don't let Alice forget me,' Polly pleaded.

'I won't, I promise. The photographs are in my handbag.' With tears in her eyes, she gave Polly a last, fleeting kiss and turned abruptly away.

Polly felt isolated among the swirl of activity on the platform as she gazed at those beloved faces at the open window. She wanted to reach out and touch them one more time – to say all the things she'd meant to say. But it was too late. The guard's whistle was blowing again, its shrill command ringing through the station and into her head. The train jolted and steam gushed in a billowing white cloud along the platform, obliterating everything in its path.

The great iron wheels began to turn, slowly at first, but gathering speed, making her break into a run to keep up with them as she shouted her last farewells.

'Bye, Polly,' shouted the twins in unison as they leant out of the open window and waved frantically. Megan was holding Alice, encouraging her to wave too as Enid blew Polly a kiss. But Alice had realised suddenly what was happening. She was crying, wrestling to be free of Megan, reaching out for her mother, her little face screwed up in anguish.

25

Polly was sobbing now, the tears running unheeded down her face as she came to an abrupt halt at the end of the platform. The train whistle blew twice as the last of the long snake of carriages emerged from beneath the vast glass roof and began to speed down the track, around the bend and out of sight.

'Huh-hem.'

Polly dragged her gaze from the empty horizon and turned to find the burly porter waiting beside his trolley. He looked neither surprised nor self-conscious at her tears, and she assumed he'd seen far too many over the past year to be affected by them any more. She scrabbled in her coat pocket for her handkerchief and hastily wiped her eyes and blew her nose. 'Sorry,' she said, although she didn't really know why she was apologising.

He tugged on the shiny bill of his railway cap, his expression not unkind. 'The train to Gloucester is already boarding, Miss. We need to get a move on if you don't want to miss it.'

Glad to have something else to occupy her, Polly took one fleeting glance back down the empty track before hurrying after him.

Chapter Two

The basement of Beach View Boarding House had once provided bedrooms for Peggy Reilly's two young sons and her father-in-law, Ron, who now lived down there in solitary squalor among his jumble of hunting, fishing and military paraphernalia with his dog, Harvey. The boys had been sent to the West Country for the duration, and every time Peggy had to do the weekly wash in the basement scullery it merely reinforced her longing for them to come home. But the war had suddenly taken a more dangerous turn, and despite her aching need to see them again, she knew they were far safer where they were.

Peggy didn't have the luxury of a washing machine, or one of those newfangled spin dryers, so washday involved a great deal of scrubbing, rinsing and wringing. As for Harvey sleeping on Ron's bed, she'd given up complaining. They all had enough to contend with without her making a fuss over something she knew would never change. At least he didn't have the ferrets any more – Cleo and Delilah had been released into the wild once the air raids began.

Peggy turned the handle on the mangle with extra vigour, using it to vent her frustration at everything that had happened over the past few weeks. It was bad enough having to cope with the dust and the debris caused by the ever-increasing bombing raids, but rationing was tighter than ever, her husband Jim was absolutely no help at all around the house, and that poor little Polish girl, Danuta, seemed determined to remain isolated in her room with her grief.

She folded the damp sheet into the laundry basket and plunged her arms back into the water to fish out the next. Feeding it through the twin rollers of the mangle, she grasped the handle and gave it a vicious turn, the water pouring into the bucket beneath.

'You'll be having that off its moorings if you're not careful.'

She glared at her father-in-law who'd tramped in from the garden with dirty boots and Harvey, a large, shaggy, Bedlington-cross. 'Thanks, Ron. But when I want your advice, I'll ask for it.'

His rough, warm hand settled on her fingers as he smiled at her. 'Let me do that,' he said softly, 'Go and put your feet up.'

'I haven't got time to rest,' she sighed, as she stepped back from the mangle and almost tripped over the dog. 'The house is filthy, the beds need changing and I'm due at the WVS reception centre in an hour. With so many people being made homeless, I can't let them down.'

'D'you not think you're trying to take on too much?' He continued turning the handle, expertly folding the sheet into the basket as Harvey plonked himself down under the sink. 'There're six other women in the house, including Cissy and Mrs Finch. You should put your foot down and get them to help more.'

'June, Suzy and Fran work long hours at that

hospital. They're so exhausted when they come in, they've barely the strength to eat, let alone get stuck into housework. Cissy does her share when she's at home, and I don't like to ask Mrs Finch, bless her. As for Danuta,' she gave another deep sigh. 'She hardly knows where she is at the moment, and needs time to grieve for her brother.'

Ron dumped the last sheet in the basket, his weather-beaten face solemn, his blue eyes understanding as he regarded her. 'A bit of dust doesn't matter, Peg,' he said softly. 'But you do. What would become of us all if you made yourself ill?'

Peggy stared at him. Ron was in his sixties and she'd known him for more than twenty years. She'd never heard him speak like that before, and it was disconcerting to say the least. 'Hard work never killed anyone,' she said gruffly. 'But I appreciate the thought.'

Ron muttered something under his breath, hoisted the laundry basket on to his hip and carried it outside.

The gravel path ran the length of the garden, past the almost empty coal bunker, the shed and the outside lav, which had had to be rebuilt following an earlier bomb attack, and continued through the lines of vegetables to the back gate which hung lopsidedly from the one hinge that had survived on the shattered flint wall. The Anderson shelter squatted at the very end of the garden, the tin roof covered with earth; the stone steps leading down to the rough wooden door were already gathering moss, and despite the lack of rain, there always seemed to be a puddle waiting to catch the unwary.

The aftermath of the recent raids could be seen in the damaged chimneys and roofs of the surrounding houses, and in the crumbled garden walls and boarded-up windows. It had been a miracle that Beach View was still standing relatively unscathed.

Peggy followed Ron down the path to the washing line that was strung across the garden from two wooden poles. He had certainly taken the government directive to dig for victory to heart – the vegetables were flourishing. But her own heart was heavy, for she missed not seeing her two sons playing there, missed not hearing their voices – even missed not having to clear up behind them. This damned war had only just got going, but already it had changed the landscape of Cliffehaven and the very essence of her family life.

It was as if Ron could read her thoughts. 'Bob and Charlie are well out of it, Peggy, and all that fresh air and exercise down on that Somerset farm can only do them and Ernie good.'

'I know.' She began to peg out the sheets. 'Ernie's thriving, according to his Aunt Vi's letters, although the aftermath of the polio means he still gets tired far too quickly.' She blinked in the bright sunlight as she continued to peg the sheets to the line. It was a beautiful day, with no clouds in the sky, and no sign of the terrifying dogfights that had been fought overhead the night before, but, try as she might, she couldn't assuage the emptiness that seemed always to accompany her now.

'Sally's coming over at the weekend to show me Ernie's letters and drawings. She misses her little brother even more than we do, and I think it helps her to talk about him with me.'

Ron handed her the tail of the last sheet. 'She's a fair wee lass, so she is. Nice that she feels this is her home. You've been a good mother to her, Peg. You should be proud of how she's turned out.'

Peggy turned from the washing line and balanced the empty basket on her hip. 'Who'd have thought it? We were strangers a year ago, and now it's as if she's one of mine. Odd how things work out, isn't it?'

'The war does have some compensations,' he muttered. 'If she and Ernie hadn't been sent down here from London, who knows what might have happened to them.'

Peggy felt rather more cheerful. It was wearing to be cross and out of sorts and, frankly, she'd had enough of gloom and doom. 'Sally and John are getting married in November,' she said brightly. 'John's coming on so well, and he's determined to walk down the aisle without his sticks.'

'I always knew that boy wouldn't let his injuries get the better of him,' he replied. 'Sally's got herself a good man there, so she has.' He pulled his disreputable cap out of his filthy trouser pocket and rammed it over his silver-streaked thatch of dark hair. 'If you're not wanting any more help, then I'll be off to the hills with Harvey to see what I can get for the pot.'

Peggy stilled him by touching his arm. 'Thanks, Ron,' she murmured, and lightly kissed his cheek.

He flushed red and tugged at the cap. 'There's no need for all that,' he muttered, before turning away. 'Come on, Harvey. Rabbits.'

Peggy stood in the warm sunshine and fondly watched the old man and his faithful hound walk through the gate and along the twitten that ran between the rows of terraced Victorian houses that climbed the steep hill to the east of the town. Ron could be stubborn and opinionated – but he was a stalwart, and Peggy couldn't imagine this house without him.

She glanced at her watch and hurried indoors. Refusing to look at the now deserted basement bedroom which her young sons had shared, she dumped the basket under the sink and ran up the stone steps into the kitchen to find Mrs Finch busy at the draining board.

'I hope you don't mind, dear,' she said, fiddling with her hearing aid, 'but I thought I'd help prepare the vegetables for tonight.'

'You don't have to do that,' Peggy replied, rather alarmed at how close the flashing blade was to the elderly, not terribly steady fingers.

'What's that, dear? I can't hear you.' The older woman put down the paring knife and fiddled again with her hearing aid, making it whine.

It was clearly one of Mrs Finch's better days, but that hearing aid was worse than useless. 'I said you don't have to do that,' Peggy repeated loudly.

'I do, dear,' she replied. 'You can't possibly manage, and I'm beginning to feel rather useless.'

'But...'

'But nothing,' Mrs Finch said firmly, her grey head bobbing. 'I can't do much, granted. But I'll do what I can. We all have to do our bit, Peggy, and I can't sit idly by watching you work yourself into the ground.' She walked slowly and carefully to the Kitchener range, her arthritis eased somewhat by the warm weather. 'I've made a pot of tea. Sit down, Peggy, and let me spoil you for a change.'

Peggy had tears in her eyes as the old woman poured the tea and set the cup and saucer on the table in front of her. 'Bless you,' she murmured, relishing the almost forgotten taste of strong, sweet tea.

'What's that? Do speak up, dear.'

'I thought we were out of tea,' shouted Peggy.

'There's no need to bellow, dear. I'm not totally deaf, you know.' Mrs Finch smiled impishly. 'I knew we were out of tea, so I went out early and managed to get to the head of the queue at the grocer's. Being old and rather decrepit works wonders sometimes, and I'm not above playing the helpless old woman, to the hilt when necessary. It's amazing what one can achieve with a walking stick and a hearing aid.' She returned to the carrots.

Peggy sipped her tea and made a concerted effort to relax and not panic over the cavalier way Mrs Finch was using that knife. Cordelia Finch was aptly named, for she was a bird-like little woman, whose cheerful chirruping always lightened the mood. She had become an intrinsic part of the family, and Peggy had noticed how easily the three young nurses had taken to her. It was as if they saw their grandmothers in her, and Mrs Finch had taken on the role with relish, dishing out advice, soothing tears, taking an interest in everything they did. Peggy had no idea how old she was, but guessed she had to be at least seventy-five and, despite her deafness and the arthritis that plagued her, she seemed to have been rejuvenated by the knowledge that she was still useful.

Closing her eyes, Peggy let the hot sweet tea revive her as she mulled over her plans for the rest of the day. She would leave the fresh linen on the beds and they could make them up themselves for a change, she decided. If Ron couldn't get a rabbit or something for the pot, she had a tin of stewing steak in the larder that would suffice and, thanks to Ron, there were plenty of potatoes to grate up and use as a pastry topping. She let out a deep sigh. Oh, for the days of real puff pastry, so light it melted in the mouth, coming out of the oven all golden and flaky, rich with real butter.

Her daydream was broken by the sound of Mrs Finch's voice. 'Have you seen Danuta today?' She scooped the diced carrots into a saucepan, added cold water and a pinch of salt before turning to face Peggy.

'I took her up a cup of tea this morning, but I've not seen her since.'

'Poor little thing,' muttered Mrs Finch. 'Heaven only knows what she must have gone through to get here all the way from Poland.'

'She refuses to talk about it,' said Peggy with a sigh. 'But I suspect she's seen more horrors than anyone should at that age – and then to discover her brother was shot down and killed only weeks before she got here. That must have been a cruel blow.'

Peggy lit a cigarette and blew smoke. 'I tried to

tell her as gently as I could, but of course there's no easy way to impart such awful news.' She plucked at the edges of the worn, faded oilcloth that covered the table. 'Alex was such a lovely man, and although he was billeted here for only a short while, I really miss him.'

Mrs Finch poured herself a cup of tea and sat down. 'Danuta's only been here a few days, and I know she's mourning her brother, but life has to go on. She's a nurse, isn't she?' At Peggy's nod, she continued. 'Well then, she should be going to the hospital and volunteering her services. It will take her mind off herself and whatever she's been through and help her recover. There's nothing like seeing other people's misery to make one realise how lucky one is.'

'Is that how you coped after your husband was killed in the last war?'

Mrs Finch nodded. 'I wasn't trained or anything, but I helped at the hospital, running to and fro with drinks, helping them to write letters, or read them. It seemed to cheer them up a bit, and seeing them get well again was good for me – made me realise that, in a very small way, I was helping to win the war.'

Peggy nodded. 'That's why I've volunteered to help with the WVS,' she replied slowly and carefully so Mrs Finch could read her lips. 'It cheers me up no end to be able to find all those poor souls housing and clothes, and to see the kiddies tuck into a decent meal. Reminds me of how lucky I am this place is still standing.'

'Talking of which, shouldn't you be on your way to the centre by now?'

'Good heavens,' Peggy gasped. 'I didn't realise what time it was.' Stubbing out her cigarette, she swiftly dragged the scarf from her head and untied her wrap-round apron, flinging them both on a nearby chair. Running a comb hastily through her dark wavy hair, she snatched up her handbag and gas mask, and slung a cardigan over her sprigged cotton dress. 'I'll be back at six unless there's another raid. You will promise to go into the shelter, won't you, if there is?'

'I might be old, but I'm not senile just yet,' Mrs Finch replied with some asperity. 'As much as I hate that shelter, I'll be inside it the minute the sirens go.' She flapped her hands. 'Now go, Peggy, and don't worry about supper. I'm perfectly capable of managing.'

Peggy rather doubted it, and dreaded the state of her kitchen on her return. But she kissed the soft cheek gratefully and hurried out of the kitchen, into the hall and through the front door.

Pausing for a moment on the top step, she eyed the narrow road which was in shadow now the sun had gone behind the terrace of houses opposite. Beach View Boarding House had been in the family for years, and this street had once been her playground, the witness to her wedding day and to where she'd returned when her parents had retired. She'd raised her children here and run a successful bed and breakfast business until the war had stopped people coming to the seaside for their holidays. The neighbours were old friends, their homes as familiar as her own; their lives somehow entwined as they'd survived the first war and the terrible financial depression and flu epidemic that had followed.

This new and terrifying war had changed it irrevocably and, had her parents still been alive, they would have been devastated to see it thus; for where there had once been an elegant terrace of fine Victorian villas, there was now a gaping hole at the end of the street to the east, boarded-up windows and toppled chimney pots, rubble-strewn gardens and damaged pavements. Families had been forced to move out, their children sent far from home and into the care of strangers; their husbands, sons and brothers fighting abroad.

To the west, beyond the street that led up the hill from the seafront, lay the broader Camden Road which ran past the local parade of shops and on to the school and hospital until it reached the High Street of Cliffehaven town centre. The school was closed due to a block of flats falling on it during an early bombing raid, the children swiftly evacuated to safety, the teachers, like her eldest daughter Anne, enlisting into the various services. The hospital had, thankfully, escaped damage but the new factory Solomon and Gold-man which had opened only weeks before had not been so lucky, and production had been seri-ously affected. It was a miracle no one had been hurt.

Peggy tutted, slung the straps of her gas-mask box and handbag over her shoulder and hurried westwards towards the High Street and the town hall where the WVS had set up a reception station for the homeless and dispossessed. She supposed she should be grateful they weren't receiving the same treatment from the enemy as London, but being directly beneath the shortest route from the continent to the capital meant they were getting their fair share.

It was a shame she'd been born a woman, she decided as she walked determinedly past the Anchor, Ron's favourite pub, because she'd have liked to have shown Mr Hitler just what she was made of.

Danuta Chmielewski heard the front door slam and, from behind the curtains of her first floor bedroom window, she looked between the criss-cross of white tape down on Peggy Reilly as she paused on the steps before striding purposefully to the end of the street and crossing over to Camden Road. She followed her progress until she was out of sight, lost among the other housewives who were hurrying to join the queues outside the local shops.

Peggy was, Danuta guessed, in her early forties, with a bustling, no-nonsense air that was evident in the way she walked. Dark haired and pretty, despite the weariness that seemed to shadow her eyes, Peggy had been kindness itself. Danuta knew only too well how hard it must have been for her to tell her about Aleksy – God knew, she'd had to impart such awful tidings herself too many times not to know how she felt. It never got any easier, either, she silently admitted.

Danuta pulled the curtains on the bright sunlight, unable to bear its cheerfulness. She turned her back on it and stood in the broad bay, trying desperately to find some essence of Aleksy in this room he'd once slept in. It was a pleasant room at the front of the house above the dining room, furnished with a highly polished oak wardrobe, chest of drawers and dressing table. The two single beds stood opposite the door, the eiderdowns covering crisp linen, the home-made rag rug between them on the varnished floorboards. There was a gas fire with a shelf over it, and a mirror above that. A comfortable chair sat to one side of it, a padded stool stood in front of the dressing table, and a little rattan table held the bedside lamp and the few precious photographs she'd managed to rescue from the rubble of their home.

It was luxurious compared to the shelled-out barns, ditches and ruined farmhouses where she'd had to sleep over the past months, and although she was dreading having to share it with the mysterious Nurse Brown when she eventually arrived, it was certainly more comfortable than the cramped, cold apartment her parents had rented in Warsaw. The thought of those tenement rooms only made the homesickness more unbearable and, at this moment, she would have given anything to roll back this last year and be with her family again. But they were gone – all of them – and no amount of wishing could bring them back.

Danuta moved slowly across the room and sank on to her narrow bed, her gaze fixed to those faded, creased photographs that she'd carried so far from home. The beloved faces smiled back at her, but it was as if they were already looking out from another world – a distant plane that she could no longer see or understand, their features blurred and almost ethereal.

She felt the weight of the gold medallion, warm

in the palm of her hand. Their father had given it to Aleksy when he'd left to fight the war in Spain, and it was a tangible reminder of how Aleksy had not forgotten who he was or the family that had loved him so much. Had Aleksy foreseen his death, was that why he'd not been wearing it when he'd been shot down over the English Channel? Was that why he'd asked his friend, and Peggy's son-in-law, Wing Commander Martin Black, to give it to Peggy for safe-keeping? Had he, in some strange way, known she would come to find him, and that this little circle of gold would bring her some kind of comfort?

She gazed at it now, turning it over and over in her hands, watching how the dull gold glinted in the light that seeped through the curtains. The Madonna and child etched into the precious metal had not protected him, the prayer on the back meaningless now in this godforsaken world that seemed intent upon destroying itself. Danuta had witnessed too much to be swayed by religion any more; she had managed to survive on her wits. And yet this was an intrinsic part of her brother, something he'd cherished, and therefore more valuable than the metal from which it was made.

She curled on to the bed, the medallion held tightly in her fist. She was weary beyond belief. Drained of all emotion, the spark of determination and life that she'd kept burning so brightly over the past year, finally extinguished. She knew she couldn't stay in this room forever, or avoid the noisy, cheerful people she heard moving about the house. She also knew her skills as a nurse would be sorely needed now England was being bombed so regularly and with such devastating effect. But she'd been fighting this war since the Germans had occupied Poland almost exactly a year ago, and it was as if Aleksy's death had killed her spirit, and she simply didn't have the energy to fight any more.

And yet, as she lay there, she felt the flutter of the new life inside her and knew that if she gave in to this terrible despondency, she would be betraying not only the memory of Jean-Luc, but the child they'd made together. She softly ran her fingers over the barely discernible mound of her belly which she'd managed to camouflage with baggy clothes. She had to fight on to help win peace – had to reignite that battling spirit to ensure that this child, sown with love during the darkest days of her life, would survive and flourish in a world free of conflict.

Danuta slowly rose from the bed and stood in front of the dressing-table mirror, almost afraid of what she would see, but knowing she could avoid it no longer. Her reflection showed a short, thin young woman in shapeless trousers and loose shirt, who looked far older than twenty-three. The ordeals she'd suffered during her time with the resistance in Poland and her escape through a war-torn Europe were etched, not only on her mind, but in her face and the green eyes that had witnessed too much. Her short, black hair looked lifeless, her skin dull, and her once elegant hands had been roughened, the nails bitten almost to the quick.

Turning her back on this unedifying sight, she

41

took a deep breath and strengthened her resolve to pull herself together and begin the next phase of her life.

Polly had had to change trains several times during the past three hours, and now they were on a small branch-line which would eventually bring them to a main station and the final leg of her journey. Polly had little real idea of where they were, for she'd never been outside Hereford-shire before and all the signs on the platforms had been taken down. The countryside was un-familiar, the small towns and villages they passed so very different to the ones at home, and she wondered if her little family was experiencing the same sense of disorientation as they travelled north to Liverpool.

Exhausted by the emotional events of the day, and lulled by the regular clickety-clack of the wheels and the warmth of the bright sun coming through the window, she dozed off.

It was only a small train of five carriages and a guard's van. The other occupants of Polly's com-partment were middle-aged or elderly civilians who kept up a desultory conversation about the inconveniences of war and the lack of any real information from the government. The corridor outside was jammed with Canadian servicemen and their huge kitbags. Despite their loud voices and sudden bursts of laughter, Polly's doze was not disturbed.

The urgent volley of sharp blasts from the train whistle woke her immediately. One glance out of the window into the almost blinding sun was enough. 'Get on the floor,' she shouted. 'Enemy planes.'

The eight of them scrambled to the floor as the guard furiously blew his whistle and ordered everyone to get down. Polly could feel the train speeding up, could hear the first deadly rat-a-tat-tat of bullets and the roar of the two fast-approaching Messerschmitts. The train was now screeching along, jolting them hard against one another, the wheels rattling over the rails, smoke and soot streaming from the funnel.

Polly tried to make herself as small as possible in the tight gap beneath the seat as the train hurtled along, the carriages swaying alarmingly as it took a curve in the tracks far too fast. She could hear the enemy planes returning; could see two of the foolhardy young Canadians lean out of the corridor window and cock their rifles.

Enemy bullets thudded and whined, pinging off metal, splintering wood and shattering glass. The carriage window exploded, showering them with deadly shards. Someone screamed and Polly curled into a tighter ball, head buried in her arms

The answering salvo of gunfire from the corridor was deafening above the shouts and the thunder of the racing train wheels. Polly remained tightly curled in the sooty dust and cobwebs that lay beneath the seat. She could feel the stiff terror of the woman beside her and reached for her hand, seeking comfort as well as giving it.

'Cease fire immediately that soldier!' The roared command came from the end of the corridor and was obeyed instantly.

The train continued its hectic pace, iron thun-

43

dering over iron as the vibration of the turning wheels shook the carriages and reverberated through the huddling passengers.

After what felt like hours, Polly realised the enemy planes had gone, and the train's pace had slowed. She dared to peek from beneath the seat so she could scan the small area of sky to be seen from the shattered window. The sun glared from an empty, cloudless blue.

'All-clear!' shouted the guard. 'All-clear!'

Polly eased out from her hiding place and looked at the others. 'Is anyone hurt?'

'If you could just help me up, dear, the old knees don't work as well as they used to.' It was the elderly woman who'd clung to her hand so tightly throughout the raid.

Polly tried to keep her balance in the swaying compartment as she helped the woman to her feet. 'You aren't hurt, are you?'

'Bless you, no, but thank you for holding my hand,' she replied, straightening her dusty hat and clutching her capacious handbag. 'I'm not usually so timid, but I really thought I was a goner there.'

Polly noticed that despite her cheerful words, her smile was fleeting and barely reached her fearful eyes. 'Sit down for a minute and catch your breath,' she advised. 'We've all had a bit of a shock.'

Polly settled her comfortably and tried to dust herself down as she took stock of the damage to her clothing. Her cotton dress and cardigan were filthy, there was a ladder in her stockings, her hair was a mess, and she'd banged her head at some point, for she could feel the swelling just above

44

her eye. She cleaned up as best she could and foraged for her handbag and gas-mask box which had been flung to the other side of the compartment, then sat down with a thump. Her legs suddenly felt as if they were stuffed with cotton wool.

'I do feel rather queer,' said the older woman. 'Sort of shaky and a bit sick.'

'It's the shock,' replied Polly, taking her wrist and checking her racing pulse. 'We could all do with a strong cup of sweet tea.' She looked at the others who were equally distressed, although they were stoutly trying to hide the fact as they tidied themselves. 'Anyone got a flask by any chance?'

There was general chatter as two flasks were produced, and they waited in turn to use the cups. Now they had something else to concentrate on, they were more at ease, and the mood lightened.

Polly waited until everyone had had their tea before she took the cup. She had just taken a deep, grateful swallow when a shout went up from the guard.

'Is there a doctor on board? We've got casualties.'

Polly quickly drained the cup and handed it back to its owner. Sliding the compartment door open, she waved her hand and caught the man's attention. 'I'm a nurse,' she called. 'What sort of injuries?'

'Serious enough to need attention before we get to the next station.'

The soldiers pressed themselves to one side to let her through and willing hands steadied her as she clambered round the kitbags, squeezed past uniformed chests and tried to avoid tripping over highly polished boots.

Thanking them, she turned to the guard, whose expression was grim. 'Show me the worst ones first,' she said quietly, 'and see if you can find a first aid kit.'

'There's one in me van,' replied the guard, holding the door open into the next carriage. 'You'd better see to this bloke first. I don't like the look of 'im at all.'

Polly knelt to examine the young Canadian who was slumped on the carriage floor in the arms of a portly middle-aged woman. His face was the colour of old parchment and blood was pouring from a head wound just above his ear and seeping into the woman's blouse. 'Does anyone have something to mop away the blood so I can get a look at the wound?'

The woman dug into a cardigan pocket. 'Here, use my handkerchief,' she ordered.

Polly took it and managed to stem the bleeding enough to take a closer look. 'It's all right,' she reassured the other woman. 'It's only a flesh wound, but by the looks of his colour, he'll probably have concussion.'

'But he's bleeding so badly, surely it's serious?'

Polly made a pad of the handkerchief and held it over the wound. 'Injuries to the head always bleed copiously,' she explained with a gentle smile. 'If you could apply some pressure to that pad and hold it there until I can bandage it properly, he'll be fine.'

As she dealt with the minor cuts and bruises of the other passengers nearby, the guard fought his way back from his van at the rear of the train, armed with a large wooden box marked with a red cross. Polly hunted out rolls of gauze, cotton wool, and a pair of scissors. Gently removing the handkerchief, she made a pad of cotton wool to place over the wound and swiftly bandaged it in place with the gauze.

'He needs to lie down,' said the woman, who was clearly used to giving orders. 'Come on, you lot, make room.' She glared at the others in the compartment, and they swiftly did as they were told.

The guard helped Polly to lift the young man on to the seat and make him comfortable. He was still out cold, but his colour was a little better, which was a good sign.

'Can you keep an eye on him? I warn you, though, he could be copiously sick when he wakes up.'

'Don't you worry, dear. I've had six children. I can handle anything.'

Polly smiled her thanks and left her to it, following the guard to another carriage where she had a sprained ankle and wrist to deal with, several bumps and abrasions, and a couple of nasty cuts from flying glass. By the time she'd finished bandaging and cleaning and mopping up, the first aid box was sadly depleted.

She closed the last of the compartment doors behind her and leant against the handrail that ran beneath the window as the train rocked and swayed in its hurry to reach its destination. The shock of the attack was beginning to take effect, and her legs felt decidedly unsteady again.

'How long before we reach the next station?'

47

she asked the guard.

He pulled the watch and chain from the top pocket of his uniform waistcoat. 'Ten minutes.' He dug into his trouser pockets and pulled out a small, silver-coloured brandy flask. 'Here, love. Have a sip of that before you keel over. You're as white as a sheet.'

'Thanks,' she breathed. The brandy was warm in her throat, burning its way down, clearing her head and making her feel more steady. She handed the flask back. 'I'll just check on the young man's head wound again before I go back to my carriage. Will the station master be able to get hold of an ambulance, do you think?'

He frowned. 'Thought you said it weren't serious?'

'All head wounds need looking after, and he's in no fit state to travel anywhere else today but hospital.'

'Thank you, ma'am, but the Canadian army will look after him now.'

Polly turned and found she was staring at a broad, khaki-covered chest adorned with medals. She looked up into a clean-shaven, ruddy face and a pair of brown eyes that had a no-nonsense glint in them. The peaked cap covered in gold braid was so low it almost touched his patrician nose.

'Colonel Samuel J. Johnson, ma'am. Thank you for your medical assistance.'

Polly's hand was swamped by his. 'Polly Brown,' she replied. 'It was the least I could do, but he will need further attention before he can travel again.'

'The Canadian army will see to that, ma'am.'

Polly nodded and made her way through the crush to her carriage. She fielded the numerous questions as she took her smaller suitcase and her coat from the overhead rack and sat down.

'I saved you the last of the tea,' said the older woman with the jaunty but rather dusty hat. 'It looks like you've earned it.'

'You're very kind, thank you,' Polly murmured. Sipping the welcome tea, she closed her eyes against the bright sunlight and tried to relax, but it was proving impossible. Hereford had escaped the attention of the enemy so far, and news reports of air raids and bombings elsewhere had somehow been softened by distance and lack of involvement. Today's experience had shaken her badly – had brought the terrifying realities of war much too close for comfort.

She stared out of the window, not really seeing the passing countryside as her thoughts whirled. Cliffehaven might be directly beneath the path of enemy bombers, and within sound of the guns across the Channel, but Alice and the others would soon set sail into the Atlantic, with enemy submarines hunting them down. 'Dear God,' she prayed with silent fervour. 'Keep them safe.'

Chapter Three

Danuta had once dressed carefully and imaginatively despite having little money to spend on such things; now she possessed only the clothes she'd had to borrow. The practical trousers, shirts, boots and sweaters had seen her through the worst of the winter as she'd made her slow and sometimes terrifying passage across Europe and into northern France.

One of the other women in Jean-Luc's resistance group had provided her with the peasant's clothing she now wore, and it had served her well, but the drab skirt, blouse and cardigan, the headscarf and sturdy lace-up shoes were far from flattering. The canvas shoulder bag she'd carried all the way from Warsaw was battered and stained, but it had become a sort of talisman, and she went nowhere without it.

With the gas-mask box and canvas bag bouncing against her hip as she walked, Danuta knew she looked a fright, but in the scheme of things, she didn't really care. Vanity, and the small pleasures of make-up and a pretty dress, were in the past, for there were more important things to think about, and today she must concentrate on finding work at the hospital. Her appearance would surely not be judged, for she had many skills to offer. She could run a ward efficiently, work in the theatre alongside the best surgeons in Poland, and speak three languages almost fluently – but would it be enough to secure a post here?

She stood on the pavement and looked up at the vast grey building that stretched the length and breadth of the block. A white portico with impressive pillars shadowed the main entrance and the steps leading up to the reception hall. Long, elegant windows looked over the wide strip of tarmac where two ambulances had just drawn up outside the double doors leading to the Accident and Emergency Department. Nurses, doctors and orderlies were scurrying by as visitors arrived and left, and patients were carefully taken from the ambulances and hurried inside.

There was a small grassed area off to one side, and Danuta smiled as she watched the group of young men who were sitting in their wheelchairs under a spreading chestnut tree. They were enjoying the sun despite their heavy bandaging, and the game of cards was obviously entertaining them.

Taking a deep breath, Danuta ran up the steps and entered the echoing reception area. It was an old building, and very grand, with black and white squares of marble on the floor and a sweeping staircase with more marble used for the balustrades. She looked up and saw an ornate glass cupola from which was strung an enormous chandelier. How either delicate adornment had escaped the bombing, was a mystery.

Danuta felt a little daunted. Everyone seemed to know where they were going, the nurses bustling in their crisp white aprons and caps, the doctors running down the stairs and looking important in their white coats, the porters wheeling trolleys with panache. But the scents and sounds of this familiar environment were welcoming, and she began to relax.

She caught sight of a middle-aged porter pushing an empty bed, and hurried towards him. 'Please would you show me where to go to apply for a nursing job here?' she asked in her clearest and best English.

'You'll be wanting Matron, love,' he said, resting on the heavy iron bedhead and eyeing her from head to toe. 'Down that corridor, up them steps, and it's the first on yer right.'

'Thank you. You are most kind.'

He grinned at her. 'Watch yer step, love, she's a bit of a tartar is our Miss Billings. Don't take too kindly to pretty young girls.'

Danuta smiled fleetingly at the well-meant compliment and hurried away. Running up the steps, she stopped for a moment to compose herself. All matrons were formidable, and she steeled herself for the coming interview as she rapped on the appropriate door.

'Come.'

She opened the door and stepped inside. The room was spotlessly clean and lined with shelves of files, and a multitude of metal cabinets. There was nothing feminine about it, not even a wilting pot plant. Danuta softly closed the door behind her and waited to be acknowledged.

The woman sitting behind the big desk didn't look up from the papers before her, and Danuta took those few moments to see what she was up against. Miss Billings was clearly on the wrong

52

side of fifty and wore a flowing white cap over iron-grey hair that had been tortured into a thick, tight bun. The starched white collar, cuffs and apron were quite startling against the dark blue of her uniform, and the only adornments to be seen were a watch pinned above her formidable bosom, and a highly polished buckle on her straining belt.

Danuta was getting rather impatient at the lack of response and cleared her throat.

'There's no need for that,' said the woman, still not lifting her gaze from the paperwork. 'If you have a cough, I suggest you make an appointment with your GP.'

'I am here to apply for work, Matron,' stammered Danuta.

The grey eyes held little warmth as they regarded her from head to toe. 'And what work can you do, exactly?'

'I am a theatre nurse,' Danuta replied. 'I wish to offer my skills to this very fine hospital.'

The eyebrows lifted, the expression hardened. 'You're foreign, aren't you? Where are you from?'

'Poland.' Danuta's gaze didn't waver from the other woman's cold scrutiny.

The strong, capable hand with the square, spotlessly clean fingernails reached across the desk. 'Your identification papers.'

Danuta scrabbled in the shoulder bag and handed them over.

Ragged and crumpled, stained from much use, they didn't look particularly wholesome, and Miss Billings held them gingerly as she scrutinised the faded photograph and the various official stamps. 'I will need to see proof of your qualifications.'

'So sorry, but I do not have them. They were lost during the siege of Warsaw, but I was trained at...'

'Without proof of your qualifications I cannot possibly let you loose in my hospital.'

'But I am skilled theatre nurse,' she blurted out. 'I have worked with some of the best surgeons in Poland.'

'What they do in Poland means nothing here,' said Matron with a sniff. 'And I'm far too busy to have to keep an eye on you all the time. As it is, your English is questionable, and I don't think our patients would appreciate having some foreigner looking after them.'

'My English is very good,' Danuta protested. 'As is my French and German.'

'German?' The mouth thinned and the eyes were gimlet as they studied her. 'I can assure you there is no German spoken in *my* hospital.'

'Of course, of course,' she stammered. 'I was only trying to impress upon you my skills.'

'It takes a great deal to impress me,' Matron said coolly. She sifted through the papers on her desk. 'I have a vacancy in the laundry, but the post does not come with accommodation. Meals can be taken here when you are on shift, and I expect a high standard of obedience, cleanliness and efficiency.' She eyed Danuta's shabby clothing with disdain. 'Uniform will be provided, but it will be up to you to see it remains in pristine condition.'

'Thank you, but I would be of more use on the wards than in the laundry. Please, Matron, at least give me a chance to prove what I can do.'

She was not to be swayed. 'I don't have time to deal with foreigners who might or might not have proper training. It's the laundry or nothing.'

Danuta realised she could get no further with this bigoted woman. 'Then I will take it,' she said with a sigh of capitulation.

Her identification papers were pushed towards her along with a printed sheet. 'Fill this in and leave it at the desk in reception. You will begin tomorrow morning at six, and your uniform can be collected from stores.'

Danuta stuffed everything in her bag and swiftly left the room before she disgraced herself completely by bursting into tears. After all she had gone through, she was shocked at how easily one spiteful old woman could knock her confidence and make her feel worthless.

Within moments of disembarking, Colonel Samuel J. Johnson had commandeered the station master's telephone and organised an ambulance, as well as a fleet of jeeps from a nearby Canadian army base. Polly and the other passengers watched with barely disguised envy as the young men were driven away, for they would be stuck here for at least an hour while their train was being thoroughly inspected for any serious damage.

Shearing Halt was on the outskirts of a tiny farming hamlet and consisted of two short platforms, a signal box and a waiting room. The station master and his wife lived in the neat red brick cottage next to the tracks and clearly loved their country idyll, for there was a flourishing vegetable and flower garden, and sprawling, sweet-scented roses climbed over the roof.

Beyond these few buildings lay miles of open country, with cows grazing and fields of wheat undulating in the warm breeze. Distant figures worked in the fields, the heavy horses pulling the reapers as the wheat was stacked in sheaves and tossed into enormous wagons. A narrow lane ran past a collection of whitewashed cottages, and much further along, among the gentle hills, Polly could see the roofs of isolated farmhouses and barns.

It was a pleasant pastoral scene, and if Polly hadn't been so frustrated by all the hanging about, she would have enjoyed it more. The station master and his wife were doing their best to make their short stay as pleasant as possible, but Polly was already several days late for her nursing post at Cliffehaven and her landlady, Mrs Reilly, must surely be wondering by now if she should let her room to someone else. She bit her lip as she mulled over her predicament, and then asked the station master if she could use his telephone.

'It can only be used in emergencies,' he replied.

'This *is* an emergency,' she persisted. 'If I don't make this call I could lose my job and my lodgings.' She smiled up at him, willing him to agree.

He tipped back his peaked hat and scratched his head. 'I suppose it would be all right,' he muttered. 'But make it short.'

Polly was shown into his office, and she reached for the large black telephone on his desk and dialled the number she'd written down in her notebook. It seemed to ring for ages, and she was about to replace the receiver when she heard an

56

elderly voice at the other end of the line.

'Hello? Who's that?'

'It's Polly Brown. Is that Mrs Reilly?'

'Mrs Reilly's out. Who did you say you were, dear? Do speak up.'

Polly took a deep breath and raised her voice. 'This is Staff Nurse Brown, and I'm ringing to let you know I should be in Cliffehaven by tomorrow. Please will someone inform the hospital that I'm on my way?'

'You're in hospital? Oh dear.'

Polly closed her eyes and tamped down on the frustration. 'Just tell Mrs Reilly I rang,' she said. 'I'm not in hospital; I'm waiting for a train.'

'It's not raining here,' said Mrs Finch. 'But I'll tell Peggy you called.' The line was abruptly disconnected.

Polly giggled as she replaced the receiver. Lord only knew what sort of message the old dear would give Mrs Reilly.

She thanked the station master who'd been hovering nearby and returned to the platform, where she perched on the larger of her two suitcases in the shade of the platform roof and watched the driver, stoker and guard laboriously tap wheels, check the bullet holes in the carriages, and closely inspect the engine. They seemed to be taking forever, standing about and talking as they drank tea and smoked cigarettes – why couldn't they just get on with it?

She realised she wasn't alone in her frustration, for there was a general muttering of annoyance among the other passengers. But it seemed such inconveniences had become commonplace, and

57

everyone soon began to settle down for the long wait. The primitive facilities of the station master's scullery and outside lavatory soon became the scenes of long, patient queues, and Polly had to accept she was stuck here for as long as it took, so she might as well make the best of it.

As the summer day waned, she wandered down the lane and leant on a fence to watch the lovely Shires plod sturdily back and forth through the wheat. It was a scene that reminded her of her childhood, and although it looked very pretty from here, she was all too familiar with the realities of life on a farm to be fooled by it. Harvesting was back-breaking work, with stinging insects worrying the sweat on your face, flies buzzing and bits of corn and wheat getting stuck in your clothes and making you itch.

But there were also joyous times that took the edge off the weariness and discomfort, and she smiled as she remembered how she and Adam had realised they were in love during a harvest festival dance at the local village hall. She remembered their first kiss beneath the full harvest moon, and the happiness of riding together on the back of one of those faithful Shires as they made their weary way home from the fields.

Tears sparked and she blinked them away, determined not to let the worry cloud this beautiful day. And yet, as she slowly made her way back to the tiny station platform, she couldn't dismiss the fear that seemed to be entwined through everything she thought and did. Adam, her childhood sweetheart, lover and best friend was lying in hospital, his future uncertain. And Alice, sweet, precious little Alice, would have already boarded the steamship *City of Benares* and, in the morning, Convoy OB-213 would set sail for Canada. The life she and Adam had planned on that magical harvest night had been scattered to the winds.

Peggy came out of the town hall and paused for a moment in the lee of the huge piles of sandbags to slip on her cardigan. There was already a bit of a chill in the air once the sun began to go down, and although they were only in the second week of September, she could already scent the coming winter.

She glanced up the steep hill towards the station, wondering fleetingly if Nurse Brown had arrived yet. She was terribly late, and although the Billeting Office had assured her she was on her way, Peggy wondered if she shouldn't give her place to someone else. It seemed very poor form to have an empty bed when so many poor souls were homeless, and if she should turn up later, the hospital could surely provide suitable accommodation.

Realising she could do nothing about it today, she hurried down the High Street towards the seafront, past the burnt-out remains of Woolworths and the pile of rubble that had once been a very smart department store, and weaved her way through the long queue outside the Odeon cinema...

She glanced automatically up the side alleyway. Jim worked as a projectionist at the Odeon and could often be found having a quiet smoke in the alley between performances. About to hurry on, she caught a glimpse of him emerging from the side door and was on the point of hailing him, when she realised he was not alone.

A peroxide blonde had followed him outside and was looking up at him coquettishly as she leant against the brick wall and tossed back her hair. Jim moved nearer to her, resting one hand on the wall close to her head, effectively making their little exchange more private. He said something that made her giggle, and she playfully slapped his arm.

Peggy watched as Jim lit her cigarette and continued to flirt with her. The pain she felt was immense, tearing through her so swiftly it took her breath away. She'd known Jim Reilly was a rogue even before she'd married him all those years ago and she'd learnt to hide the hurt – learnt it was better to believe him when he said it had only been a bit of harmless fun, that all men flirted, and of course he would never be unfaithful. Well, she'd been tested over the years, that was for sure, and when she'd seen the signs he was getting too involved elsewhere, she'd nipped it in the bud very quickly. But to see him like this when she'd thought he'd outgrown all that nonsense was so painful, she couldn't bear to watch any more.

Aware of the curious looks of those standing so patiently outside the cinema, and recognising one or two of them, she hurried on down the street, her face on fire, her pulse racing.

Jim had never been able to resist a pretty face or a dodgy deal, and if he was up to his tricks again then she'd soon spike his guns just as she'd had to do rather too frequently throughout their marriage. She doubted there was anything serious in his behaviour, but there had been one or two close calls in the past, and she didn't want a repeat performance. The peroxide blonde was young enough to be his daughter, for heaven's sake, and it was high time Jim Reilly realised he was far too old to be making such a fool of himself.

Peggy was so angry and upset that she walked even faster as she turned sharply east from the High Street and into Camden Road, which ran parallel to the seafront. Her footsteps echoed as she passed the factories, the hospital and the remains of the school, and she found she was soon out of breath.

Slowing down, she glanced into the local shop windows to see if there were any notices of new deliveries arriving. There were always rumours of tinned salmon, fresh batches of eggs and joints of pork, but they usually amounted to nothing, and half a day could be wasted queuing up for a scrag end and a handful of dubious mince.

The noise coming from the Anchor pub spilled out into the street, and she waved to Rosie Braithwaite, the landlady, who was closing the shutters over the ancient diamond-paned windows. Ron had a thing for the luscious Rosie, but at least he was entitled to flirt, she thought sourly – he'd been a widower for years.

It was getting dark much earlier now, but with no street lights and every window covered with blackout, it made walking along the damaged pavements rather hazardous. Peggy caught the toe of her shoe in a jagged piece of paving and just managed to save herself from falling by grabbing the edge of a rough stone wall.

She winced as she felt her wrist twist and her skin grate against the stone, the pain of it stoking her humiliation. How dare Jim shame her like that in front of all those people? And how dare he think so little of her and their marriage to carry on like that with a little tart barely out of school? She'd put up with his shady deals, withstood his previous forays into extra-curricular entertainment, and worked herself into the ground to make a good life for them and their children – and she'd had enough. Jim Reilly was about to discover that the world did not revolve around him, and that if he wasn't very careful, he'd lose the part of his anatomy which seemed to be his driving force.

She came to the end of Camden Road, crossed the main road that led down to the seafront and the pier and hurried along Beach View Terrace. Number sixty-four was in darkness, just as all the other Beach View houses were, and Peggy slowly climbed the steps, her gaze flitting mournfully over the shattered lamps that had once stood so proudly at the end of the concrete balustrades. Their sad state of repair seemed to be an analogy for her marriage.

She stood on the top step and made a concerted effort to calm down before unlocking the door. She had become adept over the years at hiding her sorrows, and Jim would be the only member of this household to discover how angry and hurt she was.

Plastering on a smile, she was greeted by the

lovely smell of cooking and the happy chatter of voices as she went into the kitchen. 'Sorry I'm late,' she said cheerfully. 'Has everyone had a good day?'

The train had finally left the country halt two hours behind schedule, which meant Polly had missed her ongoing train and had to wait another hour for the next one. It clattered and rattled through the gathering gloom, the heavy shutters tightly fastened over the windows to blot out any stray splinter of light coming from the compartments.

Polly tried to sleep but it was impossible. She hated being enclosed, hated not being able to see the towns and villages she suspected they were passing through, and when a train hurtled past on the other line, she flinched at the sheer force of its down-draught.

She arrived at Victoria Station at ten o'clock and within minutes found herself caught in an air raid. The sirens were screaming, their plaintive wails echoing in the high ceiling and reverberating through the vast concourse.

Guards were shouting orders to get into the shelters immediately, and Polly looked round for some clue as to where they might be. People were milling about and all was confusion.

A porter rushed up to her and grabbed the heavier suitcase. 'The shelter's this way,' he shouted. 'Quick, quick, they'll be here in a minute.'

Polly ran beside him, the weight of her overnight bag dragging on her arm, the gas-mask box and handbag thudding against her hip. She hesitated momentarily as he ran down the steps to the underground, and then had no choice but to follow him as a surge of people pushed round her. Down they went beneath the ground, the smell of soot and grime and overheated bodies growing ever stronger in the dim electric light.

She could almost feel the great weight of earth above that gloomy tunnel as she was swept along in the tide of people hurrying down the steep flight of stairs. As the tide dispersed through the various tunnels at the bottom, she experienced a moment of panic. She couldn't see the porter who had her case.

'This way love. Over here.'

With a sharp stab of relief, she followed him through a narrow archway and on to the platform. Bemused and feeling slightly claustrophobic in the crush of humanity, she looked round.

The long platform that ran down one side of the single set of rails was full of people who were lying on mattresses and blankets, sitting on chairs and upturned crates, making themselves at home for the duration of the air raid. The sound of their voices was strangely muted beneath the continuous wails of the sirens, and no one seemed to mind the lack of space and privacy as they carried out their nightly rituals.

Polly stared down the line to the yawning mouth of the great black tunnel, and up to the curved ceiling that loomed over them all. 'Is it safe down here?' she asked fearfully.

'Safer than up there,' the porter replied cheerfully. He put down her case, tipped his hat and strolled along the platform to a group of railway workers who were playing a game of cards on the top of an upturned beer crate.

Polly found a space close to the exit, placed her case against the tiled wall and sat on it. She was exhausted and fearful, and having never been in the London Underground before, was finding it hard to believe they wouldn't suffocate down here. As the sirens continued to wail she heard the distant boom of several big guns and clutched the gas-mask box, huddling into her coat.

No one else seemed to notice the terrible thuds of exploding bombs nearby, or the sharp retort of gunfire and the throaty roar of heavy bombers. They continued to read and chat, or play board games and cards, and someone at the far end even began to sing 'Goodnight Irene'. Which, in the circumstances, Polly didn't think at all appropriate.

Polly remained perched on her suitcase, stiff with anxiety as she gripped the gas-mask box and listened fearfully to the terrible noise coming from above ground. Everything seemed muted, but that didn't lessen her terror as the force of exploding bombs shook the earth beneath and around her.

Just how deep could those enemy missiles go? Would they all be killed in here, trapped like the rabbits she and her father used to hunt from their burrows? She hugged her waist as particles of loose tiling and cement clattered down and a wave of dust spewed along the track. She needed to get out, to escape, regardless of the mayhem above ground.

She was about to gather her things and run for the stairs when a strong hand on her arm stilled her. 'Don't you go worrying about all the whizz-bangs,' said the man sitting next to her. 'You get used to it after a while, and they can't touch us down here.'

Polly realised he'd been drinking, and wondered if that was his way of coping. 'I just hate being so far underground,' she said nervously.

'Better than being up there,' he slurred. He proffered her a sip from his whisky bottle, and when she politely declined, shrugged and finished it off. Within minutes he was snoring.

Polly envied him. She was longing to sleep, longing to lie down in a proper bed away from the stench of railways and the sounds of war. Determined to quell her fear and accept the situation, she rested her head back against the rather violent-green tiles and closed her eyes. If she could just shut out the noise from above and the sight of those looming ceilings, she just might be able to relax.

Chapter Four

Mrs Finch's partridge stew had been a triumph. The three birds had been plucked and marinated in the pint of beer Ron had fetched from the pub, before being slowly stewed with the vegetables until the meat fell from the bones. The thick, delicious gravy had been very satisfying, each precious drop mopped up with bread and potato until the plates were clean.

'I thought I'd do a fish pie tomorrow,' she trilled, as she and Peggy sat over their teacups much later on. 'Ron's promised to take me to the fishing station tomorrow morning.'

'It's quite a walk,' murmured Peggy. 'Why don't I nip down there for you?'

Mrs Finch's faded blue eyes became steely. 'That's not the point of the exercise,' she said firmly. 'You've far too much to do already, and I'm quite enjoying having the kitchen to myself. I'd forgotten how much I liked cooking – of course there was little point once the boys left for Canada and I was alone. But with such a house-ful to feed, I'm feeling quite excited about digging out my old recipe books.'

Peggy lit a cigarette and leant back in her favourite kitchen chair. The washing-up was done and the house was quiet. Ron was at the pub, Jim at work, and the nurses were having an early night to prepare for their morning shift at the hospital. Cissy was performing with her dance troupe at the Apollo Theatre, and poor little Danuta had scurried back to her room, no doubt finding the other nurses' hospital gossip too hard to take after the crushing rejection by the matron.

Peggy's soft heart went out to her, and she wished she could do something about her predicament. But rules were rules, and although she didn't like the way the woman had treated Danuta, she could understand why she'd had to refuse to employ her as a nurse. Laundry work was tough, though, and she wondered if the frail-looking girl would be able to manage without doing herself an injury.

'Oh,' exclaimed Mrs Finch, 'I almost forgot. Nurse Brown telephoned this afternoon.'

'Is she still coming?'

Mrs Finch frowned. 'I'm not at all sure,' she replied. 'She wasn't making much sense and the line was very crackly.'

Peggy suspected it was the hearing aid that was at fault, but let it pass. 'What did she say exactly?' she coaxed.

'She said something about falling at the hospital, and then went on to tell me she was waiting in the rain.' She shook her grey head, her frown deepening. 'Why she felt it necessary to talk about the weather, I don't know.'

Peggy smiled. 'I think you'll find she was waiting for a train,' she said, 'and no doubt wanted me to call the hospital to let them know she was on her way.' She smiled fondly at the old woman's confused expression and decided it was definitely time to persuade her to get a new hearing aid. 'I'll phone the hospital in the morning to let them know. Poor girl, she's awfully late in getting down here. I hope that matron doesn't treat her too harshly.'

'Let's hope not,' muttered Mrs Finch. 'That woman sounds a fright, and I'm glad *I* don't have to face her.'

'I'll have to warn Danuta, too,' murmured Peggy. 'I know she doesn't really want to share her room, but it's better to have the two latest arrivals together. The other three are very settled, and Suzy's room's a bit small for two beds.'

'Another shed? Why do we need two? Ron has enough clutter as it is.'

'No, dear,' said Peggy patiently. She paused and smiled. 'Perhaps we should go to the doctor and get you a better hearing aid tomorrow?'

'It would be a complete waste of time,' Mrs Finch retorted. 'This one is perfectly all right once I get the volume correctly balanced.'

The sound of a key turning in the latch made Peggy look up, and her worries over everyone fled as her eldest daughter Anne walked into the kitchen. 'Darling,' she breathed as she gave her a hug and kiss. 'What a lovely surprise. Are you staying the night?'

Anne kissed Mrs Finch's cheek and gave her a gentle hug. 'If that's all right,' she replied.

'Of course it is. Your old bed is still in Cissy's room, all it needs is clean linen.'

'Thanks, Mum.' Anne poured a cup of tea and pulled a chair out from the kitchen table. 'It's lovely to be out of those barracks and back in this kitchen again. Not that I don't have huge fun with the other girls,' she added hastily, 'and of course the work we do is exciting and challenging. But home is always best.'

'How are you getting on up there in your cliff caves? The thought of all that chalk over my head would have me screaming mad within minutes.'

'You forget where you are,' Anne replied. 'The plotting of enemy aircraft and shipping takes every ounce of concentration, and when the shift is over, or we're stood down in a lull, we're so tired, we sleep most of the time.'

'Have you managed to see Martin very much?'

Anne sighed as she twirled the rings on her finger. 'We've only been married a matter of months, and I could count the days we've had to-gether on one hand.' A smile teased at the tiny dimple in her cheek. 'But he's thinking about buying us a little house we've seen that's only a few miles from the airbase, so that could soon change everything.'

'But you'll be working day and night with the Observer Corps, and he'll be flying endless missions now the Germans are attacking our cities and ports. How will buying a house make any difference?'

The dimple deepened, and Anne's brown eyes were alight with excitement as she looked at Peggy. 'In a few months' time I'll be a lady of leisure,' she said. 'No more barracks, no more night shifts and endless map plotting for me, just the ordinary, everyday chores of a housewife.'

'But...?' Peggy suddenly understood and she was flooded with warm happiness. 'You're pregnant.' She leapt from her chair and hugged her daughter, the joy spilling over 'How far gone are you? When is it due?'

'We think it must be a honeymoon baby, because the doctor has given us a delivery date in February.'

'Oh, Anne,' said Peggy through her happy tears. 'How lovely.'

'Congratulations, my dear,' chirped Mrs Finch. 'Come and give me a kiss and then pass me that knitting bag. I'm sure I have some white wool in there and I've the perfect pattern for a matinee jacket.'

Peggy and Anne exchanged delighted smiles as Mrs Finch fussed and twittered and rummaged through her vast knitting bag, muttering to herself.

'Oh, Mum,' Anne breathed, 'I'm so happy, and Martin's over the moon. Once we have that little house, everything will be just perfect. I do so hope nothing spoils it all.'

'Of course it won't,' Peggy said briskly, deliberately misunderstanding her daughter's worries over Martin's safety. 'All new mothers panic a bit at first, thinking the worst could happen. But it rarely does, and just think, Anne, in a few months you'll be holding your baby and wondering what all the fuss was about.' She took Anne's hand. 'Has Martin told his parents yet?'

The happy glow remained, but Anne's eyes dulled. 'We decided to wait until the baby's born,' she replied. 'His family have all but ignored us since the wedding and they've made it plain they're not interested in anything we do. Martin and I have decided not to let them spoil our happy news.'

'Quite right too,' agreed Mrs Finch. 'They don't deserve any consideration from you after the way they carried on.' She looked up from the tangle of wool she was trying to unravel and smiled. 'Well done, Anne.'

Peggy made a fresh pot of tea to celebrate and, as she waited for the kettle to boil, she thought of Martin's snooty family – his mother in particular. What a fool the woman was, she thought, to shun her son's wife, and thereby risk losing all the pleasure and excitement of her first grandchild – and all because she regarded Anne as unworthy of her son and the family name.

She filled the pot and forcibly rammed the knitted cosy over it and placed it rather too firmly on the table. If that woman ever showed her nasty, self-righteous face here, she'd let her have a few home truths, and no mistake.

She was about to question Anne more closely over what the doctor had said when the siren began to wail.

Like a well-oiled machine the occupants of Beach View Boarding House swung into action and, armed with pillows, blankets and the box of necessities Peggy kept well stocked, they helped Mrs Finch down the stone steps to the basement and out into the garden.

The searchlights were already piercing the night sky, the siren's banshee wails echoing all along the seafront, reverberating off the chalk cliffs and through the dark streets as the ARP warden shouted orders to turn off lights and get in the shelters. Despite the precautions, no one could black out the moon which gilded the rooftops and cast deep shadows. The conditions were perfect for an enemy raid.

Peggy settled Mrs Finch in her deckchair in the corner and placed the full teapot on the unlit primus stove. Having checked the level of kerosene in the hurricane lamp, she lit the wick with a match from the box of Swan Vestas she always kept to hand, and then made sure everyone was comfortable.

June, Fran and Suzy were in their nightclothes and slippers, but Danuta was still dressed in her drab skirt and cardigan. The contrast between the girls was startling, even in this flickering light,

Peggy realised sadly. The three young nurses were rosy with health, their skins glowing, eyes bright, figures trim and radiating boundless energy. June and Fran were natural blondes, and Suzy had a head of flaming hair that no amount of pins could tame, whereas poor little Danuta looked washed out and dowdy, and several years older than she really was.

'This is my eldest daughter, Anne,' she said by way of introduction. 'She's about to make me a grandmother,' she added proudly.

'Not right this minute, I'm hoping,' said Suzy, her soft southern Irish voice rising through the cacophony outside. 'It's been a while since I did midwifery.'

Anne laughed. 'There's a few months to go yet,' she assured her, 'and I'm determined to have this baby in a nice safe hospital bed, not this dark, cold dungeon with enemy planes screaming overhead.'

'To be sure that's what every mother wants,' said Suzy, with a twinkle in her eye, 'but babies have a way of coming at the wrong time and in the wrong place.' She grinned impishly. 'And I should know, sure me mam's had eight, and not one of us was born in a bed. I came in the middle of the matinee at the Majestic cinema – caused a proper old fuss, I can tell you.'

'That doesn't surprise me one bit,' laughed Peggy, 'but I think we need to change the subject. Anne doesn't want to hear all the horror stories, and this tea is getting cold.'

Danuta sat in silence, the warm cup cradled in

73

her cold fingers, her gaze drifting repeatedly over the other girls as they chattered and laughed and settled down for the duration of the raid. They looked so fresh and innocent; untouched by the horrors she'd had to witness, still eager for life even in these dangerous times. She had little in common with them, their youthful vitality and cheery outlook making her feel dull and dowdy by comparison, but she really should make an effort to get to know them better. After all, she acknowledged, this wasn't the first time she'd been the stranger among close-knit groups, and she'd learnt very quickly that it was important to fit in.

She sneaked a glance at Anne, who looked radiant with happiness, her skin clear, her eyes shining, her whole demeanour proof of her robust health and confidence. Did she realise how lucky she was to have such a wonderful home and supportive family? She hoped she did, for Danuta would have given anything for that right now.

She felt the tiny flutter in her own belly and shielded the barely discernible mound by surreptitiously drawing her cardigan over it. Her baby was as eagerly awaited and just as precious as Anne's – if not more so. For it had been conceived in the last few weeks of its father's life, and was the last tangible proof of the love they'd found amidst the horrors of this war. But the ensuing trauma of her desperate race to escape the SS firing squad, and the lack of medical attention and good, wholesome food must surely have had an adverse effect on that tiny, half-formed being inside her?

She closed her eyes as the menacing drone of enemy aircraft grew louder and the crack of gunfire split the night. The heavy, booming thunder from the guns along the seafront and on the cliff-tops shook the earth beneath her feet, but after the terror of hiding in ditches from enemy tanks and fighter planes, she felt ridiculously safe under this bit of tin in the back of an English suburban garden. The sound of the Dorniers and Messerschmitts was overhead now, and it was clear that it would be a massive raid – probably on London again.

She listened as the others chattered. It was still difficult to tune in to the different accents, and she felt a little shy when she did try and make conversation, not wanting to make a mistake with her English, all too aware that her accent set her apart and that she must appear strange to them. The interview with Matron had reinforced this wariness, and she felt the shame flood through her again as she thought of how proudly she'd told them she was also a nurse. Had Peggy told them about her humiliating rejection and the lowly laundry post she'd been forced to take? She hoped not, but realised it wouldn't remain a secret once she started her shift in the morning.

She took a deep breath and forced herself to concentrate on a more pressing matter. She felt surprisingly well considering what she'd been through, but she knew she must find a doctor and have a proper prenatal check-up. And that could pose another serious problem, for he would have to have no connection with the hospital if she was to keep her pregnancy secret and not incur the wrath of Matron, and the very real possibility of getting sacked.

The all-clear startled Polly awake, and she peered at her watch to discover it was seven in the morning. She'd fallen asleep perched on her case, and now she had a stiff neck, a crick in her back and didn't feel at all refreshed. The thought of yet another long day of travelling made her wearier still.

She became aware of the activity surrounding her, and scrubbed her face with her hands, trying to bring some life to her cold flesh. Everyone was bustling to collect their belongings, and already, there was a crush as people began to climb the long flight of stairs that would take them above ground. Polly slowly gathered her things together and, with a renewed determination to get this endless journey over with as soon as possible, struggled after them.

She emerged into a smoky dawn which stank of burning wood and hot metal, and was heavily laden with thick black dust and flying ash. Horrified by the sight that met her and incapable of moving, she let the others swirl round her as she looked at the smouldering skeletons of once-graceful buildings, the high jets of water spewing from a blasted water main, and heard the sharp bells of ambulances and fire engines.

Men were working furiously to clear rubble from the roads and trolley-bus tracks, and make buildings safe, while firemen were battling to keep their powerful hoses concentrated on a large fire that was consuming a public house on the far corner.

Polly could taste the dust and soot, could feel the grime and grit of it in her hair and on her skin. They were minor irritations and could be washed away, but she knew that the images of that day would remain with her forever.

And then she smiled, a bubble of mild hysteria and amusement growing as she watched a man in a bowler hat delicately pick his way through the rubble. Complete with furled umbrella, briefcase and three-piece suit, he was clearly off to work, and his determined expression told Polly that the aftermath of a bombing raid was the last thing to stop him.

Heartened by the sight, Polly picked up her heavy bags and staggered on to the concourse to find the train that would finally take her to Cliffe-haven.

No one had had much sleep and they'd all emerged from the Anderson shelter bleary-eyed and yawning, the long day ahead stretching before them. The dawn was grey with the plumes of smoke rising from a distant bomb crater, and the usual smell of charred wood and buckled, over-heated metal hung in the air where ash and soot floated in the early breeze.

Danuta and the three nurses hurried to get washed and dressed for work, and Anne and Mrs Finch prepared a hasty breakfast while Peggy went down the street making sure everyone was all right, and that there had been no serious injuries or further bomb damage to the houses.

She helped to make tea in kitchens where the fire had gone out and everything was covered in dust. Sat for a few minutes to ease tears and give a bit of sympathy, and helped one old chap clean his bedroom where the ceiling had collapsed. Armed with a shopping list and ration book from Mrs Cole two doors down who couldn't walk far, she wearily headed back to Beach View Boarding House.

She caught sight of Danuta hurrying down the road in her usual drab skirt and cardigan, and wasn't surprised she'd left the house early. The poor little thing was clearly devastated about not being allowed to nurse, and probably didn't want to add to her humiliation by accompanying the other girls to the hospital. They were a close bunch, those three, but Peggy was determined to find some way of encouraging them to let Danuta join in. The poor girl could do with a bit of fun, and it must be horrible for her to be so far from home.

'Oh dear,' she sighed as she picked up the milk bottles from the doorstep. 'I forgot to warn her about Nurse Brown.' She stood there for a moment, deep in thought. Perhaps having another girl to share her room would ease Danuta's loneliness? She had no idea how old Staff Nurse Brown was, or anything about her family circumstances, so she mustn't jump to conclusions. But that didn't stop her hoping she might become Danuta's friend.

Peggy emerged from her thoughts and slowly made her way through the front door and into the hall where dust motes danced in the early sunlight. The night had been long and tiring, and there was still no sign of Cissy, Jim or Ron. Her previous anger had dwindled throughout the night, and she'd come to the conclusion that she would carry on as usual. It might seem as if she was being weak and woolly-minded, but Jim was her husband and, despite everything, she still loved him and couldn't imagine life without him.

She had closed her ears to her mother's warnings all those years ago and married him anyway, and she'd invested too much in this partnership to falter now. She had made her bed, now she must lie in it, and although some women might have seen her capitulation as weakness, Peggy knew it would take a great deal more strength to keep her marriage together than to walk away from it.

The thought of the coming grandchild warmed her heart as she entered the kitchen, and she smiled down at Anne who was sitting at the cluttered breakfast table with Mrs Finch. She had too much to lose, and divorce had never been an option, she acknowledged, as she placed the bottles of milk on the stone slab in the larder. She would knuckle down and carry on – deal with Jim and his peccadilloes, and ensure the smooth running of this household as she always did: quietly, determinedly and without histrionics.

'Will you be able to stay for a while?' she asked Anne.

She shook her head, making her lovely dark hair bounce against her shoulders. 'Sorry, Mum. I'm expected back before one, and it takes a bit of time cycling up all those hills.'

'Should you be using that bicycle now? I mean,

it's not very comfortable, and what if you fall off?'

Anne laughed and took her hand. 'The last time I fell off a bike I was eight,' she said. 'Don't fuss, Mum. I'm pregnant, not unbalanced and feeble.'

The three of them turned as June, Suzy and Fran clattered down the stairs and shouted their goodbyes before hurrying out of the front door. 'They seem a lively bunch,' said Anne, returning to her cup of tea.

'They certainly keep me on my toes,' agreed Peggy, 'but I like having them around. The house seemed so empty once you and Sally and the boys left.'

Anne patted her hand in sympathy, and then glanced at the clock on the mantelpiece above the range. 'Shouldn't Cissy be back by now?'

Peggy looked at her watch and frowned. 'Yes,' she murmured. 'I wonder what's keeping her?'

As if on cue, Cissy's key turned in the lock and she hurried into the kitchen. 'Sorry I'm late. There was a bit of a flap on because the costumes had been left out during the raid, and half a ceiling of plaster fell on them. I've just spent two hours trying to get them clean enough to wear tonight.'

She smiled at Mrs Finch as she pushed back the blonde hair she'd styled like Dorothy Lamour's and sat down. 'Hello, Anne,' she said through a vast yawn. 'Good to see you. You're looking well. Any more tea in that pot? I'm parched.'

'Anne's got some lovely news,' said Peggy as she added more water to the pot and swirled the leaves round, hoping it wouldn't be too weak.

'Oh, yes?' Cissy clearly wasn't really listening as she scrabbled in her handbag for a handkerchief.

'I'm expecting a baby,' breathed Anne.

Cissy's blue eyes widened momentarily. 'Congratulations,' she murmured, dabbing the handkerchief under her nose. 'When's it due?'

'Sometime in February,' replied Anne with a frown.

'That's nice.' Cissy balled the handkerchief in her fist and stared into her cup as she stirred the spoon round and round in the weak, sugarless tea.

Peggy could see she was distracted, Anne's happy news hardly registering. Her youngest daughter had always been rather self-centred, but she and Anne had been close despite their different aspirations, and it was most unlike Cissy to be almost dismissive of such momentous news. Deciding she was probably tired and out of sorts, she let it pass for now. 'How did the show go last night?'

Cissy shrugged. 'Okay. The air raid didn't help, of course.'

Peggy surreptitiously watched her daughter as she continued to stir the tea. Cissy was almost nineteen, and she and Jim had reluctantly agreed to her joining a travelling troupe of artistes on the understanding they didn't go further than the county borders. It was all Cissy had ever dreamed of – although it was a very small troupe, with no famous names attached to it, and it was unlikely to provide the fame and fortune Cissy had craved ever since her first dance class at the local church hall. But the enthusiasm and ambition for show-business life seemed to have waned over the past few weeks, the cheery, breathless excitement that had always been such an intrinsic part of Cissy had withered, and Peggy couldn't help but notice the dark shadows under her eyes.

'But everything's all right, isn't it?' she persisted.

Cissy's smile was a little too bright. 'Of course, why shouldn't it be?'

'I just wondered.' Peggy was alerted by that false smile. Something was definitely wrong with her youngest daughter. 'It can't be easy working with a new troupe and a new manager. This latest schedule of shows seems awfully hectic, and you're looking tired, darling.'

Cissy avoided her mother's eyes as she drank the tea. 'It's hectic, yes, but if I want to make a name in this business I have to be prepared for hard work.' She put the cup back in the saucer and pushed away from the table, still avoiding Peggy's gaze. 'I hope the water hasn't been turned off. I need a bath after cleaning all those costumes.'

'The mains can't have been hit last night; there's plenty of water. But that doesn't mean you can fill the tub to the top and lounge about in there half the morning,' replied Peggy. 'There's housework and shopping to do and, with Nurse Brown arriving today, I want to give her and Danuta's room a good clean.'

Cissy rolled her eyes. 'I'm exhausted, Mum. Housework is the last thing on my mind.'

'I expect it is, but that doesn't mean you can get away with ignoring it. I expect you back down here within the half-hour,' said Peggy.

Cissy scowled, grabbed her cardigan and slung it over her shoulders then, without another word, left the kitchen.

Peggy heard her light footsteps on the stairs, and the slam of the bathroom door. She couldn't ignore it any longer, she realised. There was definitely something not right with Cissy. The change had come about when Jack Witherspoon had persuaded her and Jim to let her join the small troupe of entertainers he managed. It had meant a bit of travelling, but that was what Cissy had wanted, and it was obvious by the hectic timetable of shows that the troupe was doing rather well. Peggy had initially put the edginess and short temper down to the long hours Cissy worked, but now she suspected it went deeper than that, and it worried her.

Anne broke into her thoughts. 'I must say, Cissy could have shown a bit more enthusiasm over my news. Perhaps it's because she thinks becoming an aunt will make her feel old?'

Peggy buried the anxiety and patted Anne's hand. 'She's probably a bit tired after prancing about on a stage and spending half the night in a shelter. I'm sure when the news sinks in she'll be as enthusiastic as the rest of us.'

She pushed back from the table and began to clear the dishes. If there was one thing she knew for certain about her youngest daughter, it was that she found it impossible to keep things to herself. At some point in the busy day she had ahead of her, Peggy was determined to find the time to sit her down and find out just what it was that was worrying her.

The bombing raid had left several long sections of railway line impassable, and the final leg of Polly's journey to Cliffehaven had proved as difficult and frustrating as the rest of it. She'd lugged her bags off the train and on to one of the buses that had been provided to get her to the next station, only to have to repeat the exhausting process once again within a few miles of her destination.

When the bus finally set her down outside Cliffehaven station, she wanted nothing more than to rest and have a cup of tea. But even that was proving impossible, for the station buffet was shut and there was no sign of a welcoming WVS canteen.

The gulls shrieked and circled overhead as she looked down the steep hill of what appeared to be Cliffehaven's main street to where the sea glittered at the bottom. She had only been to the seaside once before, her parents taking her and her sister to some tiny bay in Wales. She'd been eight or nine, and she remembered huddling beneath a big umbrella each day in her knitted swimsuit, shivering with cold as the rain lashed down, and the sea and sky melded into an unappetising grey. Their picnics had been gritty with sand, and her dad had insisted upon rolling up his trouser legs and tying a knotted hanky on his head.

She smiled fondly at the memories, although, at the time, she'd hated every minute of that holiday. Bringing her thoughts back into order, she took stock of her surroundings. With a name like Beach View, her lodgings had to be down by the seafront somewhere. But as she looked round she realised there were an awful lot of places with sea views – some of them right up in the surrounding hills – and, as it was clearly a fairly large town, she didn't have the energy to walk for miles only to get lost. It was time to ask for directions.

A very pleasant elderly gentleman directed her to the trolleybus stop, which was halfway down the hill. He doffed his hat and wished her luck. Polly thanked him and, with a deep sigh of weariness, lugged her bags to the stop.

She waited for what felt like an age before the trolleybus arrived. Confirming that it would drop her close to Beach View Boarding House, she clambered on board, paid her fare to the young girl who didn't look old enough to be out of the schoolroom, and stowed her big case at the back before sinking gratefully into the nearest vacant seat.

The bell clanged as the engine whined, sparks flew from the overhead electricity lines, and the wheels rattled over the rails that were set in the middle of the main road. She gazed out of the window at the bombed-out shells of buildings and the still smouldering craters the firemen were hosing down. Servicemen strolled along in groups, appreciatively eyeing the local girls who pretended not to see them, and a gang of workmen were busy trying to fix a telegraph pole that had come down on someone's roof. There were piles of sandbags stacked outside the town hall and various official-looking buildings, and long queues had formed outside the few shops that were still open.

Polly noted that the Odeon cinema was showing *Goodbye, Mr Chips,* with Robert Donat and John Mills. She and Adam had enjoyed going to the pictures every Saturday night, and she would have loved to have seen it; John Mills was one of her favourites. But the thought of going without Adam, and the knowledge that there would be little time for such pleasures, made her dismiss the idea completely.

The trolleybus reached the bottom of the hill and turned east along a promenade heavily armoured with gun emplacements. The sea glittered with sun-diamonds beyond the coils of barbed wire and around the huge barricade of concrete blocks that effectively cut off the sand and shingle bay from the Channel. The pier looked sad and rather lonely, cut adrift from the beach, and the white cliffs at the end of the promenade appeared rather daunting as they towered over the fishing station.

Cliffehaven was nonetheless far removed from the Welsh beach of her childhood, and was clearly a bustling, busy town. The sunshine had brought people out to enjoy the fresh air as they strolled along what was left of the promenade, and although many of the big houses had been boarded up for the duration, one or two of the grander hotels along the seafront had been commandeered by the forces. There appeared to be countless numbers of servicemen enjoying the warm day, sitting, walking, watching the girls pass by or playing football and French cricket on the grass strip that ran in front of their hotels.

Polly could just imagine it in peacetime, with

86

colourful deckchairs and parasols, a band playing on the pier, flashing lights exhorting people to put a penny in the slot and try their luck at winning a soft toy. She could almost hear the hurdy-gurdy music, could almost smell the candyfloss and toffee apples and the lovely aroma of vinegar on hot fish and chips.

Her daydream was shattered by the sound of the conductress's voice.

'This is your stop,' she said as the trolleybus pulled up beside the fishing station. She pointed up the steep hill. 'It's a bit of a climb, I'm afraid. You'll find Beach View Terrace three streets up on your right.'

Polly thanked her and hauled her suitcases off the trolleybus. She stood on the pavement for a moment to breathe in the lovely crisp, clean air, then sorted out the straps of her handbag and gas mask and began the long, slow climb.

She was soon out of breath and her arms ached as she swapped the heavier case from hand to hand, and it was only through sheer bloody-mindedness and a determination not to be beaten, that she finally reached Beach View Road. Setting the cases down, she took a long hard look at where she would be living for the duration.

Beach View Boarding House was halfway down a side street that looked the same as all the others she'd passed. The steep hill she'd climbed from the seafront went on and on, and it seemed the Victorian designers and architects of this part of town had decided that long terraces of villas were the most pleasant way of giving everyone a glimpse of the sea. It was within walking distance of the local shops in Camden Road and conveniently close to the hospital, which was a relief.

Polly stepped back to get a better view. The area had suffered quite a bit of damage, and she could see a huge crater at the end of the road, where she guessed there had once been a continuance of the terrace. Like the other villas, the boarding house was tall and fairly narrow, with three storeys and a basement, the window of which she could see beneath the broad white steps that led up to an impressive portico. This ornate piece of Victorian artistry sheltered the front door, which had a brass knocker in the shape of a lion's head, but sadly was missing most of the coloured panes surrounding it.

The house looked a little battle-scarred despite the polished brass and pristine white nets at the windows. The white stucco was smoke-stained and chipped in places, some of the window panes in the bays had been replaced with hardboard, and the elegant lamps cemented into the ends of the sweeping balustrades had been mangled and shattered beyond repair. But Polly could imagine how nice it must have been before, and had high hopes that her room would prove comfortable and that the landlady would be pleasant. She carried the bags up the steps and rapped the knocker.

Chapter Five

Danuta had run all the way to the hospital, but she was still almost two hours late for her shift. She stood, out of breath and frantic, wondering where on earth she was supposed to go to fetch her uniform, when she caught the terrifying sight of Matron approaching like an ominous man-o'-war in fully starched sail.

'Why are you standing about here? Your shift began two hours ago.'

'There was an air raid,' Danuta replied, determined not to be cowed by this woman. 'I couldn't come any earlier.'

'This hospital does not grind to a halt because of air raids,' said Matron, puffing out her formidable bosom. 'It is your duty to make sure you arrive on time.' She eyed Danuta's clothing with disdain. 'Where is your uniform?'

'That's what I was trying to find out, but...'

'Really, Chimpsky, it is your duty to find out things like this beforehand so you don't waste valuable time.'

'My name is Chmielewski,' Danuta said stonily.

Matron's glare hardened. 'Go down those stairs to the basement, find Stores and put your uniform on. You will work an extra two hours at the end of your shift to make up for the time you have lost.' She looked down her long nose. 'If you are late again, *Chimpsky,* you will be dismissed immediately.' She turned on her heel and bustled away, every step making the starched apron crackle.

Danuta balled her fists and resisted the urge to walk right out of this hospital and keep going. Matron was a *kurwa* – a bitch – and it was clear she'd taken an instant dislike to Danuta. If this was a foretaste of what life would be like working here, then it certainly wouldn't be easy.

She ran down the steps and headed for the basement stores. Perhaps it was a good thing she wasn't on the wards, and beneath that woman's constant glare, for sooner or later she would tell her just what she thought of her. At least, down here in the bowels of the hospital, she could escape her and get on with her work until she could find something better to do with her skills.

'Staff Nurse Brown?'

Polly smiled at the neat little woman who stood in the doorway, wrapped in a floral apron. 'At last, yes. But please call me Polly, Mrs Reilly.'

'I'm Peggy. Come in, dear. You look as if you've had the most awful journey. I expect you'd like a nice cup of tea and something to eat while you put your feet up for a bit. I'll take you to your room later.'

The thought of tea and something to eat made her stomach rumble and, as Polly hoisted the cases over the doorstep and dumped them in the hall-way, she remembered she hadn't eaten since the previous lunchtime. A swift glance took in the faded paint and wallpaper, and the worn carpet on the stairs – but Peggy Reilly was clearly a pleasant little woman, and she could smell furniture polish and the homely scent of cooking.

'I'd love a cup of tea and a sandwich,' she said, taking off her coat and scarf and shaking out her hair. 'And a minute to sit down and enjoy it,' she added with a grin. 'It feels as if I've been travelling for days.'

Peggy grinned back. 'Come on into the kitchen. The kettle's boiled, and there's a comfy chair just waiting for you.'

Polly followed the bustling little figure through the hall and into a cheerful and homely kitchen where an old lady was quietly snoozing beside the black Kitchener range.

'Don't worry about Mrs Finch,' Peggy said cheerfully, 'she's had a busy morning making fish pie, and she always has a nap around this time of day. Her hearing aid is switched off, so we won't disturb her.'

Polly took in her surroundings. There was a large framed portrait of the King hanging above the mantel, which was clearly the depository for ration books, leaflets, calendars and lists. Shelves housed pots, pans and crockery, the wireless took pride of place on a highly polished dresser, and in the centre of the room was a big table with at least six chairs round it. The square stone sink was beneath the only window, the wooden draining board covered in freshly washed crockery. Everything from the lino on the floor to the oilcloth on the table was faded and rather shabby, but it felt welcoming – felt like home.

'You'll have to excuse the mess,' said Peggy, swiftly gathering newspapers and magazines from the table, and stuffing Mrs Finch's knitting bag out of the way. 'We're all at sixes and sevens today, what with the raid last night.'

'I got into London just as it started,' said Polly.

'How is it up there?' Peggy was plumping the cushion in the other chair that sat by the range. 'Sit down, dear, and I'll get you that tea and sandwich. It'll only be a bit of spam, I'm afraid.'

'Spam sounds lovely,' she replied, sinking into the chair with a sigh of gratitude. 'As for London – it was awful, and I pity all those poor souls who have to sleep in the underground every night. I don't know how they do it.'

'My sister Doreen is up there,' murmured Peggy, running her hands down her floral wrap-round apron. 'I do worry about her, but she seems to be coping admirably as always.'

Polly didn't really know what to say to this. 'We've been lucky in Hereford, with no raids at all as yet, so it was a bit of a shock getting caught in the middle of it all. But the Londoners seem to have become inured to it and made themselves quite at home underground.'

'I'm surprised you've come down here if Hereford's so safe,' said Peggy as she hastily spread a thin layer of margarine on some bread and added sliced tomato to the spam. 'We're being called "bomb alley" by the press, and I suspect you've seen some of the damage our town has suffered on your way up here from the station.'

'I did indeed,' Polly acknowledged. She took the sandwich and cup of tea Peggy handed her and realised there would be little chance of quietly relaxing, for the other woman was settling down on a kitchen chair preparing for a good gossip.

'The crater at the end of our road was due to a gas explosion,' explained Peggy. 'We've been quite lucky, considering.'

Polly sipped the welcoming tea and munched the sandwich as she glanced at the old woman who was softly snoring in the other chair. She found she had to make a concerted effort not to fall asleep herself.

'I see you're married,' said Peggy, her gaze settling on Polly's wedding ring. 'What does your husband think of you leaving the safety of Hereford for this place?'

Polly conceded Peggy had a right to know who her lodgers were and the reason for them being there, but it was hard to talk about Adam. She finished the sandwich and sipped the tea before answering. 'My husband doesn't know I'm here,' she said finally. 'He was injured in France and is now at Cliffehaven Memorial, which is why I came down to help nurse him.'

'Oh, my dear, I'm so sorry. I didn't mean to pry.' Peggy fell silent and drank her tea, her dark eyes still bright with curiosity despite her words. 'Do you have family back in Hereford?' she asked moments later.

Polly bit down on a smile. It was clear Peggy hadn't finished her inquisition. 'We have a daughter, Alice,' she said, 'but she's gone with the rest of my family on one of the convoys to Canada. I have an uncle there, and they will stay with him until it's safe to come back.'

At the thought of Alice, she felt the tears well

93

and sniffed them away. 'I could have gone with her, of course, but my husband needs me, and after what I've witnessed these last two days, I now know she'll be a lot safer in Canada than here with me.'

'It's always hard to let your children go,' murmured Peggy. 'My two boys have been evacuated to Somerset, and this house feels very empty without them.' She cocked her head, the dark, wavy hair falling over her brow. 'Charlie's just turned nine, and Bob's thirteen. How old is your Alice?'

'She's five.' Polly's voice broke. Talking about Alice was too painful, and she changed the subject quickly. 'I will need to wash and tidy up before I go to the hospital. Could you show me my room, please?'

'But surely you should rest before dashing off again?'

Polly drained the cup of tea and smiled ruefully. 'I'm already a week late, and if the matron at the Memorial is half as particular about timekeeping and rules as the one at Hereford Royal, I'm already in deep trouble.'

'I'm afraid she is,' murmured Peggy. 'Poor Danuta's already had a run-in with her, and the other girls say she's an absolute dragon.' She put down her teacup and stood. 'Come on then. I'll show you where everything is.'

Polly was shown the cellar steps to the back door and listened closely as Peggy went through the evacuation routine they followed when the air raid siren went. She looked out of the window at the Anderson shelter and the garden. 'That's quite a show,' she said in admiration of the vegetable patch. 'Who's the gardener?'

'My father-in-law, Ron,' Peggy replied. 'He lives in the basement with Harvey.' At Polly's frown, she hurried to explain. 'He's a Bedlington-cross, what Ron calls a lurcher, and has the unfortunate habit of sleeping on Ron's bed.' She sighed and shrugged. 'I don't really approve, but Harvey's become rather adept at finding people under the rubble and is quite the celebrity.' She paused and smiled. 'He hates the sound of the siren, though, and howls to the heavens until it stops. But he's as good as gold during the bombing. Which I find very strange.'

'Is he used to loud noises then? My dad was a farmer and had several gun dogs. Nothing much frightened them, either, but anything high-pitched used to set them howling.'

'Ron takes him hunting, but he and Harvey are laws unto themselves,' confided Peggy dryly. 'You'll meet them at tea along with everyone else.'

She bustled into the hall, showed Polly where the dining room was and took charge of the smaller bag. 'Jim and I have the back bedroom down here,' she said. 'It's nice and central, and I can keep an eye on comings and goings.' She grinned. 'With so many pretty young girls in the house, and so many servicemen chasing after them, I've got my work cut out. But nothing much gets past me. I ran a bed and breakfast business here before the war, you know, and you wouldn't believe some of the shenanigans that went on.'

'I don't expect I would,' Polly murmured. Peggy

was lovely and friendly, but her endless chatter was draining Polly of any energy she had left, and at this moment, all she wanted was to lie down and shut out the rest of the world for a few minutes.

'We have quite a houseful,' Peggy continued cheerfully as she led the way upstairs. 'There's June and Fran who share the middle room right at the top, and Suzy who has the single one next door. They're nurses too, so you'll find plenty to chat about, I'm sure.' She paused for breath and hurried on. 'My daughter Cissy's room is the third one on that floor, and she shares with her sister Anne when she's off duty at the OC. Anne's married now, and she and Martin are about to buy their own little home.' Her eyes sparkled with happiness. 'She's expecting our first grand-child, which is very exciting.'

'How lovely for you,' murmured Polly, who was getting confused with all the names and relation-ships. No doubt they would be easier to remember once she could put faces to them.

They reached the first floor. 'That's the bath-room. I'll show you how to light the boiler with-out losing your eyebrows in a minute. Mrs Finch sleeps in that room, and this one is yours.'

For the first time in half an hour, she fell silent. Then she smiled hesitantly. 'I'm sorry, dear, but you're going to have to share with Danuta.'

'Oh. I didn't realise. Isn't there another room? Only I'll be coming in at odd hours and I don't want to disturb anyone.'

Peggy shook her head. 'Only down in the base-ment, but that's in a terrible state with all Ron's clutter and the smell of dog. You'll be much better up here, I assure you.'

'I see,' murmured Polly. 'You've mentioned Danuta before. Who is she?'

'She's about your age and Polish,' gabbled Peggy, who was clearly trying to persuade Polly that Danuta would make the perfect room-mate. 'She's very sweet, but terribly shy and awkward, and needs taking out of herself a bit more. I expect she feels a little lost at the moment, what with everything being so foreign, and that matron not letting her do her nursing.'

Polly thought she'd come to the end of her explanation, but Peggy snatched a breath and hurried on.

'Her brother was billeted here for a while, you know, but he was killed only weeks before she arrived, and of course that has hit her hard. It will do her good to have a bit of company, and I'm sure you'll get on like a house on fire.'

Peggy finally ran out of breath and looked at Polly hopefully.

Polly tried to absorb this flood of information. She didn't want to share a room with a complete stranger – especially someone who was in mourning and probably couldn't speak much English. But there seemed to be no other option.

'I'm sorry, dear. I know it isn't what you expected, but Danuta turned up out of the blue looking for Aleksy, and of course I couldn't possibly turn her away.'

Polly realised she was making a fuss over nothing, thereby upsetting Peggy, who didn't deserve it. 'It's all right,' she hurriedly assured her. 'I'm sure we'll get on fine.'

Peggy smiled brightly and opened the door with a flourish. 'There we are then, dear. That's your bed, and of course there's plenty of space for your things in the wardrobe and chest of drawers.' She lowered her voice. 'Danuta brought hardly anything with her from Poland,' she confided, 'and most of that is only fit for the ragbag.'

Polly wasn't at all sure about the sound of this young woman but decided it would be unfair to judge her before they'd even met. The irony was that Danuta might not want to share either, in which case, they'd just have to knuckle down and make the best of it until another room became free.

'I will need your ration book, dear, and I'm sure I don't need to remind you to keep the blackout curtains shut after dark – and of course you will need sixpences for the meter.' Peggy's smile was hesitant still, as if she was aware of Polly's uncertainty with the arrangements. 'I change the towels and linen once a week. Breakfast is at seven, lunch at midday and tea at six-thirty. Of course with all you girls doing shifts at the hospital, mealtimes are adjusted accordingly, but I'd appreciate you letting me know what your shifts are.'

Polly placed the heavy suitcase on the floor. 'It's a lovely room,' she said truthfully. 'I'm sure I'll be very comfortable here.' She walked into the bay and looked out of the window through the criss-cross of white tape. There was no view of the beach at all, which was rather disappointing.

Peggy seemed to read her thoughts. 'The only room with just a glimpse of the sea is at the top of the house – but even then you have to stand on tiptoe.' She smiled and shrugged. 'It doesn't really matter,' she continued. 'None of us has any time to sit and look at the view any more, and the seafront isn't as pretty as it was anyway.'

Polly followed her into the bathroom, listened carefully as Peggy demonstrated the mysteries of lighting the boiler and thought longingly of a bath and a few minutes of peace before she had to go out again.

Peggy's expression was understanding. 'I'll leave you to it, but be sparing with the water, dear. All these raids mean we have to conserve every drop.' She headed back to the landing and hesitated on the top step. 'I do hope you and Danuta get along,' she said softly. 'She needs a friend.'

Polly stood on the landing and watched her hurrying down the stairs. Peggy Reilly was warm and caring, the very opposite of the seaside land-ladies lampooned on postcards and by the musical hall comedians, and Polly counted herself very fortunate. Turning back to the bedroom, she closed the door and leant against it, taking in the room more carefully.

It was comfortable and spotlessly clean, the sunlight streaming through the window on to polished furniture and floorboards. Compared to the accommodation provided by the hospital when she was a student nurse, it was luxurious, for although she had to share, there was plenty of room for both of them, and the beds looked temptingly soft.

She moved away from the door and approached the small rattan table that stood beside Danuta's bed. Looking down, she saw the faded, creased and water-stained photographs. Without touching them, and feeling a little guilty at her prying, Polly regarded the faces of the elderly couple who seemed to be sitting at a table in a sunlit garden. There was a snapshot of a younger couple with a little girl, and another of the same handsome, dark-eyed young man in the uniform of the Polish air force. Polly studied the faces, and wondered if this was the brother Danuta had lost.

Realising it was none of her business, she set about unpacking. But as she opened the drawers and found the few shabby bits of clothing that must belong to Danuta, she felt a twinge of pity. The poor girl clearly possessed very little, and Polly knew enough from the newscasts to realise that Danuta's journey here must have been fraught with danger. No wonder she was finding it hard to settle.

As she hung her dresses in the empty wardrobe and placed her shoes at the bottom, she couldn't dismiss the memory of those haunting photographs. Had Danuta left her family behind in occupied Poland – or were they dead?

Polly closed the wardrobe door and placed her own precious photographs on the mantelpiece before pausing for a moment in deep contemplation. Peggy had said Danuta needed a friend – well, she did too. Perhaps sharing this room wasn't such a bad idea after all.

Polly pushed the empty cases under her bed and resisted the urge to lie down on the tempting eiderdown. If she closed her eyes now, she would probably sleep for hours, and she had to get to the hospital without further delay. Grabbing her washbag and clean clothes, she plucked the towel from the bed and hurried to the bathroom.

The Apollo Theatre had been built in the latter part of the last century when the railway had opened up the way to Cliffehaven and people began to take their holidays at the seaside. It stood squarely on the corner of Cliffe High Street and Queen's Parade, which ran the length of the promenade, and had, so far, survived the air raids.

There were elegant doors leading into a grand foyer where large chandeliers had once graced the ornately decorated ceiling – these had been taken down for the duration – and sweeping staircases led to the different sections of the auditorium. The balconies, boxes, pillars and ceiling were heavily gilded, the walls covered in thick flock wallpaper, and the velvet tableau curtain which drew up and back from the stage was deeply fringed with gold tassels. At night the theatre took on an air of mystery and grandeur, but in the harsh light of day, it merely looked tatty.

The small troupe of dancers, singers, musicians, comedians and acrobats were playing at the Apollo for a week before they went on the road again. It was a respite for all of them, for the travelling had proved exhausting, and it was good to be in one place for more than a night.

Rehearsals were in full swing that afternoon and the dancers were being put through their paces before the evening show. Cissy was wearing a leotard beneath her wrap-round cardigan and shorts, but despite the fast tap routine she'd been rehearsing with the other girls, she was chilled by the draught which always blew from the wings. She could also feel her nose twitching from the dust that rose from the stage with every pounding step, and tried to sniff away the urge to sneeze.

'Cecily Reilly! Concentrate!' The dance master hit the floor with the gold-topped cane he always carried. 'You have the grace and aptitude of an overfed carthorse.'

Cissy glared at him and caught up with the others as Mrs Philips hammered out the tune on the upright piano. Horace Dalrymple was a vicious old queen who considered himself far too gifted and important to be stuck in Cliffehaven with a bunch of hoofers he regarded as having little talent. He was habitually dressed in a dark suit and black fedora, with a gaudy cravat tied at the open neck of his flamboyant silk shirts. His hair was a shade too long, and several shades too black for a man in his sixties, and the cane was not an added affectation – he liked nothing better than to rap ankles and knees with it when he was displeased.

Cissy and the other dancers had eagerly awaited his arrival, for he was considered to be one of the best choreographers in the business, but they were soon to be disappointed. His star had clearly been extinguished some years ago, and his routines proved very ordinary, with no flare or imagination to set them apart, and Cissy could have danced them in her sleep.

Thinking of sleep, Cissy stifled a yawn as she executed the kick-ball-changes, twirled the straw boater above her head and advanced, high-stepping with the others, to the front of the stage for the finale. The previous night had felt endless and she'd only managed a couple of hours' disturbed sleep before having to help dust down all the costumes. Then her mother had insisted she help with the housework, and she'd only just had time to do her make-up and hair before she was due at the theatre for rehearsals.

The thought of another show tonight, and the very real possibility that she would be spending yet more sleepless hours in the shelter beneath the theatre, didn't lighten her mood. But it wasn't the cold, the long hours or Horace's continued sniping that was really bothering her. It was the fact that her mother suspected something was wrong – which it was – and that she could never confide in her about it. For Jack Witherspoon's worrying ultimatum was not a subject to be discussed with anyone, least of all Peggy.

'Eyes and teeth,' shouted Horace, 'and stick out those tits. It's what the punters want, God help them.'

Cissy plastered on the false smile and stuck out her meagre chest as, with a clash of chords, the music ended.

'Hold the pose. Now, bow and flourish those hats.' The cane rapped the floor. 'Together!' he roared.

Cissy sneaked a glance at her best friend Amy, and they shared a grin as they bowed and flourished to order.

'Enough.' Horace drew a pristine handkerchief from his jacket pocket and delicately mopped his brow. 'How on earth I'm supposed to work with these people, I have no idea,' he muttered to himself. 'Ghastly, absolutely ghastly.'

He swept off the stage, ignoring Mrs Philips who usually bashed out tunes at the Jolly Sailor, but who'd been roped in to play the piano for rehearsals when the pianist was too drunk to oblige. 'Take ten,' he shouted from the wings. 'Then you'll do the whole routine again until I'm satisfied you know what you're doing.'

Cissy and the other girls quickly grabbed their overcoats and bags from the wings and hurried into the freezing corridor. The dressing rooms downstairs weren't up to much, but someone had brought in a kerosene heater and they could huddle around that until they had to be back on stage again.

Cissy was about to follow Amy down the narrow stairs when her way was barred by the troupe manager, Jack Witherspoon. Her low spirits plunged further as she looked up at him and realised the moment had come to make a decision.

Jack was about the same age as her father, with dark hair and eyes and a luxuriant moustache of which he was very proud. Broad-shouldered, handsome and always immaculately dressed, he wore a wedding ring and looked as trustworthy and urbane as a bank manager – which was why her parents had agreed to her joining the troupe. But Cissy had learnt to her cost that Jack Witherspoon was not at all what he seemed.

'We need to discuss those publicity photographs,' he said.

She tried to keep the tremor out of her voice. 'I

don't mind doing the usual sort of thing, but that's as far as it goes, Jack.'

'Now, Cissy, be reasonable, darling.' He put his arm over her shoulder and firmly steered her along the corridor. 'You do want to get noticed, don't you? And those shots won't go to just anyone, but to some very high-powered people in the industry who are always looking for new talent.'

Cissy found herself in his office with the door shut and Jack barring the way out. 'Of course I want to get noticed,' she replied, 'but not like that.'

He reached out a hand and wound a strand of her bleached hair round his finger. 'You're very lovely, you know, and quite the little star. I only want what's best for you, Cissy, and after all the years I've worked in this business, I've got the contacts to do something very special for you.'

'But...' Cissy tried to edge away from him, but his other hand snaked round her waist, tethering her to his broad chest.

'Oh, Cissy, Cissy,' he murmured in her ear. 'You're so lovely, so desirable. It would be a terrible shame for it all to go to waste when you could have so much more.'

She froze in his embrace as his lips travelled over her cheek and down her neck. It wasn't as if his kisses were unpleasant, in fact they did strange and rather wonderful things to her insides – it was just that it didn't feel right at all to be kissed by someone as old as her dad. 'Please, Jack,' she managed. 'Don't do that.'

'But, darling,' he said, his brown eyes widening.

'You do want to have star billing, don't you?'

She nodded reluctantly.

'Then you must act like a star and not get all prissy and camera-shy,' he crooned, holding her more tightly. 'Do you think the big Hollywood stars think twice about showing a bit of flesh? Of course they don't, and I know how ambitious you are, Cissy. It would be a shame to ruin everything when I can help you achieve all you've ever wanted.'

'I know you think I'm being silly,' she began, 'but I don't feel comfortable about it, and Mum and Dad wouldn't like it.'

He stepped back from her, his dark eyes stormy. 'Oh, grow up, darling. This is show business, not the school playground, and if you want to succeed, you'll do as I say.'

Cissy was in a quandary. In fact, she'd been in a quandary for several days. Jack was sophisticated and worldly, and in a position to further her career. In her naïvety, she'd fallen right into his trap weeks ago, flattered by his attention and enjoying his flirting as she fended off his advances – until she'd heard the other girls talking and discovered she was just the latest in a long line to have been fooled by his charms.

But some of those girls were now working with Gracie Fields, Tommy Trinder, George Formby and a host of other variety stars. They were even travelling abroad to entertain the troops, and some of them were in London at the Windmill. Not that she wanted to show her breasts off at the Windmill, but Jack Witherspoon hadn't been lying when he said he had contacts – he knew people in high places, and it wouldn't do to upset him.

Jack strode across the room and poured a tot of whisky from a nearby decanter then drank it down. Perching on the corner of his desk, he took his time lighting his cigar, his gaze never straying from her face. 'You've had two weeks to think about it, Cissy. Now it's time to come to a decision. The photographer is in the other room. Two hours and it'll all be over, and then I'll take you out to dinner at the Grand Hotel after the show.'

'Will I have to take everything off?' Her voice was small and hesitant.

He smiled and smoothed his moustache. 'Always leave them wanting more, Cissy. Just push everything off your shoulders and do the best with your cleavage,' he said quietly, his gaze watchful. 'The photographer knows his stuff. You'll be fine.'

'I don't know,' stammered Cissy. 'I've never posed like that before.'

He slid from the desk and regarded her through the cigar smoke. 'Then it's time you learnt,' he said evenly. 'You have two choices, Cissy. Go in that room and be the starlet I know you really are, or go back and moulder in the chorus. There'll be no second chances, and there's plenty of other girls out there who would give their eye teeth for such an opportunity.'

Cissy dipped her chin, the tears blinding her. 'All right,' she whispered.

Chapter Six

Polly had bathed and changed into a clean dress and cardigan and, with her hair freshly brushed and tied back at the nape, she'd applied powder and lipstick in the hope that Adam wouldn't think she looked too much of a fright.

She looked in the mirror and realised with a jolt that her weariness no longer showed, and that the excitement of seeing him again had enlivened her eyes and brought colour back into her face. She just prayed that the information she'd been given by the hospital had been correct, and that he really was on the slow road to recovery.

The walk to the hospital didn't take long, and she took the opportunity to glance into Camden Road's shop windows before passing the abandoned shell of the primary school and entering the hospital grounds. A quick check on the large board in the reception hall told her that Adam's ward was on the ground floor.

The hospital was a maze of confusing corridors, but she found it eventually and took a deep breath before entering Men's Surgical. As the double doors swung behind her, she became aware of the great silence in the room. There were twelve beds in all, each one occupied with what looked like a seriously injured patient, and although she looked at each in turn, it was impossible to spot Adam. She experienced rising panic. Perhaps he'd been moved to another ward? If so, where on earth could he be?

'Can I help you?' The nurse was a probationer in a blue candy-striped uniform and plain starched cap. Her name tag said she was Student Nurse Barker.

'I'm here to see my husband, Sergeant Adam Brown,' murmured Polly. 'Is he on this ward?'

'Visiting hour isn't until six o'clock.'

'I've come all the way from Hereford to be with him,' said Polly, 'and tomorrow I will be working here as a staff nurse. Surely a few minutes won't hurt?'

The girl looked nervously over her shoulder. 'Matron is very strict about visiting hours,' she breathed. 'I'll be in the most fearful trouble if she finds you in here.'

'But he is here, isn't he?'

Student Nurse Barker nodded reluctantly. 'But I think you should wait until Sister Morley comes back from the sluice,' she said. 'She left me in charge, but I'm not allowed to...'

Polly had had enough of this shilly-shallying. 'I'll just have a peek at him, and then go and find Sister to make sure you don't get into trouble,' she said kindly. 'Which bed is he in?'

The little nurse sighed, looked nervously towards the swing doors and bit her lip. 'He's in the bed over there on the end, but he's very poorly, Mrs Brown. Please don't do anything to disturb him.'

Polly's heart thudded and her breath caught in her throat. 'I was led to believe he was over the worst?'

'I don't know who told you that.' The probationer's eyes widened. 'He's had extensive surgery, and although Mr Fortescue says the operations went well, he's still concerned at the time it is taking for Sergeant Brown to recover.'

'Can I see his notes?'

The little student nurse hastily stood in front of the desk where the patient notes were neatly stacked. 'I can't let you do that,' she gasped.

Polly realised she was overstepping the mark and that the girl could get into serious trouble if caught handing patients' notes to strangers. She turned from her and headed for Adam's bed.

As she drew nearer, her gaze became fixed on the gaunt, still man that looked so frail and shrunken beneath the white sheet and blankets. If it hadn't been for the heart-shaped birthmark on his lower arm, she wouldn't have recognised him, for he bore little resemblance to the brawny, handsome husband she'd kissed goodbye so many months before. Her fear for him rose and threatened to choke her. He was clearly far more seriously injured than she'd been led to believe, and seeing him like this not only broke her heart, but made her very angry. Why couldn't they have told her the truth?

She sank on to the chair, taking care not to knock the drips that hung by his bedside, and gently took the wasted hand that lay on the blanket. The broad palm and long, capable fingers that had once wielded engineering tools with ease were now soft and pale and lifeless in her hand.

Polly was aware of the little nurse hovering close

by as she eyed the many drip feeds that were snaking into his arms, and read the labels on the bags suspended above her. She felt a stab of fear as she realised how serious Adam's condition must be. For this was the man she'd adored since childhood. The man who'd held her and loved her, who'd been her rock and her best friend, the father of their precious Alice – and now he was fighting to stay alive.

Tears blinded her as she took in the heavy bandaging that almost obscured his face, and most of his chest. His left leg was in plaster, his right arm suspended in traction. His chest rose and fell in shallow, ragged breaths beneath the swathe of bandages, the sharp lines of his collar-bones jutting nakedly above the linen sheet.

'Oh, Adam, my love,' she breathed, kissing the lifeless fingers. 'I nearly lost you, didn't I?' She pressed the palm of his hand against her cheek. 'But I'm here now. We'll get through this to-gether, my darling.'

'What is that woman doing in here?'

At the sound of the booming voice, Polly swept away her tears and turned to see the probationer quailing before a large woman who could only be Matron Billings.

'I... She... It's Mrs Brown, Matron,' the nurse stuttered. 'She's come all the way from Hereford to see her husband, and I didn't think...'

'It is not your place to *think,* Barker, but to obey the rules. Wait there. I will deal with you later.' Her expression was grim as she swept towards Polly, the steely eyes boring into her, each step crackling with starch.

Polly stood and watched her approach without flinching. She was used to formidable matrons and would not be cowed. 'Student Nurse Barker obeyed the rules, Matron,' she said quietly. 'I chose to ignore them. If anyone should be punished, it is me.'

'And who are you to flout my orders?' The cold gaze trawled over her.

'Staff Nurse Brown,' she replied evenly.

'You were supposed to be here a week ago.'

'Due to severe staff shortages, I was needed at Hereford County Hospital until two days ago. I sent a telegram to let you know I would be delayed.'

'I have received no such telegram.' The expression was unrelenting.

'Well,' said Polly, 'I'm here now, Matron.'

'It simply isn't good enough,' she snapped. She folded her hands at her waist and took a deep breath, making the buttons strain over her cliff-like bosom. 'I will *not* have my wards disrupted with visitors out of hours. You will *learn,* Staff Nurse Brown, that it does not pay to take liberties with my express orders.'

Polly could well imagine that was so, but she said nothing as she reached once again for Adam's hand.

Matron's gaze flickered over the united fingers, and her lips pursed. 'Sergeant Brown needs his rest.' She took Adam's hand and tucked it firmly beneath the blanket before she checked the watch on her bosom. 'I have a very busy evening ahead, but as you're here you might as well come into my office so I can organise your shifts.'

Polly was about to protest when she caught sight of the probationer silently pleading with her not to upset the old battleaxe further. She took a swift glance at Adam, who hadn't moved since she'd arrived, and hurried after the sturdy figure sailing towards the doors.

Matron's office proved to be as tightly ordered as the woman who now sat behind the vast desk. Polly took in the filing cabinets and shelves of folders, noted the lack of flowers and photo-graphs and the absence of a chair for her to sit upon. She hitched the straps of her handbag and gas-mask box over her shoulder and prepared for the undoubted tongue-lashing she was about to receive.

'Your tardiness has already disrupted my schedule,' Matron said as she flicked through the neat pile of papers on her desk. 'I have assigned you to Women's Surgical, and you will start tomorrow at one o'clock'

'I would prefer to work on Men's Surgical,' said Polly.

'You will work where I assign you, Brown. I can't have relatives in charge of my patients. It simply won't do.'

'But I'm qualified to nurse him,' she persisted, 'and surely it will help his recovery if he knows I'm there?'

'You may visit him during the allotted hour – as long as you are not on duty,' Matron Billings looked up from the papers, and something soft-ened in her expression. 'Your husband's recovery is taking longer than Mr Fortescue expected, but I can assure you he is in very capable hands.'

'His injuries seem far more serious than I expected. Does Mr Fortescue consider he'll make a full recovery?'

'He does – but it won't be helped by you getting emotional, Staff Nurse Brown. Which is why you will be working in Women's Surgical.'

'Would it be possible to speak to Mr Fortescue about his treatment?'

'Mr Fortescue is not only a very important man, but a busy one. You may be able to speak to him when he does his rounds in the morning – but you are not to bother him for more than a few minutes. Any time you spend away from your duties must be added to your shift. You are here to work, Staff Nurse Brown, not to pester the consultants.'

Polly was about to argue when Matron Billings checked her watch again and pushed back the chair. 'You will sign for your uniform downstairs in Stores, and it is your responsibility to ensure it remains in pristine condition. Any damage or loss will be deducted from your wages.' She plucked a folder from her desk. 'I will come down with you. A new girl started in the laundry today, and I need to check on her.'

Polly's thoughts were whirling as she followed Matron out of the room and down another flight of steps. She'd been working on Men's Surgical since she'd qualified and it was ludicrous to keep her apart from Adam. It looked as if Matron was determined to make life as difficult as possible.

As they reached the hospital basement she was greeted by the humidity and fragrance of hot water, soap and wet cloth, and the steady rumble of large machinery. As Matron pushed open the laundry door Polly had a glimpse, through clouds of steam, of numerous ironing boards, vast tubs and mangles and a number of drably dressed women wrestling with quite alarming amounts of bedding.

'Stores is that way,' said Matron. 'Make sure you sign for everything.' She pushed through the door and into the steam. 'Chimpsky!' she roared. 'Mind what you're doing. That sheet is about to fall on the floor.'

Polly felt a pang of pity for whoever was getting the sharp edge of Matron's tongue, and hurried along to the stores.

She was measured for her uniform, which consisted of a loose-fitting light blue dress, with detachable starched collars, and an elasticated belt to which she would add the buckle she'd been awarded in Hereford following her final qualifying exams. There was a navy blue woollen cape with a red lining, which had to be worn outside regardless of the weather. Two pairs of thick black stockings were added to the pile, along with a cap, apron and sturdy black lace-up shoes.

Checking everything was in order, she signed the clipboard and then wrapped the clothes in the large piece of brown paper provided by the woman behind the counter, and secured the bulky parcel with string.

Hampered by the parcel, her handbag and gas-mask box, she struggled past the laundry and made her way up the two flights of stairs to the entrance hall. She would have to tell Peggy she would be late for supper, for there was just time to get back to Beach View and hang everything up before snatching a cup of tea and coming back for visiting hour.

As she hurried along Camden Road and past the shuttered Anchor pub, she felt the anger return and the tears well. Matron Billings had no heart – in fact she suspected the woman had iced water running through her veins.

Polly was suddenly overwhelmed with weariness and fear and she stumbled on a loose paving slab as she blinked away her tears. She had survived the terrible journey here, had sacrificed everything in the hope she would be allowed to nurse Adam, but Matron Billings – rot her soul – had made that impossible.

She reached Beach View Boarding House, ran up the short flight of steps to the front door and turned the key. Stepping into the hall she could hear the murmur of voices in the kitchen, but she was in no mood for idle chatter. She needed time to think and plan, for there had to be some way of snatching extra time with Adam, and she was determined to find it – even if it incurred Matron's wrath.

Ron hadn't been surprised when Rosie Braithwaite asked him to stay behind after she'd closed the doors on the other customers at two o'clock. It had become a fairly regular thing to change barrels and bring up the heavy crates of bottles for her from the cellar, and he didn't mind a bit of clearing up when it gave him an extra hour or so in her company.

He'd shifted the tables and chairs back into

116

place, emptied the ashtrays and hung the regulars' clean pewter tankards back on their hooks above the bar. Rosie usually gave him a glass of whisky for his troubles and, once the place was clean and ready for the six o'clock opening, he'd perched on a stool to drink it as Rosie polished the huge slab of oak that served as the counter.

It was a magnificent sight, that bosom, gently undulating beneath her blouse as she leant over the bar and swept the duster back and forth. Ron could have sat for hours watching it.

'Don't you ever get tired of the scenery, Ron?' she asked with an impish grin.

'To be sure it's a fine figure of a woman ye are, Rosie. A man would have to be blind not to appreciate it.'

'You'll go blind, more like,' she muttered good-naturedly.

Ron carried on watching her. He knew he was in danger of being thought a dirty old man, and he didn't want to make a complete fool of himself – but he simply couldn't help it, and it was at moments like these that he counted his blessings.

Rosie had been the landlady of the Anchor for years, and her charms were admired by every red-blooded male who stepped over the pub threshold. But despite their efforts to ensnare her, there had been no rumours of men friends or casual liaisons and, as far as Ron knew, Rosie kept herself to herself. Legend had it that there had once been a Mr Braithwaite, but no one could ever remember having seen him, and Rosie refused to confirm or deny his existence.

Her age was unknown, and she wasn't telling,

but the consensus was that she had to be over fifty. However, she wore her years well, her warm, endearing personality making her seem much younger. She was the sort of woman who dressed to show off her figure; her hair was pale gold, her eyes blue and her smile mischievous. She knew how to flirt, how to stop a fight and how to deal with drunks – but she didn't allow liberties, either with her pub or her person. In short, Rosie Braithwaite was Ron's ideal woman, and he'd been in love with her for years.

She slung the duster under the counter and put her hands on her hips. 'I don't know about you, but I could do with a cuppa and a nice sit-down in a comfy chair. My feet are killing me.' With this, she eased off the high-heeled shoes and wriggled her toes.

Ron knew this was his cue to leave. He clicked his fingers at Harvey who was asleep under a table. 'We'll be off then,' he said reluctantly.

'Don't you want a cuppa then, Ron?'

He felt a jolt of happy surprise. 'Are ye askin' me to take tea with you, Rosie?'

'I'm asking,' she said through her smile. 'But don't get any ideas, Ronan Reilly. The only thing on offer is tea, and perhaps a digestive biscuit.' She winked at him and led the way up the creaking, narrow stairs.

Ron ordered Harvey to stay where he was and took his time to follow Rosie up the stairs so he could admire her shapely legs, and the way her behind moved in that tight skirt. It was a complete mystery to him that some man hadn't snared Rosie years ago. If he'd had half a chance, he wouldn't have had to be asked twice.

'Sit down while I put the kettle on.' Rosie padded barefoot across the undulating floor-boards and disappeared into what Ron guessed was the kitchen.

He slowly eased himself down in the comfortable chair and looked round him. It smelled lovely up here, he thought, breathing in the scent of bath cubes, shampoo and other womanly delights. The room wasn't bad either, a bit fussy and cramped for his liking with all those dark oak beams across the ceiling and the chintz curtains and chair covers, but very pleasant.

'Here we are,' said Rosie, appearing with a tea tray.

Ron suddenly remembered he was still wearing his cap, and swiftly snatched it off and stuffed it in his trouser pocket. He took the delicate cup and saucer and carefully balanced them in one hand as he helped himself to a biscuit. Easing back into the cushions, he suddenly couldn't think of a thing to say to her. It was easy to chat to her when she was serving drinks from behind the bar, but up here he found he was overtaken with an unusual and crippling shyness, which was most disconcerting.

Rosie sipped her tea and watched him over the rim of her cup. 'How are things at Beach View?' she asked when the silence had grown between them. 'Peggy well, is she?'

'Well enough.' Ron discovered he had to clear his throat. 'To be sure, 'tis full of women at the moment. Jim and I are outnumbered, so we are.'

'I'm sure that's not something either of you

should complain about,' she said dryly, reaching for her packet of cigarettes.

'Oh, I'm not complaining,' he said hurriedly, 'they're a nice bunch of wee girls, and Peggy seems much happier now she's so many chicks to mother.'

'She's lucky,' murmured Rosie. 'My chick is this place.' She smoked in silence for a moment. 'We've known each other a long time, Ron. How come we've never done this before?'

'You never asked me,' he said, his smile hesitant.

Rosie grinned back at him. 'How very thoughtless of me,' she murmured. 'Perhaps we should make this a regular thing, once or twice a week. Get to know one another a little better.'

Ron regarded her and tried not to show how delighted he was at the thought.

She finished her tea and set the cup back on the tray. 'It's odd really,' she mused. 'I think of you more as a friend than a customer, and yet this is the first time we've really had a chance to talk.'

'It's not easy to talk to anyone with a bar full of people and someone hammering on the piano.' He eyed her thoughtfully. She was a lovely woman, but he could sense there was a loneliness in her and that made him feel sad, and rather protective of her.

'That's the trouble with running this place,' she said as she stubbed out her cigarette. 'It's difficult to make real friends when the pub takes up all my time, and I'm in quite a vulnerable position here – on my own. I wouldn't trust half of them down there as far as I could throw them.'

'Then I'm flattered you trust me enough to offer me tea and biscuits,' he replied. He began to fill his pipe, feeling easier now, starting to relax. There was a vulnerability about her that he found endearing, for this was a very different Rosie to the one who ran her pub with an iron fist, albeit in a velvet glove. 'I'm yours for another hour at least,' he said gruffly. 'What would you like to talk about, Rosie?'

Peggy hadn't had a chance to talk to Jim yet, other than to tell him the wonderful news about the coming grandchild. With all the comings and goings there had never been an opportunity to get him alone, and he'd left straight after an early lunch for his shift at the cinema.

There would be little time to speak to him tonight either, for he was on fire watch duty and would probably only call in to collect sandwiches and a flask of tea before rushing off again. As for Cissy… She'd managed to avoid all her mother's questions and had run off to afternoon rehearsals. With an evening performance to get through, she wouldn't be home until very late.

'You're looking fretful, dear. What's the matter?' Mrs Finch eyed her over her spectacles.

Peggy checked on the fish pie and closed the range door. It was very hot in the kitchen, despite her having opened the window, and she could feel her dress sticking to her back. 'I meant to do so much today,' she said on a sigh, 'but time has run away with me.'

'At my age it goes in the blink of an eye,' Mrs Finch replied dryly.

Peggy didn't want to discuss her worries over Jim and Cissy – some things were just too personal to share – so instead, she smiled down at the knitting in the older woman's lap. 'That matinee jacket is coming on a treat,' she said. 'Anne will love it.'

'Hello. Something smells nice. When's tea? We're all starving.'

Peggy grinned at the three young nurses who'd come into the kitchen. 'At the usual time. Don't they feed you at that hospital?'

'Not with anything you'd be wanting to eat,' said Suzy, who'd become the spokeswoman for the three of them. 'It's all boiled cabbage, potato and fish.'

'Nothing wrong with that.'

'There is when it's watery and tastes like rubber.' Suzy pulled a face.

'Well, you've got fish pie tonight, and I can assure you, it won't be tasteless,' chirped Mrs Finch. 'I made it myself, so I should know.'

'Go and get out of those uniforms and into something more comfortable,' advised Peggy. 'It's a lovely evening out there, and it would be a shame to waste the last of the summer. The old deckchairs are down in the basement.'

'Um, Peggy.' Suzy's auburn curls were like a halo around her elfin face as she took out the pins. 'Would you mind if we asked some friends to tea next Sunday?'

Peggy noticed how none of the girls could meet her eye and she bit down on a smile. 'Would these guests be male, by any chance?'

Suzy tossed her hair from her shoulders. 'To be

sure they are, Peggy. Aussie boys, actually. They were patients of ours, and now they're on the last few days of leave before they're shipped off to wherever the army sends them. They're ever so much fun, and to be sure, you'll love them, so you will.'

'I'm sure I will,' she said dryly. She'd been married to an Irishman for too long to be swayed by sweet talk, flashing eyes and a lilting brogue.

'We told them all about you and Beach View. To be sure I said you and Mrs Finch were wizards at cooking up a good meal.' Her blue eyes were wide with appeal. 'They're ever so far from home, Peggy, and we thought it'd be nice for them to come and enjoy some home comforts before they got stuck into the fighting again.'

'I can't just magic three more meals out of what I can get out of the rationing,' Peggy murmured. 'Things are tight already, and young men have vast appetites.'

'Oh, you're not to be worrying yourself about that,' said Suzy hurriedly. 'They've promised to bring some meat with them, so they have. In Australia, they cook their meat outside on something called a barbie – but I'm sure it would taste the same cooked on your range.'

'All right. But they stay downstairs where I can keep an eye on them. I've heard about some of the things those Aussies get up to, and I'll have none of it in this house.' She eyed them sternly, but couldn't quite manage to maintain it.

Suzy threw her arms round Peggy's neck and gave her a hug. 'Sure, and you're a saint, Peggy.'

'I'm far from that,' she said, untangling herself

with a chuckle. 'Now get out of my kitchen and take your blarney with you.' She followed them into the hall, preparing to lay the table for the evening meal, when a thought struck her.

'Just a minute, Suzy. Did you see Danuta at the hospital today? Do you know how she got on?'

'I haven't seen her at all today, Peggy, but then I have no reason to be going down to the laundry.'

Peggy shooed them up the stairs and walked into the dining room. She still found it strange not to see Sally's sewing machine in the corner, or the trunk with all her finished clothes lying under the bay window. But Sally had moved on, and now her home dressmaking business was flourishing in the front parlour of her friend Pearl's little house down by the fishing station.

Peggy sighed. So much had changed in the year since war had been declared. Pearl was married and expecting her first baby, and Sally was engaged. Quiet little Edie, who'd been billeted with them for only a matter of weeks, was a land girl and courting a farmer. Aleksy was dead, and Anne was pregnant, about to move into her own little house. Now she was about to be inundated with Australian soldiers.

'Whatever next?' she breathed. But, as she set out the cutlery, she couldn't quite dismiss the little thrill of pleasure at the thought of all those young people enjoying themselves in her home. The war was hard on all of them – what harm could it do to let their hair down for a few hours?

Chapter Seven

Polly heard the girls' laughter and chatter as they pounded up the stairs to the floor above. They certainly sounded a lively bunch, and she was looking forward to meeting them, but that would have to wait until later.

Her two uniform dresses and the cape were already hanging in the wardrobe, and she'd finally managed to work out how her cap should be pinned. It was a complex arrangement of starched pleats which didn't sit too easily on the thick bun of hair at her nape, and she'd spent some time fiddling with both to get it right. Satisfied she was prepared for the following day, she was about to dig in the drawer for a thicker cardigan when a voice made her start.

'Who are you? What are you doing in my room?'

Polly felt ridiculously guilty as she stood to face the pale, thin young woman who glared at her from the doorway. 'Peggy had no other room so she put me in here,' she said hastily. 'You must be Danuta. I'm Polly Brown.'

The large green eyes regarded her evenly. 'I did not think you were coming.'

'I was delayed,' replied Polly, rather stung by this cool reception.

Danuta's gaze flitted to the uniform hanging in the wardrobe. 'You are nurse?'

'I start at the Memorial tomorrow.' Polly took in

the drab brown dress which did nothing to enhance the other girl's wan colouring, and realised it was the same as that worn by the hospital laundry staff. 'If our shifts coincide, perhaps we could walk there together?'

'I work in the laundry,' Danuta said flatly. 'My hours are different. But I too am a nurse.'

'Really?' Polly was struggling to understand her coldness.

'Yes, really. But Matron say I must work in the laundry because I am Polish. She calls me Chimpsky, but my name is Chmielewski.'

'How very rude of her,' muttered Polly, remembering Matron's shouted command as she'd stepped into the laundry.

Danuta walked further into the room and eyed Polly's photographs on the mantelpiece. 'I am theatre sister in Poland.'

'That's a very responsible post,' replied Polly. 'I'm surprised you couldn't get a job at the Memorial. It's a busy hospital.'

The other girl turned from her scrutiny of the photographs. 'I do not have the pieces of paper which prove I am qualified. They are lost in siege of Warsaw. But Matron not believe me. She is not nice woman.'

'She's a complete cow,' muttered Polly with feeling.

A smile lightened Danuta's expression, making her almost pretty. 'In my country we call such women *kurwa*. It means the same, I think.' The smile remained as her gaze travelled over Polly's photographs again. 'These pictures are of your family?'

126

Polly nodded and, in the hope of keeping up this friendlier dialogue, pointed out her family members. 'This is my mother, and this is my sister with her two boys – and this is my husband Adam with our daughter Alice.'

'You are very lucky, I think,' murmured Danuta, as she fingered her own photographs on the bedside table. 'My family are gone, and I am alone in this strange country, not able even to do my nursing.'

Polly could hear the bitterness in her voice and was able to understand it. 'That must be awful for you. I'm so sorry.'

Danuta shrugged. 'It is not for you to be sorry,' she murmured. The smile had faded and her green eyes were almost accusing as she regarded Polly. 'You are staff nurse?'

Polly nodded. 'And I'll be coming in at all hours,' she said hastily. 'I hope I won't disturb you – you see I didn't realise I'd have to share a room.'

Danuta eyed her solemnly. 'I did not think I would have to either.'

Polly grabbed the thick cardigan from the drawer and slung it over her shoulders. She was wasting precious time, and it was clear Danuta had little intention of even trying to make friends. 'Well,' she said evenly, 'it looks as if we're stuck with one another, so we'd better make the best of it.'

Danuta shrugged. 'It is no matter to me. I am only laundry woman, not important nurse like everyone else in this house.'

Polly took a deep breath. 'Look, Danuta. It is not my fault that I have a nursing post and you don't. Not my fault we have to share a room. But it would be nice if you could at least *try* to be friendly.'

'For why?' She looked genuinely puzzled. 'You English do not like foreigners, even though my brother died fighting for your RAF.'

'That's most unfair,' snapped Polly. 'You know nothing about me, and you can't tar us all with the same brush just because you've had a run-in with Matron.'

'Then I am sorry if I have upset you,' Danuta said, lowering her gaze.

Polly relented, and had to control the urge to hug the other girl. She looked so defeated. 'And I'm sorry I snapped,' she said, 'but I've had one hell of a journey here, and my husband is lying in a hospital bed, far more seriously injured than I thought. Visiting hour begins in less than half an hour and I don't want to be late.'

'Then you must go,' breathed Danuta.

Polly grabbed her handbag and gas-mask box and headed for the door. She turned on the threshold to find that Danuta's expression had softened, and that there was the shadow of something she couldn't interpret in her eyes. 'We can talk when I get back,' she said. 'I would like us to be friends, Danuta. Goodness knows there's enough trouble in the world without us being prickly with one another.'

'I too would like to be friends,' she murmured. 'I am sorry if I was rude to you.'

Polly glanced at her watch. 'I'll see you later.'

Without waiting for a reply, she hurried down the stairs and into the kitchen. 'I'm sorry, Peggy, but I'll be late for tea. Visiting's from six until seven, so it will be a regular problem.'

Peggy smiled. 'I'll keep a plate warm for when you get back. But surely you don't have to stick to the visiting hour? Not with you being on the staff?'

'Matron's rules,' Polly said, pulling a face. 'I'll be back after seven.'

'Did you get to meet Danuta?' Peggy called after her. 'I heard her come in but didn't have time to warn her you were here.'

Polly nodded. 'We've introduced ourselves,' she said shortly. Not wanting to elaborate and waste any more time, she fled out of the door and down the steps.

There were few visitors in Men's Surgical, which led Polly to think that most of the patients must be servicemen, far from home and family, the travel restrictions making it impossible for their loved ones to visit.

She was all too aware of them watching her as she walked down the middle of the ward towards the end bed, and gave each of them a warm smile. Poor men; she knew from her experience in Hereford how desperate they must be to see their loved ones – knew how disappointed they were when yet another evening passed with no sign of a familiar face. The volunteer hospital visitors from the WVS and the Salvation Army did their best to bring cheer with their gifts of books and newspapers, but Polly understood how their kindness barely touched the longing for the sight and sounds of those closest to them.

She could see no change in Adam and sank into the chair beside his bed and watched him breathing. 'Hello, my darling. It's Polly, and I'm going to be seeing you every day from now on, so you've got to wake up.'

His hand was cool in hers, and he didn't seem to have a temperature, which meant he was clear of infection. She felt his pulse. It was steady but weak, but there had been no reaction to her voice or her touch – and she realised he was so deeply sedated, he was unaware of everything. 'Oh, Adam,' she breathed. 'There are so many things I want to say to you, my love.'

'Mrs Brown?'

Polly turned to see the ward sister standing at the end of the bed and wondered if she was about to be reprimanded again.

'I'm Sister Morley. I hear you had a bit of a run-in with Matron this afternoon.' A smile was hovering on her lips, the brown eyes kindly in the motherly face. 'I shouldn't take it personally,' she said at Polly's nod. 'She barks at everyone.'

'So I understand,' murmured Polly. 'I do hope she didn't tear that probationer off a strip. It really wasn't her fault.'

The smile broadened. 'Student Nurse Barker is tougher than she looks.' She approached the bedside and looked down at Adam. 'It must have been quite a shock to see him like this,' she murmured. 'Would you like me to go through his treatment and prognosis with you?'

'Please. Although, by the looks of the drugs he's being given, I can tell his situation must be serious.'

130

Sister Morley opened the folder she'd been carrying. 'Adam took the brunt of a mortar blast,' she said quietly. 'He was lucky to survive, and the medics on the hospital ship did a sterling job on him during the time it took to get him here. Apart from the tib, fib and femur fractures, he also has a compound fracture of the radius. Three of his ribs were broken, one of which pierced his lung, which is why he has that chest wound.'

She looked up from her notes and placed a warm, caring hand on Polly's shoulder. 'The head wounds were rather more serious, I'm afraid.'

'Go on,' murmured Polly.

'Mr Fortescue had to remove several shards of shrapnel from his skull. According to the theatre sister, it was a long, delicate operation, and they had to resuscitate him twice before it was over.'

Polly gripped Adam's hand, her tears blinding her. 'Will there be brain damage?' she asked fearfully.

'There is a possibility,' Sister Morley warned softly. 'We won't really know until he wakes up.' She squeezed Polly's shoulder in sympathy. 'He's heavily sedated, as you've probably realised. But the morphine is keeping him out of pain while his body has a chance to heal.'

'Thank you, Sister Morley.'

'Please, call me Mary. I've only come back to nursing since war was declared and my children were sent to Wales. As we're going to be colleagues, it seems silly to be so formal.'

'I'm Polly,' she sniffed, rummaging in her handbag for a handkerchief. She shot Mary a watery smile and blew her nose. 'It's all come as a terrible shock,' she said. 'When I rang the hospital from Hereford, they said he was comfortable and expected to make a full recovery.'

Mary frowned. 'When did you last ring?'

'About a week ago.'

Mary sighed. 'They weren't lying to you, Polly,' she said softly. 'He was doing very well once the bones had been set and his lung was repaired. Five days ago he had a fit, and that was when Mr Fortescue took him back into surgery. You see, it was thought all the shrapnel had been recovered from his head wound, but X-rays showed there was one small fragment still there – and it was pressing on part of his brain. Mr Fortescue managed to retrieve it, but...'

'I see.' Polly held Adam's palm against her tear-streaked cheek.

'Do you have any family down here, Polly? Anyone to support you through this?'

Polly shook her head, the tears running faster now. 'They're on their way to Canada on one of the convoys. Our little girl Alice is with them. Oh God, Mary. I've known him all my life – loved him for as long as I can remember. What if he dies and I never have the chance to speak with him again?'

Mary hastily drew the curtains round the bed so they could have some privacy. She folded the sides of her apron carefully over her lap and broke all the rules by perching on the side of the bed. 'You have to keep strong, Polly. Not just for Adam, but for your little Alice. You're a nurse. You must have seen cases like this before – and they don't all end in tragedy.'

Polly smeared away the tears and blew her nose again. 'I know,' she whispered. 'But it's so much harder when it's someone you love.'

'Of course it is,' Mary murmured, 'and although you might not think so right this minute, Matron was right to assign you to the women's ward.' She stilled Polly's agitated hands, thereby stifling her protest. 'We have twelve very sick men in this ward, and each of them deserves our full attention. It wouldn't be fair on you or anyone else if you worked here, because regardless of your professionalism, Adam would become your priority.'

'You're right, of course you are,' Polly sniffed. She made a concerted effort to be mature and sensible about the situation, but realised it could be a while before she had her emotions under control. The past week had been the most difficult of her life, but now she must put her own cares aside and concentrate on Adam and the job she was here to do.

'Thanks, Mary,' she murmured. 'You've been a brick, you really have.' She shot her a watery grin. 'And I promise not to break down again.'

'Tears are as healing as sleep,' Mary said quietly and gave her a soft smile. 'If you've come all the way from Hereford, I suspect you're worn out and in need of a good night's rest before you get stuck in on Women's Surgical tomorrow.'

Polly nodded. 'I could probably sleep for a week if I didn't have so many things to worry about.'

Mary looked thoughtful as she chewed her lip. 'Look, Polly, I know this is breaking all the rules,

133

but if you want to see Adam out of visiting hour, I'm sure we can devise a plan.'

Polly couldn't suppress the joy and hope as she looked back at Mary. 'But what about Matron?'

Mary winked. 'I know when she has her meal breaks and when she's in conference with the consultants.' She stood and smoothed her starched apron into place and drew back the curtains. 'I'll leave you now, but come to my desk before you go and I'll give you a list of times when it's safe to visit.'

Polly softly held Adam's hand, and leant her cheek lightly on his stubbly chin. 'Did you hear that, my darling?' she whispered. 'I think I've just made a friend.'

The fish pie had gone down a treat and Mrs Finch had blushed at everyone's praises, and promised to think of something equally delicious for tea the following day.

As the three girls chattered happily over their meals and discussed their plans for the evening, Peggy had nursed the hope that they could persuade the almost silent Danuta to go with them to the fund-raising dance at the church hall.

It was for a good cause, and billed, 'From the frying pan into the Spitfire', so most of her old pots and pans had been commandeered as donations. The girls had certainly made an effort to coax Danuta out, but she had turned down their invitation by saying she had to be in bed early because her shift in the laundry started at six-thirty.

Peggy had caught Mrs Finch's eye. They'd both

seen the look that passed between the other girls and realised the invitation wouldn't be made again. Peggy had felt sadness sweep over her. She wanted so much for Danuta to fit in, to feel this was her home, but it seemed the girl was determined to keep herself to herself.

She'd turned her attention to the others. They were a close-knit bunch, those three girls, having nursed at the Cliffehaven Memorial since they qualified, and they looked so pretty in their summer frocks, with their lipstick and high heels – so animated by the thought of dancing the night away with their admirers.

Poor Danuta was just plain dowdy beside them, her lack of social graces setting her even further apart from the rest of the household, and Peggy's soft heart went out to her. Perhaps the real reason behind her reluctance to go with them was because she didn't possess a stitch of decent clothing?

After the girls had left for their evening out, Peggy persuaded Danuta to stay at the table and have a cup of tea before rushing back to her room as she usually did. Her gaze flickered over the girl as she poured the tea, but her thoughts were on Aleksy. She would be letting him down if she didn't help his little sister, but she would have to tread warily. Danuta was quite prickly, and very proud. She might not appreciate Peggy's interference, and perhaps even resent the cast-off clothing that Peggy had begun to set aside from the WVS rehoming centre.

Determined not to dwell on Danuta's unfortunate circumstances, Peggy turned her attention to her father-in-law. Dressed in his Home Guard uniform and highly polished boots, he looked cheerful, and there was a glint of something in his roguish old eyes that she couldn't decipher.

'You're looking pleased with yourself, Ron. What have you been up to?'

'Mischief, I'll be bound,' muttered Mrs Finch, with an impish grin. 'Old scallywag.'

He puffed out his chest, making the brass buttons on his khaki jacket wink in the electric light. 'Well now,' he drawled. 'That's fer me to know, and fer you to be worrying about.'

'I bet it has something to do with Rosie Braithwaite,' Peggy murmured, a smile touching her lips.

'Maybe,' he replied, his eyes twinkling, 'and maybe not.' He drained his cup of tea and pushed back from the table. It took a moment for him to place the tin helmet over his head, the canvas satchel and gas-mask box over his shoulder, and pick up his rifle. 'I'll be off to me Home Guard duties,' he said gruffly. 'See you in the morning.'

'Have you got those sandwiches I made?'

'Aye, and the thermos.' He whistled to Harvey, who trotted after him as he marched into the hall and out of the front door.

Peggy smiled at Danuta who was silently clearing the table. 'Well,' she said, 'it looks as if us womenfolk have the evening to ourselves. What do you both say to a game of cribbage after we've done the washing-up?'

'I do not know this game,' said Danuta with a frown.

'I'll teach you, dear,' offered Mrs Finch, who

was struggling to get out of her chair. 'Quite a dab hand at crib, even if I do say so myself.'

Danuta rushed to help her, and once she was on her feet the old woman looked up at her and cocked her head. 'Thank you, dear, but you know, you'd look and feel so much prettier if you smiled,' she trilled. 'I do so like happy faces, don't you?'

'I am sorry,' murmured Danuta, her green eyes doleful. 'I would like to smile, but my heart is empty. I am a stranger here, and every day it is clear that I do not fit in.'

'What utter nonsense,' said Mrs Finch, quite startling Peggy with her uncharacteristic fierceness. 'Of course you fit in – but you have to make the effort, dear. Don't you see? A smile earns a smile. A good word earns a good word.' She patted Danuta's hand as if to make up for her strong words. 'I know you're mourning Aleksy, and that you're disappointed at not being able to nurse. But you're safe here with us and we want you to be happy.'

'I am sorry,' murmured Danuta. 'It is just that everything is so strange, and I feel I am – what is the saying – a fish out of the sea.'

'We all feel like that at times,' murmured Mrs Finch. She softly patted the girl's cheek. 'Chin up, my dear.'

'Thank you, Mrs Finch,' mumbled Danuta. 'You are most kind, and remind me very much of my *Babunia* – my grandmother. She too had the strong words and the soft heart.'

'Then you may call me *Babunia,* if you wish,' she replied, stumbling over the word a little. 'I have yet to meet my own grandchildren, who live in Canada, and at my age it is an honour to be regarded fondly as someone's granny.'

Peggy found she had to clear the lump in her throat before she could speak. 'Right, let's get this washing-up sorted before...'

The siren began to wail, the chilling crescendo cutting off any further conversation.

Peggy grabbed Mrs Finch's handbag and gas mask. 'Take her down to the shelter and pick up pillows and blankets on the way,' she ordered Danuta. 'I'll get the box of supplies.'

The front door crashed open as Peggy reached the hall. 'Polly,' she breathed, hand on heart. 'You gave me a fright, and no mistake.'

Polly was out of breath. 'I ran all the way home,' she gasped. 'The sirens were already going off on the far side of town, and I had some warden chase me down Camden Road.'

'That'd be Wally,' Peggy muttered. 'Hurry up then, dear, we're going into the shelter. Grab your tea out of the stove on your way, but mind – the plate will be hot.'

The searchlights were already tracing the sky for enemy planes as Peggy hurried down the path after Danuta and Mrs Finch. The wailing siren continued its shrill warning as she lit the lamp and settled the box on the bench. 'I think I've got everything in there,' she muttered, 'but it's been such a busy day, I can't remember if I replaced the biscuits we finished last night.'

Danuta helped Mrs Finch into the deckchair that had been firmly wedged in the corner of the Anderson shelter. The old lady had a habit of falling asleep and sliding to one side, so Danuta surrounded her with pillows. 'You are comfortable, *Babunia?* You would like a blanket?'

'I'm fine, dear,' she assured her. 'I'll just switch off my hearing aid so I can get to sleep. Such a shame we can't have that game of cards.'

'We will play another time,' murmured Danuta with a soft smile as she placed a blanket beside Mrs Finch.

Peggy peeped out of the doorway in search of Polly as the distant drone of approaching aircraft came from over the Channel. 'Where's that girl got to?'

Polly emerged from the basement doorway, gingerly holding her hot plate of dinner with a tea towel. She scrambled down the stone steps and into the Anderson shelter and plumped down on the bench. 'Whew,' she breathed as she closed the door. 'I thought I'd never make it.'

'You have seen your husband?' asked Danuta hesitantly. 'He is making good progress, I hope?'

Polly shot her a weary smile. 'He's not very well at all,' she admitted, 'but he's in the best place and being looked after extremely well.' She stared down at the plate on her lap. 'But his injuries mean he can't be moved to the shelter during a raid, so I hope he'll be all right.'

'I'm sure the hospital will make sure he's safe,' said Peggy above the gathering cacophony of the bombers overhead. 'Now you eat your tea, love. You must be half-starved by now.'

She watched Polly tuck into the fish pie with relish. The girl looked exhausted, but at least she was safely home, and once Hitler had stopped

139

dropping bombs on them, they could all go to their beds and have a good night's sleep.

Cissy heard the siren and the deep-bellied rumble of the fast approaching enemy planes. The music came to an abrupt halt as everyone scrambled for the shelter beneath the theatre, and the curtain swept across the stage. She raced with the other dancers to the wings to grab her gas mask, bag and coat before hurtling down the stone steps to the basement.

It was cold and damp and very unpleasant in that basement shelter, and, with so many people crammed into every space, she felt quite claustrophobic. Cissy huddled into a corner, wrapping the coat around her to ward off the chill, as the other girls lit cigarettes and began to gossip.

Cissy did her best to join in the chatter but she was all too aware of Jack Witherspoon, who was sitting a few feet away, and could feel his steady, disapproving gaze on her. She gave up on the gossip and closed her eyes as she huddled further into the shadows, her shame warming her face. She felt cheap and dirty, appalled that she'd allowed Jack to bully her into doing something so sleazy for the sake of her career.

She grimaced at the thought. Her career – that was a laugh. Those two hours in the back room of the theatre had opened her eyes and made her see how things really were. She was a hoofer, just one of the back row of the chorus without any real talent. How stupid she'd been ever to believe Jack Witherspoon, how naïve, to think that a few smutty photographs would get her noticed and

140

into the spotlight. She'd be noticed all right, she conceded bitterly, but not by famous Hollywood producers or theatre managers – but by dirty old men.

Her skin crawled at the memory of that horrid photographer. He'd been old with claw-like hands and thick, wet lips, and his reptilian eyes had run over her, making her shiver with disgust. She should have known then, should have walked away and refused to do it. But she'd stayed, and the shoot had begun with her posing in front of a backdrop of a tropical beach.

She'd relaxed and smiled and began to have fun until he'd ordered her to push her clothing off her shoulders, to lean forward and press her breasts together to enhance the cleavage. He'd licked his lips continuously as he'd clicked the camera shutter, and she'd flinched as he'd barked out his orders to show more, to pout, to get more of her breasts on show – to take the top off altogether and give the punters a real treat. That was the moment she'd fled the room in tears.

Cissy glanced through her lashes at Jack, who was now in deep conversation with a young dancer who'd just joined the troupe. He'd given Cissy no sympathy and offered no comfort. In fact, he'd called her a stupid little girl who wasn't worthy of his time and trouble, and had told her to go back to the chorus where she belonged and not bother him again.

A tear seeped through her lashes and she hurriedly dashed it away, glad for once that the lighting down here was so poor. She'd wanted to go home after that photo session – desperate to feel her mother's arms around her and to know that she was safe and loved and forgiven. But she knew she couldn't, and that had made everything worse.

As the enemy planes rumbled overhead and the first crump of an exploding bomb made the building shudder, she looked back over her short life and wondered how she could ever have been so stupid as to think she was anything special. She could dance well enough, and her singing voice wasn't too bad, but she was no more talented than a thousand other pretty young girls.

She'd been starry-eyed for as long as she could remember, determined she was destined for stardom on the stage, perhaps even in film. She'd begged and pleaded to be allowed to join ENSA, and had seen her parents' capitulation over this small troupe as a major breakthrough – the first step on the ladder to fame and fortune. How could she now go home and admit it had all been a terrible mistake? How to tell them that life in the theatre was a sham, and that the men who wielded such power were predatory, feeding off young girls' dreams in order to make them debase themselves?

Another enormous blast shook the very foundations of the building, making people cry out and the lights flicker. Cissy curled up in the corner with her misery, dreading the moment the raid was over, for it meant going home – meant acting out a lie until she could find some way to escape her predicament. But there was no getting round it: her parents had signed a year's contract only the month before.

Chapter Eight

Polly was terrified. It had been bad enough in the bowels of the London Underground, but cowering here beneath this thin bit of corrugated iron which was half-buried in sods of earth was beyond hair-raising. How could such a thing be remotely safe when she could so clearly hear the deep-throated roar of the bombers overhead, and the light buzz of the swifter fighter planes that accompanied them?

She huddled into her coat as the regular booms of the Bofors on the seafront and along the cliffs gave a bass note to the demonic orchestra, the ack-ack guns interspersing the thunder with their sharp volleys. Perhaps she would have been better off obeying the ARP warden and going to the public shelter? She would have been deeper beneath the ground there, further from the noise and the certain death that was about to rain down from those enemy planes.

She cried out as an explosion made the earth tremble and rattled the shelter. Curling into the corner, she whimpered, convinced she was about to die. Two more explosions followed, each one rocking the ground and making her curl ever more tightly, the gas mask clutched in her fists. They seemed close – too close. And now she could smell burning.

Controlling her fear enough to peek through the

gap at the top of the ill-fitting door, she stared, awestruck, at the horrifying sight above her. Searchlights raked the skies, revealing layer upon layer of enemy aircraft heading determinedly inland as the anti-aircraft missiles traced fire through the skies. Then she saw what appeared to be parachutes drifting down from some of the bombers, but they were too tiny to carry a man, so what could they possibly be?

As she watched them float ever nearer, to be lost among the surrounding roofs, she heard the explosions and saw the sudden orange glow in the night sky. There were hundreds of them, and they were carrying incendiaries.

She almost jumped out of her skin as Peggy moved suddenly from the shadows of the shelter and grasped her hand. 'It's all right, love,' Peggy murmured. 'I know this doesn't feel terribly safe, but it's better than risking having the house fall on us.'

'If we take a direct hit, none of us will survive,' said Polly, who knew her face was ashen and her eyes wide with horror.

'If we take a direct hit, then none of us will know anything about it,' shouted Peggy over the thunderous roar above them.

Polly was all too aware of the fact, and although Peggy was trying to comfort her, the thought of dying without ever seeing Adam or Alice again didn't ease her terror – it enhanced it.

Peggy's arm was strong round her waist. 'Take deep breaths, Polly,' she shouted. 'Have faith that we'll get through this – that we're not the prime target.'

Polly nodded and made a concerted effort to control her breathing and her fear, but every part of her was on alert, her muscles rigid as she heard the continuous blasts of exploding bombs and incendiaries.

Peggy nudged her and cocked her head towards Danuta, who was wrapped in a blanket and curled up on the bench, fast asleep.

Polly stared at the other girl in amazement. How could she sleep through this? It was enough to wake the dead. But, she reasoned, Danuta must have experienced raids like this in Poland, perhaps survived things she couldn't begin to imagine. Then she glanced at Mrs Finch, who was calmly carrying on with her knitting, and felt ashamed of her cowardice. She took a deep breath and let it out slowly, concentrating on relaxing the taut muscles and her racing pulse, forcing calm where there was chaos. She was not alone, she could get through this.

'Good girl,' murmured Peggy in her ear. 'That's right. I know you think you'll never get used to it, but you will. You'll be surprised.'

Polly gave a tremulous smile as Peggy grasped her hand. She was feeling a little calmer, but she couldn't help but flinch as another heavy explosion rocked the shelter and thrummed through the iron walls. How could she ever become inured to this? It was too loud, too real – and far too close. And what about the hospital? Was Adam all right? Had they decided to risk moving him because the raid was so fierce?

She closed her eyes, thinking of him, so vulnerable in his hospital bed and yet so unaware of the horrors that were going on around him. Then she was haunted by thoughts of Alice and the rest of her family. Were they being hounded by enemy planes, hunted by U-boats, cowering on deck in their life jackets waiting for the dreaded moment when they must abandon ship?

A chill ran to her core. She couldn't afford to think like that or let her fear get the better of her. If the Germans were concentrating on London and the south-east then the convoy would make it through, just as all the others had done. It was vital she keep strong-minded and positive.

Peggy understood Polly's fear, for she'd experienced it herself during those earlier raids when she'd been convinced that none of them would survive. That was not to say she was without fear now – she'd just learnt to control it, to live with it and steel herself for the next attack.

She could feel Polly begin to relax, so she left her side and lit the primus stove to boil the water in the tin kettle she always kept in the shelter. The numbers of enemy aircraft seemed to be lessening now, the explosions fewer, and there was the distinct buzz of Spitfires harassing the enemy. She thought of Martin and all the other brave boys who were defending this beleaguered island, and prayed that they would all return to base safely.

As she smoked a cigarette and waited for the water to boil, she kept an eye on Polly. It was clear the girl had troubles, and she suspected she was thinking about her injured husband and the rest of her little family. The poor young thing

146

must be finding it so hard, and Peggy realised she had a lot to be thankful for. At least her children were safe in the country, not risking everything in the Atlantic where merchant ships had already been attacked and sunk.

Her thoughts turned to Jim and Ron, who would be out in this hell trying to fight the fires and rescue people from bombed-out buildings. And then there was Cissy and Anne, and the three girls who'd gone to the dance with their young Australians, and...

She shook her head as if to clear it from those defeatist thoughts, and quickly made a pot of tea. They would be all right, she thought determinedly. They'd come home and life would continue She had to believe that – otherwise what was it all for?

The last of the bombers and fighter planes had gone, but the all-clear didn't sound, and half an hour later she realised why. They were coming back, dropping the last of their bombs and incendiaries over the seaports, towns and villages of the south coast before they were chased back across the Channel by the air force boys.

It was just before dawn when the all-clear rang out, and Peggy caught Polly's eye, realising they both feared what they might find when they left this shelter.

Peggy shrugged and tried to make light of her worries. 'We've come through unscathed before,' she said in the deafening silence that always fell once the sirens stopped. 'I expect everything will be all right. If it's not, then we'll just have to make the best of things.'

Danuta woke up and yawned. 'It is over, yes?' She swung her legs down from the bench and quickly folded the blanket round the pillow before checking her watch. 'I must prepare for work. If I am late this morning Matron will be very angry, I think.'

'I don't know how you do it,' sighed Peggy in admiration. 'You've managed to sleep right through the whole thing. At least Mrs Finch has the excuse of being stone deaf.' She glanced across at the old lady who was snoring softly in her deckchair.

'I was very tired,' said Danuta, with a dismissive shrug.

'So was I,' muttered Polly, 'but I couldn't sleep a wink.'

'But this is the first time you have experience of such things, I think,' Danuta said evenly. 'It is different for me. I have seen many such raids and know that if I am to die then I will die whether I am asleep or not.'

'Right,' said Peggy, gathering her coat round her, determined to get on with things. 'Let's see if the house is still standing before we wake Mrs Finch.'

The stench of burning accompanied the palls of smoke that drifted in the pearly stillness of the hour before dawn. The sky was a hazy orange from all the fires, and the shrill clamour of distant ambulance and fire-engine bells rent the silence made so profound by the enemy's departure.

The dread was a leaden weight as Peggy led the two girls up the shallow steps into the garden. She stood by the vegetable patch, her heart hammering as she dared to look up at the house. By

148

some miracle Beach View was still standing and, apart from a few missing tiles on the roof and a buckled length of guttering, it appeared to be unscathed. 'Thank God,' she breathed. 'Now let's hope the rest of the street is all right.'

She hurried indoors, the two young women following closely as she made a swift check on the basement before running up the stone steps to the kitchen. Everything was as she'd left it, although there seemed to be a lot of dust about. She was about to turn the taps to see if there was any water when she heard Polly calling her.

'Peggy. You'd better come and look at this.'

She experienced a sharp, icy jab of fear as she forced one foot in front of the other and went into the hall. With a gasp of distress, she realised Beach View had not escaped the bombardment.

The front door had been blown off its hinges and now lay in a shattered, splintered wreck amongst the glass that littered the hall floor and the stair carpet. The door knocker sat in solitary splendour on the overturned hall chair. 'Go up and see what the damage is on the other floors,' she said through a throat tight with tears.

She was hardly aware of their pounding foot-steps on the stairs as she carefully made her way across the glass and splintered wood to the dining room. The window had suffered the same fate, the glass glistening on the rug and in jagged icicles from what was left of the frames and the white tape.

She felt the tears well as she saw how her lovely curtains had been ripped to filthy shreds and, as she slowly took in the rest of the room, she rea-

149

lised there had been a prodigious fall of soot from the chimney, and everything was covered in its black dust. It would take a month of Sundays to clean up, and right this minute she didn't have the energy to think, let alone roll up her sleeves and get on with it.

Wandering back into the hall she met Polly coming down the stairs. 'It's bad, isn't it?'

Polly took her hand. 'Nothing so bad it can't be mended or swept up,' she said with a wan smile. 'Our window and the one above us has been smashed, and it's very dusty up there, but the other rooms seem to have escaped any damage.' She gave Peggy's fingers a gentle squeeze. 'Don't worry. I'll help clean up as best I can before I have to be at the hospital.'

Peggy swallowed her tears and carefully negotiated the debris in the hall before slowly making her way down the front steps to the pavement.

Beach View Terrace had survived, but the lovely old houses were looking the worse for wear in the hazy light made ochre by distant fires. Curtains hung limply in shattered windows, front doors bore the scars of shrapnel and flying debris, garden walls had crumbled in places, the flints and mortar strewn across the cracked and uneven pavements.

As Peggy slowly walked to the end of the street and looked down towards the sea, she understood why the ruinous blast had touched them all. For halfway down the hill was a vast, smoking crater where there had once been a road lined with boarding houses, private apartments and small hotels. She stilled and stared in dumb disbelief. The buildings that had stood at the end of their side streets for decades had been blown to smithereens.

'Dear God,' she whispered as she covered her mouth with trembling fingers. 'No one could have survived that.'

'Come away, Peggy. Let the firemen and wardens do their job.'

But Peggy resisted Polly's gentle tug on her arm, for she couldn't take her eyes from the knots of shell-shocked people who stood about in helpless confusion as the warden took a roll-call against his long list of residents, the firemen hosed down the smoking rubble, and a team of men risked their lives to search the still smouldering wreckage for survivors. Were Jim and Ron amongst them? Or were they doing the same thing on the other side of town?

She looked down Camden Road, which seemed to be reasonably unscathed, but noted the clouds of smoke coming from the far end which was closer to the town centre, and the unmistakable glow of a distant fire. The town had taken a beating and they'd been lucky to come out of it alive. But where was Cissy – where were the three young nurses, and Ron and Jim? Had they escaped?

Her pulse raced as a sturdy figure in a filthy khaki uniform appeared through the smoke, a large dog at his side. She would have recognised them anywhere, and she began to breathe more easily, determined to believe that everyone from Beach View had got through the raid unhurt.

With thudding heart and dry mouth, she

151

watched Ron order Harvey to begin his search. Harvey was clearly relishing his work, for his tail was wagging like a metronome as he kept his nose close to the rubble and traced and retraced his steps until he came to a halt with a bark. He began to dig frantically, and in an instant many willing hands helped him.

A shout went up, and more frantic digging ensued until someone was lifted out and gently placed on the ground. Eight more people were slowly and painstakingly brought up from the cellar of the shattered house as Harvey continued to wag his tail and bark his approval.

'I'd better go and see if I can do anything,' said Polly.

'I will come with you.' Danuta had changed into her drab brown dress, ready for work, and Polly would have protested if it hadn't been for the determined glint in the other girl's eyes.

Peggy watched them hurry down the hill. There was no sign of an ambulance yet – no doubt they were busy somewhere else – and it looked as if the voluntary services were stretched to the limit. The rescue team had moved to the other side of the crater now, and Harvey was once again trawling the rubble with his delicate nose.

Knowing she could do little to actually help, but still fretting over Cissy and the others, she hurried back to Beach View Terrace. After gently waking Mrs Finch and getting her installed buttering bread at the kitchen table, she went to check on her neighbours.

Most of the houses had suffered similar damage, but some of the women were finding it harder to cope than others, so she rounded them up and brought them back to her kitchen to help prepare tea and sandwiches for the rescue teams.

There was comfort in doing ordinary, everyday things, she realised, even if the downstairs was covered in soot and there wasn't a window left to speak of. People would still want tea and something to eat, and it helped to focus the mind on something other than one's own fears and misfortune.

Polly quickly assessed the injuries. There was a man with a head wound that looked worse than it was, a young woman with what could turn out to be a broken wrist, and an elderly woman who seemed unscathed but was shaking with shock. She was about to ask the warden for his first aid box when Danuta beat her to it.

'You have medical box?' Danuta demanded.

The man nodded but hesitated before handing it over. 'Do you know what you're doing?' he asked.

'I will need all boxes,' she commanded, snatching it from him. 'And water to clean wounds. If you have tea in that flask, give it to that woman. She is in shock.'

Polly smiled. Danuta certainly didn't stand any nonsense. She turned her attention back to the elderly woman, who couldn't seem to stop crying. Having gratefully accepted a cup of the warden's tea for her, she carefully guided her over the rubble and sat her down on the remnants of a low wall, some distance from the still-smoking crater.

She glanced across at Danuta, who was swiftly

and expertly cleaning the man's head wound and bandaging it before moving on to the young woman with the suspected fractured wrist. As Polly watched, Danuta gently examined the wrist and swiftly made a sling for it before checking over the cuts and bruises the girl had sustained. It was clear Danuta knew what she was doing, and Polly could fully understand how frustrated the girl must be to have to work in the laundry when her undoubted skills were so sorely needed elsewhere.

There were surprisingly few injuries considering they'd been buried under a four-storey house, and even after Harvey had found another few survivors, it was clear that most of them wouldn't need an ambulance. These lost souls stood about clinging to their loved ones as they stared in disbelief at the ruins of their homes and wondered what was to become of them now they'd lost everything.

Danuta was applying plasters and ointment to cuts and scrapes, so Polly remained with the elderly woman who was still trembling in her arms despite the hot, sweet tea. The lady flinched as she felt a damp nudge on her arm and looked down.

'Hello,' she said, and grinned as she ruffled his head. The furry face seemed to grin back at her, the brown eyes gleaming with intelligence and fun below the shaggy brows as he licked the old woman's outstretched hand. 'Who's a clever boy, then? Quite the hero of the hour, aren't you?'

'His name's Harvey, sure it is. And indeed he is a hero.'

Polly looked up at the square-built, sturdy man whose Home Guard uniform was covered in dust, soot and grime. 'You must be Mr Reilly,' she said. 'Peggy told me about you and Harvey.'

'Did she now?' His blue eyes twinkled in the weather-beaten face as he straightened his tin helmet. 'And who might you be, young lady?'

'Polly Brown.' She shook his filthy hand.

'You decided to turn up then,' he said round the stem of his pipe. 'How are ye enjoying your stay at the seaside?'

'It's been eventful,' replied Polly dryly. A sudden movement caught her eye, and she looked across the crater to what remained of the pavement on the other side.

Danuta was on her knees, swiftly rolling a man on to his side and checking his airway. He was in the throes of a fit, his legs and arms thrashing in the rubble as his back arched and his neck stretched.

Polly half-rose from the low wall, ready to assist, for this was a most unusual way to treat someone having a fit, and she was concerned the man might choke. But it was clear they did things differently in Poland, and Danuta seemed to have everything under control. Polly watched thoughtfully as the Polish girl grabbed a wooden tongue depressor from the medical box and wedged it firmly in his mouth before shouting for a blanket. She was holding tightly to the man in an attempt to stop him doing more injury to himself, and when the blanket was handed to her, she quickly wrapped him tightly in it and continued to hold him close, and on his side.

'She's a clever wee lass, that one,' muttered Ron as he sucked on his smoking pipe. 'Sure, and 'tis

155

a shame she can't do her proper job.'

'Yes,' Polly muttered, her thoughts whirling. 'But perhaps Matron will change her mind once she realises just how good she is.'

'"Tis no easy matter,' murmured Ron. 'The wee girl has no papers to prove she can do the job, and that Matron's not for bending, so she's not.'

Peggy arrived with three other women, each laden with tin trays of tea and sandwiches. 'Have you seen Jim?' she asked Ron.

'Aye. He's in the town, helping to clear the road. Barclays Bank took a direct hit and brought down the last of the Woolworths building with it. It's chaos down there, with burst water mains and gas pipes. I'll be drinking this and going to help. They need every pair of hands they can get.'

'I don't suppose you've seen Cissy, or any of the other girls?'

He shook his head, drained his tea and stuck his pipe back into his mouth. 'They'll turn up,' he said, patting her shoulder.

'I'm sure they will, but...'

'Now, Peggy,' he said gruffly, 'don't you be fretting, girl. For all the noise and hullabaloo the damage was minimal, and I know for a fact that the Apollo Theatre is still standing. They'll be fine, so they will.' He put the empty mug back on the tray and took a fish paste sandwich from the plate which he fed to Harvey. 'I think you've earned that, you old so-and-so. Come on. We've no time to be sitting on our laurels, there's work to do yet.'

'Oh dear,' sighed Peggy. 'And to think we all tried to persuade Ron to have Harvey put down at the beginning of the war because we thought it would be kinder than letting him suffer.'

'He doesn't look as if he's suffering at all,' laughed Polly. 'In fact, I think the pair of them are lapping up all the attention.'

Peggy laughed and was about to reply when she was interrupted by the sound of an approaching ambulance. It came to a halt at the end of the street, and the driver and his assistant clambered down. Peggy and Polly could hear the brief conversation between Danuta and the driver.

'This man have epileptic fit. Is over now, but will need to be seen by doctor to make sure no wound to the head.' She helped roll the inert figure on to a stretcher, and watched as he was loaded on board the ambulance before beckoning to her two other patients. 'You will also take man with head injury, and woman with fractured wrist.'

'We ain't got no room for no more,' the driver said sullenly.

'You have plenty room.' Danuta moved to the front of the ambulance, arms folded, expression stony. 'I not move until you agree.'

'We ain't allowed to take more'n one patient at a time. It's the rules,' he said obdurately. 'You can stand there all day, but I ain't breaking the rules.'

'Then it's time the rules are changed,' she retorted. 'Get into ambulance,' she ordered the man and woman who were hovering uncertainly by the back doors.

''Ere, you ain't got no cause to be ordering us about,' protested the assistant.

'I am nurse. You will do as I say in the interest

of my patients.'

The two bandaged casualties looked from her to the driver and his assistant, and then back to each other. Wordlessly, they climbed into the back and sat on the floor.

Danuta pushed past the driver, slammed the doors and turned to glare at him, arm outstretched, finger pointing towards Camden Road and the hospital. 'Go,' she said in a tone that brooked no argument.

He and his assistant exchanged glances then meekly clambered into the front cab of the ambulance. With a defiant clang of his bell, the driver clashed the gears and drove away at speed.

'Well done, you,' said Polly. 'It's ridiculous not to take more than one patient at a time. I'm sure that's not really in their rule book.'

Danuta shrugged, gratefully took a cup from Peggy's tray and drank it down. 'I must go to work now. Matron will be very angry, and I do not wish to lose my position, even though it is poor.'

'If you wait until I get washed and changed, I'll come with you,' said Polly.

'I will be too late,' she replied, her little face screwed up with anxiety. 'I cannot wait, Polly. I am sorry.' With that, she finished the last dregs of her tea, snatched up two sandwiches, and ran down Camden Road, her gas-mask box bouncing against her hip.

Polly quickly found someone who was happy to take in the elderly woman, who seemed much calmer now, and hurried back to Beach View. She felt very guilty about leaving Peggy in all the mess, but she would be needed at the hospital if they were inundated with casualties. And she needed to see Adam – to reassure herself that he was all right. Then, before going on her ward, she would check on Danuta to make sure Matron hadn't vented her spleen over her lateness.

As she quickly washed and changed into her uniform, she came to the conclusion that Danuta might be a tough, battle-hardened little thing, but she was vulnerable to women like Miss Billings, and would need someone to help stand up to her.

Polly had met women like Matron before. Like most bullies, she no doubt always picked on the ones who couldn't defend themselves, and Polly was determined to make sure that didn't happen to Danuta. Prickly she might be, resentful at not being able to nurse, certainly – but Polly suspected Danuta was using that tough facade to hide the bewilderment and homesickness she must be experiencing.

'Lord knows,' breathed Polly as she eyed her reflection in the mirror, 'it's hard enough for me to be so far from home and family. Poor Danuta has no one.'

Spurred on by this thought, she quickly secured the starched cap over the thick knot of hair she'd twisted low on her nape, picked up the heavy woollen cape that was far too warm for such weather, and hurried downstairs.

She found Peggy in the kitchen, surrounded by chattering, tearful women and a pile of unwashed china. There were dark shadows of weariness under her eyes, but her smile remained determinedly bright as she bustled round the room and tried to bring some order.

'I'm so sorry, Peggy, but I need to be at the hospital. With so many casualties...'

'You go, dear,' interrupted Peggy. 'I've got all day to sort things out here, and Cissy will help when she turns up. Once Jim and Ron get back, they can make a start on the door and windows.'

Polly shot her a grateful smile. 'Don't worry about our room,' she said. 'We can clean up when we get back.' She hurried into the hall, picked her way through the debris and down the steps. It was only seven-thirty in the morning, but it already felt as if she'd been awake for a week.

The walking wounded were waiting patiently on the rows of extra chairs that had been placed outside the Accident and Emergency Department. Ambulances arrived with clanging bells to disgorge their injured passengers, and nurses were scurrying back and forth trying to get everyone where they should be as porters pushed laden trolleys to X-ray and the theatres.

Polly could see that her services would indeed be needed but, at the moment, her only priority was Adam. She hurried to Men's Surgical and peeked through the circular windows in the double doors, hoping that Matron was elsewhere and that Mary was on duty. With a sigh of relief, she spotted her down by Adam's bed and hurried on to the ward.

Adam looked exactly the same as he had the night before, and she didn't know whether to feel relieved or saddened.

'I didn't think it would be long before you

appeared,' teased Mary as she finished taking his temperature. 'There's no change. I'm sorry.'

Polly could see the darkness beneath the other woman's eyes, and the weariness in the droop of her shoulders. 'Have you been here all night?'

Mary nodded. 'The sirens went off just as I was about to leave, so of course I stayed. It's quite a palaver getting these patients down to the shelter, even if we are on the ground floor, let me tell you.'

'But I thought Adam couldn't be moved?'

Mary stifled a yawn. 'Neither he nor Freddie in the next bed can be moved, but once all the shutters were over the windows, I stayed and kept an eye out for them.' She gave a wry smile. 'The conversation was a little lacking in content as they're both out cold, but we were nice and safe behind the shuttered windows, and I actually managed to read a whole newspaper without interruption.'

Polly took Adam's lifeless hand from the blanket and held it to her cheek. He felt warmer today, and there was a bit of colour in what she could see of his face. 'Thank you for looking after him, Mary.'

'It's my job,' she replied, 'just as you knew you would be needed here this morning.' She glanced at the watch pinned to her starched apron-bib. 'You'd better make yourself scarce,' she warned. 'Matron's due to do her rounds.'

'Thanks, Mary. Will I see you later?'

'I'll be here until my opposite number comes to relieve me, so I doubt I'll see you again today.' Her smile was warm as she patted Polly's free

161

hand. 'But Sister Warner's a good sort and hates Matron as much as we do. I'll warn her you might be in at lunchtime.'

'I'd better go,' murmured Polly. She kissed Adam's hand and, with a sigh, prepared to leave. 'Perhaps we could get together for a cup of tea sometime?' she said hopefully. 'It would be nice to get to know one another better.'

'That would be lovely. Come in and see me tomorrow evening and we can sort something out.'

Polly left the ward and just managed to avoid being seen by Matron by darting round a corner. She weaved her way through the milling people in the vast reception area, and headed down the steps to the basement laundry.

The smell of wet linen and wool assailed her and she walked into a steam-filled room that seemed to vibrate with the heavy drumbeat of machinery. There were at least twenty women and four men working here, and she received some curious looks as she tried to find Danuta.

Polly finally spotted her, standing at one of the many sinks, wrestling with the mangle as another girl helped to guide the sodden sheet through the rubber rollers and into a wooden tub. Her expression was grim, her chin set in a defiant square as the sweat poured down her face and darkened the brown dress. Then she seemed to realise she was being watched, and her dark, angry eyes found Polly. 'What you do here?'

'I came to see whether you managed to avoid Matron,' said Polly, determined not to be put off by the other girl's rudeness.

'She speak to me. I tell her why I am late. She not believe me and tell me I must work one extra hour.' She carried on turning the handle on the mangle. 'You go now, please. I will be in trouble again if she catch you here.'

'Let's meet for lunch,' said Polly. 'In the canteen at twelve?'

'I will see.' The anger suddenly went from Danuta's eyes and, as if she'd realised how curt she'd been, a hint of colour touched her cheek. 'Thank you, Polly,' she said. 'I will try.'

Polly left her to it. She ran back up the stairs and had just reached the reception area when she saw Matron bearing down on her. There was no avoiding her this time.

'Staff Nurse Brown,' boomed Matron. 'Thank you for coming in. It is always gratifying to know that my nurses have a sense of duty. I understand there was an incident close to your billet this morning?'

The old bitch was testing Danuta's story. 'There certainly was,' she replied. 'Our billet suffered some damage, and Miss Danuta and I had to deal with several casualties and wait for the ambulance, which is why she was rather late.'

Matron sniffed. 'It seems Miss Chimpsky has an excuse for being late every day.'

Polly gritted her teeth as she forced a smile. 'The Polish names are impossible to pronounce, aren't they?' she said with a lightness she didn't feel. 'They're quite a mouthful, and I've come to the conclusion it might be easier and quicker for everyone if we all called her Miss Danuta. What do you think, Matron?'

Matron held her gaze for several beats of silence as she tried to work out whether Polly was being insubordinate or practical. 'It would certainly save time,' she agreed with clear reluctance. 'Now hurry along, Staff Nurse. Women's Surgical needs you.'

Polly bit down on a smile as the woman swept past. 'Round one to me, I think,' she murmured.

Chapter Nine

Peggy had managed to get the other women to help clear the washing-up while she swept away the debris in the hall and wrestled the ruined door outside. Now the women were calmer, she felt easier about sending them back home to clear up their own mess. She worked better on her own, when she didn't have to keep stopping to tell people where things were or how she liked the chores done.

The three nurses rushed in shortly after the women had left, and within twenty minutes they had cleaned off their make-up, changed out of their pretty dresses and were running back down the street to the hospital fresh-faced in their uniforms. They had told Peggy they'd spent the night in a public shelter and, by the sound of it, it had turned into quite a party, with bottles of beer and gin being passed round and music coming from a wind-up gramophone someone had brought in with a stack of records.

The warden in charge of the shelter had tried to enforce the rules about alcohol and riotous behaviour, but he'd been outnumbered, and they'd danced to the music of Glenn Miller and his band, and sung all their favourite songs while the raid went on overhead. Peggy had listened to all this and envied them their energy – she felt like a wrung-out dishcloth.

She and Mrs Finch tied on their wrap-round aprons and covered their hair with knotted scarves to ward off the worst of the dust and soot. Once the glass had been cleared from the dining room rug, and the tattered, filthy curtains unhooked from the pole above the window and chucked into the back garden, Peggy used a brush to get the worst of the soot from where it lay on the picture rails, grate, floor and mantelpiece. When this was done, Mrs Finch wielded the Hoover back and forth until the floor and the rug were passably clean.

The rug would need taking up and giving a good thrashing, Peggy realised, but it was a heavy old thing, so it would have to wait until Jim and Ron came back. The floor would need a good scrub as well, she thought with a weary sigh as she looked at her watch. It was mid-morning and still there was no sight of them or Cissy.

As if her thoughts had winged their way to her youngest daughter, Cissy appeared in the dining room shortly afterwards, out of breath. 'I'm so sorry I'm late, Mum,' she panted. 'But there was an unexploded bomb down on the seafront, and none of us were allowed to leave the theatre. I tried to ring, but the telephone lines are down again, so we just had to wait it out.'

'Thank goodness you're safe,' breathed Peggy, taking her into her arms. 'I was getting awfully worried.'

Cissy kissed her cheek and gave her a hug. 'You wouldn't be you if you weren't worried, Mum,' she said fondly. She swept back her blonde hair and slung her gas-mask box and handbag on to a dusty chair. 'I saw what happened down the road. Was anyone hurt?'

'A couple of minor injuries,' replied Peggy. 'We were all very lucky.'

'Mmm. There was quite a bit of damage in the town as well, and it looks like this old place has taken a bit of a bashing too,' she murmured. 'What can I do to help?'

'Don't you have rehearsals this afternoon?'

Cissy shook her head, her gaze still on the damage. 'They decided we'd rehearsed enough. I don't have to go back until just before six.'

'In that case, you can help me roll up this rug, sweep the rest of the soot from the floor and cover everything with dust sheets, so we can begin to clear up the rest of the mess.'

Peggy sighed as she looked at the ruinous streaks of black on her lovely wallpaper, and the dark rim of it that still powdered the picture rail, dado and the ornate plaster rose in the centre of the ceiling. 'It will take forever,' she sighed, 'but if the three of us use a bit of elbow grease, we're bound to get rid of the worst of it.'

Cissy went to change into trousers and shirt then fetched an apron, headscarf and a pair of rubber gloves to protect her pretty hands and nails. Once the rug was rolled out into the hall they swept the floor and mopped it clean, then laid the big dust sheets. Having pushed the furniture to the other end of the room, they set to work with scrubbing brushes and cloths.

Mrs Finch couldn't get on to her knees, so she brushed down the upholstered chairs and polished the tables before she got a wet cloth and enthusiastically cleaned the window sill, dado rail and mantelpiece. 'I always had a girl come in to do the rough work,' she trilled, 'but this is rather fun.' She rubbed at a spot on the window frame, discovered it was where the paint was chipped and moved on to the next bit. 'Mind you,' she continued, 'I don't think I could do this every day.'

'Neither could I,' said Cissy with a grimace. 'It's lethal on the hands and nails, and I dread to think what all this soot is doing to my complexion.'

Peggy rested back on her heels and laughed. 'I don't think you're in any danger of losing your looks, Cissy, and a bit of hard work won't kill you.'

Cissy continued scrubbing the hearth. 'I work hard at the theatre,' she muttered. 'It's not easy doing two shows a night after rehearsing all afternoon.' She wiped the wet cloth over the black hearth and rinsed it out. 'I'll just finish this bit and then get us all a cup of tea,' she said. 'This is thirsty work.'

Peggy wondered if this was the right moment to question Cissy more closely. 'Is everything all right, Cissy?' she asked. 'Only you don't seem to be your sunny self these days.'

'I'm fine,' she replied, dropping the cloth into the dirty water and wiping her sooty forehead with the back of her arm. 'I'm just fed up with this war, that's all.'

'Aren't we all?' muttered Peggy. 'It seems that no sooner do I get the place straight, than it's filthy again.' She wiped the damp cloth over the skirting board and sighed. 'We'll have to get the chimney sweep in. I don't want to risk this happening again.'

'I'll get that tea.' Cissy pulled off the rubber gloves and got to her feet. 'Is there anything to eat? I'm starving.'

'I saved some sandwiches and biscuits for you,' said Peggy. 'They're in the larder under a plate.' She watched Cissy leave the room. It wasn't the war getting Cissy down, though God knew it was enough to try the patience of a saint – there was something else, something the girl didn't want her to know about.

Peggy wrung out the cloth and resumed the cleaning, her mind working through all the possibilities, her imagination in danger of running riot. Cissy had always confided in her, had always discussed her plans and her dreams, had joyously related the funny incidents at the theatre and happily brought her friends home for tea. But suddenly that well of information had dried up; she'd stopped asking her friends to visit, and she'd become quieter and more introspective. In short, Peggy realised, Cissy had changed, and it had all started shortly after she and Jim had finally given in to her pleas and agreed to her joining the travelling troupe.

168

Resting back on her heels, she went over the interview she'd had with Jack Witherspoon. He'd been a very pleasant, fatherly sort of man and both she and Jim had agreed that Cissy would be all right with him. Now she wasn't quite so sure.

She absent-mindedly ran the damp cloth over the skirting again, her thoughts whirling. She must not let her imagination run away with her. Cissy could very well be fed up and tired from the hectic schedule at the theatre – and Jack Witherspoon had promised to keep an eye on her, and let them know if there were any problems. She really must stop imagining the worst, she decided, and trust that Cissy would eventually tell her what was bothering her. She'd probably fallen out with some of the other girls. They could be a catty lot, and that peculiar man who was in charge of choreography sounded a complete tyrant.

Putting her worries firmly to one side, she eyed the ruined wallpaper. There was little point in trying to do much about it. There would be more raids like the one last night, and a lick of paint or new wallpaper would be a futile waste of time. The war had escalated since the daylight raids had begun back in August, and now with Russia and Italy allied with Germany and the Vichy French, it could only get worse.

'Here we are,' said Cissy. 'I've done some more sandwiches, but we're now out of bread and anything to put on it.' She set the tray down and handed round the cups of tea and plate of sandwiches. 'Do you want me to go to the shops?'

'You could try,' muttered Peggy as she sank on

169

to one of the chairs, 'but I suspect there won't be much on the shelves at this time of day.' She bit into the sandwich that had the merest hint of marge and a slither of tomato inside. 'We've got corned beef hash tonight with plenty of vegetables from the garden, so we won't starve.'

Cissy drank her tea and munched her way through three sandwiches in quick succession. 'I'll give it a go anyway,' she said. 'You never know, I could be lucky.'

Peggy and Mrs Finch sat in silence, the smell of soot still permeating the air, as Cissy fetched the ration books and left the house. 'I don't know what I'm going to feed everyone tomorrow,' said Peggy after a while. 'With Ron not going hunting so frequently, and the shops empty of almost everything, it's getting harder and harder to make ends meet.'

'What's that, dear?' Mrs Finch twiddled her hearing aid. 'Cold meat? I didn't think we had any.'

Peggy shook her head, too weary to explain.

The hospital canteen was busy and noisy, and it took Polly a while to find two seats together. She smiled at the other chattering nurses and introduced herself, then placed the plate of vegetable stew on the table and sat down.

She was very hungry, having missed breakfast, but the stew didn't taste as good as it looked. There was no seasoning, the gravy was thin and watery, and the vegetables had definitely passed their prime. But it was hot and filled the gap, and she'd almost finished when she saw Danuta come into the room.

Catching her eye, she waved and, as Danuta collected her food, Polly finished her stew and pushed away her plate. 'How did it go this morning?' she asked as the other girl sat down beside her.

Danuta pulled a face. 'It is hard work, but I manage.' She gave a nod of acknowledgement to the other nurses at the table who were looking at her with open, but friendly curiosity.

'This is my friend, Danuta from Poland,' said Polly to them. 'We share a billet.'

They smiled and murmured a welcome before making their apologies and returning to their wards.

Polly realised Danuta was just as hungry as she'd been, and she sipped her tea as the other girl wolfed down the stew. When she'd pushed her empty plate away and reached for the thick china mug of tea, Polly asked the question that had been plaguing her since that morning.

'I have never seen someone rolled on to their side during a fit,' she began. 'We're taught to keep them flat on their back, with their necks arched to keep the airways open.'

Danuta eyed her over the rim of the mug. 'In Poland we follow the method advised long ago by one of your English doctors at the London Hospital. It has been discovered that by putting the patient in such a position saves many lives. You do not know this?'

Polly shook her head. 'It's not in any of our nursing manuals.'

'Then it should be, I think,' Danuta said solemnly. She sipped her tea. 'I have been to Accident and Emergency,' she continued. 'The head injury and the broken wrist have been discharged. But the man with the fit is being kept in overnight for observation.'

Polly felt rather ashamed that she'd forgotten all about them. 'I've been to see Adam,' she said. 'There's no change in his condition and, due to his heavy medication, he's unaware that I'm even here.'

Danuta's expression softened as she put down her empty cup. 'It must be very hard for you to be in the hospital but not able to be with him. What are the injuries that keep him here?'

Polly took a deep breath and told her about the series of operations he'd had. 'He's heavily sedated,' she finished, 'and no one will really know much until he wakes up. It's all very worrying and...'

The sirens screamed out with deafening urgency.

As one, the staff rose from their tables and began to hurry in an orderly fashion to their posts as the shutters were slammed down over the canteen counter. Polly and Danuta swiftly joined the flow.

'I'll see you later,' shouted Polly over the ear-splitting racket as she and Danuta prepared to go their separate ways. 'What time does your shift finish? Maybe we could walk back together?'

'I will finish in three hours. But I have something I must do before I return to Beach View.' Danuta gave her a hesitant smile. 'Sorry always to say no. But it is important I do this thing today.'

Polly didn't get the chance to ask what was so

important, and she let everyone swirl around her as she watched Danuta head for the steps to the basement. She was a strange girl and clearly preferred to keep things close to her chest – but at least Polly had managed to get a smile out of her.

She realised she was getting in everyone's way, and quickly ran up the stairs to Women's Surgical. There was quiet order as the ward sister orchestrated the evacuation. Nurses and porters quickly helped patients into wheelchairs, or steered the bedridden out of the ward and down the specially made ramps towards the vast shelter that had been built below the grounds at the rear of the hospital.

Polly took charge of a young woman who was recovering from an appendectomy and helped her into a wheelchair. The woman was frightened, and it took a while to calm her down. The corridors and staircases were jammed with walking wounded, beds, casualties and staff, and the noise they made almost drowned the awful wail of the siren.

Making sure the nervous young woman was as comfortable as possible and calm enough to be left, and ensuring she was positioned near the other women from her ward, Polly returned to Women's Surgical.

It was deserted and she hesitated on the threshold, torn between the desire to see Adam and the knowledge she would be risking Matron's wrath if she didn't return immediately to the shelter.

The need to see Adam won and, as she entered Men's Surgical, she found the same orderly evacuation being orchestrated by Sister Warner,

173

who was plump and bustling and had kind brown eyes. 'You must be Polly Brown,' she said with a warm smile, 'and you should be with your own patients in the shelter.'

'I know, but I wanted to see Adam quickly, if that's all right.'

Sister Warner looked at her watch. 'You have two minutes.'

'Thanks,' she breathed, already heading for Adam's bedside. 'Hello, darling,' she murmured to the still figure. 'I've just come to say a quick hello before I go down into the shelter. Can you hear me, my love? Do you even know I'm here?'

Adam didn't move, and his hands remained lifeless and pale against the white hospital blanket.

Polly watched the rise and fall of his chest and wondered if it was her imagination, or whether his breathing seemed a little easier today. His colour was certainly better, and his hands were warmer than before, and as she studied the drip, she realised the dosage of morphine had been lessened. She felt a spurt of hope and kissed his freshly shaved chin. 'You'll be fine, darling, and when you wake up, I'll be here.'

'You must go now.' Sister Warner's voice was soft but her tone brooked no argument.

'Thanks for letting me see him,' said Polly. 'I'll come back for a quick look at him after the raid – if that's all right?'

'Only if Matron's not prowling. Perhaps it would be better to wait until visiting hour at six?'

Polly swallowed her disappointment and fled as the sound of approaching enemy planes rumbled overhead.

Peggy had stuffed a cardboard box up the chimney in the hope that it would stop any further fall of soot. She had emptied the filthy water into the butt Ron had put outside the back door so he could water his vegetables, and was about to light a cigarette and put her feet up for a few minutes when the siren went off.

'Bugger,' she muttered, dragging herself out of her chair and reaching for her gas mask. 'Am I not to have any peace today?' She crossed the kitchen and gently shook Mrs Finch from her doze. 'The siren's going. Come on, we have to go downstairs.'

'I'd love some pears, dear, but how on earth did you get hold of any?'

Peggy shook her head and helped her to her feet. 'Air raid,' she yelled just as Mrs Finch managed to get her hearing aid switched on.

'There's no need to shout, dear,' she said, grabbing her bag of knitting and her library book. 'I can hear you perfectly well.'

Peggy closed her eyes momentarily and then helped her down the steps and into the shelter. It felt strange to be in here in the middle of the day, but it seemed the Luftwaffe was determined to disrupt everyone's life and make things as difficult as possible.

She settled Mrs Finch in her deckchair, lit the lamp against the gloom, sank down on to the bench beside her and pulled out the packet of Park Drive from her apron pocket. Having lit her cigarette, she leant back against a pillow and tried to relax – but it wasn't easy. Cissy was at the

175

local shops and Jim and Ron were somewhere in the middle of the town. It had been a long, weary night, and now it seemed they were in for an even longer day.

Peggy smoked her cigarette as Mrs Finch read her library book. She could hear the planes overhead now and braced herself for the onslaught. The guns were booming out from the cliff-tops and the sharp rat-a-tat-tat of tracer fire could be heard piercing the deeper rumble of the bombers.

She closed her eyes, wishing she could have the radio down here in the shelter. She'd become used to listening to the music programmes and 'Workers' Playtime' as she got on with her chores – and of course it provided news of everything that was happening outside Cliffehaven. It had become a ritual to sit and listen to the news every night, unless there was a raid on, and although it wasn't cheering, it certainly made her feel she wasn't alone, that she was a very minor part in what Churchill was calling 'The Battle of Britain'.

The airfields and factories all over the south coast of England had been targeted back in August, and the number of daylight raids was increasing. Central London had become the prime target, of course, and the British air force had retaliated with a massive raid on Berlin. Germany's answer had been to increase its efforts by targeting not only London, but Southampton, Bristol, Manchester and Liverpool. It seemed no part of this island was safe, and she just had to pray that her sons would survive to come home – and that there would still be a home to come back to.

The all-clear went an hour later, and Peggy and Mrs Finch returned to the house. There had been no bombs or incendiaries this time, for which they were thankful, but some poor souls somewhere must have taken the full brunt of the attack.

'I'm feeling a little tired, dear,' said Mrs Finch. 'I think I'll go and have a nap.'

Peggy helped her up the stairs and, once she was settled, came back to the kitchen to begin preparing the evening meal. It was a chore she'd come to hate, for there was very little variety in the food available, and the last of the summer vegetables were beginning to look rather sorry for themselves. But at least they could fill up on potatoes, and the onions Ron had hung in the shed would provide a bit of flavour to the hash.

Cissy felt awful. The shock of her fall and the knowledge that there was blood on her face was nothing compared to the pain in her ankle. She managed to haul herself up the steps, but had to bite her lip to stifle the yelp of pain as she inadvertently put her weight on her ankle while trying to dodge the dining room rug which had been rolled into the middle of the hall.

'Mum,' she said plaintively on finally reaching the kitchen. 'Mum, can you help me?'

Peggy turned from the sink and gasped in horror before rushing to help her sit down. 'Cissy? Oh, Cissy, what happened?'

Cissy felt like a rag doll as she slumped into the chair, the string bag of groceries falling to the floor from her limp fingers. Her head was pounding and she felt sick. 'The sirens went and, in the rush for the shelter, I tripped and banged my head,' she stuttered. 'And I've done something to my ankle. It really hurts, Mum.'

'So I see,' murmured Peggy. 'It does look horribly swollen.'

'I think it's broken,' Cissy said with a hiss of pain as she tried to move it.

'If it is, then I'll have to get you to the hospital,' said Peggy. 'Oh dear,' she fretted. 'I have a house full of nurses and just when I really need one, none of them are to be seen. What a to-do.' She eyed the swollen ankle and then turned her attention to the blood on Cissy's face. 'Let's clean you up first,' she murmured. 'Then we'll think about what to do with that ankle.'

Peggy rushed to get a clean cloth which she soaked with cold water. 'I'll be as gentle as I can,' she soothed, 'but I need to clean away this blood so I can see what the damage is to your face.'

'Is it very bad?' Cissy's headache was pounding in time with the throb in her ankle, and she winced as the cold cloth dabbed at her sore cheek.

'You've got a nasty graze there,' murmured Peggy, 'and a lump the size of a pullet's egg on your forehead. I wouldn't be surprised if you ended up with a black eye.'

Cissy looked at her in horror. 'I can't go out with a black eye,' she gasped.

'You won't be able to dance on that ankle either,' muttered Peggy as she put a cold compress against the swelling. 'Put your foot on that chair and keep it there. It might help ease the pain.'

Cissy covered her face with her hands and,

although she remained dry-eyed, she let out a few dramatic sobs for good measure. Her mother would expect her to cry, but actually she was thinking fast. The accident could be turned to her advantage, and although the injuries were painful and probably made her look ugly, they would be far easier to bear than having to face Jack Witherspoon tonight.

At the thought of the awful events of the previous day she felt tears well, and now she was truly sobbing. 'But I can't let everyone down,' she said, hoping she sounded stalwart and brave. 'They'll be furious if I don't turn up.'

'There will be no point in you going,' said Peggy firmly as she ran cold water over another cloth. 'You won't be able to dance with an ankle like that. I'll telephone the theatre and tell them you won't be back for at least two days.'

Cissy dipped her chin, her blonde hair falling in a waterfall over her face so that her mother couldn't see the relief that was flooding through her.

Polly had been kept busy on her ward for the rest of her shift, and now she was so tired she almost had to drag herself back to Beach View. Stepping through the entrance that had once held a front door, she peeked into the dining room and realised Peggy had been extremely busy, for it looked almost back to normal.

She dumped her gas-mask box and cloak over the newel post, stepped over the roll of carpet and went in search of a cup of tea. The sight of the young girl being fussed over by Peggy made her falter. 'Oh, my goodness,' she breathed. 'What's happened? You weren't hit in that raid, were you?'

Peggy looked up, her worried expression clearing. 'Thank goodness you've come back, Polly. This is my youngest daughter, Cissy,' she explained quickly. 'She's had a bit of a fall, and I think she might have broken her ankle. Would you mind taking a look at it?'

'Of course I will.' Polly knelt beside the girl. 'Hello, Cissy. I'm Polly Brown.' She looked into a wan little face streaked with tears and saw the dark bruising that was already spreading round one of her blue eyes. 'You've got a bit of a shiner coming and will need a drop of iodine on it to help the bruising go down quickly,' she said lightly. 'But let me look at that ankle first. Is it very painful?'

'It is a bit,' Cissy replied, and winced as Polly gently felt the delicate bones of her foot and pressed against her toes.

Polly smiled reassuringly at her. 'No bones broken, but it's a nasty sprain. The swelling should go down if you rest it for a couple of days.' She took the little bottle of iodine and the roll of bandaging Peggy had dug out of her cupboard. 'Thanks, Peggy, and a cup of sweet tea wouldn't go amiss, if you wouldn't mind. I suspect she's a bit shocked.'

'I think you could both do with one,' replied Peggy as she set out the cups and put two spoonfuls of precious sugar in each. 'But the tea's awfully weak, I'm afraid.'

'Wet and warm will do,' said Polly before turning back to Cissy. 'Peggy tells me you dance with a theatre troupe. That must be such fun, with all

180

the lovely costumes and the music and every-thing. Me and Adam used to go to the theatre a lot before Alice came along.'

Cissy gave her a wan smile over the lip of her teacup. 'You must come and watch sometime,' she muttered with little enthusiasm. 'I can always get you free tickets.'

'Perhaps once you're feeling better,' murmured Polly. 'You won't be up to dancing for a few days, I'm afraid. That ankle has to rest.'

'I've telephoned the theatre and warned them,' said Peggy. 'Mr Witherspoon was very under-standing.'

Polly had quickly bandaged the swollen ankle and was now carefully dabbing iodine on the swelling above Cissy's brow. She frowned as she caught the fleeting gleam of contempt in the girl's eyes at the mention of his name. Whoever Mr Witherspoon was, he clearly didn't rate highly in Cissy's estimation.

'Does it hurt anywhere else?' she asked softly.

Cissy set aside her tea and rubbed her fore-head. 'I've got the most awful headache,' she said. 'I think I'll go to bed.'

Polly frowned. She didn't like the sound of that. 'Perhaps it would be better if you sit in that chair by the range for a while. Peggy, do you have any aspirin?'

Peggy dug into her cupboard again for the tin box where she kept such things. 'It's not serious, is it?' Her dark eyes were clouded with concern as she handed over two aspirin.

'She might have concussion, so she'll need to be watched for a while. It's always difficult with head injuries, one never knows what sort of damage might have been done.' Polly saw Peggy's look of horror and rushed to reassure her. 'I'm sure she'll be fine,' she said. 'Let her fall asleep in the chair here, but if she's sick, then ring the hospital immediately.'

'But surely, with you in the house...'

'There's only so much I can do, Peggy. I'm sorry. If she has concussion, then she needs to be seen by a doctor.' Polly looked at the watch pinned to her starched apron. 'Talking of hospitals,' she sighed. 'I need to get some sleep before I go back to visit Adam.'

She helped Cissy into the fireside chair and covered her in a blanket. The girl's colour had improved even though the bruising was already darkening one eye. A quick check of her pulse told her it was steady and strong, and it didn't feel as if she had a temperature, so she didn't think there was too much to worry about.

Leaving the kitchen, she collected her cloak, bag and gas mask from the newel post and trudged upstairs to her room. Peggy had certainly been busy, for the glass had been cleared and a sheet of hardboard covered the window, and although Polly was immensely grateful, she was so tired she couldn't think straight as she stripped off her uniform and hung it up. With a sigh of pleasure, she sank into her bed, set the alarm, and was asleep within seconds.

Peggy rescued the string bag from where she'd slung it on to the table and dug out a loaf of bread, a few ounces of margarine, a packet of tea and a pound and a half of stewing beef. It was quite a haul for so late in the day. She was about to congratulate Cissy when she realised the girl was asleep. Her colour was back to normal, her breathing was easier, and all in all, she suspected Cissy would be as right as rain before morning.

Peggy moved round her kitchen trying to make as little noise as possible so she didn't disturb Cissy as she prepared the dinner and tidied up.

A while later, she heard the tramp of heavy footsteps coming up the front steps and rushed into the hall. 'Jim,' she breathed thankfully. 'At last. I thought you were never coming home.'

'And where else would I be, me darling?' he murmured, staring in puzzlement at the lack of a front door. 'What the devil happened here? Are you all right?'

'Everyone's fine, except for Cissy who fell over and hurt her ankle. The door was blown off along with the front windows during the raid last night.' She looked at his weary, dirt-streaked face, his lank hair and filthy clothes, and realised he was probably even more tired than she. 'I'm sorry, Jim, but you'll have to find something to replace them before it gets dark.'

'I've still got some plywood in Dad's shed. I'll do it after I've had something to eat and drink and a bit of a sit-down.' His dark blue eyes fell on the rolled up rug. 'What's that doing here?'

'We had a fall of soot from the dining room chimney,' she said shortly. 'All in all, it has been quite a day.' Peggy looked up into his handsome face and returned his weary smile. 'Come on into the kitchen,' she said softly, 'but mind Cissy.

She's asleep.'

The usual twinkle in Jim's blue eyes was dimmed by his tiredness as he sank into a kitchen chair. He was covered in dust and soot and grease, his usual dapper appearance discarded on a bomb site somewhere in the town. He eyed his sleeping daughter with a frown. 'She's all right, though, isn't she?'

Peggy explained as she quickly made a pot of fresh tea and toasted some bread for him which she slathered in home-made jam to hide the fact there was so little margarine.

He smiled fondly at Cissy and gave a vast yawn. 'As long as there're no broken bones,' he murmured. 'B'jesus, I could kill for a few hours' sleep, Peg. Me and Da have been at it all night.'

'Where is Ron?' Peggy poured the tea and passed him the toast. 'The last time I saw him was this morning at the bomb site down the road.'

'He'll be here in a minute,' mumbled Jim with his mouth full of toast. 'He's gone to check on Rosie Braithwaite, and help her change the barrels and get those crates up from the cellar before she opens at six.'

Peggy settled on one of the wooden kitchen chairs and lit a cigarette. 'You both must be dead on your feet,' she murmured. 'I'm sorry you've got to sort out the doors and windows before you can rest.'

'So am I,' he muttered, 'but needs must.'

'I hope you don't have to go in to the cinema tonight?'

'No, thank goodness. I'm off now until tomorrow afternoon.'

Peggy eyed him as he slurped his tea and munched his toast. 'I see they've got a new usherette at the Odeon. She looks about the same age as Cissy. Nice girl, is she?'

'Nice enough,' he muttered. Raising one dark brow, he eyed her quizzically. 'Nothing much gets past you, does it, Peg?'

'No,' she replied, holding his gaze, her expression speaking volumes.

Jim broke the eye contact first, finished the toast and drained the last of his tea. 'I'll sort out the door and windows, then I'm for me bed.'

Peggy watched as he strode across the kitchen and hurried down the stairs. Within minutes he was back, armed with several sheets of plywood, a hammer and a bag of nails. 'We'll have to use the back door until I can get a replacement,' he muttered as he crossed the kitchen.

Peggy listened to the hammer blows and the occasional curse. Jim had never been very good at doing things about the house, but at least he was trying his best, so she didn't have the right to complain. She eyed her daughter, a little concerned that she could sleep through the racket.

Jim reappeared almost an hour later. 'The house is secure, and I'll go down to the scrapyard tomorrow and see if Bert has any doors.' He dropped the hammer and bag of nails on the table. 'I'm for me bed now, Peg. I could sleep for a week.'

'You'll have a bath first,' she said, alarmed at the thought of all that muck on her nice clean sheets. 'Leave those clothes in the bathroom and I'll wash them tomorrow.'

Mindful of the state of his clothing, he carefully

185

gave her a hug. 'You're the only one for me, Peg Reilly, and don't you ever lose sight of that,' he murmured.

She gently pushed him away. 'It's you who needs to remember that,' she chided softly, 'not me.'

He gave her one of those smiles which usually made her go weak at the knees. 'Why not come upstairs and scrub me back for a minute? I'm sure you could do with a bit of a lie-down yourself.'

'There's a loofah in the bathroom,' she retorted mildly. 'I've done enough scrubbing today to last me a lifetime.'

'Are ye sure I can't persuade you?'

'Get out of here, Jim Reilly,' she said on a giggle. 'I thought you were tired?'

He gave a deep sigh. 'That I am, me darling. Dog tired. So don't wake me if there's another raid. If Hitler's going to get me, then it'll be in me own bed. I'm past caring.'

'Funny you should say that,' said Peggy. 'Ron voiced the same sentiment when the Anderson shelter arrived a year ago, but he sits in there along with everyone else when there's a raid on.'

'Not me, and not tonight.' He kissed her, leaving a smudge on her cheek, and then trudged upstairs.

Within minutes, Peggy heard the bathwater running. She finished peeling the vegetables and made the corned beef hash, her thoughts drifting from Jim to Ron to Cissy. She hadn't needed to say much to Jim, he'd understood she was on to him. As for Ron, he was free to do what he liked, and if Rosie was his choice, then good for him.

She eyed Cissy, who at last seemed to be stirring from her deep sleep.

'I'm feeling ever so much better,' she said through a vast yawn. 'Was that Dad coming in?'

Peggy nodded and told her about the windows and door. 'He's having a bath now, and will probably sleep right through, so don't disturb him.' She cocked her head and smiled. 'That black eye's coming on a treat, by the way.'

Cissy grimaced as she gingerly touched the lump on her forehead. 'Thanks, Mum. I really wanted to know that,' she said ruefully.

'Here, borrow this old walking stick I found in the cellar. Are you feeling well enough to go upstairs and get changed out of those clothes? You've got some blood on your shirt that will need to be washed out.'

Cissy nodded. 'If I take it slowly, I can manage just fine.'

Peggy was poised to rush and help as she listened to the girl make slow progress up the two flights of stairs. But it seemed Cissy had recovered enough to reach her bedroom and slam the door with her usual carelessness.

With a deep sigh, Peggy returned to setting the kitchen table. They would have to eat in here tonight, the dining room furniture was still stacked against the wall, and she hadn't had the heart to ask Jim to shift it.

'Can I help you, Mrs Reilly?'

Peggy turned and smiled. 'No thank you, Danuta. Everything is under control.' She noted the dark circles beneath the girl's eyes and the weary droop of her shoulders beneath that drab brown dress and shabby cardigan. 'I see you managed to find your way round the back, but you look like you could do with a cup of tea. Was it very tiring at the hospital?'

'Thank you, I would like some tea. And yes, it is hard work, but maybe I can find other job where I am of more use.'

'Ye'll not be finding it easy without those bits of paper,' muttered Ron as he lumbered up the basement steps and into the kitchen with an equally filthy Harvey at his heels. 'What else can you do besides nursing?'

Peggy gave them both a cup of tea and lit a cigarette. 'Don't interrogate the girl, Ron,' she chided softly. 'Can't you see she's worn out?'

'I can speak French and German as well as English,' said Danuta, 'and when I was with the resistance, I learn many other things – but these are not needed in Cliffehaven, I think.'

'Well now,' said Ron thoughtfully, his gaze steady on her wan face. 'There are many different skills needed in these dark times. Maybe...' He fell silent and drank his tea to the background noise of Harvey slurping from his water bowl.

'You think these skills would be useful?' Danuta was watching him closely.

He didn't answer her question directly. 'Did the authorities not ask you any questions when you arrived in England?'

Danuta shrugged. 'Of course, and I had to stay in a camp before they would let me come to Cliffehaven. But I have identification papers, and I told them about my brother and my nursing

188

skills. I did not think it very wise to tell them I could speak German.'

His eyes twinkled as he grinned. 'You were probably right. German isn't the favoured language at the moment. Still...'

'You are thinking of something, Mr Reilly?' Danuta's interest was clearly piqued.

He gave a vast yawn. 'I'm thinking I need a bath and a few minutes to read me paper,' he replied, getting to his feet.

Danuta's disappointment was clear, but she continued to sip her tea.

'What are you doing tomorrow, girl? Would you consider coming with me up in the hills with Harvey? It's about time I got some meat for the pot, and I always like a bit of company.'

Danuta eyed him thoughtfully. 'I do not work until day after tomorrow,' she replied. 'I would like to see your English hills.'

'Good, that's settled then. Be ready straight after breakfast, and I'll show you what me and Jim and everyone else in this country is fighting for.'

Chapter Ten

Polly was woken by her alarm clock and she lay for a moment, bleary-eyed and disorientated. Then she heard the shrieking gulls squabbling on the roof across the road, and smelt the saltiness that was carried on the wind from the sea, and

189

remembered she was in Cliffehaven. With a wry smile, she realised that although she'd been here for two days, this had been the first chance she'd had to actually sleep in her bed.

She luxuriated in a long stretch and rolled over to discover Danuta was watching her from the other bed. 'I'm so sorry,' she said quickly. 'I hope my alarm didn't wake you.'

'No matter. I was only resting,' Danuta replied, rising on to one elbow. 'You sleep well?'

'Like a log,' Polly replied. 'But I could have done with at least another eight hours,' she added ruefully. She swung her legs off the bed and padded across the room in her pink liberty bodice and camiknickers. 'I'd better get washed and ready for visiting,' she murmured, grabbing her dressing gown from the hook on the back of the door.

Danuta curled back into the soft blankets, and was still there when Polly returned to the bedroom to get dressed. 'You have very nice hair,' she said, as Polly ran a brush through it and left it to swirl around her face and shoulders. 'I once had long hair, down to my waist. But it was not practical once I had to leave my apartment in Warsaw.'

'It's not really that practical as a nurse,' muttered Polly as she stepped into a sprigged cotton frock and began to fasten the buttons that went from neck to waist. 'But Adam loves it, and I just haven't had the heart to cut it all off.'

She surreptitiously glanced at her watch as she slid her feet into her sandals. She didn't really have much time to talk, but it seemed that Danuta was at last opening up to her, and it would be awful to deny her the chance. 'Was it very bad in Warsaw?'

'When the Germans came we lost everything,' Danuta said with little emotion. 'I cut my hair and sold it for food. The man made wigs for the women who consorted with the enemy soldiers.' She grimaced, her eyes dark with disgust. 'For some women it was the only way to survive – but I could not do that.'

Polly fastened the belt and smoothed the cotton dress over her hips. She was intrigued, despite the lack of time. 'How did you survive, Danuta?'

'I sell things, steal things, live like a rat in a trap.' She sat up in bed and pulled the blanket up to her bony shoulders with a shiver. 'There is no work for me at the hospital, but I must find food for Mamma and Papa, and when Aleksy's wife, Anjelika, and their baby come to my hiding place, it is almost impossible to find enough for us all.'

Polly sank on to the bed beside her. 'So, what did you do?' she asked softly.

'I survived,' Danuta replied, her gaze steady, her little face working against the tears and the memories and the pain. 'Mamma and Papa die, and then Anjelika and baby are taken away. I have no one to care for, so I leave Poland and join my friends who are fighting in the resistance.'

Polly wanted to hug her, to assure her that no matter how much she hurt, she would always be able to confide in her. But she had the feeling that Danuta would not appreciate any tactile sympathy – she just needed to talk. 'You're very brave,' she murmured, resisting the urge to take Danuta's hand.

'I didn't want to die without fighting back,' Danuta replied. 'It's not about being brave – it is, how you say, instinctive.' Throwing off the blanket to reveal a washed-out liberty bodice and pants, she grabbed the shabby dressing gown Peggy had given her and wrapped it tightly round herself before she faced Polly again. 'I have new life now,' she said firmly. 'I must forget Poland.'

Polly suspected she never would, but didn't argue the point. She sat on Danuta's bed and watched as the girl briskly brushed her short, dark hair. She couldn't begin to imagine the sort of life Danuta must have had during the occupation of Poland, and she suspected the tale she'd heard today was only a tiny glimpse into that terrible time. No wonder she was so edgy, so unwilling to open herself up to more hurt or rejection. Matron's attitude must have almost destroyed her – and Polly knew it would have certainly broken her if she had been in Danuta's shoes.

Danuta turned from the mirror above the gas fire. 'I do not ask for pity, so please don't look at me that way, Polly. We are the same age, I think, but our lives so far have been very different. Perhaps, now we are sharing this room, we can learn to understand each other a little bit, no?'

'I hope so,' murmured Polly.

Danuta put the hairbrush on the bedside table and glanced at the clock. 'You will be late for Adam,' she said. 'I will see you later.' She picked up a towel and left the room.

Polly's thoughts were still occupied with Danuta's sad story as she slowly pulled on a thick cardigan over her dress – the weather was changing and it got cold once the sun went down. The girl had obviously survived far worse things than the fall of Warsaw, and Polly wondered how deeply the scars of those experiences went – and how much damage had been done.

Everyone had finished their tea and the washing-up had been done, the kitchen tidied. Peggy had put a plate of dinner by the hob to keep it warm for Polly, and another plate for Jim in the larder in case he woke in the middle of the night wanting something to eat. The three girls had gone out again to meet their Australians, Ron had disappeared to his Home Guard duties after visiting the pub, and Mrs Finch was busy with her knitting.

'Thanks for helping to clear everything up, Danuta,' she said. 'It's a bit of a squash trying to feed everyone in here, but we'll be back in the dining room tomorrow.'

'It is nice to have everyone together in this kitchen. It reminds me of home,' Danuta said shyly. 'And although it is often that I cannot join in, I like to listen to the conversations and hear the laughing. It is good, I think, to keep the spirits high.'

'It is indeed.' Peggy smiled hesitantly. 'Danuta, I have something for you. It's not much, and I hope you won't be offended, but it is given with the best of intentions.'

Danuta frowned as Peggy rushed into the hall. 'What is this, *Babunia?*'

'I have no idea,' twittered Mrs Finch, 'but knowing Peggy, it'll be something very nice.'

Peggy returned bearing two large brown paper parcels. She fiddled with the knots in the string and carefully wound it into a ball to be used again before folding back the brown paper. 'I thought these might do you until you have enough coupons to get yourself something new,' she said hurriedly. 'I've washed and ironed everything, so it's all clean, and the shoes have hardly been worn.'

Danuta's eyes widened as she lifted out two dresses, a floral skirt and white blouse, two cardigans, a blue jacket and a very smart navy raincoat. The second parcel revealed white sandals with low heels, warm slippers and a sturdy pair of walking shoes. 'These are for me? But how you get them?'

Peggy felt herself blush. 'I work at the rehoming centre for the WVS, and we're always being given clothes and suchlike for those who've been bombed out. I explained your situation to my supervisor, and she gave me permission to hunt out a few of the better bits for you. I do hope you don't mind?'

'Oh, Peggy, they are lovely. You are so kind. So very kind.' Tears glistened in Danuta's eyes as she slipped on the warm jacket and caressed the good cloth. 'It is so long since I had anything pretty to wear.'

Peggy had to clear her throat before she could speak. 'Go and try everything on. I can always change them if they don't fit.'

Danuta's tears were yet to fall as she softly kissed Peggy's cheek. 'Thank you,' she breathed. 'Thank you for thinking so kindly of me.' She flashed Peggy and Mrs Finch a grin that made her look years younger. 'Now I can feel like the real Danuta again.'

Peggy watched her run up the stairs, her heart full, the tears brimming. It was such a little thing that she'd done, but the reward was enormous – for Danuta's smile was worth more than gold.

Polly reached the hospital just as the clock struck six. Mary was at her desk in the centre of the ward, keeping an eye on the probationer who was writing a letter for one of the men who had both arms in plaster. Two other nurses were quietly reading to those who had bandages over their eyes, and another was going through a trolley loaded with books and magazines for one of the younger men who was sitting in a wheelchair.

With a glance towards Adam, she smiled at Mary. 'I thought he looked a bit better this morning,' she said. 'What do you think?'

Mary smiled back. 'He's breathing much easier and Mr Fortescue has reduced the dosage of morphine. He hopes that by doing so, Adam will wake up. But it's a slow process, as you very well know, and it's vital the medication is not withdrawn too quickly.'

Polly couldn't help grinning at the news as she made her way down the ward, and it seemed her mood had been caught by the other men as they cheerily greeted her.

Adam's skin had taken on a better hue, but he was still unaware of everything. She sat down and took his hand. 'It's been a really hectic day,' she began, and then proceeded to tell him everything that had happened, and to describe the house and the people where she lived, in the hope that he might be able to hear her.

The hour seemed to fly by, and when the bell went for the end of visiting, she reluctantly kissed his chin and prepared to leave. 'I'll be back tomorrow,' she promised as she softly put his hand back on top of the blanket before turning away.

'Polly?'

His voice was cracked and hesitant, but it was unmistakeable, and Polly whirled back to him. 'Adam? Oh, darling, yes. I'm here. I'm here.' Her heart was thudding and she could barely speak through her tears of joy as she took his hand and felt the answering grip of his fingers.

'Polly,' he sighed. 'I knew you'd come.'

Mary bustled over, took his pulse and his temperature and grinned. 'Welcome back, Adam,' she said with soft delight. She turned back to Polly. 'Well, it looks like our sleeping beauty has finally woken up. I'll need to keep a close eye on him if you don't mind, but you can stay a few minutes more, Polly, as it's such a special occasion.'

Polly grinned up at her before returning her attention to Adam. 'That was Mary,' she said. 'She's the ward sister who's been very kind to me by letting me come in out of visiting hour.'

'She sounds nice,' he muttered with a terrible weariness.

Polly grinned again as Mary checked his notes. 'She's got lovely brown hair and eyes and a smile that warms your heart,' she told Adam.

'Why can't I see?' His free hand tentatively touched the bandages. 'What's happened to my eyes?' His voice rose and trembled as his fingers made a more desperate search of the bandaging.

'They put the bandages on to cover your head wounds,' Mary explained quickly, stilling his hands. 'They're over your eyes to protect them from the bright lights. You're not blind, Adam. I promise you.'

'Polly?' He turned his head towards her, seeking reassurance.

'It's true, my darling,' she said, battling her tears. 'The bandages are only temporary.'

He sighed and lay still. 'How long have I been here?'

'It's Monday the sixteenth of September, 1940, and it's ten past seven in the evening. I've been in Cliffehaven for two days, and they tell me you've been asleep for about a week.'

He digested this for a while in silence, his grip never lessening on her fingers as if he was afraid she might not be real – might disappear at any moment. 'Where's Alice? Is she with you?'

Polly licked her lips as she glanced up at Mary, and decided it wouldn't do Adam any good to know everything – not yet, anyway. 'I didn't bring Alice, my love. She's with Mum and Megan and the boys.'

'So, she's safe?'

'Of course she is,' she soothed, hoping to God she was telling him the truth.

'I'm tired, Pol,' he sighed. 'So tired. Love you.' His head slumped on the pillow and he began to snore.

Polly giggled. Adam's snoring had always been a bone of contention, for it had often kept her awake at night, but today she wouldn't have minded if he snored forever.

'You'd better go,' said Mary quietly as she checked his pulse again. 'One of my nurses has just seen Matron go into the ward up the corridor.'

'But...'

'Go, Polly. You can come in tomorrow at ten-thirty for a few minutes while she has her tea break – but if she catches you here now, then I can't promise anything.'

'He will be all right, won't he?'

Mary's expression softened. 'He's sleeping naturally. He'll be fine. How about we meet up at the Daisy Tea Room after our shift, and I can fill you in on what the consultant says tonight?'

'He'll come in?'

'Mr Fortescue ordered me to let him know if Adam woke up. Now shoo, or we'll both be in deep trouble.'

Polly kissed Adam and almost danced down the length of the ward. Adam was going to get better – and once this war was over and Alice was safely back in England, they could be a proper family again, and put all this behind them.

The week had flown by, and although the household routine had been interrupted constantly by raids day and night, Peggy was at peace. The house was still standing, although the front windows had been boarded up, and she was very proud of the new front door which Jim had carefully painted a lovely blue. The chimney had been swept, the rug beaten, and her dining room had been returned to what passed as normal these days.

Now it was Sunday, and although it was gloomy and cold, with the sea crashing against the defences and the gulls screaming as they hung like kites in the wind or squabbled on the rooftops, Peggy was finding the long bicycle ride back from the church bracing.

She always enjoyed morning mass, and didn't mind at all that the clouds were lying thick above her, the wind was threatening to steal her headscarf, and that it was getting harder and harder to pedal against it. She felt at peace and optimistic about the weeks ahead, the wind blowing away the cobwebs and setting her up for what she hoped would be a happy afternoon.

It had been a lovely week, she thought, as she turned off the seafront and swung down from the bike so she could push it up the long, steep hill to Beach View Terrace. Sally and Pearl, who'd once billeted with her, had come for their regular Saturday visit the previous day, and they'd chatted for hours over cups of very weak tea as they discussed Sally's forthcoming wedding, caught up with the gossip, read the children's letters and planned what to send them as a treat.

The thought of her sons stilled her for a moment and, as she leant on the bicycle's handles and caught her breath, she stared up the hill to the crater, and acknowledged that although it was hard not to have them home, they were much safer in Somerset. Since tight travelling restrictions were in place she couldn't go and visit them, see where they lived, or be a part of their lives again, if only for a few days. They had to be growing up fast, growing away from her – and this had always been her greatest fear. And yet she had to keep faith that the ties of love and family would remain no matter how far apart they were, or however long it would take before they could come home. Their letters were proof that they thought of home often, even though their new lives were fulfilling, and she silently blessed Sally's aunt for all her kindness in taking them in and loving them as her own.

Continuing at a slower pace, she dismissed these darker thoughts and smiled at the memory of how happy Sally was now that her John was making such a rapid recovery from the terrible wounds he'd sustained at Dunkirk.

He'd promised Sally he would walk unaided down the aisle in two months' time, and Peggy knew he wouldn't break that promise. She had known John Hicks since he was a boy in short trousers, and he'd become the sort of man who would always defy his injuries and make the best of his new tin leg – why, he'd already gone back to work at the fire station as an area co-ordinator, and was proving to be just as efficient and hard-working as he'd always been as a fireman.

Peggy circumnavigated the crater which had only been partially filled in. The buildings on either side were just piles of rubble now, but at least no one had been killed. Her bicycle wheels jolted over the rough surface of what had once been a pavement, making her handbag and gas mask bounce about in the wicker basket that was strapped to the handlebars.

As she reached the smoother tarmac, her thoughts turned to Polly. Adam also seemed to be making a recovery, but it was painfully slow, and although the girl's whole demeanour had lightened, her laughter ringing out as she joined in the fun with the other girls, Peggy had seen the shadows behind those bright smiles and knew Polly still fretted over the rest of her family.

There had been no news of the convoy in the papers or on the radio, no letters or cards arriving at Beach View, and Peggy understood the agony of not knowing – she'd experienced it when Jim and his brother Frank had gone with the armada of little boats to Dunkirk, and there had been no news for five days. But, she reasoned, Polly's family would surely be in Canada any day now, and no doubt would write as soon as they were settled.

She reached the end of Beach View Terrace and stood for a moment taking in the yawning gap at the other end where once there had been four houses. Boarded-up windows looked blindly out on the street where garden walls had toppled and weeds had pushed their way through the paving slabs. It was a sad sight.

Peggy experienced a moment of blinding clarity as she looked at the street she'd known all her life. In the devastation lay hope, for, like her, the inhabitants of Beach View Terrace were proof positive of what was being called the 'bulldog spirit'. They still fought on, living each day to battle with air raids, dust, rationing and every other privation and inconvenience so they could win this war. People all over England were falling in love, getting married, having babies and making plans for the future – to think otherwise would be to give in to the enemy. As Churchill had said in one of his rousing speeches, 'There will be no surrender.'

She hoisted the bicycle up the steps and smiled as she dug into her handbag for her door key. Even Danuta seemed to be slowly coming out of her shell now she had new clothes, and Cissy had given her a very fetching bobbed haircut. The Polish girl at last seemed to be settling in and, despite the difference in age, had built a real rapport with Ron as they'd tramped the hills and come home victorious with rabbits, hares, pigeons and blackberries. It was as if she'd found a new lease of life, and Peggy was delighted that it had been Ron and Harvey who had provided it.

Peggy was still smiling as she opened her new front door. Mrs Finch had proved an absolute whizz in the kitchen, and Peggy had happily left her to it on the three afternoons she helped at the WVS, and on the other days while she got on with her other household chores.

It was amazing what people could turn their hand to in times of crisis, she thought, as she took off her hat, gloves and coat and put them away in her bedroom. But what on earth they were going to feed those young Australians this lunchtime, she couldn't think. Their promise of meat was all very well, but what if they couldn't get any? A few wood pigeons wouldn't be enough to feed them – young men that age had hollow legs!

A burst of laughter rang through the house as she crossed the hall to the kitchen. Curious, she hurried to see what was going on.

Fran and Suzy were standing barefoot on the kitchen table, their skirts lifted up to their camiknickers as June and Danuta carefully applied some sort of brown stain to their legs.

As Peggy stood in the doorway and gazed upon the scene with amazement, she began to join in the laughter, for Cissy was now inexpertly attempting to draw a pencil-line from the top of Suzy's newly tanned thigh to the heel of her right leg.

'Do keep still, Suzy,' Cissy admonished. 'You're making the line all wobbly.'

'It tickles,' protested Suzy, her wild red hair springing around her head as she twisted and turned and tried to see the effect. 'Are you sure you know what you're doing, Cissy? To be sure that looks terrible crooked.'

'It wouldn't if you stood still,' retorted Cissy, who still had a bit of a black eye, and a bandage round her ankle. 'And as this is my best eyebrow pencil, I'd appreciate it if you'd do as you're told.'

'Yes, sir.' Suzy executed a mock salute and stood ramrod straight for all of five seconds.

Peggy sidled into the room and went to sit next to Mrs Finch, who was watching all this with a twinkle in her eye. 'What are they using to colour their legs?' Peggy asked over the babble of voices and laughter.

'Gravy browning.'

'But there's hardly any left, and I'm going to need it for tomorrow's stew.'

'Suzy managed to get some the other day. Don't fret, Peggy, there's plenty more where that came from.'

'But gravy browning? Won't it run the minute it rains?'

203

'Of course it will,' said Mrs Finch with a chuckle. 'That's half the fun.'

Peggy watched as Cissy finished drawing the lines and stood back to admire the effect. 'They can't possibly think anyone could be fooled into thinking they were wearing stockings, surely?' she murmured.

'You'd be surprised,' Mrs Finch replied dryly. 'I remember doing much the same thing with cold tea back in 1919, when there was a shortage of decent stockings.' She stuck out her spindly legs and grimaced. 'Not much point now,' she muttered. 'No one would give these a second glance any more.' She heaved a sigh and fondly watched the lovely young girls who were so unaware of how beautiful they were in their youthful exuberance. 'I used to have legs like that.'

'Youth is a wonderful thing,' Peggy murmured, thinking of the varicose veins that now threaded her own thighs.

'There. Is finished.' Danuta stepped back from the table and brushed back her newly cut fringe as she eyed her handiwork. 'You want me to do your legs now, June?'

'Yes please, Danuta. Can't have those two taking all the limelight.' She clambered on to the table, making it rock, and hoisted up her skirt to reveal long, slender legs that seemed to go on forever.

'You've got amazing legs, June,' breathed Cissy. 'You should be a dancer at the Windmill with legs like that.'

June laughed uproariously. 'Not on your life. I've heard about that place. Don't the girls dance

204

half-naked?'

Cissy nodded, her concentration fully occupied with drawing the line on Suzy's other leg.

'Hey, girls,' said Suzy, 'let's hope it isn't raining tonight, or our smashing new tans will just wash away. Can you imagine it? We'll look like streaks of bacon, so we will.'

Peggy and Mrs Finch exchanged glances and laughed along with them. It was good to have some fun for a change, and as long as the clouds remained thick in the skies, there would be no air raid to spoil it.

Polly sauntered along the street, the wind at her back whipping her cloak against her legs. It had been a long night shift at the hospital because two emergencies had come in, and she'd been asked to stay a while longer to settle them after their operations.

She'd managed to snatch a few minutes with Adam but he'd been asleep most of the time, and she'd had to be satisfied with simply holding his hand and having a one-sided conversation. At least now the bandages had been removed from over his eyes he looked a little more like the Adam she'd kissed goodbye all those months before.

Mr Fortescue was pleased with him, according to Mary, but Polly was still concerned that his recovery was taking too long. Each day she'd looked hopefully for some tiny sign that he was improving – and had been disappointed. His speech was still rather slurred, his attention slipping from one thing to another, and although he'd begun to eat again, he was still far too thin.

She slowed as she reached the end of Camden Road. Everything was shut because it was Sunday, and there was something mournful in the seagulls' cries as they hovered and swooped overhead. But the freshening wind and scudding clouds invigorated her after the airless warmth of the hospital, and she strode across the main road into Beach View Terrace.

The girls were all upstairs in their bedrooms when Peggy heard the loud knock on the door. She pulled off her apron, patted her freshly washed hair and hurried to answer it.

Three handsome young men in long brown waterproof coats and slouch hats stood grinning on her doorstep. 'G'day, Mrs Reilly.' They spoke in drawling unison as they whipped off their hats.

'Good afternoon,' she replied, rather taken aback by the fact one of them was carrying a dustbin with holes in it, and what looked like two wire shelves from an oven. 'Please, come in.'

'Thanks, Mrs Reilly. It's real nice of you to ask us to dinner.' The spokesman had blue eyes and a mop of shaggy brown hair. 'The name's Joe,' he drawled, 'and this is Davy and Mike.'

Peggy could see no sign of the promised meat and was beginning to panic. They were big lads, none of them less than six feet tall, with the ruddy, strong faces and broad shoulders of boys who liked their food. 'It's a pleasure,' she murmured distractedly as they filled her hallway.

The thunder of running feet on the stairs rescued her. 'That sounds like the girls,' she said gratefully. 'Why don't you all go into the dining room?' she suggested. 'There's more room in there than in my kitchen.'

The three young men grinned as the girls reached the hall and, having deposited the dust-bin and metal grilles at the bottom of the stairs, quite happily let them lead them into the other room.

Peggy dashed into the kitchen where Mrs Finch was rather shakily adding a touch of lipstick and powder to her face in honour of the visitors. 'Mrs Finch, they're here,' she said in a hoarse whisper. 'And they haven't brought anything that looks remotely like food. You've got to help me sort out something for them to eat.'

Mrs Finch frowned as she tipped the lipstick and powder compact into her ever-present hand-bag, and turned up her hearing aid. 'Well, there's the three pigeons, I suppose, and that bit of scrag end. But it will take a bit of time to cook it.'

'Um, Mrs Reilly.'

Peggy whirled round to find the one called Joe standing in her kitchen doorway. There was some-thing very odd going on under that long coat – it appeared to be moving of its own accord. 'Yes?' she asked distractedly.

'Mrs Reilly, we was wondering if you'd like these?' He opened the coat.

Peggy couldn't believe what she was seeing. The coat was like the one Ron wore when he went poaching and, as Joe held it open, four chickens poked up their heads from the inside pockets and began to cluck with annoyance, their black, beady eyes glaring malevolently back at her.

'Oh, my goodness,' chuckled Mrs Finch. 'Well, I never.'

'Where did you get them?' Peggy managed to splutter through her laughter.

'Well, I reckon you don't really want to know that,' Joe drawled, his blue eyes full of mischief. 'Let's just say these chooks were liberated from their prisoner of war camp, and are now only too willing to lay eggs for you in return for their freedom.'

Peggy was laughing so hard she had to sit down. 'The girls said you'd bring meat,' she managed, 'they didn't warn me it might be covered in feathers and running about the place.'

'Oh, that,' said Joe, unperturbed. 'The chooks are just a bit of a thank-you present. They're not dinner.'

Peggy and Mrs Finch watched, open-mouthed, as he dug into several other pockets and drew out a dozen tightly wrapped packets.

'The steak's not as tender as we get back home – but it'll hit the spot, I reckon.'

'Steak?' Peggy gasped, unable to take her eyes off those parcels. 'Real steak? All of that?'

'Well, yeah.' He shifted his feet as if suddenly unsure of himself. 'You do like steak, don't you?'

Peggy nodded, unable to speak.

He gave her a relieved smile. 'Don't worry, missus, it's bonzer stuff all right, and I made sure there was enough for everyone.' He dug in yet another pocket and very carefully drew out a brown paper bag.

'There's a dozen eggs to go with it, as well,' he said, placing the bag carefully on the kitchen table.

She looked up at him, overwhelmed to the point of being dumbstruck.

'*You* are a scallywag,' scolded Mrs Finch with a chuckle. 'I've heard the stories about you Australians. Rogues to the last man.'

'G'day, Mrs Finch.' He bent and gently shook her hand. 'I reckon you could be right,' he murmured with a wink, 'but you know, I don't reckon you'd really like it any other way.'

She shot him an old-fashioned look and went pink. 'That would be telling,' she giggled.

His smile was wide as he turned back towards Peggy, and she noticed how it made his blue eyes crinkle most attractively in that handsome, tanned face. She was getting as daft as Mrs Finch, she thought crossly, and really must pull herself together otherwise the day would simply descend into further chaos.

But then, as she looked up at him, she couldn't help but acknowledge what fun he was, and how much she was enjoying his bright, open-handed, cheerful company.

'I could always take the eggs back,' he said, 'but it wouldn't be a proper Aussie dinner without steak and eggs.'

'Did I hear the words steak and eggs in the same sentence?' Jim appeared in the doorway closely followed by Ron.

The Australian turned and stuck out his large hand. 'Yeah, that's right, mate. You must be Jim, and Ron. Pleased to meet ya.' They all shook hands and Joe glanced across at the silent, stunned Peggy before turning back to Jim with a worried frown. 'I reckon your missus don't know what hit

209

her, mate. Perhaps I shouldn't have brought the chickens.'

'Chickens?' said Ron, his eyes widening. 'What chickens?'

'These.' Joe opened his coat again and several feathers drifted to the floor as the birds made a second escape bid. 'I have it on good authority that they're excellent layers, though they might come in handy if you're a bit short of dinner one night.'

'Bloody hell,' breathed Jim in admiration. 'You Australians certainly know how to make the best of things. But we'd better get them tidied away quick. Dad, put them in the shed for now, and see if you can find them something to eat. We'll build a proper pen tomorrow.'

'I reckoned you might be needing some chook feed.' Joe dug in an outside pocket this time and came up with another brown paper bag. 'That should see 'em right for the next day or so.'

Harvey whined and danced on his hind legs as Ron and Joe managed to get the furious birds out of the pockets. Holding them by the legs and away from Harvey's inquisitive nose, Ron carried them squawking down the cellar steps and out to the shed.

'I expect you'd like a beer?' said Jim, rooting about in the larder. 'I got a few crates in from the Anchor, so I did.' He pushed back the cork that was held in place with sturdy wire hinging and handed it over. 'Cheers, Joe. Thanks for everything.'

'No worries, mate. Good on yer.' Joe took an appreciative swig of the rather warm beer, and then caught sight of Cissy who was lurking in the doorway. His face lit up. 'Who's this then?'

'My youngest daughter, Cissy,' muttered Jim, as he lifted two crates of beer out of the larder. 'I'll take these into the other room before the lads die of thirst.'

'G'day, Cissy. The name's Joe Buchanan. Nice to meet you.' He smiled down at Cissy as he swamped her small hand in his giant fist. 'Gee,' he said, giving a low whistle. 'How'd you get the shiner? What's the other bloke look like?'

Cissy went bright pink. 'I fell down during an air raid. It's nothing,' she said with unusual shyness, as he continued to look down at her for rather longer than was necessary. When he at last released her hand, she too seemed dumbstruck.

Peggy watched the little scene with a sense of misgiving. Cissy and Joe had instantly 'clicked' as the youngsters called it, which could only cause trouble. For he was here as one of the other girls' guest, and if he kept looking at Cissy like that there would be tears and tantrums before bedtime, and no mistake.

She heaved a great sigh. It was probably a good thing he'd be leaving Cliffehaven within the next few days, she thought sadly, for although he seemed to be a very nice young man, he was far too attractive for his own good – and young Cissy was clearly smitten. Still, she decided, at least he'd brought a smile to her face and cheered her up a bit. She'd been far too gloomy of late.

Ron came back into the kitchen and kept a very firm hand on Harvey's collar as they both eyed the parcels of steak. 'That's a wonderful bounty,

211

so it is,' he breathed. 'I can't remember the last time I ate steak. I'm hoping me old teeth are up to it.'

Joe tore his gaze from Cissy and grinned. 'Then I'll make sure we cook you the best steak you've ever had, mate. A real Aussie steak.'

'You're going to cook?' Ron stared up at him in amazement.

'Too right.' Joe smiled and winked at Cissy, who was gazing up at him. 'Now come on, ladies,' he said, 'out of the kitchen so me and my mates can get on. I don't know about you, but my stomach thinks me throat's been cut.'

He helped Cissy to her feet and she blushed becomingly as she took his arm. 'We don't want you falling over again, love,' he said. 'Not with that bad ankle.'

Peggy was about to say something sharp to Cissy, but found that she and Mrs Finch had been rounded up like sheep and were being firmly herded into the hall. 'But my kitchen,' she protested. 'You won't know where everything is and...'

'No worries, missus. We'll have it all clean and tidy before we leave. I promise.'

Peggy walked dazedly into the dining room to discover that everyone had settled down with Jim's beer, and were all talking nineteen to the dozen as their cigarette smoke rose to the ceiling and the music of Glenn Miller drifted across the chatter. Someone had unearthed the old gramophone from under the stairs, but she had no idea where the records could have come from. The last time she'd listened to that old thing, it had been Bessie Tucker who was all the rage.

'Right, you blokes. Follow me,' shouted Joe from the doorway. 'And don't forget to bring you know what with you.'

Everyone watched in amazement as the two brawny men grabbed their discarded coats and hurried with enthusiasm to join Joe in the kitchen.

'Well, I never,' breathed Jim. 'Would you look at that?'

'It's a lesson you could learn, Jim Reilly,' teased Peggy. 'Pass me one of those beers. I'm going to put my feet up and wait for my lunch to be cooked for me for once.'

Polly had snatched a couple of hours' sleep and now she managed to persuade Danuta to come with her downstairs and join in the fun. She had lent the girl some powder, mascara and lipstick, and nodded approvingly as she chose one of her new dresses to go with the moss-green cardigan that did wonderful things to her eyes.

'You look really lovely,' she said. 'Now come on, or we'll miss all the fun.'

Danuta followed her uncertainly down the stairs and into the dining room where the other four girls were jigging about to the music as they set the cutlery and glasses on the tables that had been pushed together.

'You look nice,' said Cissy. 'I'm glad you let me cut your hair, it really suits you with a fringe.'

Danuta blushed and hurried to help sort out the chairs.

'Where are our visitors?' asked Polly.

'Out the back, probably making a terrible mess

213

in my kitchen,' said Peggy, 'but I don't care. We're having steak and eggs this lunchtime instead of scrag-end and pigeon stew. Won't that be a treat?'

Jim shook his head and frowned, still clearly bothered by the Australians' apparent eagerness to be in the kitchen. ''Tis a poor thing when men are doing women's work,' he muttered. 'I thought those Aussies were supposed to be rough and tough. What do you think, Dad?'

'I don't care who does it, as long as they don't burn that steak,' Ron said round the stem of his pipe as he folded his hands over his belly and leant back in his chair.

Polly smiled, helped herself to a beer and tiptoed into the hall so she could have a peek at what was happening in Peggy's kitchen. She frowned when she discovered it was deserted, and then simply looked puzzled as she heard the loud voices and barks of laughter coming from the garden.

Crossing the kitchen, she looked out of the window and giggled. The three Australians were standing around what looked like a dustbin with a blazing fire inside it. On the top of this strange object were two grilles – probably the shelves from someone's oven – and on top of them was a frying pan full of chopped onions, and at least a dozen steaks sizzling in the heat and sending up the most heavenly aroma.

Harvey was lying panting at their feet, tongue lolling, eyebrows twitching as his eyes followed their every movement. One of the men threw him a titbit, and he snapped his jaws round it, swallowing it without even bothering to chew first.

Polly's mouth was watering at the wonderful

smells drifting up to her as she stood in the kitchen and watched. They turned the meat and sipped their beers, their drawling conversation not quite reaching her. They didn't seem to notice the scudding clouds and darkening skies that threatened rain; they were too engrossed in their cooking to notice much of anything.

She ducked out of sight when one of them looked up, and hurried back into the dining room. 'You don't need to worry about your kitchen, Peggy,' she said as she sat down. 'They're cooking our lunch in the garden.'

Peggy's eyes widened in horror. 'In the garden?'

'On a dustbin they've turned into some kind of brazier.'

'I wondered why they brought a dustbin,' murmured Peggy. 'How very strange. Still, they *are* Australians, so I suppose we shouldn't be surprised.'

'Tucker's up,' said Joe some while later. He stepped into the dining room ahead of the others and they placed the loaded plates on the table and pulled the chairs out for the women. 'There you are, ladies, what d'ya think of that?'

Like everyone else, Polly stared at the plate before her, her mouth watering and her stomach gurgling with anticipation. The succulent steak was capped with a glistening fried egg, and nestled between sliced onion and a handful of early mushrooms. None of them had seen food like this for a year.

Murmurs of appreciation floated round the room but then, as they picked up their knives and forks and began to tuck in, there was almost complete silence.

It had been so long since Polly had eaten steak that she'd forgotten how delicious it could be. She closed her eyes and savoured the perfectly cooked meat, letting the flavour sing in her mouth as she slowly relished each morsel. Pricking the bright yellow yolk, she watched it ooze over the meat before she mopped it up with a slither of the crisp, brown fat that ran along the top of the steak. It was nectar – food for the gods. And she doubted an egg had ever tasted better.

The meal continued with only murmurs of delight and the scraping of cutlery against china to disturb the silence. And when it was over, each of them almost reverently placed their knives and forks together and leant back with a deep sigh of satisfaction tinged with regret that the meal had come to an end.

'To be sure, that was the best meal I've had in years,' said Jim, voicing everyone's thoughts. He lifted his bottle of beer. 'I salute you, boys. Well done, and thank you.'

Everyone talked at once, giving their thanks, and going over every morsel they'd eaten, trying to describe the sheer magnificence of the meal as the Australian boys became ever more bashful.

Peggy caught Polly's eye. 'I'll make a pot of tea,' she murmured.

'I'll come with you.'

They slipped out of the room, then Polly almost walked straight into Peggy, who'd come to a complete standstill in the kitchen doorway. 'What is it? They can't have wrecked the place, surely?'

Peggy shook her head. 'Far from it,' she murmured. 'In fact I've never seen it so clean. And look,' she breathed. 'Look what they've given us.' She pointed to the shelf above her immaculate, shining range where there sat four large packets of tea, and two bags of sugar. On the draining board, next to the spotless frying pan, stood three packets of lard, and one of butter.

'Oh, Polly,' she sighed. 'They've been so very kind to us. We don't deserve it.'

'You've made us feel at home, Mrs Reilly,' said Joe, who had silently followed them into the kitchen. 'This place is like my ma's kitchen back in Sydney, and she'd like to know you've been good to us blokes.'

'But I've done nothing really,' she protested.

'You've been like a mum to those girls in there, and that's enough. Without them nursing us back to health, we wouldn't be here today, and that's a fact.'

'Oh dear,' sniffed Peggy, scrabbling for the handkerchief she always kept up her sleeve in case of emergencies. 'I think I'm going to make a complete fool of myself.'

'Aw, fair go, missus. Don't be doing that. You go and sit down. I'm sure Polly won't mind making the tea, will you, love?'

'Of course not.'

Polly was grinning as she set the large kettle on the hob and made herself busy with cups and saucers. She could easily understand why Fran, Suzy and June were so besotted with these young Australians. Their smiles and cheerful, relaxed outlook on life seemed to bring the very essence of their hot, red homeland right into this kitchen

217

– making it sunnier, somehow, even though the sky was grey and it had begun to rain.

She frowned as she heard furniture being moved and wondered what on earth they were doing in the dining room. She took the kettle off the hob again, and peeked round the door.

The tables had been pushed to one side, the rug rolled back into the bay. Music was already playing, and the three girls had been swung into an enthusiastic dance by their Australian admirers.

Polly tapped her feet to the music as she watched, but she noted the envy in Cissy's eyes as Joe danced with June, and the wistfulness in Danuta's. It was strange how music played with the emotions, affecting everyone in a different way, but touching them all the same. For Polly it was the memory of those barn dances after harvest when Adam would twirl her round until she was breathless. For Danuta, she speculated, perhaps it was wilder dances to strange music in gloomy stone castles and cobbled streets, and for Mrs Finch, perhaps memories of her youth?

She laughed as Jim grabbed a protesting Peggy and whirled her round enthusiastically, and applauded when Ron sedately led Mrs Finch on to the floor and proceeded to dance a quite admirable two-step in the corner where they wouldn't get crushed in the mayhem of the boogie-woogie that was all the rage at the moment.

Polly decided to leave the tea for now. Everyone was still drinking beer, and tea didn't seem to fit the occasion any more. She smiled as she sat down next to Danuta. She would have a lot of lovely things to tell Adam tonight.

Chapter Eleven

Danuta wished that Polly hadn't had to leave for the hospital so soon after helping to do the washing-up. But she was on night shift, and wanted to spend some time with Adam first, so Danuta had steeled herself to join in the fun, not really certain whether she would fit in.

It seemed that she did, and Danuta hadn't protested at all when Davy grabbed her hand and swung her into a hectic dance. She was enjoying herself – enjoying the music and laughter and these precious carefree hours when they could all forget the war, and just be young again.

Having danced until she was breathless and giddy, she collapsed into the chair beside Mrs Finch and took a long draught of the lukewarm beer that tasted so different to Polish beer, which was always served ice-cold.

'It's good to see you having a bit of fun,' shouted Mrs Finch above the noise. 'I must say, these Australians know how to have a good time.'

'I'm thinking you are having fun too, *Babunia*,' she teased. 'I saw you dancing in the corner with Ron. You make a lovely couple.'

Mrs Finch tried to look offended and failed. 'I was merely joining in with the spirit of the party,' she said. She leant closer. 'But Ron and I are of the generation where people dance properly,' she confided, casting a bewildered eye over the shenanigans going on before her. 'There was none of this hoogie-googie nonsense in my day.'

'It's boogie-woogie, *Babunia*. Joe says the dance comes from America.'

Mrs Finch sniffed, with derision. 'I might have known,' she said. 'The Americans never did have any taste – and certainly no stomach for war. They didn't come into the last one until 1917, you know, and I suspect they'll leave it until the last minute before they join in this time.'

Danuta didn't really want to get into politics with the old lady, so she sipped her beer, leant back in her chair and watched the fun.

Cissy was dancing with Joe now, the music a little softer and slower, his arm round her waist as she blushed prettily and rested her forehead lightly against his broad shoulder. The ankle seemed to have made a miraculous recovery, Danuta thought wryly – this morning she'd used it as an excuse to get out of cleaning the dining room.

Peggy and Jim were waltzing happily, looking content with each other, and Fran was dancing with Davy, June with Mike. But June was not concentrating on Mike; she was too busy shooting jealous darts at Cissy, who was now dreamily embraced against Joe's broad chest as they swayed to the music.

Danuta could see only trouble ahead, and was wondering what to do about it when Peggy stepped in.

'This is a lady's excuse-me, I think,' she said brightly. 'Come on, Joe, give an old lady a bit of a dance, will you? Jim's feeling his age and can't keep up the pace.'

Cissy stuck out her bottom lip and flounced back to her chair as her mother waltzed off with Joe. It would have been quite funny, thought Danuta, if only Joe hadn't looked like that over Peggy's shoulder to Cissy, and June hadn't glared at both of them. It was clear their attraction was mutual, but June could cause serious trouble if it went on much longer.

The party finished two hours later and, after putting the room to rights and washing all the glasses and cups, the Australians and the three nurses prepared to leave for another fund-raising dance, this time at the Town Hall.

'Will you be coming with us, Danuta?' asked Suzy, her little face lit up with a bright smile as she clung to Davy's arm.

Danuta shook her head, even though she would have loved to have joined them. 'I have very early start tomorrow,' she said sadly. 'Perhaps next time?'

'I'll keep you to that,' replied Suzy. 'And what about you, Cissy? That ankle looks as if it'll hold up.'

'I don't think Cissy ought to risk doing *further* damage to that ankle,' said June coolly, 'and I'm sure she doesn't want to go out with that black eye *just* yet.'

Cissy was clearly torn between her desire to put June in her place and go out dancing, and the knowledge that she looked a fright with all that bruising round her eyes. 'I could cover it with make-up,' she said hopefully.

'You look fair dinkum as you are, love,' said Joe,

blissfully unaware of the friction between the two girls.

June's glare could have stunned a mule – but Joe seemed impervious to it as he grinned at Cissy. 'As a nurse,' June said, digging into his ribs with a sharp elbow, 'I wouldn't recommend her dancing any more on that ankle. As it is, she's had to give up her place in the dance troupe, and I don't think her manager would appreciate catching sight of her prancing about at the Town Hall.'

Joe looked down at her and frowned. 'Strewth, love,' he breathed, 'I only said...'

'I think enough has been said,' said Peggy, as she chivvied everyone out of the room. 'Come along. The dance starts in half an hour, and you don't want to be late, do you?'

Joe looked over his shoulder at a mournful Cissy as he pulled on his large coat and settled his hat firmly over his hair. 'It's been a pleasure, Mrs Reilly,' he drawled. 'Me and the other blokes are real grateful for your hospitality.'

The three of them shook hands with everyone, and called Mrs Finch 'little Ma' as they gently kissed her cheek – which made her blush and twitter like a flustered robin.

'Will we see you before you leave for wherever you're going?' asked Jim.

June's lips formed a thin line as she caught the glance Joe gave to Cissy – and this time Joe noticed her displeasure. There were spots of high colour on his cheeks as he replied. 'I reckon we might be a bit busy, mate,' he replied, not quite meeting Jim's gaze. 'We've a lot to do before we're shipped out.'

The wind had got up during the afternoon, the clouds thickening, the promised rain coming down like stair-rods. It was barely seven o'clock, but the night was drawing in fast. Danuta and the others stood shivering on the steps as they waved their last goodbyes and watched them hurry through the downpour and out of sight.

'God bless,' whispered Peggy through her fingers as the tears filled her eyes. 'Keep them safe.'

'Now, Peg, don't be getting over-emotional,' said Jim gruffly, putting his arm over her shoulder. 'Those boys will come through just fine without your tears.' He drew her back into the house and sat her down by the range where the coals glowed warmly. 'Let's sit awhile and enjoy the fire now we have some coal to burn,' he murmured. 'I have to be on warden duty in half an hour.'

Danuta wandered into the dining room and found Cissy curled up in a chair and looking sullen as she fiddled with a cigarette packet. The Aussies had given each of them a pack, which was a real treat, even though Danuta and Cissy rarely smoked. 'You can go dancing another time,' she said softly.

'I know, but it would have been nice to dance with Joe again.' She fell silent, her gaze wistful. 'I wish he wasn't leaving so soon,' she said finally.

Danuta picked up her cardigan and slung it over her shoulders. 'I think June will be disappointed too,' she said carefully. 'It will be nice for them to have these last few days together before they are parted.'

Cissy gave a deep sigh. 'I suppose so, but I wish...'

'If wishes were pots and pans, we'd all be tinkers,' said Ron cheerfully. 'Either of you two feel like walking off that lunch?'

'With this ankle?' Cissy eyed him balefully. 'And it's raining.'

'The ankle didn't stop you bouncing about earlier,' he replied, the twinkle in his eye belying the soft reprimand. 'And a bit of fresh air might do you some good after lounging about the house all week.'

Cissy looked mutinous as she snatched up her cardigan. 'I'm going to my room,' she muttered, and hobbled rather dramatically into the hallway.

'I'll come with you, Ron,' murmured Danuta. 'Just give me time to get changed, please?'

'Right you are. I'll be in the basement.'

Danuta hurried upstairs, carefully hung her dress and cardigan in the wardrobe and changed into her baggy old trousers, sweater and sturdy shoes. Covering everything with her raincoat, she slipped the packet of Australian cigarettes and a box of matches into her trouser pocket and hurried downstairs.

'I'm going out with Ron,' she told Peggy and Jim, who were sipping tea by the range and listening to a music programme on the wireless. 'I don't expect we'll be too late.'

'God help us,' sighed Jim. 'The auld fella never sits still. You shouldn't encourage him, Danuta.'

Danuta shrugged. 'I like to walk with him,' she said simply, and then ran down the steps to the cellar.

'I've found you some wellington boots. They should fit,' said Ron gruffly. He waited for her to try them on and nodded with satisfaction as she grinned back at him in delight. 'Here, lass, ye'll be soaked through in that t'ing,' he said, handing her one of his older poaching coats. 'Put this on, and ye'll be as dry as a bone.'

Danuta carefully hung her lovely raincoat on the peg behind the back door and wrestled into Ron's coat. It was heavy and reached to her ankles, and there was a funny odour clinging to it. 'What is this smell?' she asked, wrinkling her nose as she did up the buttons.

'That'll be me ferrets,' muttered Ron.

Danuta would have liked to ask him what a ferret was, but Ron was already stomping down the garden path and she almost had to run to catch up with him.

With Harvey loping ahead of them, they tramped along the alleyway between the backs of the houses and began to climb the steep track that would finally lead to the brow of the hills that formed a protective embrace between Cliffe-haven and the rest of the county.

As usual, they didn't speak until they reached the top, and then they stood in companionable silence in the lee of a small copse of trees and waited for their hearts to stop racing. It was dark now, the rain still coming down hard.

Danuta's hair was plastered to her head and dripping coldly down her neck, but she didn't mind a bit. She loved being up here at night with Ron – enjoyed the freedom and the sense that they were alone in the world with only the scent of grass, earth and sea to accompany them. It was a world away from the hospital laundry – and another world away from the cobbled streets and poor, crowded tenements she'd known in Warsaw.

'Sure, and I should have asked them Aussie boys if they had a few of those hats spare,' muttered Ron. 'They'd be ideal to keep off the rain, so they would.'

He shoved his unlit pipe in his pocket and pulled out a powerful torch. 'Let's see if we can find a few rabbits,' he said. 'But we won't be using the nets tonight, it's too dark, so I hope you aren't squeamish.'

Danuta shook her head. She'd seen enough death not to worry over the demise of a few rabbits.

'This is called "lamping",' Ron explained, 'and it's highly illegal in this country, so keep an eye out for rangers – though what they'd be doing up here on such a night, I wouldn't know,' he added.

Danuta walked beside him, chin tucked into the neck of her coat, hands buried deep in the pockets as Harvey raced back and forth, nose to ground, and the torchlight beam wavered over the grass and hillocks.

'There we are,' murmured Ron, coming to a standstill. 'A nice fat bunny for the pot.' He kept the beam on the startled rabbit which seemed frozen to the spot. 'Go, Harvey,' he whispered.

Harvey took off like a rocket.

The rabbit broke from its trance and began to race away, darting back and forth in a desperate attempt to shake off its pursuer and reach the safety of its burrow beneath the trees.

Ron kept the beam on the rabbit, jiggling it back and forth to confuse the creature as Harvey closed in. With one swift pounce, the rabbit was captured, and Harvey carried it proudly back to Ron, who finished it off by wringing its neck.

The dog wriggled his eyebrows, tongue lolling as he waited for Ron's pat on the head, and once Ron had secreted the rabbit in one of his many pockets, Harvey received his reward along with a bit of biscuit.

The rain stopped some time later as they tramped over the hills beneath a sky of scudding clouds which raced over the slither of moon. The great silence was broken only by the owls which hooted in the trees, the occasional, distant shriek of a vixen, and the rustle of the wind in the grass. It was awesome, that silence, and Danuta felt as if she was treading in the footprints of the ancient men of England as Ron led her further and further into the great open spaces that lay north of Cliffehaven.

Harvey and Ron had now caught five rabbits and, having decided there were enough for a decent stew, Ron led Danuta down into a valley to a stone building she hadn't noticed before. It was tucked away in a thicket of trees, and almost buried in gorse and brambles. There was a sturdy door with an even sturdier lock attached to it, and there was no way of seeing inside, for there were no windows.

'This was an old shepherd's hut before the war,' he explained, as he settled on a fallen log and got his pipe going. 'There used to be a farm here, but the army commandeered it, and the farmer, Bill Watson, was given the option of relocating to another farm in Scotland, or moving into a bungalow somewhere near Worthing.'

He puffed contentedly on his pipe, his eyes distant with memory. 'Bill was a man of the land through and through. He would have rather died than move to Worthing.'

'But it is very far to Scotland, I think?'

He nodded. 'That it is, lass, but for a man like Bill it was the only solution. Him, his wife and their three kids, along with two farmhands and their families, loaded everything they possessed on to two wagons and herded those cows right through the middle of Cliffehaven to the station.'

He chuckled. 'It was quite a sight, I can tell you, seeing those lovely old Shires pulling those wagons, and Bill sitting proud on his cob. There was not a soul in Cliffehaven who didn't come to see them off. We all thought the circus had come to town, so we did.'

Danuta could imagine the scene, but she was still puzzled. 'But what did the army want with this place?'

'See over there?' He pointed the beam of his torch towards the valley, illuminating a tumbledown wreck of a place surrounded by equally dilapidated barns and outbuildings. 'That was once a fine farmhouse, two labourers' cottages and three barns. The army used it to train the gunners, and look at it now. Poor old Bill – I hope he never comes back to see it. He was mighty proud of his farm, so he was.'

'But they have not used this building for target practice,' said Danuta. 'Why is that, do you think?'

'Well now,' Ron said, shifting himself into a

228

more comfortable position, 'that's because it has other uses.' He regarded her steadily for a moment as if considering what he should say next.

'Go on,' she prompted.

'To the inquisitive, it is an emergency food store, so it is,' he muttered, 'but to those in the know it is far more important.' He fiddled with his pipe for a while and then looked at her from under his bushy brows. 'You have told me something of your journey from Warsaw to Cliffehaven, Danuta, and trusted me with the secrets you've carried along the way. What I'm about to tell you is closely guarded by those at the very top of our government. Can I trust you?'

Danuta was intrigued. 'You can trust me,' she said evenly.

He held her gaze for a long moment before speaking. 'Then I will tell you a story,' he said. He puffed on his pipe for a moment, his gaze fixed to a distant spot in the darkness.

'When France fell in May this year, there was – and still is – a very real threat of Hitler invading our island. Winston Churchill ordered a Colonel Gubbins to create a force of civilian volunteers, recruited primarily from the ablest Home Guard personnel. These recruits were to be trained to operate from secret underground bases located behind the enemy lines of occupation. In other words, they were to be our secret line of defence against enemy invasion.'

Danuta felt for the packet of cigarettes in her trouser pocket and lit one. She had an idea where this was going, and strangely was not at all surprised, for Ron had always struck her as being a man with a secret.

'Initially, these men were set up in patrols of six to eight men, led by a sergeant and co-ordinated by a local commander, usually a captain or lieutenant. Ideal recruits are countrymen, farmers, foresters, gamekeepers,' he grinned, 'and old poachers like me.' He smoked his pipe and stared into the night. 'I had experience of sabotage in the last war, and although some might say I'm past it, I know enough to teach the young ones a trick or two.'

Danuta watched the smoke from her cigarette curl away. 'So,' she murmured, 'you are part of a secret army, but you wear the uniform of the Home Guard.' She grinned. 'Is that why you keep going away? Peggy thinks you are with Rosie at the pub.'

'I wish I was with Rosie, but she and I don't have that kind of friendship,' he admitted ruefully. 'I'm away helping to train the latest recruits, or sitting it out in one of the operational bases which are hidden all along the coast.' He patted the solid wall behind him. 'This is an arsenal,' he said, 'but the base is hidden well away from here.'

He must have noted her frown, for he carried on, 'I can't tell you much more about what I do, Danuta. As I said, it is top secret. But the special reserve battalions are now spread all across England. If we are invaded by the Hun, then we will carry out sabotage: target supply dumps, railway lines, convoys and enemy occupied airfields. We won't let them take our land without a fight, so we won't.'

Danuta stamped out the cigarette, and through force of habit, put the butt in her coat pocket. She rarely smoked anyway, and tonight it was making her feel a little nauseous. 'I know how it feels to have your country invaded, Ron, but why do you tell me this top secret?' she asked quietly.

'Because of what you've been through, and what you just did,' he replied. 'Not many people would think of taking their fag ends with them.' His gaze was steady beneath his thick brows. 'You have experience and skills that are sorely needed, Danuta. I told you that tale tonight because I think you would be the ideal recruit for Special Duties.'

She returned his steady gaze, but her pulse was racing at the thought of actually doing something useful and challenging again. 'And what would these Special Duties involve?'

'It would be a secret recruitment, so you could tell no one,' he replied. 'You would be trained to provide intelligence gathering, spying on and observing enemy formations and troop movements. It would mean leaving here to be trained in fieldcraft, sabotage, codes, telegraphs and unarmed combat. And then you would go through an intensive course to make sure your German and French were good enough to pass as a local. You will go through long, and probably harrowing, interrogation sessions to measure your ability to withstand such things, and ultimately, I suspect, you would be parachuted into enemy territory.'

Danuta's heart was hammering. 'I would love to do this,' she breathed. 'I know already about sabotage, silent executions, and guerrilla fighting, and my languages have already proven good enough to let me pass as German or French.'

'So you'll do it?'

She shook her head, the tears blinding her. 'I cannot. I am so sorry.'

'But why? I don't understand.'

She took a deep breath. 'I am four months pregnant, Ron, and this baby is far too precious to risk such things.'

Ron gave a very deep sigh. 'I see,' he murmured. 'I wish I'd known before I told you everything.'

Danuta put her hand on his arm. 'It will remain a secret, Ron. I promise. And, who knows, maybe I can do something once the baby is born?'

'Once that wee bairn's in your arms, you'll not be wanting to risk your life, Danuta.' He eyed her for a long moment. 'But you could still train to work with the Observation Corps. My granddaughter Anne's with them.' He gave a deep sigh, 'But of course with the baby on the way, they probably wouldn't take you. Anne will have to leave soon. They don't like pregnant women on base.' He stood and whistled up Harvey. 'It's late, so let's be getting home, lass.'

Danuta stood beside him and touched his arm again. 'We both have secrets, Ron. Please don't speak of this baby.'

'You have my word, lass, as I have yours. Let that be an end to it.'

Peggy was dozing by the fire as the sweet orchestral music poured from the wireless. Cissy and Mrs Finch were upstairs, and everyone else was out. It was bliss to have these moments to herself, even though she'd thoroughly enjoyed having a houseful all afternoon.

She was falling deeper into sleep and would have missed the sound of someone knocking on the front door if, at that moment, there hadn't been a lull in the music. Frowning, she dragged herself out of the chair, rammed on her slippers and went to see who it was at her door after nine o'clock on a Sunday night.

She frowned at the two middle-aged women who stood very solemnly on her doorstep in their sturdy shoes, enveloping overcoats and sensible hats. She knew both of them through her work with the WVS, and their unexpected appearance was unnerving, for they were welfare workers, and house calls were made only in the direst of emergencies. 'Miss Jackson, Mrs Friar?' she managed through a constricted throat. 'How can I help you?'

Miss Jackson's expression didn't change. 'Good evening, Peggy. I'm sorry, but this isn't a social call. We're here to see Mrs Polly Brown.'

'Polly's at the hospital on night shift,' Peggy replied, her heart beating a rapid tattoo. 'She's not due home until about six tomorrow morning. What is it? What's happened?'

Mrs Friar pulled her coat collar in. 'It's a brisk night, Peggy, and it will take some time to explain everything.'

'Of course, oh, do come in,' she said, flustered at having forgotten her manners. 'I'm sorry. You rather caught me on the hop.'

'We realise it's very late,' said Kate Jackson as they stepped into the hall and shed their coats.

'But the matter has only just come to light and is rather urgent.'

'I see.' She didn't see at all, in fact her mind was in such a whirl that she couldn't think of anything very much as she dumped their coats over the newel post and led them into her kitchen.

'I don't usually bring visitors in here,' she said hurriedly, 'but we had a bit of a party in the dining room this afternoon and it's all a bit of a mess still. And anyway, I can't have two fires going and the kitchen is cosier with the range and everything and...' She realised she was babbling, and fell silent.

Agatha Friar pulled off her gloves and plumped down in a kitchen chair. 'Peggy, your kitchen is absolutely fine, and I think we've known one another long enough not to have to stand on ceremony,' she said in her deep contralto.

Peggy's hand was trembling as she turned off the wireless and sank into her chair by the fire. 'What is it?' she breathed. 'Why do you need to see Polly so urgently?'

Kate Jackson sat next to her colleague and quietly and calmly told Peggy the reason for their late-night visit.

Peggy closed her eyes as the full import of what she'd been told began to sink in. She yearned for someone, anyone to walk through that door and help shoulder part of this terrible burden. But the only sound in the house was the tick of the clock above the mantel, and the spitting of wood-sap in the fire.

'I'm sorry, Peggy,' said Kate Jackson after a long interval. 'We don't usually divulge such information before we speak to the person concerned, but in this case, I think it's right that you should be fully prepared. Mrs Brown is in your care, and she will need a great deal of help and support in the coming days – and we both know that your enormous capacity for compassion will be of infinite comfort to her. She's lucky to have you, Peggy. I'm only sorry you've had to be burdened with this.'

'You do realise her husband is critically ill in hospital?' muttered Peggy, the tears blinding her. 'Something like this could tip her over the edge.'

'I know, and in normal circumstances it would have been up to the hospital almoner to speak to her. But we thought it better to visit her at home where she has more privacy, and is surrounded by people she trusts.'

'But why was there no news of this on the wireless?' breathed Peggy, 'Surely something as terrible...?'

'The Prime Minister has put a block on any press coverage until everyone involved has been informed. A tragedy like this cannot be revealed in the press, or by telegram – it is too shocking, and with the post being so unreliable at the moment, Mr Churchill himself decided it would be best if we in the Welfare Department visited personally to break the news.'

Agatha rose from her chair and put the kettle on the hob. 'There will be a letter arriving for Mrs Brown in the next few days from Mr Shakespeare, who is the Under-secretary for the Dominions, and Chairman of the Evacuation Board.' She collected cups and saucers and busied herself with making the tea. 'It's a small gesture, but hopefully it might help her realise that she is not alone.'

Peggy lit a cigarette and smoked furiously as she regarded the two women, her thoughts jumbled, her emotions in turmoil. 'Surely you don't expect me to sit here all night waiting for her to come home with this preying on my mind? What words could I possibly find to tell her such a thing?'

'Of course not,' soothed Kate. 'And you won't have to break the news, Peggy. We will do that. As this needs to be done as soon as possible, would you mind if I use your telephone to call the hospital?'

'But you can't tell someone something like this over the telephone.'

'I have no intention of doing so,' murmured Kate, as Agatha placed the teacups in front of them. 'Drink your tea, Peggy. It might help to restore you.'

Peggy ignored the tea, smoked her cigarette and stared into the fire as Kate walked out of the kitchen. She heard the 'ting' as she lifted the receiver and the murmur of her voice as she asked to be put through to Matron's office at the hospital. Throwing the cigarette butt into the fire, Peggy buried her face in her hands and began to sob.

Chapter Twelve

Polly was still buzzing with the liveliness of the lunchtime party and felt happier than she had in a long while. She'd managed to have a fairly long chat with Adam during visiting time – even though it was mostly her doing the chatting – and he'd seemed a little more conscious of what was going on around him before he'd once again fallen asleep.

Her patients also seemed in a better frame of mind tonight, as well, but Polly put that down to the lack of any raids throughout the day. They had sat and knitted and gossiped and read magazines, and then had enjoyed the short visits from their friends and relatives before quite happily settling down for the night after their cocoa.

Now the ward was quiet, Sister was on her break, and Polly was sitting in the pool of light cast by the table lamp which sat on the edge of Sister's desk. She was going through the medical notes of each patient, making sure everything was up to date. Two of them would be going home tomorrow, so there would be a bit of a change-round in the morning.

'Staff Nurse Brown.'

Polly started; she hadn't heard Matron creeping up on her. Did the blasted woman never sleep? She quickly rose from the chair, wondering if she was about to be torn off a strip for visiting Adam out of hours – or worse, that Adam's condition had suddenly deteriorated – but Matron's expression was unreadable. 'It's not Adam, is it, Matron?' she asked fearfully.

'Your husband is sleeping quite peacefully, Staff Nurse.'

Polly saw something approaching hesitation and reluctance in those steely eyes and it made her mouth dry and her pulse race. 'What is it?' she breathed.

Matron took her arm and firmly led her through the double doors into the corridor. 'It seems you are needed back at Beach View Boarding House,' she said quietly. 'Mrs Reilly will explain everything when you get there.'

'What's happened? Is someone hurt?'

Matron reached into the tiny room set aside for the nurses to make tea during their breaks, and pulled Polly's cloak, handbag and gas mask from the coat-stand. Her expression softened as she held them out to Polly. 'I understand there has been a fatality,' she said with a gentleness no one had witnessed before.

Polly thought her heart would burst from her chest as she struggled into the cloak and grabbed the rest of her things. 'A fatality? But who?'

Matron put her warm, soft hand on Polly's shoulder. 'Mrs Reilly needs you, Nurse,' she said softly. 'I can't tell you anything more, I'm sorry.'

Polly flew along the corridor and hurtled down the stairs. Her thoughts were going a mile a minute as her footsteps pounded the pavement and echoed through the silent streets, and her heart thudded against her ribs.

Who could have died? Surely not Mrs Finch – or Ron – or Danuta? Oh God, it felt as if Beach View Terrace was miles away instead of just a few hundred yards down the road.

She skidded to a halt at the bottom of the steps and looked up as the door opened. Peggy was standing on the threshold, and it was clear from her reddened eyes and swollen lids that she'd been crying.

Polly slowly climbed the steps, her dread growing when she realised Ron and Danuta were also in the hall, and their solemn expressions made the fear rise and lodge like acid in her throat. 'What is it?' she managed as the terror squeezed coldly round her heart. 'Who ... what...?'

Peggy put her arm round her shoulders and drew her inside before closing the front door. 'Come into the kitchen, Polly. There's something we have to tell you.'

Polly allowed herself to be stripped of her cloak before being led into the kitchen. She stared at the two women who were standing there, wondering who they were.'

'These ladies are from the Welfare Department,' said Peggy.

Polly nodded at them, still baffled by their presence. 'Welfare Department?' she murmured. 'But what...? Why...? Matron said there'd been a fatality.'

'Sit down, dear,' said Peggy. 'They'll explain everything.'

Polly found she was being pressed into the fireside chair by Peggy. She perched stiffly on the very edge of it, her terrified gaze flying between the two silent women who now sat by the table, to Ron and Danuta who stood by the door, and back to a clearly distraught Peggy. 'You're frightening me,' she whispered. 'Please tell me what's happened.'

The taller, thinner and slightly younger woman cleared her throat. 'Mrs Brown, my name is Kate Jackson, and this is Agatha Friar. We work for the Welfare Department, and it is our sad duty to inform you that a German U-boat attacked and sank the *City of Benares* during a storm in the Atlantic, causing a tragic number of fatalities. I'm sorry, Mrs Brown – Polly – but none of your family is on the list of survivors.'

Polly stared at her, unable to take it in. 'No, you've got it wrong,' she said with heavy calm. 'They're in Canada. They were due to arrive at least two days ago. There's been a mistake.'

Kate reached for her hand. 'We wouldn't be here if there had been the slightest doubt that any of them had survived,' she said softly. 'I'm so sorry.'

Polly looked at each of them in turn, the strange calm slowly being undermined by an icy, jagged fear. 'They're in Canada,' she repeated flatly. 'They're with Uncle Peter in Ottawa.' She looked to Peggy for reassurance.

'It's no mistake, my dear,' said Peggy, her voice gruff with unshed tears. 'Eighty-three of the ninety children on board were killed along with two hundred and eleven passengers and crew. Alice and the rest of your family were among them.'

Polly's mind simply couldn't accept what she

was hearing. 'But how could that happen, when the convoy was being escorted by navy destroyers? How did a U-boat manage to get anywhere near them?'

Peggy's tears were spilling down her face. 'I don't know,' she said softly, grasping Polly's hand. 'But it did happen, Polly, and although it must be the hardest thing you will ever have to do, you must try and accept they are gone.'

Polly turned to Kate Jackson, who shook her head. 'We haven't been told all the details of how the attack happened,' she confessed, 'just the salient facts of those who perished.'

'Then you'd better check those *salient facts* again,' Polly rasped, 'because I would have known if something had happened to Alice. She's my baby. I would have felt it here.' She put her fist against her heart.

'No, Polly,' said Peggy urgently. 'We all like to think we would know if such a thing happened to our loved ones, but it simply isn't true.'

'That's nonsense,' snapped Polly, rising from the chair. 'I'm going to telephone the Children's Overseas Headquarters. They'll tell me it was all a mistake, and that Alice and Mum and Megan and the boys weren't even on the *City of Benares* – and that they're in Canada, safe and well. You'll see.'

'The office is closed, Polly,' said Kate Jackson, gripping her by the arm, 'and even if it wasn't, they don't have the authority to tell you anything over the telephone.'

'But I'm Alice's mother,' she snapped, the calm unravelling into ragged tatters. 'I have a right to

241

know who told you to come and tell me this wicked pack of lies.'

'Please calm down, Mrs Brown,' begged Agatha Friar. 'This really isn't doing you any good.'

'I'll be the judge of that,' retorted Polly.

She shrugged off Kate Jackson's restraining hand and ran into the hall. 'Someone's got to know the truth,' she muttered as she reached for the receiver and tried desperately to think who she could telephone. 'They're in Canada. I'll get a postcard or a letter tomorrow, you'll see. The bombings have delayed the post, that's all. There's been a mix-up.'

Polly stared at the receiver in her hand, incapable of coherent thought as the operator asked what number she wanted.

She was barely aware of Danuta gently replacing the receiver, and continued to stare stupidly at the telephone. 'They're in Canada,' she muttered. 'They are, they really are.'

'Come, Polly. Come into the warm,' murmured Danuta.

Polly looked at the other girl and could see only her eyes – dark green eyes, sorrowful eyes bright with unshed tears. She began to tremble as drip by icy drip the truth seared through her numbed mind and into her heart.

She searched that wan little face for some sign that she was mistaken – that this was some terrible nightmare from which she would awaken at any minute. But Danuta's expression was stark with the truth of it, and Polly finally had to accept the unbearable burden of that terrible knowledge. It weighed down on her, filling her with a darkness

242

so profound it was overwhelming.

'No,' she screamed. 'No, no, no.' Black clouds enfolded and filled her, sweeping her into a void of welcoming oblivion.

Danuta gasped as Polly crumpled, but Ron managed to catch her before she hit the hard tiles on the hall floor. Lifting her into his arms, he carried her into the kitchen and set her gently down in the fireside chair.

'I heard someone scream. Whatever's happened?' Cissy raced into the kitchen, wide-eyed, and came to a skidding halt when she realised there were two strangers there.

Peggy quickly explained as Danuta fetched a glass of water.

Cissy sank into a kitchen chair. 'Oh, my God,' she breathed. 'How awful.'

Peggy was too busy trying to bring Polly round to answer her. 'Come on, Polly. Wake up, there's a good girl. That's it, now drink this,' she said softly as the girl's eyes fluttered open.

There was an instant of confusion in Polly's eyes before her gaze settled on the two women. And then memory returned. She pushed the glass of water away and tried to stand, but her eyes rolled back and she fainted again.

'I think you'd better leave this to us,' said Peggy to the two women from the Welfare Office. 'Please see yourselves out, and I'll speak to you tomorrow.'

They left swiftly and silently, almost unnoticed.

'She needs to go to bed,' said Danuta. 'I will look after her.'

Ron cleared his throat, his eyes suspiciously bright as he looked down at Polly. 'Poor wee lass,' he said gruffly. 'I'll take her up.' He lifted her gently into his arms as if she was a child, settling her so her head rested against his shoulder before he carried her into the hall.

Danuta had seen one of the women put a slip of paper on the table before she left, and, curious, she picked it up. It was a telegram delivered to the Welfare Office that evening from the Children's Overseas Evacuation Board, confirming the tragedy in stark, black, emotionless words. She scanned it quickly then folded it repeatedly until it was a tiny square. If she made it small enough, perhaps she could harness its harm.

She became aware of Cissy's wide-eyed puzzlement and shrugged as she stuffed the tiny square of paper into her trouser pocket. 'She doesn't need to see this – not tonight,' she said by way of explanation and, having picked up the glass of water, she followed Peggy and Ron as they slowly climbed the stairs to the bedroom.

Ron laid her gently on the bed, clearly affected by her plight but unsure of what to do for the best.

'Thank you, Ron. Peggy and I will see to her now,' said Danuta, catching sight of Cissy who had followed them up. 'It's all right, Cissy,' she murmured. 'Why don't you make a fresh pot of tea? I'm sure your mother would appreciate it.'

She waited until Ron had closed the door behind both of them before she turned to Peggy. 'Let's get her more comfortable before she comes round again,' she murmured.

They gently stripped her to her underwear and bundled her in a blanket before Danuta tried to rouse her. 'Wake up, Polly,' she said firmly. 'Come on. I know you don't want to, but you have to wake up.'

Polly opened her eyes, stared at Danuta and Peggy in confusion for an instant before the awful truth dawned again. Tears filled her eyes and trembled on her lashes before spilling down her face. 'I shouldn't have sent her away,' she whispered. 'I knew it was dangerous, but I let them persuade me. I thought it was for the best – thought I was doing the right thing.'

She turned her back on Danuta and Peggy as she curled like a small child against the pillows and released her anguish in great wailing sobs.

Danuta could see that Peggy was feeling as helpless as she. 'There's nothing either of us can do,' she reassured her. 'This is a battle only Polly can fight. All that is left for us is to comfort her – and even that will take time, for it will barely touch the terrible pain she's in at the moment.'

'I know,' sighed Peggy, wringing her hands. 'And I feel so useless.'

'I have something that will help her to sleep,' Danuta murmured, getting off the bed. She reached into the canvas bag she'd brought all the way across Europe, and found the small phial that had proved such a godsend during those dark days. Adding two drops to the glass of water, she set it aside until Polly was more able to actually drink it. 'I will stay with her, Peggy,' she said softly. 'You go to bed.'

Peggy continued to look down at the sobbing

Polly. 'How can I sleep, knowing that her heart is breaking? How can any of us rest with those terrible images going round and round in our heads?'

Danuta scrubbed her face with her hands. 'There is no real answer to that,' she said wearily. 'But you have been through enough tonight, Peggy. Go to bed and try to sleep. Tomorrow could be a very long day.'

'Are you sure you don't need me to stay?'

Danuta nodded as she sat on the side of Polly's bed.

'All right,' Peggy murmured. 'But I won't go to bed. I'll wait downstairs for the others to come in. They'll need to be told.' After a long, lingering look at Polly, she squeezed Danuta's shoulder in gratitude and quietly left the room.

Danuta waited until the door closed behind Peggy and then stripped off her sweater and the baggy trousers which were still damp and muddy at the hem from her walk over the hills. With the faded dressing gown wrapped over her underwear to disguise her pregnancy, she stood for a moment to look down at Polly.

To lose a child must cause the most unimaginable pain, and she couldn't begin to comprehend how she would feel if she lost her baby. But she realised that being a mother, Polly would always carry the extra guilt of believing she'd played a part in her child's tragic death – and she feared for her.

Drawing back the eiderdown, she slid in beside Polly and gently drew her into her embrace, offering the only comfort she could – that of warmth and presence and human kindness.

Polly didn't seem to notice she was even there, her heart-rending sobs continuing as she curled ever tighter into the pillows.

Danuta silently lay beside her, remembering how much she'd longed for any kind of comfort when she'd lost her own family. Her thoughts went to her parents who'd been too frail to survive that first Warsaw winter of occupation without food and warmth. She had carried them one by one back to their tenement, and had spent a terrible night digging a grave in the iron-hard earth in the back garden. Their only epitaph had been a crude cross of twigs that she'd planted in the snow.

She closed her eyes as the memories flooded back, and willed them to fade – for although their scars had begun to heal, they were merely the first cuts to be deeply inflicted, and she'd had to go through far worse before she'd managed to arrive at this sanctuary in Cliffehaven.

Polly was aware of Danuta lying beside her, aware of her solidity and warmth – and although she found some comfort in her calm, silent presence, her warmth couldn't reach Polly's icy, empty core, or begin to touch the numb horror of what she'd done.

She pushed away from the pillows and sat up. 'I should have gone with her,' she rasped. 'I should have been there.' She grabbed Danuta's hand. 'I could have saved her, Danuta, I'm sure I could have. But her mummy wasn't there – she was alone – all alone in the middle of that terrible sea. She must have been so frightened – so very frightened without me.'

Danuta gripped Polly's fingers but said nothing. It was as if she understood that there were no words to erase her guilt or her pain.

'She's only five,' she whispered, 'so tiny – so very tiny in that great big sea without me to look after her.' She had the most horrific image of Alice screaming for her as huge black waves carried her away, the echoes of those screams fading until they were silenced.

'She would have called out for me,' she murmured, the tears running hot on her face, salty on her lips. 'Do you think she suffered – was she in pain as well as terror?'

'You must not torture yourself with such thoughts,' murmured Danuta.

'But how can I not?' stormed Polly. 'I sent her away. I killed her.'

Danuta gripped her arms, her face inches from Polly's. 'You did what thousands of other parents did. You did it for the best reasons,' said Danuta firmly. 'And I'm sure your mother and sister were with her. They would have made sure she didn't suffer.'

'How do you know that?' Polly swiped back her hair and rubbed away her tears. 'How do you know that she ... that she...?' The images in her head were simply too awful to be articulated, and Polly drew her knees to her chest and buried her face in her arms as the agony tore through her again and the tears flowed.

'You need to sleep, Polly,' said Danuta softly as she moved on the bed. 'Drink this. It will help.'

'I don't want to sleep ever again. How can I rest

when I have the death of my baby on my conscience? I should never have let her go – should never have let any of them go.'

'You did not kill them,' said Danuta firmly. 'It was the Germans. Now drink this, Polly.'

Polly stared at her, bleary-eyed and overwhelmed with crippling emotion. But something in Danuta's tone made her obey the order like an automaton. She felt the cold glass on her lips and the cool, strange-tasting water on her tongue, and drank it down. She didn't care what it was – didn't care about anything but the aching need to be with Alice and the rest of her family.

'That is good,' murmured Danuta. 'Now, you lie down. Sleep will come soon.'

Polly felt like a rag doll, heavy-limbed and drained of energy as the eiderdown was settled over her shoulders. She could hear Danuta's soft, soothing murmurs, but they seemed to be coming from a long way away.

Her eyelids fluttered and the terrifying images in her head seemed to fade – to become lost in the warm, dark clouds of oblivion that were beginning to envelop her and draw her into their comforting embrace.

Peggy was grateful for Ron's sturdy and comforting presence as they waited in the kitchen for everyone to come home. He'd poured a generous glass of precious brandy for each of them and, as Harvey snored at their feet, they sat, deep in their own thoughts, as they watched the fire dwindle in the grate and listened to the solemn ticking of the mantel clock.

It felt like a lifetime ago since they'd all been dancing in the other room, and the memory of the fun and the careless laughter they'd shared served to make the tragic events of tonight even more shocking.

The three girls came in moments before Jim and, as Peggy told them what had happened, she felt the onset of tears again. Jim took her in his arms and, as she buried her face in his jacket, she realised just how badly she'd needed his comfort – his very solid, warm presence.

It was a subdued household that went to bed that night, and Peggy was not the only one who lay staring into the darkness for a long time before sleep overcame her.

It was dawn when Peggy brought in the bottles of milk from the front step and tramped into the kitchen to make a cup of tea. She felt wrung out and terribly low. As she waited for the water to boil, she stared out over the back garden and counted her blessings. Her children were safe, she still had a home, a husband and a supportive father-in-law, and soon there would be a grand-child to love and protect.

'You're up early, dear. Couldn't you sleep?'

Peggy turned to find Mrs Finch standing by the kitchen table in her dressing gown, her handbag over her arm as usual. 'No,' she said, shaking her head. 'We've had some very sad news, and I don't think anyone slept very well at all.'

Mrs Finch clearly couldn't hear a word she'd said but seemed to realise Peggy was struggling to maintain any sign of her usual sunny disposition.

She fiddled with her hearing aid. 'What is it, Peggy? What's happened?'

Peggy waited until she was settled in a chair before telling her. 'So you see,' she finished, 'we need to give Polly some time to absorb this terrible news. I don't know how she'll be, grief takes us all differently, but I think that as long as she knows we're all here to help her, she'll come through in time.'

Mrs Finch nodded. 'It's a terrible thing when the young are snatched away,' she said, plucking at her handkerchief. 'And doubly cruel that they should all have perished.' She blew her nose forcibly. 'Poor little Polly. How on earth is she going to tell her husband? Is he well enough for such news?'

Peggy made the tea and added some precious sugar to it to give them both a bit of a boost. 'I don't think he is,' she murmured, setting the cup and saucer in front of Mrs Finch. 'Polly says he's recovering slowly, but I think he's far from out of the woods yet – and something like this could set him back weeks, if not months. It's a terrible dilemma, it really is.'

'Poor Polly,' murmured Mrs Finch, 'as if she doesn't have enough to contend with.'

They sat in thoughtful silence as they sipped their tea. As the clock on the mantel struck seven, they heard the clatter of the newspapers being shoved through the letterbox. The war might have changed many things, thought Peggy, but come hail, rain, shine or air raids, the newspapers and milk arrived every morning without fail. The normality of it was comforting

251

in these troubling times.

Peggy dragged herself out of the chair, traipsed into the hall and drew the papers out of the new wire-mesh basket that hung below the letterbox. She liked the *Daily Mirror*, Ron and Jim preferred the *Mail*, and Mrs Finch would only read *The Times*.

As she shuffled back towards the kitchen, Peggy glanced at *The Times*' headlines with little interest. There were the usual reports of heavy bombing over London, and RAF retaliation over Berlin, and a follow-up article from the previous day about America's promise to increase the current monthly delivery of two hundred Flying Fortress warplanes they were manufacturing for Britain. She handed it over to Mrs Finch, wondering if, at last, the Americans would play a bigger part in this awful war.

Mrs Finch settled her reading glasses on her nose, switched off her hearing aid, and became happily immersed in the news, oblivious to everything else.

Peggy was about to set the other two papers on the kitchen table when she caught sight of the headline screaming across the front page of the *Daily Mirror* and froze in horror.

83 CHILDREN DIE AS HUNS SINK LINER IN STORM

Peggy's legs seemed to turn to water and she sank on to the kitchen chair and stared at those awful words. Polly must have been one of the last to have been informed of the tragedy, and the press had clearly wasted no time once the government ban had been lifted.

Hands trembling, she finally reached for the paper and began to read. The article wasn't very long – but it painted a terrible and tragic picture.

EIGHTY-THREE out of a party of ninety children being taken to Canada died along with 211 other passengers and crew when a British liner was torpedoed and sunk by the Huns in an Atlantic storm.

Seven out of nine adults who were escorting the children were also drowned. A U-boat committed this crime against civilians when the liner was 600 miles from land. The ship sank in twenty minutes. Huge seas swamped some of the boats which the crew managed to launch. In other boats, people sat waist deep in water and died of exposure. Many of the children were killed when the torpedo struck the ship. The disaster was revealed late last night when it was stated officially that the number of missing was 294.

'Dear God,' breathed Peggy. 'It sounds as if this happened days ago. Why did it take so long to come out?' She riffled through the pages, but there were no further details.

Setting the *Mirror* to one side with a cluck of exasperation, she found herself staring at the headline across the *Mail*.

Mercy Liner Torpedoed
83 out of 90 Children are Drowned.
Boats Swamped in Heavy Gale.

Peggy raced through the short article which chilled her to the bone.

Some of the children were trapped in the ship or killed by the explosion. Others suffered from exposure in life-boats and on rafts, which were swept by wind, waves, rain and hail for hours before they could be picked up by a British warship.

A full list of the lost children is given on page 5, and stories from the survivors are on page 6.

Peggy flicked through until she found that terrible list. And there they were, in stark black against white – William and Samuel Walters aged 7; Alice Brown aged 5.

She looked at those names for a long time before quickly trawling through the survivors' stories. All she could do was thank the Lord that Churchill had had the compassion to keep this out of the papers until all those concerned were informed. She couldn't imagine what it might have done to Polly, or to any of the other parents, if they'd come across this without warning at the breakfast table.

Peggy returned to the articles and read them more slowly. The *City of Benares* hadn't been mentioned by name, and there was nothing to say where the survivors had been taken. Six hundred miles from land could mean they'd been taken to Canada or were back in Britain. The news was so horrifying, she was amazed it wasn't splashed across *The Times* as well.

She sat and mulled this over as she smoked a cigarette. At the sound of footsteps overhead, she quickly bundled the papers together and hid them away in the dresser. The last thing Polly would need today was to see those, she decided.

Hurrying to begin preparing breakfast, she found her thoughts wandering and managed to break a plate as it slipped out of her fingers. Close to tears, she swept up the shards of china and dumped them in the waste-bin under the sink. 'This won't do at all,' she muttered crossly. 'Pull yourself together, Peggy. That girl needs you to be strong.'

She hurried down the basement steps to the shed to discover Ron was already building a coop and run for the chickens the Australians had given them. She told him quickly about the newspaper reports and Ron shook his head, his face drawn and pale.

He dredged up a weary smile as he carefully put the fresh-laid eggs in her bowl. 'You look as tired as I feel,' he said. 'But perhaps these will go some way to cheering everyone up.'

She nodded and carried them back up to the kitchen. It was a lovely idea, and a super treat, but she doubted a few fried eggs would raise much of a smile in anyone today.

There was no sign of Danuta or Polly during breakfast. Conversation was muted as the newspapers were quickly scanned and the fried eggs devoured along with hot, strong, sweet tea. Once read and discussed, the papers were consigned once again to the dresser. Polly might want to read them at a later date when she was stronger, but for now they were better kept out of sight.

When the three girls were preparing to leave for the hospital, Peggy handed Suzy an envelope. 'Would you give this to Matron, please? Danuta is needed here, and I don't want her getting into trouble. I've also suggested it would be better if Polly doesn't come in for at least two weeks. She needs time to get over this.'

Suzy nodded, her little face solemn for once as she tucked the envelope into her pocket and straightened her cloak. 'We'll see you after our shift,' she said quietly.

Peggy returned to the dining room once they'd left and sat down, weary before the day had even got going. 'What about you, Cissy? What are your plans for the day?'

'I think it's time I went back to work,' she said, setting aside her empty plate. 'There's nothing wrong with my ankle any more, and the bruising is easily covered in make-up.'

She flashed her mother a woeful smile. 'In the scheme of things, I admit I was making a bit of a drama out of it all and I feel rather ashamed of myself. But I'll stay here if you'd prefer,' she added hurriedly, 'though I don't know what I could do really.'

'You go, darling. It will be good to keep busy, and I know how much you've missed doing your shows.'

Cissy finished her cup of tea and began to stack the empty plates. 'I'll do the washing-up and clean my room first,' she said. 'There's no point in going too early. No one will be there.'

Polly was wide awake, listening to the noises within the house. Danuta had left the bed some time ago to go to the bathroom, and Polly had pretended to be asleep, not wanting to see the sympathy in her eyes or bear the burden of having to talk. But she knew she couldn't be here all day – knew that she would only torture herself if given time to think.

She threw back the eiderdown and, after a moment's hesitation, got out of bed. She was surprised to discover she was in her underwear, and that her uniform was hanging neatly in the wardrobe. She didn't remember getting undressed – had been aware of nothing but the awful pain.

'Don't think,' she muttered. 'Stay busy. Keep moving. There's work to do, Adam to see...' She sank back on to the bed. How on earth could she tell Adam? He was far too ill, and something like this could finish him. She felt the onset of tears again at the thought of losing Adam as well as everyone else, and angrily steeled herself against them. She would not cry. She'd shed enough tears, and they would achieve nothing – absolutely nothing.

'Polly, you shouldn't be out of bed.' Danuta was dressed, ready for work.

'I have things to do,' she replied, getting to her feet and reaching for her dressing gown.

'But Polly...'

She gave Danuta a swift hug. 'Thank you for last night,' she said, her throat raw from crying. 'But I have to deal with this in my own way. And right now, I need a bath.'

She grabbed her washbag and fled before

Danuta could protest. But once the door was locked and the water was running, she had to battle the awful pain that encircled and squeezed her heart, and the tears which sprang unbidden to burst into sobs.

It was a long time before she felt in control enough to return to the bedroom and she breathed a sigh of relief when she discovered Danuta was nowhere to be seen. The girl had been kindness itself, and she'd felt comforted by her presence during the night, but that very kindness weakened her resolve, and she didn't have the courage yet to talk – couldn't begin to voice the thoughts, images and emotions that were beleaguering her.

Still, she had to get dressed and face Peggy and the others before she could escape the house and seek out the freedom of the wind and sun up on the hills, where she could walk in solitude and try to come to terms with what had happened before she had to face Adam.

Cissy stood outside the theatre and looked up at the garish poster advertising the revue. It promised gorgeous dancing girls and splendid singers, along with a cheeky comedian, and several speciality acts.

She felt a little flutter in her stomach as she eyed the photographs in the glass case on the wall beside the main doors. There she was, one of the chorus, long legs and a bright smile staring back at her. She'd wanted to be a star for so long – had believed she could be until the other week. Now she didn't know what the future held, only that it wouldn't involve Jack Witherspoon.

'G'day, Cissy. I thought I might find you here.'

She whirled round to find that Joe was leaning against a lamp post, his long wiry frame looking at ease as he grinned at her from beneath the broad-brimmed hat. She grinned back, feeling foolish but unable to help herself. 'You're lucky I decided to come today, then,' she replied.

He pushed away from the lamp post and sauntered over. 'Then I'd've come to the house.'

'I don't think June would be very pleased if you did,' she said, reddening.

'But would *you* have liked me to come?' His eyes were mesmerising as they held her from beneath the hat-brim.

She nodded and dipped her chin.

'Look, Cissy,' he began, 'I'll be off tomorrow, so I don't have long to get to know you properly, but would you come for a cup of tea, or a walk – or something?'

'I'm supposed to be getting warmed up for rehearsals,' she replied ruefully. Then she looked back into his eyes and saw the way they crinkled at the edges. 'But I'm sure it wouldn't hurt if I took just one more day off.'

Joe held out his arm. 'Then let's get acquainted,' he said, his smile making the cobweb of lines around his eyes deepen in that tanned face. 'I reckon we should be able to get a cuppa in the town.'

'Not so fast, Miss Reilly.'

The dismay was like a heavy weight in her stomach as she looked at Jack Witherspoon who had emerged silently through the theatre doors.

'Joe's being shipped out tomorrow,' she said, her nervousness making her voice tremble. 'We're just going...'

'You have a show to rehearse,' he said, barely giving Joe a glance. 'And you've already had a week off. Get inside, or I'll dock your wages.'

'You can't talk to the lady like that, mate,' said Joe, moving his shoulders threateningly inside the confines of his large coat.

'She's my employee and has a contract to prove it,' said Witherspoon. 'I can speak to her any way I like.' His dark eyes settled on Cissy. 'Unless she wishes to break that contract, of course. But that would be extremely foolish, considering how much she stands to lose, wouldn't it, Cissy?'

Cissy swallowed the lump in her throat as she nodded. His veiled threat was all too clear. 'You'd better go,' she murmured to Joe.

'Will you be all right with him?' Joe shot Witherspoon a warning glare.

'I'll meet you here at one, when I've got a break,' she murmured hurriedly, loath to let Witherspoon overhear their conversation. 'I'm sorry Joe, but I've got no choice.'

'Come along,' said Witherspoon impatiently. 'You've wasted enough time this morning and rehearsals are about to begin.'

Cissy gave Joe a nervous smile, ran up the steps and into the foyer. Without waiting to see if Witherspoon was following, she dashed down to the deserted dressing room and locked herself in the lavatory.

The other girls were on stage; she could hear the music and the tramp of their feet, could smell

260

the veil of dust sifting through the boards. She stood with her back to the door and tried to control her racing pulse. This moment of respite could only be temporary though, she realised, for she would have to come out sooner or later – would have to face him.

The tap on the door startled her, and she gave a yelp as if she'd been burned. 'Go away,' she cried out.

'Come out of there, Cissy,' growled Witherspoon. 'We've got unfinished business, you and I.'

'I've nothing to say to you,' she retorted. 'Go away.'

'If you don't come out, I'll break the door down.'

Cissy knew he meant it, for he'd done it once before when one of the other girls had tried to defy him. She reached out a trembling hand and pulled back the rusting bolt.

Opening the door, she was confronted by an angry face and a pair of glittering black eyes. 'I want my photographs back,' she said, her brave words marred by the quaver in her voice. 'The negatives too,' she added.

He merely smiled a cold smile, grabbed her arm and forced her into the deserted dressing room. 'Get ready for rehearsals, and I'll speak to you later.'

'I only came in to get those pictures and give in my notice,' she said, trying hard to sound brave and determined. 'I don't care if I do have a contract. I don't want to dance here any more.'

He grabbed her chin and held it between thumb and finger so tightly it made her wince. 'You will

261

do as you're told, Cissy, or I'll show those pictures to that boyfriend of yours. You never know, he might like seeing his girl half naked, and even if he doesn't, I'm sure his mates will approve.' He gave an unpleasant grin. 'I have a lot of contacts, Cissy. You could be famous within minutes.'

'You wouldn't?' She looked up at him through the tears and realised that indeed he was perfectly capable of doing such a thing. 'But why? Why can't you just give me those photos and let me go? I'll get a job working in a shop or something, and I'll be out of your hair – and I won't tell anyone, I promise.'

His smile reminded her of the wolf from one of her childhood fairy-tale books. 'But you're bought and paid for, Cissy, and I like to keep what's mine,' he said softly as he brushed his lips against her cheek. 'The contract can only be broken if your parents sign on the dotted line, and I don't think you really want them involved, do you?'

She dumbly shook her head.

'Good girl,' he murmured, patting her bottom. 'Now get changed and join the rehearsals. I'll see you in my office at lunchtime.'

Cissy's legs threatened to fail her. She plumped down on a hard wooden stool and listened to his retreating footsteps. She was trapped and had nowhere to turn, for there was no one she dared trust with her dirty little secret. To expose him for what he was would reveal her own stupidity and the lengths to which she'd gone in search of promised fame and fortune. And the thought of her parents finding out made her skin crawl with shame.

Chapter Thirteen

Polly tramped the hills until the sun was so high it cast no shadows at her feet. She had never felt so drained, and every part of her ached, but her thoughts would not be still and she couldn't dispel those terrible pictures in her head, no matter how far or fast she walked.

She finally sank to the springy turf and looked out over Cliffehaven. In the short while she'd been here, she'd not had time to walk along the promenade which ran the length of the horseshoe bay, from the towering white cliffs at one end to the rolling green hills at the other. She gazed out past the gun emplacements, the acres of barbed wire and mined shingle to the abandoned pier which had been cast adrift from the shore to prevent enemy landings. The fishing fleet was making its slow, steady way around the concrete blocks that formed a ragged barricade across the bay, the queue of eager housewives already forming nearby to purchase a share of the precious catch.

Polly watched as the sails were furled and the boats rushed in on the rolling waves to beach on the area of shingle that wasn't mined. The sun on the water hurt her eyes, and she shielded them with her hand as she regarded that broad sweep of blue that looked so benign in the early autumn sunshine. How could something so beautiful be so cruel? How could it roll glassily on to shingle with barely a splash, when it was capable of rising like a leviathan to rip her world apart?

The grief and despair were overwhelming, for there were too many to mourn – too much to take in – too many regrets to count. She wanted the comfort of her mother, to feel her kiss and hear her voice; to be her little girl again. Needed to tell her sister she was sorry for snapping at her on that last morning, and longed to hear those bright-headed little boys racing through her kitchen with their paper planes.

But most of all she ached to feel Alice, warm in her arms, the sweet scent of her drifting to her as her baby slept. What she wouldn't give to have those last precious moments of that morning again – what she wouldn't do to breathe in her essence, and to hear her piping voice as she prattled on about her day.

She hugged her knees, the scene blurring before her as the tears returned. It didn't feel real – it was incomprehensible – and yet it was fact – cold, bitter, indisputable fact. Alice was gone – they were all gone, and those moments would never return. All she could do now was keep them alive in her heart and in her memories until it was time for them to be together again.

A surge of longing gripped her. 'If only Adam was stronger,' she murmured. 'If only we could share this terrible thing.' She sniffed back the tears and got to her feet. There was little point in wishing things were different, for she couldn't change them. All she could do now was carry that terrible knowledge alone. Adam *would* get better, and when he was strong enough, she would tell him, but not today – and probably not for some time. She silently prayed that she had the strength to shoulder that burden for however long it might take.

Cissy dashed off the stage the moment rehearsals were over. Knowing she had only minutes to change out of her shorts and leotard before Witherspoon came looking for her, she yanked them off and dragged on her dress. Kicking off the tap shoes, she stuffed her feet into her sandals, grabbed her bag and gas mask and raced for the stage door.

If Witherspoon caught her then the game was up, but she was determined to avoid him and, as the door slammed behind her, she didn't waste time congratulating herself but dashed round to the front of the theatre.

Joe was waiting for her, but he wasn't alone. Witherspoon was talking to him.

Cissy skidded to a halt and, pulse racing, hid behind the shrubs that grew beside the low stone wall of the theatre entrance-way. She watched as the two men talked but couldn't hear what they were saying – neither could she read anything in Joe's expression for his hat shadowed his face. She bit her lip and moved further into the shadows, unsure of what to do.

'What on earth are you doing, Cissy? Who are you hiding from?'

'Shh. He'll hear you,' she replied furiously, grabbing Amy's arm and pulling her behind the shrubbery.

Amy frowned as she peered through the leaves.

'What's going on, Cissy? You're acting very strangely.'

Cissy looked at her best friend mutely, longing to confide in her but knowing she couldn't. They had met at their very first dance class when they were five years old, had gone to the same school, danced in the same revues, and swooned over the same boys. Until now, they'd shared their secrets – but this was not the time to reveal her darkest one. 'That's Joe talking to Witherspoon, and we're supposed to be stepping out for the afternoon. But Witherspoon's got other ideas,' she said gloomily.

Amy frowned and tucked her long dark hair behind her ears. 'What sort of ideas?'

Her gaze was level and too probing for comfort, and Cissy had to look away as she felt the heat rising up her neck and into her face. 'I just need to get him away from Joe without him seeing me.'

Amy eyed her thoughtfully. 'Tell you what. How about I distract Jack, and you try and catch Joe's eye?'

'Would you?'

'Only if you promise to tell me what all this is about.'

There was that probing look again, which made Cissy feel very uncomfortable. It was as if Amy knew something of her predicament and was simply waiting for her to voice it. Cissy blanked out the thought – she was letting her overheated imagination run away with her as usual. What could Amy possibly know? Witherspoon was far too clever to risk being caught alone with her, and the incident over the photographer had happened long after everyone had left the theatre.

'I'll tell you tonight after the show,' she promised.

'You'd better keep that promise, Cissy,' Amy said solemnly. 'You've changed, you know, and I'm worried about you.'

Cissy felt a pang of regret and shame. 'Thanks, Amy,' she murmured, taking her hand. 'But I'm all right, really I am, and I'll tell you everything later.' She peeked agitatedly through the shrubbery. 'Why doesn't Witherspoon just go?' she hissed. 'What on *earth* can they be talking about that takes so long?'

Amy swung her handbag and gas-mask box over her shoulder and straightened her jacket. 'Leave this to me.' She strode away and headed straight for the two men who were talking on the pavement outside the theatre. 'Jack, can I have a word?' she called. 'It's very important and simply can't wait.'

Cissy watched as Amy tucked her hand into Jack's arm and steered him back up the steps into the theatre foyer. What she'd thought to say to him was a mystery, but Amy had always been quick-witted and a consummate actress, for which Cissy blessed her. Perhaps it wouldn't be too awful to confide in her after all, she thought fretfully – and it might help to ease the burden of having to deal with Witherspoon on her own every day.

Joe was looking at his watch and clearly getting impatient. Cissy banished all thoughts of Witherspoon and waved to him as he turned in her direction. Her heart fluttered as she returned his smile and watched his loose-limbed, ambling approach. He was very handsome – especially in that uniform.

'What are you doing hiding over here?' he drawled.

'I wasn't, not really,' she said, flustered by the intense way he was looking down at her. 'I just didn't want to get involved in your conversation with Jack Witherspoon.' She tucked her hand in the crook of his arm, forcing him to walk away from the theatre.

Her heart was still pounding and her mouth was dry as she dared to ask the question that had been bothering her ever since she'd seen them together. 'It seemed to be quite a serious discussion between you,' she said carefully. 'What on earth did you find to talk about?'

'Nothing much,' he replied. 'Just discussing the war and the weather.' He grinned. 'The usual things you Poms talk about when you've nothing much else to say.'

Cissy felt so relieved that her legs almost failed her, and she had to grip on to Joe's arm to keep her balance.

'Whoa there,' he muttered. 'Is that ankle still bothering you?'

She nodded. 'It is aching a bit,' she confessed truthfully, 'but that's probably because I've been dancing on it all morning.' She smiled up at him. 'Don't let's waste this lovely afternoon talking about my silly ankle, Joe. We're supposed to be getting to know each other, remember? Why don't you tell me everything about Australia and your family, and what you do there?'

He raised one dark brow, his eyes twinkling. 'I reckon it could take a while to tell you *everything*,' he drawled. 'Australia's a big place.'

She giggled. 'Then tell me about the bit you know. Is it really flat red desert, with lots of kangaroos bouncing about?'

He chuckled as they settled on one of the stone benches that were dotted along what remained of the promenade. 'There are kangaroos aplenty, but we've also got spiders and snakes and wombats and kookaburras.' He grinned. 'As for it being desert, well, some of it is – but we have lakes and rivers and mountains, and miles of bush which sometimes go right down to the sea. There are tropical islands and long sandy beaches, rainforests and mountains that are veiled in a haze of blue from the eucalyptus oil.'

He gave a deep sigh as he squinted out over the sparkling water. 'It has everything a man could wish for.'

She heard the wistfulness in his voice and could see it in his eyes as he continued to stare out to sea. 'You miss it dreadfully, don't you?' she said softly.

'Reckon I do,' he admitted. 'It's God's own country, Cissy,' he said, his gaze returning to her. 'I wish I could show it to you.'

'Describe it for me, Joe,' she said softly. 'Let me see it as you do.'

'Let's have some tucker first,' he said, as he dug into the deep pocket of his coat and pulled out four bottles of beer and a packet of sandwiches. 'I thought that as it was such a nice day, we'd have a picnic.' He carefully folded the long coat

269

over the arm of the bench and settled down to his beer, his hat tipped back, face lifted to the sunshine.

They sat in companionable silence for a long moment, just enjoying the beer, each other's company and the chicken sandwiches. Cissy was at ease with him in a way she'd never felt with a man before, and she kept glancing at him through her lashes, wondering if he realised how little she knew of the world and how naïve she really was despite her pretensions of sophistication – and if he had realised, was he bothered by it? It suddenly mattered quite a lot that he wasn't.

He seemed relaxed enough, with one booted foot on the knee of the other leg, his free arm stretched along the back of the bench within inches of her shoulder as he continued to soak up the sun and drink his beer. But then, she rationalised, he was a man of the world – a man who had seen things she could never imagine – a man who no doubt was used to sitting beside girls in the sunshine.

The sandwiches had been eaten, the wrappers stowed back in the deep coat pockets and the last two beers had been opened. Settling comfortably on the stone bench, he tugged his hat-brim low to shield his eyes from the sun's glare on the water and began to speak.

'I was born in Sydney twenty-five years ago,' he drawled in that slightly nasal twang. 'My mum and dad still live there and it's a bonzer place, but by the time I'd left school, I was restless. It's a big country, Cissy, and I wanted to see as much of it as I could before I had to settle down.'

Cissy's heart thumped at the thought he might be married.

He grinned down at her, seeming to read her thoughts. 'I'm still fancy free,' he drawled, 'if you don't count the seven hundred square miles of property and four thousand head of cattle I run on it.'

'Seven hundred square miles?' she breathed, unable to comprehend any farm being that big.

He shrugged as if this was commonplace. 'It's not much compared to some, why, there's cattle stations out there over two thousand miles square. But I do all right.'

Cissy listened to the slow, drawling voice which held the very essence of his homeland, and found it soothed and yet excited her. He was so different to anyone she'd ever met before – almost exotic, with that deeply tanned skin and strong features that could soften so quickly into a smile.

She listened as he told her how he'd moved from place to place, learning the skills that would one day help him to run his own cattle station. He described the homestead he'd built at Wallaby Creek so well, she could see the fly-screens over the door and windows, and how the sweeping corrugated-iron roof dipped past the sturdy stone chimney to shelter the deep verandah from the sun.

His words painted pictures of mile upon mile of dusty red earth that shimmered beneath a cloudless sky, and the hazy blue of a distant chain of mountains. She could almost hear the raucous chatter of the white cockatoos as they raided the grain stores, and the rustle of the hot wind in the

271

sweet-smelling eucalyptus trees that looked so silvery-grey and delicate against the cobalt sky. And when he told her about the long days he and his men had spent in the saddle as they drove the cattle to market, she could almost hear the jingle of harness, the bellow of the cattle, and taste the dust kicked up by the many hooves.

Cissy watched him as he talked of his home, and could see the love for it shining in his eyes. This was a man from a very different country – a man who belonged in the great red heart of Australia, who was at home in the awesome outback silence with his cattle and the heat and the flies. How small England must feel, she thought. How dull and colourless he must think we all are after being surrounded by such vibrancy.

'I could have stayed,' he said finally, 'beef cattle are vital for feeding the army – but I wanted to be with my mates, and I could trust Wally and Sam to look after the place while I was gone. My dad fought in the first war, and we Aussie blokes don't like sitting back while there's a fight on – we have a reputation to keep.'

He grinned as he looked back at her. 'So, that's my story, Cissy. Now it's your turn. And I want to know *everything*.' There was a teasing light in his eyes that made her blush.

'It's not half as interesting as yours,' she replied, 'and there's hardly anything to tell. I'm almost nineteen, and I've lived in the same house since I was born. After I left school, I got a job dancing and worked in Woolworths part-time until it was bombed out. I've got two much younger brothers who've been evacuated to Somerset, and an older sister, Anne, who is married to an RAF pilot. She's expecting her first baby in the new year.'

She fell silent, not wanting to tell him about her dancing and the ambitions that had dwindled over the past few weeks. It would simply make her look foolish, and she so desperately wanted him to like her. 'That's about it really,' she said shyly. 'I did warn you it was a bit boring.'

'Not at all,' he protested. 'It's just a different sort of life to mine, that's all – and if it hadn't been for this war, I would never have left home or seen anything of the world at all.' He fell silent for a moment. 'Your mum and dad seem real nice,' he murmured. 'That's quite a houseful you've got there. How are you all coping with the bombing raids and the rationing?'

Cissy grimaced. 'We manage, and although it's terrifying when those bombers come over, we're getting a bit fed up with having meals and sleep and every other thing interrupted. As for the rationing, Mum and Mrs Finch do very well, and those chickens are a godsend.' She grinned back at him. 'Thanks to you, we had fried eggs for breakfast instead of the usual powdered stuff. They were delicious.'

He shrugged off her thanks. 'No worries. I just wish we could have brought more stuff, but the MPs are keeping a closer eye on the stores. They seem to think someone's been pilfering tea and butter and suchlike.' He chuckled. 'Those flaming chickens nearly did for us, squawking and carrying on, with the guard right on the other side of the wall. Luckily he was too busy chatting to one of the WAAFs to take much notice.'

'Mrs Finch was right,' laughed Cissy. 'You are a rogue.'

'Fair go, Cissy, a bloke's got to do what a bloke's got to do. There is a war on, you know.' His smile slowly faded as he looked at her. 'Can you stay with me a while? Spend my last evening with me? Or do you have to go back to the theatre for tonight's show?'

'What about June?' she asked hesitantly. 'Won't she be expecting to see you on your last night?'

He shook his head. 'June and me had a bit of fun together, but we're just mates. She won't mind if I don't turn up with the others tonight. There'll be plenty of other blokes about to keep her occupied.'

Cissy doubted June would see it that way but wasn't going to argue her case with him. The wonder that he wanted to spend the rest of the day and his last evening with her was overwhelming, and she forgot about June, forgot about Wither-spoon and the theatre, and threw caution to the wind.

'They won't miss me if I don't turn up at the theatre,' she said quickly. 'Besides, my ankle's still too sore after rehearsing all morning.' She grinned up at him impishly. 'Let's go and find a cup of tea, and you can tell me more about Wallaby Creek Station.'

Polly had returned from her long walk and, despite the heavy weariness in her limbs, her mind was still racing. She had gone straight into the kitchen in search of something to drink, and, as she'd feared, Peggy had heard her come in and was

274

now hovering anxiously in the doorway.

'I'm all right,' she said firmly, after gulping down the glass of water. 'Please don't worry about me, Peggy.'

'But...'

'I know you mean well,' Polly said softly, 'but I really don't want to talk about anything right now.' She washed the glass and upended it on the draining board. With a glance at the clock, she gathered up her things. 'I must get ready for work. Visiting starts in an hour, and I want to see Adam before my shift starts.'

Peggy was still blocking the doorway. 'But I sent a note to Matron, telling her you wouldn't be in for at least two weeks,' she said, wringing her hands. 'It's too soon, Polly, dear. You can't possibly go back to work yet.'

'I have to, Peggy, or I shall go mad,' she said hoarsely, her throat restricted as the tears threatened yet again. 'If I sit about all day I won't be able to escape it. I'm better off working and concentrating on something useful.'

'I see,' murmured Peggy. She sighed. 'You know best, of course,' she said, her brown eyes warm with sympathy, 'but you mustn't overdo things.' She licked her lips, clearly hesitant about saying more. 'Have you decided what to tell Adam?'

Polly was on the brink of giving in to the tears, and furiously blinked them away. 'He's not well enough yet, and I can't afford for him to have a relapse – not now – especially not now.' She glanced at the clock again, desperate to be away. 'I'm sorry, Peggy, but I really must get changed.'

Peggy stood to one side as she dashed past and

275

ran up the stairs. Without giving herself time to think, Polly swiftly changed into her uniform and cleaned her teeth. Eyeing her reflection in the mirror above the gas fire, she put powder over the dark shadows beneath her eyes, mascara on her lashes and the tiniest dab of rouge on her cheeks. Her hand was shaking so badly that she had to reapply her lipstick twice.

Taking a deep breath, she looked into her reflected eyes and forced herself to smile. The muscles in her face felt stiff, the smile barely warming her grey eyes, but this was the face Adam would see tonight, she thought determinedly, and even if it was agony, she would just keep on smiling.

'See you tomorrow morning,' she called out to Peggy, who was crashing saucepans in the kitchen.

With the front door firmly closed behind her, she ran down the steps and hurried towards the hospital. She needed to see Adam, to hold his hand and hear his voice – to find the reassurance and strength his very presence always gave her. Even if it meant looking him in the eye and keeping the awful truth from him as she smiled and chattered about nothing in particular.

Mary was sitting at her desk in the centre of the ward, and when she looked up, Polly could see the shock in her eyes. It was clear that her news had spread, so at least she didn't have to go through long, painful, explanations.

'You're not supposed to be on duty tonight,' said Mary, who seemed to understand that if she touched her or tried to sympathise it would be too painful. 'Adam's asleep, I'm afraid, but he seemed a little more coherent this afternoon.'

'Thanks, Mary.'

Polly forced a smile and kept it in place as she hurried to Adam's bedside. Sitting down, she reached for his hand. It was warm and oh so familiar despite the lack of strength in the fingers and the softness of the skin. She held it against her cheek and had to bite her lip to stop herself from pouring out her pain and despair. She had never kept secrets from him before, and it was far harder than she could possibly have imagined.

'Polly?'

She rapidly pulled her thoughts together and plastered on a smile. 'Hello, darling,' she murmured. 'How are you feeling today?'

'Tired,' he said on a sigh, 'and my head hurts.' He didn't open his eyes; it seemed the light was bothering him.

She looked at him in alarm. 'You mean you've got a headache?'

'It's a blinder,' he replied, wincing as he rolled his head on the pillow. 'Do you think you could persuade Sister to give me something for it?'

'I'll ask, but I doubt she will,' said Polly. 'You're already on so many other things.' She felt his forehead. He was too warm, and there were high spots of colour blossoming on his cheeks. 'I'll be back in a minute,' she murmured, kissing his hot cheek.

She did her best to keep the panic out of her voice, but the tremor betrayed it. 'Mary, I think Adam's temperature's up, and he's complaining of a headache.'

'It was up a little this morning,' said Mary, leaving her desk, 'but he made no mention of a headache.' She bustled to Adam's bedside and took the thermometer from the small tube of disinfectant that was on the wall above his bed. Giving it a shake, she carefully placed it under his tongue as she checked his pulse.

Polly watched anxiously as Mary checked the thermometer and noted down her findings on his chart. Her friend was giving nothing away in her expression. 'He hasn't got an infection, has he?' she asked fearfully.

'I don't think so, but I'll need to get the duty doctor to come and give him the once-over.' She shot Polly a warm smile. 'Don't worry, Polly, I'm sure it's nothing serious.'

Polly remained at Adam's bedside, holding his hand, talking to him in murmurs as he lay with his eyes closed. She could tell he was in pain, and she felt utterly helpless. Why didn't the doctor hurry up?

It was almost the end of visiting time when Dr Matthews appeared. He was an elderly man with a bald head and a neat grey beard, but his gaze was kindly, his expression thoughtful as he introduced himself to Polly, read the notes and examined Adam. Polly knew from Mary that he'd come out of retirement to help out for the duration of the war, but she wondered if his experiences of being a country GP would be enough to help Adam.

'I will give you a slightly higher dose of the morphine for now,' he murmured to Adam. 'If you still have that pain in the morning, I'll get Mr Fortescue to come and have a look at you.' He patted Adam's shoulder and turned to Polly. 'I think we should leave him to rest for now,' he

278

murmured. 'I'm sure he'll be fine, and I'll keep an eye on him, don't you worry.'

Polly thanked him and watched him go into a huddle with Mary. The main fear she'd had since coming here was that Adam would get some sort of infection – and the heightened temperature was an ominous sign that this might now be the case. She turned back to him and kissed his cheek again. 'I have to go on my shift, my darling, but I promise I'll come back later. Try and sleep, Adam.'

He opened his eyes a slit and quickly closed them again. 'Don't worry, Pol. It's only a head-ache,' he murmured.

Polly tucked his hand beneath the blankets and turned away. 'I'll be on Women's Surgical if you need me,' she said to Mary 'Can I come down during my break?'

'Of course you can,' she replied. 'Just don't let Matron catch you, or we'll both be for it.' Polly was about to leave when Mary caught her arm. 'And don't overdo it, Polly,' she warned softly. 'Adam needs you, and you'll be of no use to him if you make yourself ill.'

She nodded and fled the ward, her feet pound-ing the marble as she ran up the uncarpeted stairs to the next floor. She would not cry. She would not panic. She would concentrate on the job she loved, see Adam later, and hopefully fall asleep the moment her head hit the pillow the following morning.

The all-clear had just sounded and Peggy and Mrs Finch had returned to the house, disgruntled

279

at having been disturbed yet again. The sirens had gone off shortly after seven, and again at nine – just as the BBC news was about to come on the wireless. There had been one or two explosions as the enemy planes tipped their remaining bombs over Cliffehaven, but they had been distant enough not to rattle the remaining glass in the windows.

It was almost ten o'clock, and both of them were sipping their cocoa in preparation for bed when someone rapped the knocker on the front door. Peggy looked at Mrs Finch with wide eyes. 'Oh God,' she breathed. 'What now?'

'Do you want me to go and see who it is? It can't be the welfare people,' Mrs Finch soothed, 'it's far too late at night.'

Peggy stilled her with a hand on her arm. 'It was late last night,' she murmured. 'I'll go.' She went into the hall and turned off the light before opening the door. That little Hitler, Wally the Warden, had already banged on the door complaining of light seeping through a gap in the hardboard over the dining room window, and she didn't fancy a repeat performance.

'Mr Witherspoon,' she gasped as she took in the tall, well-dressed figure standing on her doorstep with a gold-topped walking cane. 'Whatever's happened?'

He doffed his hat and gave her a short bow. 'I'm sorry to disturb you, Mrs Reilly,' he said smoothly. 'I know it's late, but I was hoping to have a word with Cecily.'

Peggy frowned. 'But Cissy's at the theatre,' she said, a dart of apprehension making her go cold.

'Cecily is not at the theatre, Mrs Reilly. I assumed she was here at home resting her ankle.'

Out of habit, Peggy opened the door wide and ushered him into her hall before turning the light back on. 'But I haven't seen her since she left for rehearsals this morning,' she said in bewilderment.

Witherspoon peeled off his leather gloves and dropped them in his hat which he placed on the hall table next to the telephone. Leaning with both hands on the gold-topped cane, he regarded Peggy sorrowfully. 'She did indeed come to rehearsals this morning, and the poor girl was clearly suffering. I had a quiet word with her afterwards, and when she didn't show up this evening, I supposed she'd taken my advice and come home.'

Peggy was flustered and embarrassed. 'I don't know where she is,' she confessed. 'I'm so sorry, Mr Witherspoon. It's very unprofessional of her to let you down after all you've done for her.'

'My dear Mrs Reilly, my own feelings are unimportant. It is Cecily who is my concern, for I had my suspicions, and it seems that she has been deceiving us all.'

'What do you mean?'

'I believe she has gone off in the company of a young Sergeant Joe Buchanan – an Australian,' he added with a sneer. 'Thereby letting not only herself down, but the rest of the cast.'

'She's gone off with Joe?' Peggy stared at him in surprise. 'But how do you know this? What made you suspect such a thing?'

'I had the dubious pleasure of meeting him this lunchtime when he was hanging about the

281

theatre.' He leant forward, his tone confidential. 'I try to protect all my girls from these young men – I understand all too well what the temptations are, and of course I always take special care of Cissy and Amy and the other two younger ones. I like to think of myself as a father figure – a mentor and protector. In short, they are like my daughters, Mrs Reilly.'

'I'm sure she won't come to any harm with Joe,' Peggy murmured. 'Cissy might be naïve at times but she's not stupid, and Joe is an extremely nice young man.'

'Of course she's not stupid,' he soothed, 'but in these troubled times we all do things we might live to regret.' He turned to pick up his hat and gloves. 'If I may, I will visit you again tomorrow morning to make sure she is all right,' he said, his voice silky and reassuring.

Peggy watched, mesmerised, as he smoothed the moustache over his top lip and smiled before carefully putting his hat on. He was such a handsome, urbane man. His wife was a lucky woman.

'Again, I apologise for my late intrusion, and I'm sure you're right. Cecily has merely had her head turned by the Australian and will no doubt see the error of her ways in the morning.'

Peggy opened the front door, her thoughts in a whirl. He was such a nice man, and so thoughtful to come all this way at this hour. She'd have a word or two with Cissy, and no mistake. Fancy letting everyone down like that – and running off with Joe to God knew where when she knew he was June's young man.

Jack Witherspoon crossed the threshold and ran

down the steps. Doffing his hat, he gave another short bow. 'I'll bid you goodnight, Mrs Reilly.'

Peggy could hear his footsteps and the tap of his cane in the stillness as he hurried out of sight. She stood on the doorstep long after he'd gone, her thoughts troubled, her anger rising. Cissy was old enough to know better, she thought crossly, and when she eventually got home, she would most certainly get the sharp edge of her tongue.

'Put that light out this instant!' Wally the Warden shouted from the street corner. 'This is the second time I've had to warn you, Mrs Reilly.'

'Oh, go and boil your head,' yelled back Peggy before she slammed the door behind her.

Chapter Fourteen

The blush of dawn was colouring the sky as Cissy and Joe ambled arm in arm towards Beach View. His uniform jacket was too big for her, but it was warm against the chill of the early hour and the scent of him was in the cloth.

Cissy didn't want their time together to end, but within a few hours he would be heading for the ship which would take him back into battle. A cold dread squeezed her heart as she thought of the dangers he would have to face, and the possibility that he might be hurt again – or worse, that he might get killed.

Joe came to a halt at the end of Beach View Terrace, opened his long coat and drew her into his embrace. 'I wish I didn't have to say goodbye, Cissy,' he murmured. 'Don't forget me, will you?'

She rested her cheek against his warm chest and listened to the steady beat of his heart through his shirt. 'Of course I won't,' she sighed. 'Tonight has been the most marvellous night, despite the raids and that warden chasing us down the street.' She looked up at him, smiling through the unshed tears. 'He was awfully cross we didn't want to go in his horrid old shelter, wasn't he?'

Joe's smile was soft and filled with regret. 'Too right he was, but we found a much better place at the Grand Hotel, didn't we?'

'It was certainly far more salubrious,' she agreed with a lightness she didn't feel. She gave a deep sigh. 'It was a wonderful night, Joe. I'll always remember it.'

'For me too,' he murmured, and softly kissed her. 'I wish I didn't have to go, Cissy,' he whispered against her lips. 'But I'll come back, I promise.'

'I'll hold you to that,' she replied, her arms tightening around his waist. 'Please make it very soon, Joe.'

He held her within the confines of his coat, his arms wrapped round her, his chin resting on her head. 'The army's in charge of my life now,' he murmured. 'I could be gone for a long time. Will you write to me, Cissy? Letters mean so much, especially when they're from someone special.'

She arched her neck and looked up at him, her pulse racing. 'Am I special, Joe?' she whispered.

'Oh, yes,' he sighed, capturing her lips in a long, intense, sweet kiss.

She clung to him, giving herself up to the delicious sensations he was arousing, and when he gently drew away from her, she felt as if she'd been set adrift like a small boat on an isolated sea. 'Do you have to go now? Can't we have just a few minutes more?'

He shook his head sorrowfully. 'I'll have to run all the way back to the barracks as it is. Goodnight, Cissy. Keep smiling that lovely smile and send me a photograph as soon as you can. I'll write with the address once I know what it is. I promise.'

Cissy took off his heavy uniform jacket and handed it to him, her skin goosing with the cold. She wanted to say she loved him, that she would wait for him – that he would be in her thoughts every moment until he came back. But she remained silent, knowing it was too soon, and that she would simply appear naïve and foolish after spending only a few hours with him.

'Take care, Joe,' she murmured. 'Stay safe, and write soon.'

He nodded, his eyes suspiciously bright as he tugged at the brim of his hat, turned swiftly away and began to run back down the road.

Cissy stood in the pearly stillness of dawn and watched until he was out of sight, then she burst into tears and fled for home.

The house was silent, and Cissy tiptoed through the door and carefully closed it behind her.

'What time do you call this?' Peggy emerged from the kitchen, her expression thunderous.

Cissy's heart jumped a beat. 'You scared me half to death, Mum,' she protested.

'And you've been out all night with Joe Buchanan,' Peggy replied coldly. 'What do you have to say for yourself?'

'I haven't done anything wrong,' Cissy retorted, her chin lifting defiantly. 'Joe and I just walked and talked and sat in a pub for a bit. Then we had supper in town and spent several hours sitting in an air-raid shelter.'

'It is five-thirty in the morning,' said Peggy, her dark eyes boring into her. 'The last raid was several hours ago. Where have you been since then?'

Despite the fact she and Joe had gone no further than sharing a few delicious kisses, Cissy reddened under her mother's accusing glare. 'We were in the lounge at the Grand Hotel for a bit, and then we went for another walk.'

She met Peggy's angry glare and refused to be cowed by it. 'We didn't do anything wrong, Mum,' she said flatly. 'Joe was the perfect gentleman.'

'Do you realise what sort of reputation you'll get by staying out all night with a man?' Peggy was clearly still furious.

'It won't happen again,' Cissy replied. 'Joe's being shipped out today.' The tears were falling again, and she wiped them away before hugging her waist. 'We just wanted to spend some time together, to get to know one another, that's all. There's a war on, Mum, and after what happened to Polly, I intend to make the most of every minute I might have left. I can't see why you're so cross.'

'I'm not cross, Cissy. I'm livid. What do you think your father will say when he finds out? And he will, Cissy, I can assure you of that.'

Cissy stared back at her mother through her

tears. 'I'm almost nineteen,' she stammered. 'I'm old enough to do what I want.'

'You're certainly old enough to know better,' Peggy snapped. 'How could you be so stupid? Don't you realise I've been up all night waiting for you? I was out of my mind with worry.'

'I'm sorry, Mum,' she whispered. 'But please try and understand. We only had the chance of a few hours together. We did no harm.'

'Really?' Peggy folded her arms. 'And what about June? Did you think of her? Or of how your actions have let everyone down at the theatre? Mr Witherspoon was terribly upset that you didn't bother to turn up for tonight's show. And I think you've behaved disgracefully considering how much that man has done for you.'

The chill went deeper as Cissy stared at her mother. 'Witherspoon was here?' she breathed.

'Indeed he was, and it was shaming to have to confess that I had no idea where you were. He'd guessed you'd gone off with Joe, you know, and I suspect you've gone right down in his estimation because of it. That man really cares about you and the other girls, and look how you've repaid him.'

It was on the tip of Cissy's tongue to tell her mother how wrong she was about Witherspoon, but it was clear she would not believe her – would see any kind of blackening of his character as merely a bit of spite to justify her actions. At least there had been no mention of photographs.

'I'll speak to him later today,' she mumbled instead.

'See that you do,' Peggy snapped. She turned

on her heel and disappeared into her bedroom, the door closing firmly behind her.

Cissy trudged up the two flights of stairs to her own bedroom. The evening had been spoiled, and all she wanted to do now was try and regain the essence of it in the peace and quiet of her bed. She opened the door and froze.

June rose from the chair, her face stiff with anger. 'What have you got to say for yourself?' she said flatly.

'Nothing,' said Cissy. 'Get out of my room, June.'

'I'm not going anywhere until you tell me why you thought it was right for you to steal my fellow.'

'You don't own him,' Cissy retorted, 'and if he didn't want to be with me, then I couldn't have stolen him.'

'Joe was happy with me until you turned on the little girl act,' snapped June. 'You were making a play for him the moment you clapped eyes on him, and you had no right to do that.'

'I'm sorry,' said Cissy wearily, 'but Joe's old enough to make up his own mind. He came to the theatre this morning and asked me to spend the day with him. What was I supposed to do?'

'If you were the decent sort of girl you pretend to be, you'd have said no, and reminded him he already had a girl,' snarled June, as she advanced on Cissy. 'Instead of that, you spent the night with him.'

'Not like that, I didn't,' she protested.

'Really?' June's tone was cold and flat with sarcasm, her gaze trawling over Cissy, making her skin crawl. 'It's clear what sort of girl you *really* are, Cecily Reilly, and men will always be men. I pity your poor mother. She must be so ashamed to have such a *tart* for a daughter.'

The slap of Cissy's hand on June's cheek shocked them both.

But June's reaction was swift, and she hit Cissy with such force it made her stumble. 'You *bitch*,' she snarled, making a grab for Cissy's hair. 'I'll have you for that.'

Cissy dodged her grasping fingers and gave her a shove which sent her stumbling across the room. 'Call me that again and I'll punch you,' she panted. 'It's not my fault Joe finds me more attractive than you, so get over it.'

With a howl of rage, June threw herself at Cissy and managed to grab a fistful of her hair. Cissy yelped at the pain, but managed to get two good blows to June's head as they staggered back and forth, wrestling in almost silent fury.

'Stop it. Now.'

Cissy felt a strong arm round her waist and the air was knocked out of her as she was flung across the room. She lay dazed on the floor by the bed as Danuta wrestled a furious June into a corner and held her there.

'Enough, June,' hissed Danuta. 'You will have whole house awake.'

'That bitch stole my man,' yelled June.

'I did not,' yelled back Cissy as she got to her feet and prepared to hit her again.

'What is going on up here?' Peggy stood in the doorway, taking in the scene with one furious glance. 'Danuta, thank you, but I will deal with this.' She turned her angry gaze on June. 'Go back to your room at once,' she ordered.

June threw a venomous glare towards Cissy. 'Sorry, Mrs Reilly,' she muttered. 'But I couldn't just let her...'

'Out,' ordered Peggy.

June pushed past her, and with a sob of distress, ran to her room.

Peggy glared at Cissy who was still trying to get her breath back. 'Pull yourself together, Cecily, and stop making such a show. This is a house of mourning – not a bear garden.'

Cissy knew she was in deep trouble, her mother never called her Cecily unless she was really angry. 'It wasn't my fault,' she muttered.

'It never is, is it?' Peggy turned in the doorway to find Danuta, Fran and Suzy watching from the landing. 'Go back to your rooms,' she commanded. 'There's nothing more to see. I will not have this sort of behaviour in my home – and you can tell June I want to see her downstairs tonight on the dot of six.' She turned back to Cissy. 'That goes for you too.'

Cissy sank on to her bed as her mother shut the door. She was shaking with anger and humiliation, and her head hurt where June had tried to yank out a fistful of her hair. It just wasn't fair, she thought as she collapsed into the pillow and burst into tears. She'd done nothing wrong, and it really wasn't her fault that Joe preferred her company to June's. And as for calling her a tart, that had been going too far. Of course she'd had to defend her reputation.

'Oh, Joe,' she sobbed. 'You have no idea how

much trouble you've caused, but it was worth it – it really was.'

Polly had had a busy night on the ward with two emergencies coming in after their operations, and all the palaver of getting everyone down to the shelter and back again because of the two air raids.

She had kept the dark thoughts at bay for most of the time, but when the grief came over her in great engulfing waves, she'd had to battle to overcome them and sought temporary sanctuary in the sluice until she had herself under control again. It hadn't been easy to keep focussed, but Sister had been kindness itself; never remarking on her short absences, never asking awkward questions or telling her to go home. She seemed to understand that Polly desperately needed to be kept occupied, and found endless tasks for her to do during the lulls between air raids.

There had been no sign of Matron, which was most unusual, and Polly had managed to slip down to see Adam during her meal break. He was asleep, and Mary had assured her that his temperature was almost normal again, and that the extra medication was helping with the headache.

She had taken another peek at him a few minutes ago, and there was no change, so she'd begun the short walk home in the soft light of a new dawn in the hope that she would find rest for her weary body, and that her exhaustion would banish the awful images that were churning in her mind.

She let herself into the house and quietly went

upstairs. It was barely six o'clock, and yet Danuta was already dressed for work. 'You must have an early start today,' she murmured, as she dragged off the heavy cape and kicked off her shoes.

'My shift begins at eleven, and I was not planning to be awake so early,' replied Danuta, 'but the noise from upstairs disturbed me.'

Polly took off her cap and shook out her hair. 'I suppose they all came in late because those Australian boys are leaving today,' she said through a vast yawn.

'There was a fight,' said Danuta, and grinned at Polly's shocked expression. 'Cissy came home about an hour ago having spent the night with Joe. She and June were snarling like cats and lashing out, making the terrible noise to wake all of us. I put a stop to it, but Peggy was very angry, I think.'

'Oh dear. I had a feeling there would be trouble in that quarter. Who won the fight?'

'Peggy.' Danuta giggled. 'She is very English, not raising her voice, but commanding all the same. She is tough lady, and I am thinking June and Cissy will hear more from her today.'

Polly grabbed her washbag and nightdress. 'Let's hope Joe proves to be worth all the trouble,' she sighed. She gave Danuta a weary smile. 'I'll just have a wash and then I'm for bed. It's been a long night, and I'm hoping I'll manage to sleep right through until teatime.'

'I can give you something to help you sleep,' said Danuta, bringing out the little bottle. 'Two drops of this in some water and you can rest with no dreams.'

'Thank you,' Polly said softly, reaching for the bottle. 'I might need some help for the next few days.'

Danuta eyed her thoughtfully as she handed it over. 'It is strong, so be careful,' she warned, 'and don't come to depend upon it too much. It can form a habit.'

'I'll only need it for a little while,' murmured Polly. She didn't bother to read the label, for she didn't care what it was if it fulfilled its purpose and stopped the dreams. She dropped the little bottle into her dressing gown pocket. 'Thanks, Danuta. I'll be careful, I promise.'

Danuta was gone by the time she returned from the bathroom, and Polly carefully used the dropper to add the clear medication into the glass of water. Drinking it down, she grimaced at the bitter taste and then climbed into bed.

With a concerted effort, she forced her aching body to relax. She lay in the darkness staring into its void, seeing the faces of her loved ones drift before her, hearing them call to her, their cries becoming more distant as the darkness enfolded her and crept right inside her, banishing all thought and softening the pain.

Polly's eyelids fluttered and she yielded willingly.

Peggy was feeling frazzled and at the end of her tether. It had been a long, disturbed and worrying night, and she really didn't feel up to dealing with anything much today after all the shenanigans that had been going on.

However, she'd come to the conclusion that it would be best if Jim wasn't told about Cissy's dawn homecoming and the fight that had ensued. He would probably start shouting and playing the heavy-handed father, and would no doubt blame her for Cissy's behaviour, which would do no good at all. She was better left to deal with this minor crisis on her own.

She gave a deep sigh as she cleared Danuta's dishes from the table and prepared her own breakfast in the deserted kitchen. She might have known there would be trouble with so many young girls in the house, and all those service boys wandering about the town looking for company. But she was mortified that her own daughter should cheapen herself that way – thank goodness Mrs Finch had slept through it all – and she was determined to give her and the others a stern talking to.

As she made the tea and toast, she wondered how Polly had managed to get through her night shift and if she'd been able to see Adam – and if so, was he yet well enough to share Polly's insufferable burden?

Peggy shivered and wrapped her cardigan more firmly about her. She could only imagine what the girl must be going through, but the thought of losing her own boys was enough to make her want to weep – how much worse it must be for Polly who'd lost all her family, and had a desperately sick husband to worry about.

Peggy placed her breakfast on the table and sat down, her thoughts drifting as the tea cooled and the toast turned to rubber.

Kate Jackson had telephoned from the welfare office the day before, asking after Polly. Peggy had

had questions of her own, and on learning that the *Benares* had been sunk a week earlier, had furiously challenged her about the delay in telling everyone. Kate had explained that many of the dead children's families came from London and Liverpool, which had been devastated by bombs. A good number of the parents had been rehoused or evacuated to safer areas, and they'd been difficult to track down. Churchill had made it clear that every last one of them must be informed before the story was released to the public.

Peggy gave a prolonged sigh. In the scheme of things, she decided, Cissy's behaviour and the earlier events were paltry matters easily dealt with, and she counted her blessings yet again, aware that she had so many things to be grateful for.

Ron came home with Harvey a short while later. He looked washed out and every one of his sixty-odd years, and even Harvey had a hangdog look about him. Refusing her offer of breakfast, Ron trudged down to the basement bedroom with Harvey at his heels, and within minutes they were both snoring.

Jim came in just as she'd finished her unappetising breakfast, and she quickly fried him a bit of spam to go with the freshly laid egg. Putting a slice of bread and marge on the side of the plate, she noted how tired and drawn he looked after his night of fire-watching.

'Would you listen to the auld fella?' said Jim with a weary smile. 'Sure and his snoring's enough to wake the dead so it is.'

'He's worn out,' muttered Peggy. 'How was it out there tonight?'

'Not so bad,' Jim replied as he tucked into his meal. 'There were a couple of fires over the other side of town, but the brigade got there quickly so there wasn't much damage, and no real casualties to speak of. Most of the tip and runs were over the Channel.'

'The fires weren't near Doris, were they?' Peggy had horrible visions of her elder sister arriving with her suitcases and demanding to stay. She would be welcomed, of course, but Peggy shuddered at the thought, and suspected such a visitation would lead to some terrible rows.

Jim grinned. 'To be sure, the Germans wouldn't dare bomb the very grand and important Doris,' he said, mopping up the last of the egg with the bread. 'Don't worry, Peg, she'll not be moving in yet – and besides, we've no room, unless she wants to share with Da.'

They both chuckled at the thought. Doris and Ron disliked each other intensely and made no secret of it.

Peggy smoked a cigarette as Jim poured a second cup of tea. Unlike her warm relationship with her younger sister, Doreen, she and Doris had always been prickly with one another. They were like chalk and cheese, and she still found it strange that they could be sisters at all. They had nothing in common but their parentage, and Doris had long made it clear that she considered Peggy and her brood to be several strata below her own perceived social standing.

Doris was married to Ted, who was the manager of the Home and Colonial store in the High Street, and who was probably the most boring, pompous man in Britain. They had a son who was 'something important' in the Foreign Office, and lived in a detached house in Havelock Gardens. This salubrious address was on the other side of town and considered by the residents to be a cut above everywhere else. It was certainly very pleasant with its leafy avenues and pretentious houses hiding behind high walls and fancy gates, but Peggy wouldn't have given tuppence for it.

Doris was a snob, and Peggy dreaded the first Sunday in every month when she came for afternoon tea. Why this had become a ritual had never been explained, for it was a rare occasion to be asked to tea at Doris's – and this happened only when there was some new piece of furniture or addition to the house to be admired.

Peggy sighed. Doris seemed to have forgotten that she'd been born and raised in this boarding house, by parents who'd worked hard to give their three daughters the best start in life they could afford. She took great delight in showing off her smart clothes, hats and jewellery, and couldn't help making snide remarks about how she thought Peggy had married beneath her, and consequently lived in a slum. It wound Peggy up no end, and after each visit she would fume for hours.

'I'm for me bed,' said Jim. 'Wake me before four, darlin'. I'm due at the cinema tonight.'

'Jim, you can't keep up these long hours with hardly any sleep,' she protested.

'There's a war on, Peggy, and this is the only way I know how to do my bit. Dad will tell you the same and, God love him, he's an old man, but he's getting as little sleep as I am.'

Peggy returned his kiss and watched him slowly make his way to their bedroom. They were all tired, she acknowledged, but if this war was to be won, then it was worth a few sleepless nights, surely?

Cissy had only slept for four hours, but it had been deep and refreshing, and when she woke she was very hungry. About to climb out of bed, she heard the other girls leaving for the hospital and snuggled deeper beneath the blankets, listening sourly to their bright chatter as they ran down the stairs. She would wait until she was sure they'd left the house before going down for her own breakfast, she decided, for she didn't want to run into June again, and certainly couldn't face her mother.

Her stomach rumbled and she tried to ignore it as she turned over in bed and listened to the noises within the house and the mournful cries of the seagulls. Joe would be on board his troop ship now, and probably already at sea. Was he thinking of her? Would he really write or had she simply been a pleasant diversion for his last night?

She closed her eyes, remembering the way he'd kissed her, and the look in his eyes when he'd said goodbye, and decided that if he hadn't been as smitten as she, then he was a very good actor.

Cissy smiled as she let her mind wander through the images he'd given her of his home. Wallaby Creek sounded a lonely place – far from the nearest neighbour and surrounded by miles of cinnamon earth and dusty, pale trees – but because it meant so much to Joe, she wished she could go there and see it for herself.

She set aside the small inconveniences of not knowing one end of a horse from another and that she got a nasty rash if it was too hot. All she could imagine was the two of them riding through those sunlit pastures before returning to the homestead to sit on that verandah and listen to the white cockatoos as they watched the sun go down over the distant mountains.

A tap on the door snapped her out of this daydream and she sat up, clutching the bedclothes. 'Who is it?' she asked warily.

'It's me.' The door opened and Amy stepped into the room. Her expression did not augur well.

Cissy swallowed and looked guiltily at her friend. 'I'm sorry,' she said hastily, noting the furious glint in her eyes. 'I know I promised to see you after the show, but I...'

'You were out with your Australian and forgot,' Amy finished for her. She sat down on the end of the bed and wriggled out of her jacket, tossing her long hair back from her face. 'I don't know what's got into you lately, Cissy, but I don't appreciate the way you seem to have forgotten we're supposed to be best friends.'

'I've never forgotten that,' gasped Cissy. 'It's just that things have been happening, and I needed to think about them on my own.'

There was a softening in Amy's expression, but her demeanour was still unyielding. 'What things?'

Cissy licked her lips and reached for her dressing gown. It was cold in the bedroom, and the thought of telling Amy her secret was making her shiver.

'I've decided I don't want to be in the troupe any more,' she prevaricated.

Amy's blue eyes widened. 'But dancing is all you've ever wanted – all either of us wanted.'

'It was a little girl's dream,' said Cissy, 'and I'm not a little girl any more.' She drew the dressing gown closer, garnering some warmth and comfort from its familiarity. 'Let's face it, Amy, we've been in the back row of the chorus in every show we've ever done, and I can't see that changing. Can you?'

Amy clasped her hands in her lap and stared down at them for a long time. 'It might,' she murmured. Then she sighed deeply and looked back at Cissy. 'This isn't about the back row of the chorus, is it? This is to do with Jack Witherspoon.'

Unable to speak, Cissy nodded and Amy reached for her hand. 'He's not married, you know. He only wears that ring for effect. It makes our parents think he's respectable – but he's not, is he?'

Cissy shook her head, the tears pricking. 'I've been such a fool, Amy. I believed everything he said – and then ... and then he asked me to ... to...'

'Pose for that creepy photographer.'

Cissy stared at her friend in shock. 'How did you know about him?'

'I fell for the same line, and although I didn't want to do it, Witherspoon was very persuasive with his talk of agents and theatre managers. I really thought that if I could get through that awful session it would lead to something special. But I couldn't go through with it.'

Amy shuddered. 'That awful man was like some horrid reptile, pawing over me, tugging at my clothes, and I could swear that Witherspoon was watching every move somehow. He has spyholes all over the theatre, you know – that's why we always make sure we hang our coats on the back of the dressing-room door.'

Cissy was so shocked she could barely speak. 'He spies on us?' she managed.

Amy nodded. 'I thought you knew.' She forgot to be angry and took Cissy's hand. 'Poor Cissy,' she murmured. 'You can be awfully naïve at times.'

Cissy didn't really appreciate the honesty, but as Amy was her best friend she had to take it. She decided to get back to Amy's nasty interlude with the photographer. 'When did this photo session happen? Why didn't you tell me?'

Amy shrugged. 'It was weeks ago. I didn't tell you because I was ashamed at how stupid I'd been to let Witherspoon manipulate me into such a situation.' She gave a ghost of a smile. 'You didn't tell me either – probably for the same reason.'

'Yes,' Cissy admitted. Then she had an awful thought. 'You didn't strip right off, did you?'

Amy went scarlet. 'I took my top off, but when that old lizard tried to unzip my skirt I socked him in the eye and made a run for it.'

'I ran for it too,' admitted Cissy with a relieved chuckle. She gripped her friend's hand. 'Oh, Amy, how awful that this has been preying on your mind for so long and you couldn't tell me. I'm sorry I've been such a poor friend – I should have seen that you were worried about something.'

'We're both to blame, and it's a huge relief to talk about it finally,' Amy admitted softly. 'But Witherspoon's the real villain. He gave each of us a secret we were too ashamed to share even with our best friends, and then held it over all of us so we didn't dare try and break our contracts.'

'You mean he's done it to some of the other girls?' At Amy's nod, Cissy covered her mouth with her hand and gasped. 'But how did you find out?'

'I caught Judith in floods of tears the other day, and eventually managed to get the truth out of her. She and Florence have gone through the same experience as us – and being so young, they were bullied into actually stripping right off.'

'Then we must do something about it,' said an outraged Cissy. 'Judith is only sixteen. He can't be allowed to get away with this.'

'We can do nothing unless we get hold of those photographs and negatives,' said Amy solemnly. 'All the while he's got those, he's got us. And then there are our contracts. I bet he threatened to tell your parents if you tried to break yours?'

Cissy nodded. 'He frightened me yesterday morning,' she confessed. 'He said I was bought and paid for and that from now on I must do as he says, or he'll have a long talk with Mum and Dad.'

'I've thought long and hard about that, and have come to the conclusion he probably won't,' said Amy thoughtfully. 'You see, if he tells our parents what we've done, the finger of blame will fall directly on him, and he'll be exposed for what he really is. I know my dad would get the police on to him straight away, and I suspect yours would too – after they'd given him a good pasting.'

Amy dug in her bag for a cigarette and offered one to Cissy, who took it though she rarely smoked. Once they were lit, Amy went to stand by the window which looked out over the garden to the terrace of houses at the back. 'He likes young girls, Cissy, and he's not above blackmailing us into doing what he wants.' She shuddered. 'I've managed to avoid being in his office again so far – but the time will come when...'

'If we get together with the other girls and refuse to be bullied, surely he'd have to leave us alone?'

Amy smoked in silence for a long moment, her gaze on some distant spot. 'It's worth a try, but I don't know that he would,' she murmured some time later. 'And by standing up to him, we'll give him the chance to cover his tracks.'

'You mean he'll destroy those photographs? But surely that would be to our advantage?'

Amy turned back from the window, her expression grim. 'I don't think he'll destroy them – they cost him money, and there's always an eager market for smutty pictures. He'll just move them out of that safe in his office, and then we won't ever have the chance of getting those negatives back.'

Cissy coughed and stubbed out her cigarette before opening the window to get rid of the smell. Mum didn't like smoking in the bedrooms, and Cissy didn't fancy pushing her patience any further today. 'Then what do we do, Amy? How can we ever escape him?'

Amy puffed smoke and then impatiently stabbed the cigarette out in the small ashtray by Cissy's bed. 'We have to get hold of those negatives. The only problem is, he never opens that safe when anyone's in the office, so none of us knows the combination.'

Cissy sat deep in thought as Amy restlessly paced the bedroom. 'We need to get Judy and Flo in on this,' she murmured. 'With four of us working on the problem, someone will surely come up with a good idea.'

Amy nodded and became businesslike. 'Get up, Cissy. We're not due at the theatre for two hours, and this is the perfect time to catch Judy and Flo before they leave their billet. We have to move quickly on this, because none of us can avoid him for much longer.'

As Cissy hurried to dress and Amy experimented with the lipsticks on Cissy's dressing table, neither of them were aware that their entire conversation had been overheard, and that someone was already formulating a plan.

Chapter Fifteen

That Thursday the WVS reception centre was noisy as usual with lots of people all talking at once as babies cried, small children, too young to be evacuated, ran round the room, and a wireless played lively music in the background.

Peggy had been on her feet all afternoon and

was looking forward to getting home, despite the fact that the atmosphere between Cissy and June was still frosty, even though almost four days had passed since she'd given them both a good talking to.

As she rummaged through the mounds of donated clothing people had so generously left at the centre, and tried to stack them into neat piles, she let her thoughts drift. Cissy's behaviour was worrying, and she wondered if perhaps she should have told Jim after all about her staying out all night with Joe – a loud harangue from her father might bring her up short. She didn't want the girl running wild and getting herself a bad reputation – and it seemed that nothing she said could bring her to her senses.

Peggy sighed as she set aside a couple of winceyette nightdresses and a tweed skirt. Cissy and Amy had run out of the house that Monday morning before she could stop them, and she'd had the embarrassing task of having to face Mr Witherspoon, yet again, to apologise for her daughter's absence. The poor man had looked so concerned that Cissy's behaviour might infect Amy, and Peggy sympathised with him. It must be a terrible worry not to be able to rely on his dancers when he was preparing to take the troupe back on the road in three days' time.

She continued to fold and tidy, her thoughts whirling. Cissy's bad behaviour was not her only concern. Poor little Polly was struggling to contain her grief and had flatly refused to take time off from her hospital duties. Peggy could understand that she needed to be busy and wanted to spend as much time as she could with her sick husband, but she was worried at how quiet and pale she'd become – and how little she was eating.

The girl would leave the house at five-thirty every evening and return at dawn the next morning, washed out, and so weary she could barely climb the stairs to her room. No one could carry on like that for long, and Peggy feared she was heading for a nervous breakdown if something wasn't done quickly.

She'd had a long discussion with Danuta, and they'd agreed Polly must be carefully watched over the next few weeks; but Peggy had privately come to the conclusion that it might be a good idea for her to go and have a confidential word with that Matron Billings. Perhaps she could persuade Polly to cut down her hours and start taking care of herself?

As the clock struck five, Peggy determinedly put all her worries aside and prepared to leave. She picked up the two nightdresses and the skirt which would do for Danuta once they'd been washed and ironed, and began to fold them into her basket. The weather was changing rapidly, the breath of autumn lacing the chill wind and rain that blew in from the sea, and Peggy didn't like to think of the girl getting cold at night in her threadbare liberty bodices and knickers which threatened to fall apart with every wash.

She was busy tucking the clothes away in her basket when the door opened and a gust of wind brought in a flurry of autumn leaves and her sister Doris. Peggy quickly grabbed her coat, wondering if she could avoid her sister by going out the back way. But as Doris's imperious gaze settled upon her, Peggy knew there could be no escape.

She watched her sister's stately navigation around the many tables and clothes rails, and was forced to acknowledge that Doris never let the side down by looking less than immaculately turned out. Today she was wearing a tweed suit with a mink collar, silk blouse and felt hat, her feet shod, as usual, in expensive high-heeled shoes which matched her brown leather handbag and gloves. Her make-up looked freshly applied, and it appeared she'd just come from the hairdresser.

Peggy couldn't remember the last time she'd worn make-up, or had a shampoo and set, and was all too aware of what a fright she must look in her faded cotton dress, wrap-round pinny, headscarf and hand-knitted cardigan.

'Hello, Doris,' she said, as she slipped on her coat and stuffed the second nightdress into her basket. 'What's brought you down here?'

Doris peeled off her gloves to reveal soft white hands and manicured nails. 'I don't know how you can bear working in here with all these ghastly people,' she said with a delicate dab of her lace-edged handkerchief against her nose as she eyed the rampaging children and down-at-heel adults. 'The smell of unwashed clothing is quite appalling.'

'You don't notice it after a while,' Peggy replied flatly, 'and the people we help aren't ghastly, they're down on their luck and deserve sympathy, not derision.'

Doris gave a delicate shudder and held her

handkerchief to her nose as if to combat any stray germs that might be flying about. Then her gaze fell on Peggy's basket. 'What are those doing in there?'

'They're for Danuta.' Peggy gripped the basket, afraid it might be snatched away.

'They were donated for the homeless of Cliffe-haven,' said Doris, 'not some foreign refugee who doesn't even belong here. Return them immediately.'

'Danuta has as much right to them as anyone else,' retorted Peggy 'She came from Poland with only the clothes on her back, and she can't go through winter without warm nightdresses and skirts.' Peggy took a deep breath in an effort to remain calm. 'And all the while she's living in my home she belongs here as much as you do.'

'Then she must use her clothing coupons like everyone else. Put them back, Margaret.'

Peggy bridled. Her sister was the only person who called her Margaret, and she only did it because she knew Peggy hated it. 'I will do no such thing,' she replied, and put the basket under the table and out of Doris's reach. 'Why are you here, Doris? This is hardly your usual neck of the woods.'

'Needs must in these troubled times. Being on the WVS committee means I have a duty to ensure that everything is running smoothly.'

Peggy followed her gaze as Doris looked round the large hall crammed with laden tables of clothing, kitchen equipment, shoes, toys and just about everything else, and wondered if her sister had the first idea of how much good was being done here – or if she really cared.

A team of women were helping others to find what they needed, and through the open doors of the even larger room next door could be glimpsed line upon line of camp beds where those who'd been bombed out could get meals and a bed until they were rehoused. There was a long queue of weary, defeated-looking people waiting outside the office to be seen by the housing and welfare administrators, and Peggy knew that the four women who ran those departments often felt as if they were under siege, for they had few resources, and it seemed the queues never got any shorter.

Doris adjusted her mink collar as her dark gaze returned to Peggy. 'One of my responsibilities is to ensure that no one is helping themselves to our donations in order to save on clothing coupons. I have to say, Margaret, that I'm shocked by your lack of moral fibre.'

Peggy flushed with anger. 'Lack of moral fibre?' she gasped. 'How *dare* you insinuate such a thing?'

'I dare because I'm in charge of this particular centre, and I do not expect my sister to flout the rules.'

'Lady Charlmondley's in charge, not you, and I have her permission,' said Peggy flatly. 'If you don't like it, then I suggest you take it up with her.'

Peggy got some small satisfaction from the way Doris suddenly didn't look quite so sure of herself. Lady Charlmondley – pronounced Chumley – was not only the Chairman of this local WVS, but a leading light in the heady echelons of what passed as Cliffehaven's high society. Doris had been angling to become a part of this inner circle for years – and now she was firmly ensconced on several of the doughty Lady's committees, she made full use of this tenuous contact to lord it over her less-favoured friends and relations.

'I don't think that will be necessary,' Doris replied stiffly. 'Lady Aurelia is extremely busy organising the fund-raising ball at the Manor.' She raised a severely plucked eyebrow. 'Did I tell you she has asked me to help her this year?'

'Several times,' muttered Peggy, who was underwhelmed.

'It's quite a feather in my cap, even if I say so myself.' Doris was becoming animated. 'Edward and I have been invited to sit at the top table, you know, and it is going to be the highlight of Cliffehaven's social calendar.'

Peggy nodded, but her mind was on other things. 'How much are the tickets?' she asked, not really that interested.

'We aren't having anything so common as tickets,' retorted Doris. 'It is by invitation only. That way,' she said, lowering her voice confidentially, 'we can keep out the hoi polloi, and ensure the whole evening goes without a hitch.'

Peggy had always possessed a wicked streak when it came to Doris, and she couldn't resist tweaking her tail. 'I don't know if I have anything suitable to wear to such an event,' she said with a straight face, 'but I'm sure I could get Sally to make me something from those old curtains I had in the back bedroom – and Jim does have the tuxedo he wears when he's front of house at the

310

Odeon on their gala nights. It's a little worn in places, but I'm sure it'll brush up lovely.'

Doris couldn't hide her horror. 'My dear, I couldn't possibly put you to all that trouble,' she said hastily. 'I realised, of course, how difficult things are for you at the moment, which is why I thought it kinder not to embarrass you by adding you to the guest list.'

'Why should I be embarrassed?' Peggy was only just managing not to laugh.

'Well, dear,' Doris replied, glancing either side to make sure they weren't being overheard, 'there will be auctions, and one will be expected to donate rather a lot for the cause.' She cleared her throat, unable to look Peggy in the eye for once. 'I'm sure *you'd* be fine, but this is a very select gathering, and Jim isn't really cut out to mix with the gentry, is he? After all,' she added, 'he *is* Irish, and you know how noisy *they* can get when the alcohol is flowing.'

Peggy burst out laughing. She simply couldn't hold it in any more. 'You really are the most frightful snob, Doris,' she managed finally. 'Jim and I wouldn't want to go to your pretentious function even if you paid us. We're quite happy to do our bit in our own way, without making a song and dance about it.'

Doris was furious and her glittering gaze trawled over Peggy with disdain. 'Some of us take pride in bettering ourselves, Margaret,' she said coolly, 'but I can see that you are a lost cause. Not only have you married beneath you, but you seem to have lowered your standards in personal grooming as well. You look like a washerwoman in that frightful get-up!'

Peggy was still giggling as she shrugged. 'My clothes are practical for the job I do here,' she replied. 'You'd be surprised how dirty we get sorting through all these every day.' She held Doris's baleful glare, angry now at her sister's rudeness. 'At least I'm not all fur collar and no knickers like some,' she added with asperity.

There were high spots of colour on Doris's face that had nothing to do with her careful application of rouge. 'Don't be vulgar,' she snapped.

'Then don't come swarming in here like a duchess and start throwing your weight about.' Peggy fastened the buttons on her overcoat before retrieving the basket from under the laden table. 'You seem to forget,' she said crossly, 'that I've known you since you had a snotty nose and half-mast knickers, so your airs and graces don't wash with me.' She glared at Doris. 'Now, if there's nothing else you wish to discuss, Doris, then I'm off home to get Jim's tea.'

'It's supper, Margaret,' hissed Doris. 'Tea is something you drink at four o'clock.'

Peggy grinned at her. 'We have tea at all times of the day in my home,' she said calmly, 'but especially after we've eaten our tea. Bye.' She left the hall feeling quite light-headed. Doris's visit had cheered her up no end.

It was just past dawn on Friday morning when Polly felt the metal bowl slip through her soapy fingers. She watched it fall, as if in slow motion, unable to stop it plummeting to the floor.

With a loud clang, it hit the foot of the iron

bedstead, spilling warm water, a flannel and a bar of soap all over the freshly scrubbed linoleum. She stared at the spreading pool of suds, helpless and unable to think what to do about it.

'Staff Nurse Brown, clean that up at once.' Sister Collins bustled through the curtains Polly had pulled round the bed. 'I'm sorry about that, Mrs Green,' she said to the elderly patient. 'I'll get one of the other nurses to finish your bed-bath, and then you can have a nice little nap until breakfast.'

'I'm sorry, Sister,' muttered Polly, dangerously close to bursting into tears.

'That's your third accident on this shift, Staff Nurse,' muttered Sister Collins, 'and it simply isn't good enough. Now pull yourself together and clean up this mess before someone slips and breaks a leg.'

Polly picked up the bowl, flannel and soap, and hurried into the sluice to fetch a mop and bucket. She was dead on her feet. The night had been constantly disturbed by air raids, which meant that her shift had lengthened to twelve hours, and, as it had gone on and on, she'd become more clumsy and more tearful.

'Are you all right, Polly?' Nurse Frost had followed her in to prepare another bowl of water for Mrs Green's interrupted bed-bath.

She nodded even though she was far from being all right, and gave the other girl a weary smile before hurrying back to the ward. Once the floor was dry and clean, she returned everything to the sluice room, took a deep breath, and went back to face Sister.

'It's time you went home,' said Sister Collins. 'We can manage here until the other nurses come in.'

'I don't mind staying,' said Polly. 'And after all the raids last night, they could be a while yet.'

Sister Collins was middle-aged, with a sunny disposition and gentle manner, but this morning she was clearly as tired as everyone else and not prepared to argue. 'I don't want you to stay,' she said softly. 'You've not really been concentrating all night, and I don't want to have to worry about you as well as my patients.'

'It's been a long, busy shift,' Polly protested. 'I'll be fine after I've had a nap, I promise.'

'Staff Nurse Brown, would you come to my office, please?'

Polly turned to find Matron looming. Her mouth dried and her heart banged against her ribs. 'What's the matter?' she breathed. 'It's not Adam, is it?'

Matron's expression was implacable. 'In my office, Staff Nurse.'

Polly found that a strong hand was propelling her out of the ward, past the porters pushing breakfast trolleys, and nurses hurrying on or off duty, and through the usual orderly chaos of an early hospital morning to the relative sanctuary of Matron's austere office.

Matron closed the door and indicated that Polly should sit in the chair that had been placed on the other side of her desk.

Polly's heart was hammering so loudly she wondered that the other woman couldn't hear it. Perched on the edge of the chair, she looked at

314

her fearfully. 'Is it Adam?'

'His health is of some concern, yes,' said Matron with surprising gentleness, 'but Mr Fortescue assures me that the medication he is now on will cure the infection within the next couple of days. There is absolutely no reason for you to be overly worried, Staff Nurse. This is merely a minor set-back within the healing process, and your husband is still expected to make a full recovery.'

'I see.' Polly looked down at her hands, which were tightly gripped on her lap. 'But what if the infection doesn't clear? How can I be certain that I won't lose him too?' The tears dripped on to her hands and spotted the pristine starched apron.

'Oh, my dear,' sighed Matron. 'You have far too many burdens to bear without fearing the worst for your husband. He's in excellent hands, you know. And I wouldn't lie to you about his recovery.'

Polly stared at her through her tears. 'I didn't mean... I'm sorry, but...'

'I know.' Matron reached into her navy blue sleeve and pulled out a very white handkerchief which she offered to Polly. 'You're tired and grieving, and worrying about your husband. I've seen many things in my career, and yet I couldn't begin to understand what you must be going through.'

Matron's unexpected kindness and soft sympathy just made things worse, and Polly found she couldn't stop crying. She buried her face in Matron's handkerchief which smelled strongly of rose water, and released all the pent-up tears she'd been storing throughout the night.

She was aware of Matron leaving the room and heard her return a short while later, but still she couldn't stop the flow of tears. There was the rattle of china, the clink of a spoon, and the sweet aroma of cocoa drifting towards her.

'There's nothing like a cup of cocoa, is there?' said Matron calmly. 'I find it soothes better than anything else. Dry your eyes, dear, and take a sip. It's very good, and I've made sure there's plenty of sugar in it.'

Polly's tears finally ebbed, and she blew her nose and scrubbed her face with her hands. Her eyes felt swollen and sore, her throat hurt, and she was absolutely exhausted. 'I'm sorry, Matron. I didn't mean to carry on so.'

'Drink your cocoa before it gets cold,' she replied unperturbed, as she sat opposite Polly and daintily raised her cup to her lips.

Polly took several sips of the sweet, milky drink, and discovered she felt a little better. 'Thank you, Matron,' she murmured when the cup was almost empty and she was feeling partially restored. 'You've been very kind.'

'I know I have a reputation in the hospital for being a bit of a dragon,' she replied, carefully putting down her cup and saucer. 'And it is not wholly unjustified, for I have high standards and a firm belief in efficiency and discipline. But regardless of all that, I really do care about my nurses.' She held Polly's gaze. 'Which is why I'm asking you to take some time off.'

'But...'

Matron raised her hand. 'Hear me out, Staff Nurse,' she admonished softly. 'I haven't finished.'

316

She eyed Polly across the desk, her expression understanding. 'You must have time to grieve,' she said, 'and a hospital ward is not the place to do it. I know you want to keep busy so you don't have to dwell on your losses, but I cannot put my patients in jeopardy, or my staff under further pressure. You made some forgivable mistakes tonight, but tomorrow it might be more serious.'

'I was tired, that's all,' Polly protested.

'I know,' said Matron on a sigh. 'We're all tired, but you have extra burdens on your narrow shoulders, and if you continue this way you will make yourself ill.'

Polly stared at her in misery. 'But I can't sit about doing nothing,' she murmured. 'I'll go mad.'

'Then find other things to occupy yourself,' said Matron. 'I understand you're billeted in a boarding house along with four other members of my staff, and I'm sure Mrs Reilly would appreciate help around the house with so many of you to feed and look after. And what about bracing walks. We have some magnificent countryside surrounding us – get out there and take a look for yourself, breathe in the good fresh air and blow away the cobwebs. And if none of these things help, then go and do a bit of voluntary work for the Red Cross or the WVS, or any one of the other charities who are so desperate for another pair of willing hands.'

'How long must I be away from my work?' Polly asked fearfully.

Matron pulled a sheaf of forms from her desk drawer and began to rapidly fill one in. 'I am signing you off for a month.'

'A month?' Polly gasped. 'But I can't...'

'You will do as you are told, Staff Nurse. I don't want you back here until you have come to terms with what has happened.'

'I doubt I'll ever come to terms with it,' Polly said flatly. 'How can I possibly accept what's happened my child – to my whole family?'

'I know it seems impossible now, but in time it *will* hurt less.' Matron gave a deep sigh as she sat back in her chair. 'Grieving is a long, drawn-out process and cannot be hurried. You are tearful and in pain now, your thoughts filled with those you've lost. I suspect you also feel guilty?'

Polly nodded, unable to speak.

'You're not alone in that, my dear. Those that are left behind always blame themselves for not being there, for not saying the words they should have said – for still being alive. And then the anger comes, raging at the unfairness of it, at the terrible waste of life, and it is only when that has lost its power that you can accept what has happened and begin to heal. And you will heal, Polly, I promise you. It's just that it takes time.'

'I know,' said Polly, trying desperately not to break down again. 'But it's all too raw at the moment and with Adam so ill, I ... I...'

'Would it help if I gave you special dispensation to visit Adam more frequently?'

'Yes, oh, yes please.'

Matron smiled. 'I know you've been going to see him out of visiting time but I decided to say nothing until now, and you can be assured that Sister Morley has not been admonished for breaking the rules.'

318

Polly could feel her face redden, and didn't dare meet Matron's gaze.

The older woman chuckled. 'Nothing much gets past me, Staff Nurse, as others before you have discovered.' She cleared her throat. 'It would be easier all round if I arranged for you to visit for half an hour each morning, as well as the normal hour in the evenings, and if that proves conducive to Adam's recovery, perhaps I can arrange another half-hour in the early afternoon.'

Polly regarded her with growing respect. Dragon she might be, but under that fiery exterior beat a heart of gold – a warm, caring heart that understood Polly's needs. 'That would be wonderful,' she breathed. 'Thank you so much, Matron.'

Matron waved away her thanks. 'Go home and get some sleep. No doubt our paths will cross when you're visiting, but I don't expect to see you on duty again until the end of October. Is that understood?'

Polly nodded and stood up. 'Thank you again, Matron.'

Matron dismissed her with a wave of her hand, not bothering to look up from the form she was signing.

Polly left the office and quietly closed the door behind her. She didn't see the tear that sparkled on Matron's eyelashes before it was dashed away, and could never have guessed that Matron Billings knew all about grief and that, now and again, she was haunted by the memory of the young man she'd been engaged to, who'd never come home from the Somme.

Once Polly had fetched her things from the sluice, she hurried down to Adam's ward. It was almost seven-thirty, and she wanted to catch Mary before she went off duty, for despite the age gap, they had become firm friends, and she wanted to share her happy news.

'Matron said it was all right,' she assured Mary, who was preparing to leave. 'In fact, she said I could visit every morning from now on.'

Mary smiled. 'I know. She came to see me earlier. I thought I was for it, but the old dragon was quite nice for once and didn't bat an eyelid.'

'How is he?'

'He's still got a temperature, but it's going down steadily, and his breathing is a bit easier. He's young and far stronger than he looks, and he will come through this, Polly. Really, he will.'

Polly dredged up a weary smile. 'Is it all right if I just go and have a look at him?'

Mary nodded. 'I'll wait for you outside,' she said. 'I could do with some fresh air and a cigarette, and we could go and have a cup of tea at the café now it opens so early.'

'That sounds nice,' Polly said before heading for Adam's bedside. He was sleeping, but his colour wasn't so hectic, and he was no longer struggling to breathe, which was a good sign. 'I'll be back tonight, my love,' she murmured against his cheek. 'Sleep well, my darling.'

'Pol?' His eyelids fluttered open.

She gripped his hand. 'Yes, darling? I'm here.'

'Are you all right, Pol?' he muttered sleepily. 'You look as if you've been crying.'

'I had a run-in with one of the other nurses,' she

lied swiftly. 'A bit of a spat over nothing really, but I've been on duty all night and am desperate for sleep. And you know me, I can cry at the drop of a hat when I'm tired.'

He frowned as he regarded her 'Are you sure that's all it is, Pol? You're not worried about me, are you?'

'Of course not,' she said too quickly. 'Well, perhaps a bit,' she relented. 'You have been very sick.'

'I *am* going to get better though, aren't I?'

'Of course you are,' she said firmly. 'I have it on the highest authority. Mr Fortescue and Matron are convinced this infection is just a bit of a hiccup, and that you'll soon be up and about and causing all sorts of trouble on the ward.' She smiled and kissed his cheek, desperate to banish the true depth of her worry.

'You smell nice,' he murmured, his eyelids already fluttering with sleep. 'Like roses.'

She held his hand as he went to sleep. Once she was sure he wouldn't be disturbed by her moving away, she released his fingers and hurried off the ward.

It was blustery and cold outside, the dark clouds scudding across the sky and threatening rain. Polly quickly crossed the red straps of her woollen cloak over her chest and fastened them behind her waist, glad of its warmth. The wind tugged at her cap as she hurried outside, and she had to hold on to it fiercely.

Mary was standing on a patch of grass in the lee of the trees which, during better weather, had been a favourite place for the walking wounded to sit and play cards or read the newspapers. She took a final puff of her cigarette and crushed the stub under her shoe as Polly approached. 'Come on. Let's find that cup of tea.'

The Daisy Tea Room huddled in ancient splendour between an ironmonger's and a chemist, its tiny, diamond-paned windows giving only a glimpse of the interior. Several centuries before it had been a fisherman's cottage, and now the wattle and daub walls leant towards the pavement from beneath the sway-backed tiled roof, the network of black beams stark against the whitewash. It had become a firm favourite among the hospital staff, for it provided good strong tea and the occasional treat of cake or scones.

A bell tinkled as they pushed through the door and negotiated the three narrow steps that led down to the flagstone floor of the main body of the tea room. There were already several people taking advantage of the earlier opening and enjoying the warmth of the welcoming fire in the hearth as they sipped tea and gossiped beneath the sturdy beams that ran across the undulating ceiling.

The room was cosy and warm, each table covered with a cheerful gingham cloth which matched the cushion pads on the chairs and the curtains at the window. Polly breathed in the heavenly scent of fresh baking which drifted from the kitchen, and discovered that, despite her weariness, she was ravenously hungry.

'Do you think they have scones?' she asked Mary, who was examining the menu card wedged between the salt cellar and a tiny vase of wilting wild flowers. No one had seen pepper for months, and even salt was getting scarce.

'We certainly do,' said the cheerful, and rather rotund waitress who was swathed in a vast floral apron. 'And there's home-made strawberry jam to go with them.'

'Then we'll have one each and a pot of tea,' said Polly. She leant back in her chair savouring the warmth coming from the blazing fire. 'I could go to sleep right here,' she murmured to Mary, 'if I wasn't so hungry.'

'Me too, but it's strange, the minute I leave the hospital, I seem to get my second wind.' Mary grimaced as she glanced outside. 'It's probably something to do with the weather. It certainly blows the cobwebs away.'

Mary's mention of cobwebs brought Polly's thoughts back to her interview with Matron and, as they waited for the scones and tea to arrive, she told her friend all about it.

'She was so unexpectedly kind,' she murmured finally, 'and I made an awful fool of myself by crying for ages. But she spoke a lot of sense, and I realise now that I can't carry on as I was.'

'I've heard rumours that she has a heart – but until today I never believed them.' Mary reached across the table and patted Polly's arm. 'I'm glad you've decided to take her advice. I've been worried about you, you know.'

They waited while the waitress placed the plate of scones and the pot of tea on the table. When she'd gone back to the kitchen, Mary eyed the bountiful spread as she poured the tea. 'I say,' she breathed, 'look – real tea, lovely and dark brown for a change. And there's sugar too, and even a tiny pat of butter to go with the scones and jam.

What a treat.'

Polly's mouth was watering as she carefully smeared the precious butter on the two halves of scone and added a dab of strawberry jam. It tasted heavenly, and she and Mary said very little until the last crumb of scone and the final smear of butter and jam had been devoured.

'I have to say,' Polly said eventually, 'that has to be the best scone I've ever eaten.'

Mary grinned as she poured the last of the tea into their cups. 'It's certainly set me up for my mother-in-law's visit later today. I dread her coming, you know; she does nothing but pick holes and complain. But then she's old and lonely, and while Simon's away fighting, I'm the only family she has.' She suppressed a yawn. 'We'd better go before I fall asleep at this table. What a night,' she sighed. 'I thought it would never end.'

They split the cost of their luxurious treat and the little bell rang out cheerfully as they closed the door behind them. The wind whipped at their cloaks and tore at their caps as they bent into it and struggled down the street to the crossroads.

'I'll see you tonight,' said Mary as she grimly held her cap in place. 'Polly? Polly, what's the matter?'

Polly was transfixed. She heard nothing and was unaware of anything but the newspaper headline on the board outside the shop on the opposite corner.

MERCY SHIP; 46 MORE SAVED

She stepped off the pavement, right into the

path of a cyclist who shouted at her as he swerved to avoid knocking her down and almost came off his bike. She didn't even notice he was there, for now she could see the rest of the headline, and her heart thudded with joyous hope.

Six Children 'Back from the Dead'
PLANE SEES BOAT AFTER 8 DAYS

'Polly, no,' shouted Mary, as she grabbed her arm. 'Don't let this get your hopes up. They would have told you if one of them was Alice.'

Polly wrenched away from her and ran into the shop. Scrabbling in her bag, she found the right change and almost threw it on the counter before snatching up the paper.

Forty-six people; six children, a woman and 39 men, believed drowned in the torpedoing of the mercy ship *City of Benares,* were brought safely home to port last night by the Navy. The six children were all boys.

Polly closed her eyes, the moan of despair trapped in her throat. She stood there, unaware of being watched by Mary and the shopkeeper and his wife, her heart drumming painfully as she tried to absorb the terrible news that Alice had not escaped death – that this miracle had not been meant for her.

'Come on, Polly,' said Mary, taking her arm. 'Let's get you home.'

Polly stared at her and couldn't comprehend what she was saying. 'I have to read the rest of it,'

325

she muttered. 'I must make sure. Perhaps one of my nephews survived – perhaps they both have. They were all boys, you see. All boys.'

'Polly,' Mary said softly. 'Don't torture yourself.'

'I have to know,' she rasped. Her hands trembled so badly she could barely read the rest of the article, but it seemed the survivors had drifted in the lifeboat for eight days before being spotted by a Sunderland flying boat. Rescued by a navy destroyer, they were taken to the safety of a port on the western coast of Scotland.

The list of survivors was the final proof that the hope she'd carried for these few short minutes had been betrayed – the miracle of the survivors a devastating reminder that fate had not smiled on her little family, and that she had indeed lost them all.

Polly swayed as her vision blurred and the newspaper fluttered to the floor from her nerveless fingers. The truth was a heavy weight on her heart – a leviathan of darkness that was sweeping over her just as the icy Atlantic waves must have swept over those she loved and engulfed them.

Polly opened her eyes and looked round in confusion. She didn't know this room, didn't recognise the faces that seemed to swim in front of her, or the voices that murmured close by.

'Polly? Polly, it's all right,' soothed Mary. 'You fainted.'

'Where am I?'

'In Mr and Mrs Ellis's back parlour,' said Mary, indicating the middle-aged couple dithering with concern in the doorway.

Polly frowned. She couldn't remember ever having met Mr and Mrs Ellis, and certainly couldn't remember ever being in this over-furnished, stuffy room with ornaments and pictures crowding every flat surface and wall.

She struggled to sit up, but her head began to swim again and she collapsed once more into the soft embrace of the sagging couch. 'Who are they?' she breathed. 'Why am I here?'

Mary took her hand. 'They own the paper shop, Polly. Mr Ellis carried you in here when you fainted.'

'Paper shop?' she murmured, her comprehension still muddled by her light-headedness. And then the fog cleared with vicious speed and she remembered everything. 'I have to get home,' she said, struggling with the blanket and the enveloping couch.

'In a while,' said Mary, as she gently pushed her back into the cushions. 'It's a bit of a walk, and I don't want you fainting again. Here, drink this.'

Polly stared at the cup of weak tea. She wasn't thirsty. 'I need to get back so I can telephone Miss Jackson at the Welfare Office,' she said, gripping Mary's hand and making the tea slop into the saucer. 'Papers get things wrong – keep things secret – don't always tell the truth. I have to make sure.'

'I've already spoken to Miss Jackson,' said Peggy as she bustled in. 'I did it the moment I read that article. I'm so sorry, Polly, but that report was true – every last word of it.'

'What are you doing here?'

'I came to find you. You were late home, and I didn't want you to see the paper headlines without someone being with you.' Her face crumpled as she fought her tears. 'Oh, Polly, I'm so sorry you've had such a terrible disappointment, dear.'

Polly stared at her, knowing she was telling the truth, and that she had no choice but to accept it. The emotions that had besieged her since Miss Jackson's first awful visit deserted her, and she was left feeling cold, empty and numb.

'Would someone help me out of this couch?' she asked flatly. 'I need to get back to Beach View and change out of my uniform. Our bedroom rugs need beating, and I've lots of washing and darning to do as well.'

She caught the worried look that passed between Mary and Peggy and threw back the blanket. 'Please don't make a fuss,' she said unemotionally. 'I'm quite all right, really.'

Chapter Sixteen

Almost three weeks had passed since Peggy had tracked Polly down to the paper shop. It was now near the end of October, and the war had entered another, more dangerous stage, with the signing of an axis pact between Germany, Italy and Japan. Romania had fallen, the Italians had invaded Egypt and Greece, and massive German air raids had devastated London, Southampton, Bristol, Manchester and Liverpool.

Due to the enemy bombardment of supply ships, and fierce fighting in the Channel as well as the Atlantic, rationing had been tightened even further. But, like their beleaguered countrymen and women, the residents of Beach View shouldered the tribulations, kept their grim determination, and an irrepressible tendency to break into a defiant grin even after the sirens had gone off eight times in a day, and they'd emerged from their shelters to discover that awful damage had been inflicted. They refused to be intimidated, their spirit of resistance fortified with every bombing raid and every inconvenience. Even the smallest of victories against the enemy were celebrated, and life was lived to the full, for no one knew what tomorrow might bring.

For the people of Cliffehaven, the sight and sound of hundreds of RAF bombers and fighter planes heading across the Channel had become almost commonplace, and many stood in the streets or on the hills to watch the furious dog-fights going on overhead, and to cheer on their brave boys in blue. At night they went to sleep in the shelters to the sound of hundreds of enemy planes droning towards London, and this noise soon became known as the 'Luftwaffe Lullaby'.

The continual raids and tip-and-runs by the enemy had left their scars on Cliffehaven, and parts of the town were now almost unrecognisable, especially around the station and goods yards. The military camps had been quickly moved further into the countryside to protect civilians from unnecessary danger, but the airfield where Anne's husband, Martin, was stationed had come under constant fire in the past few weeks, and the loss of planes and personnel was reaching crisis level.

Peggy closed the blackout curtains on the cold, damp Friday evening and switched on the kitchen light. She could hear the wind howling round the house, and it made the warm room feel even cosier. Mrs Finch and Anne were happily knitting by the fire as chamber music drifted from the wireless, and she returned to her chair, content to leave her own knitting for a while and just sit and watch them as she smoked a cigarette.

It was lovely to have Anne home for the weekend, and to be able to make a fuss of her. She hadn't liked the thought of her girl in that clifftop bunker, where no doubt she'd done sterling work for the Observer Corps until her pregnancy forced her to resign. Peggy felt far more relaxed now Anne was safely ensconced in the sweet little cottage Martin had bought for them in the village of Wick Cross. It was a few miles out of Cliffehaven on the other side of the hills and, because of the distance involved, it wasn't easy to get to. But there was a rather unreliable bus service and, as long as it was running, Peggy made a point of going there every Friday. It was a rare occasion for Anne to come into town, and Peggy was determined to enjoy every minute of her visit.

'I really hope this weather keeps the bombers away,' she said. 'We'll freeze in that Anderson shelter tonight, and I'd like to spend at least a few hours in my bed for a change. I do so miss my small comforts.'

Anne looked up from the matinee jacket she was knitting and smiled. 'Me too, but then I think of Martin at the airfield in his hard, uncomfortable bunk, and feel ashamed. The wind whistles through that hut, and there are very few home comforts apart from a kerosene stove which reeks and fills the whole place with most unpleasant fumes, and a couple of battered old chairs and tables.'

She sighed. 'I take over the magazines and books my neighbours give me, and Martin bought a radio to keep them occupied while they hang about waiting for the next shout. He's so tired, Mum, they all are – but there's very little let-up, and with so many missions, there's barely time to get a decent few hours of sleep.'

Peggy eyed-her eldest daughter with deep affection. Her pregnancy had made her even more beautiful, and there was a serenity about her that told of her contentment, despite the very real worry over her husband's safety.

'I thought that once they'd flown a certain number of missions, the RAF insisted upon them taking up training posts or admin?'

Anne chuckled. 'I can't see Martin being terribly happy in an office, can you?' She finished knitting the row, a little frown creasing her brow. 'His commanding officer has already offered him a nice safe post at a training school up north, but Martin turned it down.'

'Surely, with the baby coming, he should consider his safety?' chirped Mrs Finch, who was making a complete mess of the bootee she was attempting to knit.

Anne eyed her affectionately. Mrs Finch had lived at Beach View for several years now and had become so much a part of the family that Anne thought of her as her grandmother.

'He doesn't want to leave "his boys" now that they work so well together,' she explained. 'They're a tight group which includes several Poles and Free French, and he's become a bit of a good luck charm – even though he denies it. But their squadron has certainly suffered fewer losses than many others.' She grinned. 'And that's probably down to the ear-bashing Martin gave them a few months back. With so many aircraft being lost, they simply couldn't afford to be quite so gung-ho.'

'I still think he should consider you and the baby,' Mrs Finch replied. 'Men get so carried away with things like war, they can be very selfish at times,' she added with a delicate sniff.

Anne dipped her chin, letting her dark curls cover her face. 'He's only doing what he does best,' she murmured, 'and with so many losses, it would be even more selfish to pack it all in and get a nice safe desk job instead of fighting alongside his men.'

Peggy heard the tremor in her voice and took her hand. 'Don't upset yourself, Anne,' she said softly so that Mrs Finch couldn't hear. 'She's only thinking of you and the baby.'

'I know.' Anne shook her head, making her curls bounce on her shoulders. 'Let's change the subject, shall we?' she said, picking up her knitting again 'How are the plans for Sally's wedding coming along?'

'We've all been saving food coupons, and she's managed to get the extra ones she's entitled to from the Town Hall so John's mother can bake a wedding cake with a bit of fruit in it and some icing on top. John has got a new suit, and Sally says he looks more handsome than ever when he's wearing it, and his mother managed to find a lovely hat at a jumble sale, which Sally is decorating with fabric flowers.' Peggy was quite misty-eyed. She loved weddings.

'What about my dress?' asked Anne. 'It has certainly put in some good service since I wore it. Sally's must be the fifth or sixth wedding it's had – and there are at least five more girls wanting to borrow it.'

'She's finished altering it so she doesn't trip over the hem any more, and has had to take it in quite a bit since that last girl borrowed it. I'm sure she'll look every bit as beautiful as you did on your wedding day, Anne.'

Peggy smiled softly and patted her daughter's cheek before continuing. 'She's made a lovely frock for Pearl, who will be her matron of honour.' Peggy chuckled as she threw the butt of her cigarette into the fire. 'It's a good thing the wedding is only a week away. Pearl's waistline is growing by the day, and Sally's had to alter the dress countless times. We've got a little bet that Pearl's having twins – though the doctor insists she's just enjoying her extra rations of milk and cheese.'

Anne softly stroked the small mound that pushed against the waistband of her own skirt. 'I know how she feels,' she murmured with a gentle smile. 'I've had to put elastic in all my skirts, and will soon have to resort to wearing a tent – or a barrage balloon.'

They both giggled. 'I'd better see if your father can get hold of one then,' spluttered Peggy. 'They've been putting them up all over town, and I'm sure something that hasn't been tied down too well will come his way sooner or later. You know what he's like.'

Anne was still chuckling as she knitted. 'I think I'll pass up the offer,' she said finally. 'Balloon grey isn't really my colour.'

'Oh dear,' sighed Mrs Finch. 'I seem to have done something wrong.' She held up the tangle of wool which festooned her knitting needles.

'Give it to me,' said Peggy kindly. 'I'll see if I can't sort it out.'

She took the bedraggled piece of knitting and carefully began to unpick it. This bootee had been started so many times it was destined never to be finished, but as the old lady seemed to be enjoying the process, it didn't really matter. Peggy had been knitting the layette ever since Anne told her she was expecting, and now there was an entire suitcase full of baby clothes, upstairs. One tiny bootee wouldn't be missed.

'I haven't seen Polly since I arrived. How is she?' Anne asked a while later. 'Has she gone back to work yet?'

Peggy gave up on the tangle and pulled it all off the needles with a little tut of irritation – the damned thing would have to be started again.

'She's due back next week, and I think she's ready for it – though it's hard to tell. She's still

334

very quiet, and there are moments when I catch her unawares and find her crying – but she seems to have come out of herself a little more now she's involved with the Red Cross people.'

She began to wind the crinkled wool into a rough ball. 'Danuta says she's sleeping naturally, which is a relief. Those sleeping draughts are dangerous, and I was so frightened she'd come to depend upon them.' Peggy brightened. 'Ron has been an absolute brick, taking her for long walks over the hills every time he thinks she's flagging. He's even introduced her to Rosie, who seems to have taken a shine to her, and the three of them often have afternoon tea together before Rosie has to open the pub at six.'

'My goodness,' breathed Anne. 'Granddad usually keeps Rosie to himself. Things must be getting serious.'

'I doubt it,' replied Peggy. 'They're friends, good friends, and Ron's too set in his ways and a bit long in the tooth to start thinking about settling down.' She grinned. 'Even if the lady in question owns a pub and looks like a rather faded film star.'

Anne laughed and continued knitting. 'And what about the strange and rather mysterious little Danuta? She and Polly getting on all right now, are they?'

Peggy nodded as she began to cast on stitches and make a new start to the bootee. 'I was a bit worried they wouldn't at first, but it seems they've formed a close bond since the tragedy of that ship sinking. I suspect Danuta understands far more of what Polly's been going through than we ever could.'

She rapidly knitted several rows before speaking again. 'I didn't tell you, did I? Polly persuaded Danuta to take a First Aid course. Passed it with flying colours, evidently, and immediately gave in her notice at the hospital. She's driving ambulances about and thoroughly enjoying herself.' She grinned. 'Your father has seen her behind the wheel and reckons she's learning to drive on the job. She's had several close shaves already, and Jim shudders at the thought of ever having to be one of her passengers.'

'Don't they drive on the other side of the road in Poland?'

'I don't know, Anne. They might do – and it would certainly explain her hazardous driving.'

Anne smiled. 'I'm glad everything is turning out all right for her. It can't be easy living in a foreign country where everything must feel so strange.' She carried on knitting, the needles clicking in time with the music that came from the wireless. 'What about Polly's husband?' she asked a while later. 'Adam, isn't it?'

Peggy nodded. 'I haven't liked to intrude on visiting hour, so I've not gone to see him. From what Polly tells me, he seems to be making a little progress, and yet I suspect there's a very long way to go before he's well enough to be told about Alice.'

'But he'll have to be told eventually,' murmured Anne. 'You can't keep something like that a secret.'

'I think Polly's putting it off for as long as she can,' replied Peggy. 'She's simply terrified he'll blame her for Alice's death – she certainly still blames herself.' She put down her knitting and blinked away the tears. 'It's all so terribly sad.'

'My knitting is not terribly bad,' protested Mrs Finch. 'You can see what it's supposed to be – or at least you would if you didn't keep unpicking it.'

Peggy could always rely on Mrs Finch to raise a smile. 'Let's make a cup of tea and treat ourselves to a nice biscuit while we listen to the news,' she said, setting the bootee to one side. 'It's almost nine, and it looks as if we'll have no raids tonight, so I think we're due a bit of a celebration.'

Anne set her own knitting aside and went to the larder to fetch the milk and sugar before putting out the cups and saucers. 'Will Cissy be back before I leave on Monday morning?' she asked, as they waited for the kettle to boil. 'Only I haven't seen her in ages.'

'She's due back tomorrow afternoon,' said Peggy. 'And I'll be relieved to have her home again even if she does hog the bathroom for hours and is totally useless when it comes to helping about the place. I don't like to think of her travelling about with all these raids on, even if she isn't leaving the county. It's dangerous on the roads in the middle of the blackout. There have been some serious accidents over the past few months.'

'I'm sure she's absolutely fine, Mum,' Anne soothed. 'The travelling and the shows are what she enjoys best – though I can't think why. The thought of prancing about on a draughty stage in front of hundreds of braying servicemen makes me shiver.' She grinned. 'But then I'm not Cissy,

337

and I bet she's having the time of her life.'

Cissy and the other girls were not having much fun at all, although they agreed that one day they might be able to look back on this tour and laugh about it.

The boarding houses they'd had to stay in were unkempt and smelled of boiled cabbage and fish; the beds were uncomfortable, the pillows lumpy, and the succession of landladies they'd had to face were complete harridans who seemed to think that because they were dancers, they were tarts – and therefore had to be virtually kept under lock and key.

The venues Witherspoon had found weren't much better. From vast service canteens which were in the middle of nowhere, to draughty village halls and almost derelict theatres, they'd gone through their routines, accompanied by the less than skilled hammering on the out-of-tune piano they'd managed to strap on to the back of the wheezing bus.

The piano player had got so drunk one night he'd barely escaped with his life when he fell asleep on a bench in the middle of a town square and didn't even notice the fierce bombing raid going on around him. They'd left him in the hospital of the forgettable town they were passing through and two days later the piano came loose from its moorings and crashed to the road, splintering into a thousand pieces. The drummer and violinist gave in their notice, saying they'd had enough.

From that moment on, the dancers had had to

rely on Witherspoon's collection of scratched records to accompany them – which wasn't at all satisfactory, because the gramophone was very elderly and inclined to grind to a halt, and the girls couldn't hear the music above the shouts of their audiences.

At least there was a bit of enthusiasm for all their efforts, and it was quite flattering to have so many young men waiting for them after the show. Yet even that small joy was dampened by Witherspoon, who refused to let them fraternise and had them all in the coughing, spluttering bus on their way to their digs before they could blink.

The tour was limping along when the magician's rabbits went missing after they'd played at an army barracks. He threw a tantrum, upset the soprano by calling her a fat, screeching cow, and stormed off, swearing he'd rather face Hitler than look at her ugly mug again. The soprano left in high dudgeon, taking her husband with her – which was unfortunate, because he was the comedian, and rather a good one. It was discovered a few hours later that two baskets of costumes and props were missing. And that was the final straw. They had wound up the tour almost a week earlier than planned, but since the bus was incapable of doing more than fifteen miles an hour, the long journey back to Cliffehaven meant they would arrive on time.

Cissy was looking forward to being home again. Why she'd ever thought the theatre was glamorous, she didn't know. She was cold, hungry, and in need of a bath and change of clothes, for she was convinced the bites on her ankles were from one of the flea-ridden beds she'd had to sleep in. Witherspoon was in a filthy mood, which pleased her, but it didn't make for an easy or pleasant journey, as he kept shouting at everyone and making Judith, the youngest dancer, burst into floods of tears.

The bus had been threatening to break down for days, and it finally ground to a wheezing halt in the middle of a narrow country lane. The driver, who considered himself to be an excellent mechanic, clambered down to look under the bonnet and then stood there for an age scratching his head. Witherspoon stood beside him under an umbrella and everyone inside the bus could hear him ranting at the poor man.

Cissy and the other girls stared gloomily out of the window at the pouring rain and the deserted landscape. They were still several miles from Cliffehaven, and they were all hoping he'd get the bus fixed before it got dark.

'Have you thought any more about our plan, Cissy?' murmured Amy, who was keeping herself busy with the embroidery that accompanied her everywhere.

'I don't think it'll work,' Cissy replied, still staring out of the window. 'None of us wants the job of distracting him, and although Flo got a good look when he opened the safe before we left, we still only know part of the combination.'

'Flo said she'd distract him for us if we were willing to give it a go,' said Amy.

'But it could take hours to work out the rest of the combination, and we can't leave Flo with him for that long. There's no telling what he might do.'

'I think we all know what he'd do,' said Amy, her expression grim as she stabbed the needle into the half-finished tablecloth. 'You're right,' she said with a deep sigh. 'We'll have to think of something else. Though I don't know what – I've been racking my brain for days and can't think of any way we can open that safe.'

'Neither can I, and Judy and Flo haven't come up with anything sensible either.' Cissy gave a weary smile. 'At least we've all been safe for the last three weeks,' she said. 'Those landladies might have been awful, but they made certain no male darkened their doorsteps while we were there.' She giggled. 'I wouldn't mind betting that last one slept in her curlers at the top of the landing every night, rolling pin in hand, itching to catch someone trying to get in.'

They giggled at the thought of Witherspoon getting hit over the head with a rolling pin. That particular landlady had muscles in her arms that would have put a docker to shame, and she'd have given him a right bashing and no mistake.

The bus finally came to life with a loud bang from the exhaust pipe, a plume of black, noxious smoke, and a rather disconcerting whine from somewhere under the floor. It coughed and rattled and wheezed the last few miles, the windscreen wipers losing the battle with the rain. As it approached the theatre, everyone began to gather their things.

The engine sighed deeply and died, and the bus sagged on its balding tyres like a weary hen settling over her eggs.

'You'll all help to unload the bus and get everything into the theatre before you leave,' said Witherspoon, barring the exit.

There was a loud groan from the jugglers, who'd been looking forward to a decent pint, and a sharp yap from the performing dog who had already left a puddle on the floor.

Cissy and Amy clambered down into the rain and helped drag one of the baskets out of the back of the dead bus as the others trudged unwillingly to fetch the rest of what was left of their costumes and props. They trooped inside and dumped everything in the wings.

'Right,' snapped Witherspoon, who'd been watching the activity from the shelter of the doorway. 'Everyone in my office. It's time we discussed what an absolute shower you lot are, and how I'm going to be cutting your wages from now on.'

'That ain't fair,' barked one of the jugglers. 'You don't pay us enough as it is.'

'I'll be the judge of that,' retorted Witherspoon as he opened his office door.

The light was already on and Cissy stared in amazement at the two large policemen who rose from their perch on Witherspoon's desk. Sitting in his chair was another man in civilian clothes who had a grim expression and cold, accusing eyes which swept over them all from beneath the brim of his fedora.

'What the hell is going on here?' blustered Witherspoon, his gaze darting towards the safe. 'Get out of my office.'

The man in the fedora took his time in getting to his feet. 'Mr Jack Witherspoon?'

'Who wants to know?' he said belligerently.

'Chief Inspector Craddock.'

'You can't break into my office without a warrant,' Witherspoon snarled, taking a step back and almost crushing Cissy's toes.

'I have a warrant.' Craddock drew a piece of paper from an inside pocket of his overcoat. 'I also have these.' He picked up a handful of negatives and black-and-white photographs. 'Can you explain how they came to be in your safe, Mr Witherspoon?'

Witherspoon went ashen and stumbled back as the two policemen advanced on him. He turned and was about to make a run for it when Cissy stuck out her foot and he went sprawling.

'Well done, Cissy,' shouted Amy, who was jumping up and down and clapping her hands.

Chief Inspector Craddock smiled at Cissy as his officers dragged Witherspoon to his feet. 'That was quick thinking, well done,' he said.

His smile broadened as he looked round at the delighted faces of the troupe. 'Do I get the feeling that none of you are too upset about the fate of your Mr Witherspoon?'

A chorus of affirming murmurs greeted this question, and Craddock nodded. 'I don't think it has come as much of a surprise either,' he murmured. Clearing his throat, he continued. 'I'll need to take statements from all of you, but that can wait until tomorrow,' he said, before turning his attention back to Witherspoon.

Cissy heard very little of this, for her gaze was now firmly fixed on the photographs Craddock was still holding. She couldn't see any of them properly, and was terrified that some of them might be of her and Amy, and Judy and Flo. If so, she would have to prepare herself for one almighty telling-off from her father. The thought of it made her heart thud.

Chief Inspector Craddock waited until his officers had Witherspoon in handcuffs. 'Jack Arnold Witherspoon,' he said, his deep, stern voice ringing round the cramped office. 'I am arresting you for taking, or causing to take indecent photographs of minors, and for the selling of said indecent photographs.'

'I want my lawyer,' rasped Witherspoon, who'd gone a most interesting shade of green.

'You will get the chance once we've got you down at the station.' The Chief Inspector's smile was almost vulpine. 'There are a couple of your cronies already down there. You won't be allowed to speak to them, of course, but you might not feel so lonely knowing they are in the next cells.'

'What do you mean?' gasped Witherspoon, whose legs were shaking so badly he had to be held up by the two policemen.

'I'm talking about that reptile of a photographer you employed, and that nasty little queer who helps you deal in your dirty photographs. Screamed like a girl he did when we arrested him this afternoon but, seeing as how we caught him with his trousers down, so to speak, he was very keen to tell us everything he knew in exchange for leniency over the charge of gross indecency.'

Witherspoon's colouring went from sickly green to scarlet before it turned ashen as he was hauled away.

Cissy and the other three girls stared in wonder and amazement at each other, the realisation slowly dawning that they were at last free of Witherspoon.

There was movement in the corridor and they made way for the new arrival who strode purposefully towards Craddock.

'This is WPC Smith,' said Craddock. 'Please give her your names and addresses and then you are free to go. I want all of you at the police station by ten tomorrow morning.'

Having done as he asked, Cissy waited for the other girls and they quickly gathered their things and rushed out of the theatre and into the rain. It was not yet dark and the wet streets and pavements looked like glass in the pale light.

'Don't say anything until we know we can't be overheard,' said Amy, casting a suspicious glance over her shoulder. A police car was parked at the kerb, with a young woman in military uniform sitting behind the wheel. She smiled at them as they hitched up their heavy bags and gas-mask boxes and hurried away.

'I think it's best we say absolutely nothing until we know whose pictures were in that safe,' said Amy some time later. They'd found refuge from the rain in a pub where they knew they wouldn't be asked their ages, and were sitting in a far corner so their conversation was lost in the babble of noise.

'I agree,' said Cissy. 'We don't want our parents finding out unless they absolutely have to. And I don't know about you, but I dread the thought of having to stand up in court to give evidence.'

'But he has to be punished,' said Flo. 'We can't let him get away with what he's been doing by keeping silent any more. You heard what that copper said, about photos of minors – and although we're none of us yet twenty-one, I wouldn't describe us as minors. Would you?'

There was a thoughtful silence as they digested this.

Cissy shuddered. 'You mean he was taking pictures of kids?'

'It certainly sounds like it,' said Flo grimly. 'If that's the case, then I don't mind telling the police everything – from the spyholes to the photographs and his wandering hands. Men like him need to be strung up.'

Cissy thought about this as the conversation raged back and forth. 'I wonder how the police found out what he was up to?' she said finally. 'Someone must have informed on him.'

'Well, it wasn't any of us,' said Flo. 'Perhaps it was one of his cronies that he'd cheated.'

'Or perhaps it was the pianist. He hated Witherspoon enough to do it.'

'So did Cheeky Charlie the comedian,' said Flo dryly.

'It could have been anyone,' said Judy with a shiver.

Cissy gave a vast yawn and finished her glass of lemonade shandy in the hope it would take the nasty taste from her mouth. 'I don't know about you lot, but I'm going home. I'm completely shattered, and I expect Mum will want to hear all about the tour and it'll be ages before I get to bed.'

She stood up and put on her damp coat. 'What do you say we meet at Judy's place at nine-thirty tomorrow and walk to the police station together?'

This was agreed and they left the pub. Within minutes they were hurrying their separate ways, each occupied with the dark, troubling images that Witherspoon's arrest had brought them.

It had taken all Cissy's skills as an actress to hide her true feelings before she was able wearily to climb the stairs to her bedroom. Although it had been lovely to make everyone laugh about the adventures on the disastrous tour, and to catch up with all of Anne's news, she couldn't quite dismiss her worry over the interview she must do in the morning. Witherspoon's arrest had opened a can of worms, and Cissy had a nasty feeling that she and the other girls would be tainted by it.

Dragging off her clothes, she wrapped herself warmly in her dressing gown and hunted through her dresser drawer for a clean nightdress. There was a stack of post on top of the dresser and she would have left it there until she'd had her bath if she hadn't caught sight of the large brown envelope.

The address had been typed, and it felt fairly heavy. Intrigued, she opened it and shook out the contents. A sheaf of photographs and negatives spilled all over her bed.

'Oh my God,' she breathed as she stared at them. 'These must be from Witherspoon's safe. But how did they get here? Who...?'

She sifted through the photographs quickly. It looked as if all of hers were there from what she could remember of that awful afternoon, and they weren't terribly shocking considering what else Witherspoon had been up to. But those of Amy and Judy certainly were. It wasn't the poses they were in – it was the look of whipped resignation and shame in their eyes that made her feel sick.

After a hurried examination of the negatives, Cissy gathered everything up and tried to stuff it all back in the envelope. But there was something else stuck in the bottom and it took a moment to fish it out.

It turned out to be a short typewritten letter that had been folded neatly into two.

'These photographs and negatives came from Witherspoon's safe. You must do with them as you see fit. The remaining evidence in the safe does not concern you or your friends, but is enough to put Witherspoon behind bars for a very long time. My advice is to burn the photographs and say nothing to the police, for it would only hurt your loved ones to see you dragged through the courts. Your secret is safe with me, I promise.'

There was no signature, and the postmark was almost indecipherable.

Cissy bundled everything back into the envelope and buried it at the bottom of her underwear drawer. She leant against the dresser and closed her eyes. She'd been saved by an anonymous guardian angel who had somehow – and most mysteriously – known how to get them all out of the mess they'd found themselves in.

'Whoever you are,' she breathed, 'thank you. Thank you from the bottom of my heart, and I promise I'll never do anything so stupid again.'

Chapter Seventeen

It was the beginning of November, and Polly had been back at work at the hospital for a week. Although she'd enjoyed her short time helping at the Red Cross centre in the town, and had appreciated the homeliness of Beach View, and the warmth and support of Peggy and her family, she found the familiarity of the routine on the ward strangely soothing.

She still had nightmares and would, at times, be almost overwhelmed by great waves of loss, but she'd learnt to live with them – had used the pain, the guilt and the grief to keep her going. The hardest part was having to face Adam, who was still too ill to be told what had happened to their beloved Alice. She hated lying to him, but feared telling him the truth – and that was her punishment; the burden she'd been forced to shoulder because she'd been the one to send Alice to her death.

She was very aware that the day would soon come when Adam must be told and, although their marriage had been strong, their love for one another indestructible so far, the knowledge of what she'd done would always be between them and she feared it could be the wedge that drove them apart – and then she really would be left with nothing.

Polly still visited Adam at every opportunity,

and today had been no different, but she'd warned him that tonight she would not be coming in to visit at six – she had other plans. She collected her things at the end of her shift, determined to banish all the dark thoughts and terrors that besieged her, and to enjoy the evening out with Mary, and her day off tomorrow. They were planning to go to the theatre to watch the local drama company's production of *Rebecca,* which had had excellent reviews. It had been ages since she'd had a night out, and she was really looking forward to it.

The crisp autumn days at the beginning of the week had turned mild and wet, the wind rising through the nights, and she rather hoped it would stay dry long enough for her to be able to potter around the town while everyone was at the wedding tomorrow, and then tramp along the hills on Sunday with Ron and Harvey.

As she fastened her cloak and unfurled her umbrella, she thought fondly of the old man and his dog. He reminded her of her late father, for he spoke his mind, could be quite sharp at times, and knew the countryside like the back of his hand. But for all his gruffness, Ronan had a good heart and seemed to understand how much she'd needed his solid, unwavering support over the past month. Their friendship had been born out of sorrow, but it was one she would always hold dear.

The heavy drone of British aircraft filled the air as several squadrons of bombers and Spitfires headed across the Channel. Polly watched them for a moment and was about to dash down the steps and into the rain when an ambulance came splashing through the puddles and screeched to a halt.

'Danuta,' she exclaimed, looking down at the splatters on her black stockings, and the hem of her cloak and uniform. 'Do look where you're going, you've absolutely soaked me.'

Danuta clambered down from the driver's cab with a grin. 'So sorry,' she said cheerfully. 'I not see puddle.'

'You don't look where you're going most of the time,' Polly replied with a weary sigh. 'Goodness only knows how you've managed to avoid a serious accident.'

Danuta pursed her lips, her gaze darting to the sizeable dent in the front wing as she hitched up the strap of her khaki dungarees and fastened her heavy overcoat. 'I hit wall this morning, but Stan say he can fix, so no matter, I think.'

She grinned as her co-driver, the thickset and much put upon Stanley Gubbins, clambered down, eyed the dent and raised his gaze to the teeming sky. 'Stan is good man to fix things. I'm very lucky.'

'She'll kill the pair of us one day,' he grumbled. 'I reckon we're lucky to have got away with it for so long.'

'But you can fix, yes?'

He nodded dourly and climbed into the driver's seat. 'I'll take it round the back and sort it out before anyone notices,' he muttered through the open window. 'But this is the last time, Danuta.'

Danuta gave Polly a beaming smile as she took off her tin helmet. Her dark, short crop of hair was plastered to her head, but her face was radiant, her eyes gleaming with happiness. 'He does not mean it,' she said. 'He just likes to be, how you say, "grumpy" all the time.'

'Strikes me he's got something to be grumpy about,' laughed Polly.

Danuta shrugged. 'He like to have things to complain about. It makes him happy, I think.' She grinned again. 'I finish work now. We walk home together, yes?'

Polly nodded and looked up at the sky. The rain was coming down even harder now, and the wind was picking up – but still squadron after squadron of British planes headed south. Perhaps, with so many of their pilots in the air, the enemy wouldn't risk a raid tonight? 'Get your things, and I'll wait for you indoors.'

Danuta dashed off, the tails of her long, heavy coat flapping in the rising wind as she splashed through puddles and headed for the ambulance station at the far end of the hospital building.

Polly was grinning as she returned to the relative warmth of the hospital reception area. Danuta had changed so much since she'd left the hospital laundry. She had put on some weight, looked years younger, and seemed to have come alive now that she was doing something she regarded as more useful. Her cheerful chatter and endless enthusiasm for her work had helped lighten Polly's mood, and her warmth and understanding had certainly endeared her to Polly.

'It's good to see you smiling again, Staff Nurse,' said Matron, appearing from around a corner. 'Your first week back has not been too difficult, I hope?'

Polly nodded. 'I've managed,' she said simply.

Matron's steely gaze held her for a heartbeat. 'Good. Then long may it continue,' she replied before bustling away.

June, Suzy and Fran came in out of the rain and, after a brief greeting, hurried off to begin their night shifts.

Danuta came rushing into the reception area moments later. 'I am ready,' she panted. 'Come on, Polly. Peggy will have tea on the table soon, and I am starving.'

'So am I, but I do hope it isn't rabbit stew again,' said Polly, unfurling her umbrella before they ran down the steps and into the rain. 'If I eat another bunny, I swear I'll grow long ears and whiskers.'

Danuta laughed as they hurried down Camden Road. 'I think *Babunia* has made her famous fish pie today,' she replied. 'Ron was going to see his son Frank at the fishing station this morning.'

The thought of Mrs Finch's fish pie made Polly's mouth water. Because of the ever tightening restrictions, food had become rather bland, so it was a real treat to have something more exciting than corned beef hash, scrag end of something unidentifiable, or one of the awful concoctions dreamt up by the Ministry of Food.

'Are you planning anything for this evening?' Polly asked, as they reached the end of Camden Road and waited for an army lorry to trundle past before crossing into Beach View Terrace. 'Mary and I have tickets for *Rebecca,* and I'm sure we could get you one as well if you'd like to come with us.'

'I am sorry,' Danuta replied. 'But I have already made other arrangements.'

Polly glanced at her and grinned. 'That's twice this week,' she teased. 'Have you got a chap hidden away, Danuta?'

She slotted her key in the door and shook her head. 'I go to meet friend, that is all.'

Polly realised she would get no further into the mystery of where Danuta disappeared to on such a regular basis, and left it at that. It was actually none of her business, and it was lovely to see her so cheerful. Whatever – or whoever – it was, was doing her a lot of good, and she hoped it would continue.

The turn in the weather had made little difference to the activity overhead, and the constant drone of aircraft heading for Europe had become a part of everyday life. With the sirens going off day and night, and enemy raids becoming ever more frequent, this everyday life was beginning to pall. Landmines exploded under the onslaught of the heavy rains, shattering windows and rattling the very foundations of the house, and the crump of distant bombs was a reminder that they were all living on a knife-edge.

It was almost five o'clock when Peggy closed the blackout curtains on the weather and turned on the light. Polly and Cissy had just come in and were upstairs getting changed, and another wave of Spitfires and bombers was heading for the enemy ports and shipyards across the Channel. She wondered fleetingly if Martin was up there with them, and had to accept that he probably was. Poor Anne, no wonder she'd had to go for a sleep this afternoon. She must be exhausted with worry.

'I'll be off to get the evening paper,' said Jim, 'and maybe snatch a pint on the way back. Paddy at the Sailor's Rest usually has his back door open for the regulars out of hours.' He dragged on his heavy waterproof coat and wrapped a scarf about his neck before putting on his hat.

'Don't you dare be late for tea,' Peggy warned. 'We have so few nights together, and it's not often we have Anne and Cissy at home at the same time.'

'To be sure, I'll not be late for me tea,' he replied with a grin. He winked. 'I have an appetite, so I have, and as I'm home all night, perhaps we could find time for a bit of a cuddle as well?'

Peggy blushed and shooed him out of her kitchen before turning on the wireless. Jim was incorrigible but the thought of a cuddle in the comfort of their lovely bed was something to look forward to, and she settled down to listen to 'Children's Hour', the blush still warming her face.'

'Aren't you a bit old to be listening to that, Mum?' Cissy wandered into the kitchen some time later and checked on the progress of the fish pie.

'Of course I am,' she replied comfortably, 'but the boys will be listening down in Somerset, and it makes me feel a little closer to them.'

'You are an old softie,' Cissy murmured, giving her a hug and a kiss before wandering out again to see if her sister had woken up yet.

Peggy smiled. Cissy seemed to have got over whatever it was that had been worrying her. She seemed much more herself, and definitely more cheerful since she'd come home last weekend. No doubt the week off Witherspoon had given them all had restored her good nature, and she thought again how considerate he was, for the tour sounded as if it had been a complete shambles. But Cissy's spirits had been high as she'd related some of the funnier incidents, and it was good she could laugh about it – and even better that she seemed, happy to be home again.

As she listened to the story on the wireless and thought about her boys, she became tearful as she always did, and wondered when she could see them again. Sally and John were planning to honeymoon in Somerset so they could be with Sally's little brother Ernie for a while, and Peggy had knitted scarves, sweaters, gloves and socks for them to take for Charlie and Bob.

Christmas would be hard this year, for it would be the first they would spend apart, and she wondered how she would cope without seeing their bright, expectant faces on Christmas morning, and the chaos of wrapping paper and excited, piping voices urging her and Jim to get up so they could look at what Father Christmas had brought them.

Determined not to let these thoughts spoil the evening, she switched off the wireless at the end of the programme and got the fish pie out of the oven. It smelled delicious, and her stomach gurgled in anticipation. Meals had become a bit of a labour of late, and she'd known all too well that they were often bland and unimaginative – but there was little she could do about it now rationing had been tightened yet again.

On the dot of six they began to come into the kitchen, where most meals were served these days. The dining room chimney was still blocked off to prevent another soot fall, and the windows were still covered in plywood. It didn't seem practical to go to all the expense of new glass when it would more than likely be broken again, and they certainly couldn't get enough coal for two fires.

Cissy, Polly and Danuta came in with Mrs Finch. Anne followed shortly after, looking much refreshed after her long sleep. She was staying overnight for Sally's wedding the next day, and Peggy was hoping she might linger for the rest of the weekend, which would be lovely.

Peggy eyed the kitchen clock. Jim was in danger of being late, despite his promise, and she'd give him a piece of her mind if he was, and that was a fact.

Ron appeared moments later from the cellar with Harvey, who took more than a passing interest in the heaped plates.

'Get him out of here, Ron,' Peggy muttered. 'Fish makes him...'

Harvey farted and tucked his tail between his legs, a look of shame crossing his bowed head as the dreadful smell drifted into the kitchen and everyone gasped in disgust.

'Sorry about that,' said Ron, shooing him downstairs. 'I gave him the heads and guts when I was cleaning the fish earlier. I forgot what it

357

does to him.'

Peggy wrinkled her nose as the girls giggled. 'It's not funny,' she said, trying not to laugh as she sat down.

'To be sure 'tis only nature's way of dealing with his wind.'

'There's enough wind outside, without it in here,' said Peggy, still trying to keep a straight face.

They had almost finished tea when the front door slammed shut and Jim strode into the kitchen bringing the scent of fresh air and rain with him.

'You're late,' said Peggy, not really bothering to give him more than a glance. 'Tea's on the hob.'

'I don't want bloody tea,' he roared, making everyone jump. 'I want an explanation.' He slammed the newspaper down on the table between Peggy and Cissy. 'Read that,' he shouted. Dragging off his hat, coat and scarf, he threw them in the vague direction of a nearby chair and stood over his wife and younger daughter, his heavy breathing filling the shocked silence.

Disconcerted and not a little frightened by his language and his clear rage, Peggy's gaze flew across the lurid headline and then slowed as the full import of the shocking article began to sink in. When she'd come to the end, she looked at Cissy and realised the girl had gone deathly pale. 'Did you know about this?' she managed through a tight throat.

'Of course she bloody knew,' roared Jim. 'And if that bastard laid one finger on her I'll have his...' He seemed to realise the kitchen was full of startled and rather frightened women and fell silent. 'Did he touch you, Cissy?' he said gruffly. 'Did he make you do anything you didn't like?'

Cissy lifted her gaze from the newspaper article and discovered Danuta was watching her with a strange intensity. It was almost as if she was trying to tell her something. 'N-n-no,' she stuttered. 'But I knew he'd been arrested.'

'When was this? How long have you been keeping this from me?' shouted Jim.

'Last Saturday,' admitted Cissy, on the brink of tears. 'They arrested him when we got back from the tour.'

'And you came home and told us all a pack of lies,' shouted Jim. 'You sat there and said he'd given you all a week off, when all the time that ba–' He caught himself again and wiped the back of his hand over his mouth. 'You do know what he was up to, don't you?' he rasped.

Cissy nodded, unable to meet her father's fury or her mother's shocked expression. 'The policeman said he'd been taking pictures of minors and selling them,' she muttered.

'That's only half the story according to this. The man's a pervert of the worst kind – and when I think I actually let you anywhere near him – or that creep of a choreographer, I want to ... to...' He curled his fists, his face going puce.

Peggy reached for Cissy's hand, her dread clear in her expression and in her cold fingers. 'Cissy,' she said hoarsely, 'is he the reason why you've been so quiet lately? He didn't make you do anything, did he? He didn't take nasty pictures or touch you or...' Her words faded as she clearly found it impossible to voice her worst fears.

Cissy blinked away her tears and was on the point of telling her mother just how stupid she'd been to fall for his charms when she caught Danuta's eye. The Polish girl still had that tense, warning look and Cissy had a startling moment of awareness. Danuta had sent those damning photographs and negatives. How or why, didn't matter, but she knew now how to answer her parents' questions.

She squeezed her mother's cold fingers. 'He didn't touch me,' she said softly. 'From what the policeman said, he liked much younger girls than me, so I was quite safe.'

'And Amy, and the others?' breathed Peggy. 'Judy's only sixteen.'

'None of us knew what he was up to,' Cissy lied smoothly. 'We were as shocked as you when we got back and found the police waiting.'

'Then why didn't you tell us straight away?' shouted Jim, who was clearly itching to murder Witherspoon if only he could get his hands on him.

'Because I knew how angry you would be,' she said honestly. 'Once we found out what he'd been up to, we all decided to wait a bit and see what happened to him. But we've realised we don't ever want to go back to the troupe.'

'I should bloody well think not,' roared Jim. 'You step one *foot* in that place again and I'll lock you in your room until your twenty-fifth birthday.'

'Language, Jim,' snapped Peggy. 'It isn't help-ing.'

'I'll speak as I bloody find,' he yelled back. 'To

360

think I actually signed that damned contract because I thought he was a proper gentleman.'

'He had us all fooled,' muttered Peggy.

'It strikes me no harm's been done to our girl,' said Ron, breaking into the ensuing silence. 'And for that we must thank the Lord. Perhaps this will be a lesson to you, Cissy, and you'll be thinking more sensibly from now on.'

Cissy glanced at Danuta before replying, but she seemed intent upon reading the article, sharing the newspaper with Polly and Anne, and didn't look back.

'Amy and I have decided to do something useful for a change,' she said rather nervously. 'We're both going to brush up on our typing and join the WAAFs.' She looked at their disbelieving faces and lifted her chin in defiance. She would show them she was capable of more than dancing in the back row of the chorus. 'We went to the recruitment office this morning, and it seems they're crying out for more secretaries.'

Jim sank into the fireside chair with a deep sigh. 'God help the air force,' he muttered. 'Haven't they got enough on their plate without you and Amy in their ranks?'

Cissy bridled. 'There's no need to be like that, Dad. I did typing at school and I came top in my class. It won't be long before I get it up to speed again.'

Peggy was still clearly mulling over the consequences of Witherspoon's shocking downfall. 'Will you have to go to court, Cissy?' she asked, her expression fretful.

'I shouldn't think so,' she soothed. 'We all had

to give a statement to the police, and Chief Inspector Craddock said that as we knew nothing about what had been going on, we wouldn't be called to give evidence.'

'Thank God,' breathed Peggy. 'But what about the contract we signed? Will you still have to honour it if someone else takes over the troupe?'

'Over my dead body,' growled Jim. 'And if that man, or any of his cronies, comes within a hundred miles of Cissy or this family, he'll find that contract shoved somewhere incredibly dark and painful.'

Cissy giggled and Peggy smiled uncertainly.

Jim rose from the chair, fetched his plate from the hob and slammed it down on top of the discarded newspaper. The fish pie was consumed at a great rate and in complete silence.

The crisis was over and, at last, Cissy knew she could go to bed that night and sleep undisturbed by bad dreams.

Danuta pulled on the heavy Red Cross driving coat over her nightdress and sweater before shoving her feet into her slippers and leaving the bedroom. It was after midnight and Polly was sleeping soundly, but Danuta was restless, the baby kicking and squirming inside her so much it was impossible to sleep.

She crept through the silent, dark house and out through the front door, closing it softly behind her and pocketing the key. It had stopped raining and the sky was clear of clouds and studded with cold, bright stars. Breathing in the fresh, clean scent of rain-washed pavements and gardens, and the salty air of the sea, she sat down on the top step and watched the returning Hurricanes and Spitfires fly overhead.

Once they had gone, she sat huddled in her warm coat and listened to the silence. There had been no raids tonight and Cliffehaven slept peacefully for the first time in weeks. She reached into the coat pocket, took out the pack of cigarettes and lit one, before leaning back against the wall, eyes closed, her thoughts drifting.

'I thought it must be you.'

She almost jumped out of her skin, and the baby kicked out as if it too had been given a fright. 'Ron,' she hissed at the shadowy figure emerging through the front door. 'Don't sneak up on me like that.'

He grinned as he joined her on the top step. ''Tis good to know I can still creep up on anyone, what with me shrapnel wound,' he muttered. 'Did I ever tell you how I came to get such a terrible affliction?'

Danuta grinned back at him. 'Several times,' she said fondly, 'and I'm surprised you want anyone to know you were hit in the bottom while squatting in the bushes behind enemy lines.'

'Ah, well now, that's the story I tell when people need cheering up,' he said, as he filled his pipe. 'The truth of it is I've told that story so many times, I've almost forgotten how I really came by it.'

'I find that very hard to believe,' said Danuta softly.

He winked at her as he got his pipe going to his satisfaction and leant back against the door.

'Well, I remember enough to know I didn't care for it,' he mumbled round the stem of his pipe. 'Me arse was sore for weeks after.'

Danuta grinned. 'How did you know I was here?'

'Smelled your cigarette smoke through me basement window, so I did. Always a giveaway, that. First lesson we're taught when on covert exercise – absolutely no smoking, no hair preparation or strong soap.' He continued to smoke his pipe, his expression thoughtful. 'Talking of covert missions,' he said finally. 'How did you manage to get hold of those things from Witherspoon's safe?'

She stared at him in amazement. 'How you know this?' she stammered.

He clenched his teeth round the stem of his pipe as he grinned. 'Old habits die hard. I caught a glimpse of that envelope the day you went to post it, and wondered why you should be mailing something to Cissy. But I'd known the girl had been troubled for some time, and suspected that envelope might have something to do with whatever was ailing her. I'm not ashamed to admit that when it arrived that morning, I opened it.'

'But you said nothing? Why?'

'Because of the letter you put with them. I realised that you'd helped Cissy get out of a very nasty situation, and although some of those photographs were shocking, it was clear Cissy hadn't been persuaded to overstep the mark.' He regarded her steadily. 'How did you know she and her friends were having problems with Witherspoon?'

'I overheard her talking to Amy just before they were due to leave on the tour,' she admitted. 'It was easy to follow them when they left the house that morning, and once I'd established the identity of all four girls, I knew what I was looking for.'

Ron puffed on his pipe, his silence encouraging her to continue.

'I also followed Witherspoon to see where he lived,' she said, stamping out her cigarette and putting the butt in her pocket without thinking. 'There didn't appear to be a wife or family about, so once they'd left on the tour it was easy to get into his house. It took me a while to find the safe he'd hidden under the bedroom floorboards, but I guessed there would be one somewhere. Men like that keep their dirty secrets close.'

She fell silent and shuddered at the memory of what she'd found in that safe. 'It didn't take too long to work out the combination – it was his date of birth,' she said finally, 'and it was easy to take what I wanted and transfer the most damaging evidence to the office safe. An anonymous telephone call and an envelope of samples to the police did the rest.'

Ron chewed the stem of his pipe. 'You did very well, Danuta,' he said after a long moment.

'Men like him need castrating,' she hissed, 'and if I achieve little else here, at least I'll know I did the right thing.'

He patted her knee and stood up with a wince of pain. 'The damp's getting into me old bones, so it is,' he groaned. 'I'm fer me bed.'

Danuta sat for a while after he'd gone. Although it had been quite exciting to use her covert skills again, she needed time to get those awful images out of her head before she went back to bed and attempted to get some much-needed sleep. There had been a man like Witherspoon in Warsaw – he'd been hung – and she hoped the same fate awaited the Englishman.

With a sigh, she turned her mind to happier things and the appointment she'd had earlier. The baby was coming along nicely according to the lovely, gentle Dr Craig, who'd come out of retirement to run a general practice on the far side of town. He hadn't even raised an eyebrow when she explained her circumstances, but had warned her to start taking it easy now she had reached her fifth month.

Danuta looked up at the stars and the empty sky, thinking of Jean-Luc, the ache for him returning to haunt her She blinked away the tears and deliberately switched to more practical things. She was on her own, and once the baby was born her life would be very difficult – but this baby she had made with him was precious, and she would find a way to survive.

She didn't want to have to give in her notice at the Red Cross until it was absolutely necessary, and so far no one had even noticed how thick she was getting round the middle. She grinned. The overalls and heavy coat hid a great deal, but the day would come soon when someone would notice, and then she'd be sent home to face Peggy.

Danuta frowned into the darkness, trying to work out how Mrs Reilly might react to the fact she hadn't confided in her about her condition. Peggy was a sweet, accommodating woman, but Danuta suspected she would be very angry to discover how duplicitous Danuta had been from the moment she'd arrived at Beach View.

Clambering to her feet, she let herself into the house and climbed the stairs. She would deal with that problem when it arose, but for now she would just carry on as usual.

Peggy had risen early after not having slept much at all. She and Jim had talked for a long time after they'd gone to bed, and they'd fallen asleep in each other's arms, comforted that their daughter had come to no harm, and that justice would be done. But each of them bore a deep guilt at how easily they had been taken in by the man, and it was this that had brought about the disturbed night.

There were three warning sirens during the morning, and in the end Peggy was so sick of running out of the house to the Anderson shelter that she refused to do it any more. She wanted a bath and a moment of peace to get ready for Sally's wedding, and something as irritating as another air raid was not going to stop her.

Jim and Ron could protest all they liked, but then all they had to do was wash and shave and put on a suit. She had to do her hair and make-up, find a pair of stockings that hadn't been darned, and struggle into a corset before she could dress in her suit and hat and find her gloves – all of which took time and effort if she was to look her best and do Sally proud.

The rain had stopped by lunchtime, which was a blessing, and it was quite a little parade that left the house promptly at one. Ron had been told very firmly to leave Harvey behind, and the dog could be heard howling as they all set off. Jim looked handsome in his suit as he gave Mrs Finch his arm and they walked slowly down the road to the trolleybus stop.

Peggy couldn't help smiling, the pride lifting her chin as she walked beside a rather disgruntled Ron and saw how radiant her girls were, and how lovely they looked all dressed up. She was a very lucky woman.

Jim left them at the tiny church on the other side of town to walk the few hundred yards to Pearl's house where he would collect the bride. Peggy knew how proud he was to have been asked to give Sally away in the absence of her father, who was still out there in the Atlantic on the convoys, and Peggy's soft heart melted at the thought of how dear that little girl had come to be to her family.

The tiny stone church had been lit with dozens of candles. There were no flowers – it was the wrong time of year, and the florists had all closed – but the pews were packed with Sally and John's friends, and Peggy beamed in delight to see Pearl's husband Billy sitting next to John in the front row. Pearl must be thrilled to have him home now she was so close to having that baby, she thought, as she sat down and gave Ron a sharp dig in the ribs to remind him to take off his hat.

The congregation was mainly female, and Anne and Cissy started chatting to friends as the soft organ music drifted through the church. Mrs Finch put on her glasses, rummaged for a handkerchief, and opened the hymn book, her hearing aid buzzing away like a hive of bees. She didn't want to miss a word of the ceremony, for like Peggy, she loved a good cry at a wedding.

The choir entered and took their places by the altar and the organ music drifted into silence as the heavy oak door at the back of the church was opened with a creak and groan. The congregation rose as one and turned to get a glimpse of the bride.

John and Billy got to their feet as the lovely, familiar music began and Sally slowly drifted down the ancient flagstone aisle on Jim's arm. The beautiful silk dress she'd made for Anne all those months ago emphasised her elfin slenderness, the cloudy veil of lace unable to hide the brilliance of her eyes or the radiance in her lovely face.

Sally's joy seemed to light up the candlelit church, and Peggy had to dab her eyes as she saw the look of utter adoration on John's face as he leant heavily on his walking stick and watched her approach.

They stood together at the altar and exchanged their vows, and Peggy had to keep using her handkerchief to stop the tears ruining her make-up. They were meant for one another, it was clear, and the fates that had almost torn them apart had been vanquished. How long ago it seemed that Sally and her little brother had come from London to live with them – how the girl had changed, from waif to beauty – and all because she'd been given the chance to make a life for herself here in Cliffehaven.

Peggy felt a surge of deep affection which was

tinged with a certain pride. She had played her own part in the girl's transformation – she and Jim and Ron. And Jim looked as proud as any father as he placed her hand into John's, thereby giving her into his care.

She could hear Mrs Finch sniffling beside her and peeked at Betty, John's mother. She too was in tears. Oh, she thought, the tears streaming, what a happy, happy day.

As John slipped the band of gold on to Sally's finger and gently drew back her veil, the congregation held their breath and sighed with pleasure as he kissed her with infinite tenderness.

Once the register had been signed, they emerged once more to the sound of the triumphal wedding march. John had to lean heavily on his walking stick, but with Sally lightly holding his arm, he carefully and purposefully walked down the aisle. Their faces said it all, and Peggy wouldn't have minded betting that there wasn't a dry eye in the place as everyone followed them outside.

Peggy blew her nose and dabbed her eyes in an attempt to pull herself together as they stood on the church steps and watched the happy couple greet their friends. Pearl looked ready to pop as she stood in Billy's embrace, her face radiant with happiness. Peggy took a quick glance round the gathering and was thankful there was no sign of Sally's awful mother, Florrie. She'd left Cliffehaven months ago and hadn't been heard from since – which was a good thing, thought Peggy, for if she had dared to show her face again, she would have socked her in the eye.

She collected her frazzled thoughts and looked

up at Jim. 'You look very handsome, Jim Reilly,' she murmured. 'You should wear a suit more often.'

'And you're a fine-looking woman, so y'are, Peggy Reilly.' He grinned down at her, his dark blue eyes twinkling, his smile roguish. 'Or at least you would be if half your make-up wasn't running down your face.'

She gasped in horror and was about to rummage in her bag for a mirror when he stopped her with a kiss. 'You look beautiful,' he murmured against her lips. 'I was only teasing.'

'Jim Reilly, you'll be the death of me,' she giggled

He put his arm round her waist and gave her a squeeze. 'I don't know what it is about weddings,' he muttered, 'but they always make me want to marry you all over again.'

She was so taken aback by this declaration that she didn't quite know how to respond. 'You are so full of the blarney, Jim Reilly, that they should turn you into a national monument in Galway.'

His eyes lost their sparkle and his expression was almost yearning as he looked into her face. 'I know I'm not the best husband in the world,' he said softly, 'but I'd be lost without you. You won't ever leave me, will you, Peggy?'

Peggy stared up at him. What on earth had got into her husband? 'If I was ever going to leave you,' she said firmly, 'I'd have done it years ago. You're stuck with me, Jim, like it or not, so let's stop talking nonsense and concentrate on celebrating this wedding.'

The afternoon had sped by once everyone had left for the wedding. The other three girls were asleep upstairs after their night shift, and Polly had promised Peggy she would make sure they had a proper meal before they left for the hospital that evening, so she had a vegetable stew simmering on the hob.

By mid-afternoon she was pleasantly tired. It had been rather nice to have the house to herself for once, and she was enjoying being a housewife for a few hours. She had finished all the ironing she'd found in Peggy's laundry basket. There were clean sheets and towels flapping on the washing line in the brisk breeze that was coming off the sea, and the kitchen lino had been scrubbed.

She sat down for a sandwich and cup of tea at four o'clock and decided she might take Harvey for a short walk before it got too dark. The days were shorter now they were rapidly approaching Christmas, and if she didn't leave soon she ran the risk of getting caught somewhere in the middle of a raid.

Washing her plate and cup, she left them to dry on the wooden drainer and wrote a note for the other girls to help themselves to the stew if she wasn't back in time. She leant the note against the bottle of tomato sauce that stood in the middle of the kitchen table and hurried upstairs to get her coat, sturdy shoes and gas mask.

The knock on the front door came just as she was about to put on her coat, and she hurried downstairs to see who it was. When she opened the door she could only stare at the woman on the doorstep.

'Polly,' said Kate Jackson. 'Do you remember me?'

'Yes.' The muscles in Polly's face felt stiff and something cold seemed to be clutching her heart. 'What do you want, Miss Jackson?'

Kate's smile made her look positively youthful. 'Can I come in? Only there's something I have to tell you.'

The icy band round Polly's heart tightened. 'I've heard all you've got to say,' she began.

'But this is important, Polly,' Kate broke in. 'It's good news. I promise.'

Polly let her in as if she had no control over what happened. 'Good news?' She shut the front door and followed Kate into the kitchen. 'The only good news would be that my family survived. Anything else means nothing to me.'

Kate was almost hopping with excitement. 'Alice is alive, Polly.'

'What?' Polly sank into a chair and stared at her. Her brain didn't seem to be functioning at all. 'But she's dead. She drowned with Mum and Megan and the boys. You sat there only a few weeks ago and told me so.' Tears pricked and the anger rose. 'What sort of cruel game are you playing?'

Kate squatted beside her and took her hands. There were tears in her eyes too. 'I'm not playing any kind of game, Polly. She's alive. She didn't drown with the others. She's safe and well and asking for you.'

Hope surged like a warm tide, melting the ice, shattering her fear and sorrow. 'But how? Why didn't...? When did you know this?'

Kate pulled another chair close and sat down. 'She was among the original survivors of one of the lifeboats that were picked up by a destroyer, but because she'd lost her identity tag, no one could identify her. It was thought at first that she was another child, but then it was proved to be a mistake. The other child's body was found and identified by her aunt who'd been travelling with her.'

'Where is she?' Polly could barely breathe.

'She's been admitted to the Smithston Hospital in Greenock, which is in western Scotland.'

The truth was at last sinking in, but with it came confusion and a tide of questions. 'But I made sure she knew her name and address. I drummed it into her when she was old enough to understand how important it was if she ever got lost. Why didn't she tell you straight away?'

Kate bit her lip. 'According to survivors' reports, the U-boat struck in the middle of the night, and many of the children were killed before they could be put in the lifeboats. Alice's lifeboat had been drifting in the Atlantic for over eight hours before they were rescued. It was bitterly cold, with enormous waves washing over and threatening to sink them. She was badly traumatised, Polly, and suffering from exposure.'

Polly stared at her, the visions of what had happened to Alice vivid in her head.

Kate took her hands. 'Alice couldn't speak until two days ago. It was as if she had closed herself off to the outside world, and it was only after some very specialised care by trained doctors that she began to talk again.' Kate smiled. 'You taught her well, Polly. She told us her name and age, and the address where you lived in Hereford.'

Polly still couldn't believe it. She wanted to – desperately – but so many mistakes had already been made and it would be too cruel to let this hope take hold. 'You're sure?' she whispered. 'You're absolutely positive it's my Alice?'

Kate dug into her large handbag. 'The doctor took this photograph and sent it special delivery as proof.' She held it out.

Polly's hand was trembling as she took the small black-and-white photograph. 'Oh, Alice,' she breathed, 'Alice my darling, darling, precious baby. You're safe – really and truly safe.' She held the photograph to her lips and kissed the image of the little girl smiling back at her.

'As you've gone through such a terrible few weeks, the Overseas Board has arranged for you to travel to Scotland to see her. It will be a long, hazardous journey, Polly, but I'm sure you won't mind that.'

'When can I go?' she breathed.

'I have your travel pass here. You can leave first thing tomorrow morning.'

Polly threw her arms around Kate and hugged her so hard she had to gently extricate herself. 'I'm just so sorry you've been through such a bad time,' she said, dabbing at her tears. 'Some terrible mistakes have been made. But in defence of the authorities, the *City of Benares* wasn't the only ship to have been torpedoed that night. The SS *Marina* was hit too, and with so many to rescue from those terrible seas, it was no wonder one of the lifeboats was overlooked. It was a miracle it was spotted by that plane, and those children brought home to safety.' She blew her nose. 'Your Alice was one of the lucky ones, Polly. She was rescued fairly quickly, so no lasting harm has been done.'

Polly's smile was joyous. 'My baby's safe. She's safe, and soon I'll see her and hold her again. It's a miracle, Kate, an absolutely wonderful, unbelievable miracle.'

Kate nodded. 'Even in the midst of war there are miracles,' she agreed. 'I'll leave you to celebrate, Polly. And if you need me for anything, you have my private telephone number.'

Polly hugged her again, thanking her profusely right up to the moment she closed the door. Alice was alive and only a few days' journey away. Some might think that Scotland was too far to travel, but she wouldn't have minded if she'd had to go to the ends of the earth to hold her again.

She stood in the hall, filled with wonder and joy and wanting to shout her news to the rooftops. But the house was silent, the only occupants asleep. It didn't matter, she'd wake them anyway.

Pounding up the stairs she called out to them. 'Alice is alive. She's alive and in Scotland, and I'm going to be with her in just a few days.' She burst into their bedrooms. 'Wake up, wake up. It's wonderful news. Alice is alive.'

They leapt out of their beds and rushed to hug her, jumping up and down as they stood on the landing in their nightwear. Harvey barked and leapt and tried to join in as Polly was bombarded with questions and hugged and kissed. Then they all charged downstairs to celebrate with a bottle of sherry Suzy found at the back of the pantry.

Polly's head was buzzing by the time the girls left for the hospital, and she realised she'd had enough sherry, and a cup of tea might calm her down. There was a lot to do before she left tomorrow, and she needed to keep her wits. She had to ring the hospital and warn Matron that she wouldn't be able to start her week of night shifts the next day. Then she had to pack, and tell Adam...

She glanced at the clock on the mantelpiece and grabbed her coat. If she ran all the way she might just make the end of visiting hour. She'd been so busy celebrating that she'd lost track of the time.

Mary wasn't on duty, and Polly felt a stab of disappointment, for she wanted to tell everyone her wonderful news. She hurried to Adam's bedside and sat down. Reaching for his hand, she gently tried to wake him. 'Adam? Adam, it's Polly,' she said, unable to keep the excitement out of her voice. 'Please wake up, darling. I've got something to tell you.'

His eyelids fluttered and he turned his head towards her. 'I'm really tired, Polly,' he murmured sleepily. 'Can't it wait?'

She gripped his fingers. 'Adam, I have to go and see Alice,' she said urgently. 'I don't know how long I'll be gone, but I won't be able to come and visit you for a while.'

'That's all right,' he muttered, clearly not understanding.

'Adam,' she said firmly. 'Please try and listen. I am going to see Alice, and I might not be coming in to see you for a long time.'

'Alice?' he muttered as he struggled to wake. 'Why, what's the matter with her?'

Polly had already worked out what to say. 'She's not been very well and is asking for me. I've been assured it isn't serious, but I need to see her for myself. She's so little, and she needs me.'

'All right,' he said on a deep sigh. 'Give her a kiss from Daddy.'

'Adam?' He was asleep again and Polly cursed the drugs he was on. 'Oh, Adam,' she murmured, 'I so wish things were different. I need you, my darling. I need you to hold me, to be Adam again. Am I greedy to ask for more miracles tonight?'

She fell silent, accepting that she was. Adam would come through this and sleep would help him recover. She kissed his cheek, lingering for a moment in the hope that he'd know she was there. When there was no response, she left the ward to the sound of the bell ringing out the end of visiting time.

Chapter Eighteen

Polly had packed her bags, and everything was prepared for the next day. Her travel pass, identity card and tickets were carefully tucked in an inside pocket of her handbag along with her food ration book which she'd liberated from Peggy's kitchen mantelpiece. All she had to do now was clean her shoes and remember to pack her nightclothes and washbag the following morning.

Her happiness was clouded, at times, by the knowledge that there had been no miracle to save her mother, sister and nephews. They would never return – and in those quiet, still moments, she asked them to forgive her joy. She would never forget them, never stop loving them, but Alice and Adam had to be her priority now.

She decided not to go and sit alone in the Anderson shelter when the sirens went off just after seven o'clock. There was too much to do and she felt as if she was untouchable now which probably wasn't wise – but she simply couldn't believe that the fates could stop her from going to Scotland now. Why work a miracle only to have it destroyed by a Nazi bomb? It didn't make any sense.

She discovered she was singing along to the late-night concert on the wireless as she polished her shoes over a piece of newspaper on the kitchen table, and Harvey snored beside the fire. It was almost eleven and everyone would soon be home. Danuta was out in her ambulance somewhere, waiting to be called if there was an emergency, but it didn't sound as if Cliffehaven had been a target for the bombers tonight, and the only explosions she'd heard seemed to come from far out to sea.

Polly put the brushes and polish away, screwed up the dirty paper with that pervert's face on the front page and committed it to the fire in the range. The all-clear had just sounded and it was time to make some cocoa so that when the others came in they could have a nightcap to beat off the chill.

Less than twenty minutes later, she heard the sound of a heavy engine rumbling to a halt outside, and the laughter and chatter of many voices. Rushing to open the front door, she was met by such a curious sight she burst out laughing.

A fire engine was parked outside the house, and Peggy was protesting uproariously as Jim hoisted her out of the driver's cab and over his shoulder in a fireman's lift. Ron was riding shotgun on the back with the ladders and hoses, and he clambered down to pluck Mrs Finch from the cab and carry her, twittering and flustered, up the front steps. Wearing a fireman's helmet, Cissy giggled as she slid from the cab and showed rather a lot of leg to a very admiring fire officer, and Anne was in the arms of another sturdy man and blushing furiously as he set her gently on her feet.

'Put me down this instant, Jim Reilly,' laughed Peggy as Jim carried her up the steps. 'Everyone can see my knickers.'

'To be sure they're very fine knickers,' he chortled. 'And a very fine arse inside them too.' He patted said arse and gave it a pinch.

Peggy yelped and kicked as she beat her fists on his back, her face scarlet. 'Put me down this instant,' she ordered furiously.

He swung her down as if she weighed nothing, and carried her in his arms the rest of the way into the house, then dumped her unceremoniously in her favourite chair. After giving her a hearty kiss on her cheek, he began to rummage in the dresser cupboard. 'Time for a nightcap,' he said, his voice slightly slurred by the amount of beer he'd already sunk.

Polly heard all this while she waited for the others. Mrs Finch was all of a dither as she straightened her hat and thanked Ron. 'I didn't realise you were so strong,' she said admiringly. 'Goodness me, I'm feeling quite light-headed.'

Ron grunted something unintelligible and stomped into the kitchen in search of another drink.

Cissy was still flirting as Anne thanked the men and slowly climbed the steps. 'They were so kind to give us a lift home,' she murmured happily as she stretched her back. 'I do hope they don't get into trouble, but the trolleybus doesn't go after ten and none of us wanted to leave the party early.'

Cissy gave the fireman back his helmet and rushed up the steps. With a broad grin, she waved goodbye to him. 'Gosh,' she breathed. 'That was fun. I'll have to write to Bob and Charlie and tell them all about it. They'll be ever so envious.'

Now everyone had come home, it appeared they were not at all interested in cocoa. Jim had found the last of Aleksy's vodka and was slopping it into glasses as Polly returned to the kitchen.

'Before you drink that,' she said, cutting through the babble, 'I have some wonderful news to tell you.' She grinned as silence fell and they all turned to look rather blearily at her. 'Alice is alive, and I'm going to Scotland tomorrow to be with her.'

She was hugged and kissed by Peggy, Cissy and Anne, and Jim and Ron gave her an awkward pat on the back as they congratulated her.

'This calls for a toast,' roared Jim, who'd already toasted just about everything he could think of tonight. 'Here's to Alice Brown. Slainte!'

It was some time before Polly could escape to her room. She really needed to get a good night's sleep before her long journey, but Peggy's family had been so lovely in their joy at her news that it would have been rude not to have had one or two drinks with them as they talked over the wedding and her plans for the future.

As she lay in bed and listened to the noise slowly die down, and the various bedroom doors close, she wondered what her future held. To go to Scotland certainly; but then what? Adam still needed her – did she dare bring Alice here – or was it safer to leave her where she was? Peggy couldn't guarantee there would be room for her if she came back after too long, which would mean finding a new billet and one that accepted children if she dared to bring Alice with her. Her head and heart tussled with the worry of it – it was a huge dilemma, and one that she was in no fit state to solve tonight.

She was nowhere near sleep for she was too overwrought and excited, the alcohol making her head buzz. She switched on the bedside lamp when she heard someone creep upstairs and into the bathroom, and climbed out of bed, wrapped herself in her dressing gown and waited until Danuta crept in some twenty minutes later. 'It's all right,' she murmured. 'I'm not asleep.'

Danuta dumped her coat on the chair and sat down to untie her sturdy boots. 'Well, I will sleep the moment my head hits the pillow,' she said through a vast yawn. 'There was a terrible accident, and we have spent most of the night digging people out and getting them to hospital.'

'But I didn't hear any bombs hit the town.' Polly drew her knees to her chin and hugged them as she sat on the other bed.

'They didn't,' said Danuta, keeping her back to Polly as she stripped off her sweater, dungarees and liberty bodice before slipping on the winceyette nightgown Peggy had given her. 'A bombed-out house had not been made properly safe and it fell on top of the house next door, which then fell on the next. It was a terrible mess, but we managed to get everyone out, even though two of them were dead.'

'How awful,' Polly breathed, 'and to think that only a short distance away Peggy and the others were celebrating a wedding.'

Danuta, still shielded by the nightgown, stepped out of her knickers and slung them towards the rest of her things that were now strewn across the chair. 'How did it go?'

Polly frowned as Danuta moved across the bedroom. The light from the bedside lamp was meagre, and the nightdress was voluminous, but it couldn't quite hide the fact that Danuta seemed to have put on a suspicious amount of inches around her middle.

'It went very well,' she replied distractedly. 'Everyone came home in a fire engine, and we sat up drinking until gone midnight to celebrate.'

Danuta perched on her bed and frowned. 'You celebrate too? But you do not know this Sally, I think. She live here before I come.'

Polly decided the light had been playing tricks

with her. She grinned at Danuta. 'I was celebrating something far more important,' she said. 'My Alice is alive, Danuta. She was alive all the time, and tomorrow,' she glanced at the clock, 'no, today, I'm going to Scotland to be with her.'

Danuta leapt off her bed and flung her arms around Polly and, as the two young women embraced, Polly knew the light had not been playing tricks. They eventually parted and, as Polly tried to answer Danuta's bombardment of questions, her gaze kept returning to the other girl's midriff.

Danuta eventually became aware of her scrutiny and hastily clambered into bed, pulling the covers to her chin. 'I'm very tired,' she said, turning off the light. 'I must sleep now.'

Polly's whisper floated into the silence. 'You're pregnant, aren't you?'

Danuta shifted in her bed and didn't reply for a while, and when she did, it was on a sigh. 'Yes.'

'How far along are you? Five, six months?'

'Five months,' she admitted softly. She sat up and switched the light back on. Her green eyes were pleading for understanding. 'Please say nothing. I must keep this baby secret for as long as I can.'

Polly questioned her gently but firmly about her antenatal care. 'Well,' she said when she was satisfied Danuta was doing all the right things, 'at least you're not leaving anything to chance. But you're entitled to extra allowances of milk and cheese and all sorts of things now. You will have to sort that out, Danuta – and tell Peggy.'

'I am afraid she will tell me to leave,' said the other girl softly. 'It is a big disgrace, I think, to

384

have child and no husband.'

Polly heard the quiver in her voice and her heart went out to her. She'd been hiding her pregnancy for months, and despite all her steeliness and verve, she was just a frightened girl with no one of her own to turn to in her time of need.

'I'm sure it won't come to that,' she soothed, perching on Danuta's bed. 'Peggy isn't the sort of woman to turn away someone who needs help. She's far too soft-hearted.'

'But what will happen when the baby comes? I cannot expect her to let us stay.'

'I think you need to talk to her – and soon. I'm sure everything will be fine.' Polly took Danuta's trembling hand. 'I'm sorry I can't be with you for a while, but you've got friends here, Danuta. They'll look after you and the baby.'

'I wish Jean-Luc was here,' Danuta murmured, the tears glistening on her cheeks.

'Where is he? Back in Poland?'

Danuta shook her head, the tears running faster now. 'He is dead. The Gestapo take him.'

Polly held her as she wept, thinking how right it was for her to give comfort when Danuta had been so kind to her during those awful weeks when Alice was thought to be dead. She waited for the storm to subside and handed her a clean handkerchief. 'Do you want to talk about it, Danuta? Or is it too painful?'

Danuta blew her nose and took a deep breath. 'It is painful, yes, but I have learnt to live with it, and now it does not twist like a knife so sharply in my heart.' Her eyelids were swollen as she looked at Polly. 'I may tell you? It is not a pretty story, but I have kept it inside for so long, it needs to come out.'

Polly nodded, dreading what she might hear, but knowing she couldn't let this girl down. By the sound of it she'd been through a great deal more than Polly could begin to imagine, and her kindness deserved to be reciprocated.

'Take your time,' she murmured, holding her close. 'We have the rest of the night.'

Danuta felt the baby move inside her as she tried to control her emotions. The memories were flooding back, sharply cruel and bringing a return of the pain she'd thought she'd vanquished.

'I met Jean-Luc in Warsaw before the war. He was a medical student, and I was training to be a nurse. His mother was French, his father was a Pole, but his grandparents were originally from Germany, so he was fluent in all three languages. Jean-Luc's father's family had moved to Warsaw many years before. They were Jews.'

She took a deep breath. 'I am Catholic, and both families did not like us to be together. But for me and Jean-Luc it didn't matter. We were in love.'

She could feel her face lighting up as she thought back to those far-off days – days of youthful enthusiasm and laughter, days when they'd believed they had the world at their feet, and a whole lifetime to live out their dreams.

'We had such plans, Polly,' she said softly. 'Such wonderful plans. We would get our qualifications and marry, and Jean-Luc would set up his own clinic with me working as his nurse. We needed money to do this, so we were still working at the hospital when the Germans came last September.'

Danuta fell silent, the bitterness caught in her throat as the terrifying images of tanks rumbling through the cobbled streets returned. She could almost hear the shouts of the soldiers and the death rattle of their machine guns as they enforced their presence and their power.

'You don't have to do this, Danuta,' said Polly softly.

'Yes, yes I do,' she said, her voice husky with the tears she refused to let fall. 'I must tell it all.' She grasped Polly's outstretched hand and closed her eyes. 'When the Germans came, Jean-Luc was forbidden to work in the hospital, or even run his own practice. He and his family were forced to wear the yellow star on their coats – and then they and all the other Jews in Warsaw were sent to live in the ghetto.'

Danuta shivered. 'Jean-Luc was very brave; he came into the city through the underground passages they had dug, looking for food, blankets, medicines – anything he could find to help his family get through that first terrible winter.'

She angrily blinked away the tears. 'Things got worse, and I was forced to leave my work at the hospital because I had loved him, and the Germans called me a whore – a Jew's whore. But for Jean-Luc it was more terrible, and soon it was known by all in Warsaw that the ghetto was being cleared – whole families taken away in trucks to the railway station. None of us knew where they had been sent.'

She took another deep breath and battled to

387

keep her composure. 'My brother's wife Anjelika and her little girl were taken too,' she said softly. 'I don't know why. Perhaps she'd been caught stealing food, or insulted a German officer who tried to pick her up – or maybe someone had falsely accused her of being a Jew. Neighbour informed against neighbour in return for scraps of food that winter – they didn't care that their lies cost others their lives. It was sometimes the only way to survive.'

'Dear God,' breathed Polly.

'God had very little to do with it,' said Danuta bitterly. 'He turned his back on us – wouldn't hear our prayers or strike out at our enemy. We were on our own.'

She gathered her thoughts and took a moment to find calm again. 'Jean-Luc knew what was happening, but there was nothing he could do. After his parents were taken, he and several of the other men escaped the ghetto and joined the resistance. He sent me a message, and I went to meet him. I had no reason to stay in Warsaw. My family were gone.'

'You were in the resistance?' Polly stared at her, wide-eyed.

'I had a lot to learn,' Danuta replied flatly, 'and it was very hard, living in the snow, scratching for food and warmth, and shelter – and keeping one step ahead of the Gestapo who were looking for us. They got too close after we'd blown up an ammunition factory, and caused big damage to many of their tanks and soldiers. Jean-Luc had become our leader, and his reputation as a brave freedom fighter had spread. But this meant we eventually had to leave Poland and make our way over the mountains into occupied Czecho-slovakia.'

She sniffed and blew her nose. 'It was early spring by the time we arrived there, and through Jean-Luc's contacts, we joined with the Czech resistance. But we soon had to move again. They were still looking for him, and his presence with the group was jeopardising their safety. So four of us decided to head for Switzerland, which was neutral. We planned to rest there, to find money and guns and men willing to carry on the fight against the invaders.'

'My geography is vague,' muttered Polly. 'But that sounds a terribly long journey. Surely you didn't walk it?'

Danuta's smile held little warmth as she shook her head. 'We killed the border guards and blew up their station, then stole their truck along with their rifles and ammunition. The truck got us over the mountains into Austria, but it was not safe to use it too long, so we had to walk a long time before we could find bicycles. Jean-Luc had taught me German and French – I found I had a flair for languages during those early days with him, and was a quick pupil – so between us we could buy food and get the four of us out of trouble when we were stopped. We all carried false identification papers and said we were farm labourers – peasants.'

Danuta twisted her hands in her lap. 'Jean-Luc became restless in Switzerland. He wanted to fight, to be a part of the growing resistance against the enemy, but the Swiss were too comfortable on their fence – they did not want to become in-volved. Our comrades decided to remain there – they had had enough of fighting so we left them and eventually crossed the mountain border into France.'

Danuta fell silent for a moment, remembering the terrible things she had done to secure their safety as they'd crawled past guard-posts and gun emplacements, and hidden from fleets of enemy tanks which roared within inches of the ditches where they lay. She had learnt to kill during those months after she'd left Warsaw, and had become adept at slitting throats and making booby traps – but Polly should not hear this, she would not understand.

We eventually managed to join a group of French resistance men and women through Jean-Luc's family contacts in Lyon – but we had to be very careful. The Vichy French were only too happy to collaborate with the Boches, and we never knew who we could trust.'

But it had not all been dark and forbidding, and she sighed as she remembered the hot, early summer days when they'd made love in the long grass, and lay watching the celestial displays in that enormous dark sky. 'Our baby was con-ceived in France, and one day I would like to take him there. It is very beautiful, even though the memories are sad.'

Danuta gave a grim smile. 'We did a lot of damage in and around Lyon before an informer told the Gestapo where we were hiding. Jean-Luc was almost caught one night trying to get back to us after he'd sabotaged the Germans' army base, and he insisted it was time for me to leave him.'

Tears sparkled on her lashes and she blinked them away. 'We knew I was having a baby, and he was desperate we should survive, for he also knew that the Gestapo were getting closer by the day, and soon it would be too late for us to escape.'

Her voice caught and her heart thudded as she remembered those terrible last hours. 'I begged him to come with me, but he refused – there was work to be done, and he was determined to see it through for as long as he lived.'

Her voice was barely above a whisper as the pain seared through her. 'I said goodbye to him that night, knowing I might never see him again, and before dawn I left with one of the Frenchmen who would take me to another group further into France.'

Danuta's resolve faltered and she could no longer fight the crippling pain that gripped her. 'We had not left the camp more than one half-hour when we saw the convoy of Gestapo cars and motorbikes make their way along the road towards the camp. There was nothing we could do but hide in the trees and watch.'

She swallowed and blew her nose. 'Jean-Luc and the others put up a fight, but they were too few against so many. Jean-Luc was wounded, but they didn't kill him. He was thrown into a truck and driven away to Gestapo headquarters.'

Silence fell for several minutes as Danuta tried to compose herself. 'I wanted to make the Gestapo headquarters explode,' she said bitterly. 'I wanted to run after that truck and shoot them all

391

down, even if it meant killing Jean-Luc. At least then they would not torture him.' She heaved a deep, sad sigh. 'But of course I couldn't. Jean-Luc had entrusted me to look after our child, and I had to honour that trust by staying alive.'

'And so you have, you brave, brave girl. Oh, Danuta.' Polly swept her up in a hug as their tears flowed.

'I am sorry, Polly,' Danuta finally managed. 'It is not a good story to tell before sleep, and it is after three o'clock. You will be very tired for your journey.'

'It doesn't matter,' said Polly. 'I can always sleep on the train. Come on, Danuta, let's cuddle up under the eiderdown and talk about other things until we get too tired to dream.'

Danuta nestled into Polly's embrace and, as the minutes ticked away and their talk became desultory, she felt her eyelids droop. Sleep came softly and dreamlessly for the first time in months.

Polly had left Danuta once she was sure she was sleeping soundly, and clambered into her own bed. She'd fallen asleep almost immediately, but now she was having a strange and disturbing dream in which Alice was in a lifeboat and the Gestapo were shooting at her. Somewhere in the distance there was the sound of a telephone ringing, and now she was in an unfamiliar room and they were at the door, knocking on it, calling her name.

She sat up abruptly as the door opened. Her heart was hammering with fear, for the dream still entangled her, and she fully expected an SS officer to step into the room. But it was only Peggy, and she was looking flustered. Feeling incredibly silly for being so easily frightened, Polly glanced at the clock; it was barely five.

'Polly, Danuta. I'm sorry to disturb you both, but this is important.'

Polly stiffened as Peggy came to stand next to her bed and reached for her hand. She tried to read the other woman's expression, and her heart thudded painfully when she realised that no good news came at such a time of day. 'What is it?' she breathed.

Peggy licked her lips. 'Polly, there's been a telephone call, dear. From the hospital. Adam has had some kind of fit and he's being prepared for theatre.'

Polly leapt from the bed and began to drag on her clothes. 'What kind of fit? Why does he need an operation? How serious is it?'

Peggy was wringing her hands. 'Matron just gave me the bare facts. I'm sorry, I don't know.' She chewed her bottom lip anxiously as she twisted the cord of her dressing gown between restless fingers. 'But she did say it was important you get there as quickly as possible.'

'I come with you.' Danuta clambered out of bed and was dressed before Polly could get her coat on.

Polly shot her a grateful glance and was out of the door and charging down the stairs. Her heart was beating a tattoo in time with her running footsteps as she raced along the pavement. She couldn't lose Adam – not now.

Chapter Nineteen

Matron was waiting outside the ward. 'Your husband will be taken up to theatre in a few minutes. Mr Fortescue is already preparing for surgery.'

'What happened?'

'He woke this evening complaining of being in pain. Within a few hours he had a fit, and Mr Fortescue thinks there must be something pressing on his brain. He had hoped all the shrapnel had been extricated, but he fears something could have been missed.'

'But you told me...'

Matron's glare silenced her. 'Surgery is not always straightforward, Staff Nurse Brown. Mr Fortescue is the best neurosurgeon in the country, and he has been known to work miracles, but nothing is ever certain in these cases.'

Chastened, Polly dipped her chin. 'Can I see Adam?'

'He's been prepped for theatre and won't know you're there,' warned Matron.

'It doesn't matter,' replied Polly, 'I want to see him anyway.'

Matron threw a stony glance at Danuta, who was looking very dishevelled and out of breath as she trudged towards them. Matron had never forgiven her for leaving the laundry, and decided to ignore her.

She turned back to Polly. 'I cannot permit any

other visitors at this time of the morning,' she said firmly. 'Your *friend* should wait outside.'

Polly nodded at Danuta and hurried after Matron, who was already striding down the ward to Adam's bed. Mary wasn't on duty, the curtains were drawn, and a nurse she didn't recognise was taking his pulse and temperature.

'You may stay one minute,' said Matron, chivvying the nurse out and snapping the curtains shut behind them.

Polly looked down at Adam and a chill of dread ran through her. He was the most ghastly colour, his eyes sunken above his sharp cheekbones as his breath rasped in his throat. She took his hand and realised he was already deeply sedated. 'Don't leave me, Adam. Please don't leave me,' she whispered desperately. 'Alice and I need you so much.'

His fingers twitched in her hand and, encouraged that he might be able to hear and understand what she was saying, she continued. 'Alice is well, my darling, and safe – and soon we will go and see her and be a family again. Oh, my darling, I love you so much,' she murmured, her tears falling on their entwined fingers. 'Please, please don't leave us.'

'That's quite enough of that,' said Matron brusquely as she swept back the curtains to let the porters through with the trolley. 'Go to the relatives' room, Staff Nurse, and I'll get someone to bring you a cup of tea.'

She didn't want tea; didn't want anything but reassurance – and that was clearly not on Matron's agenda. Polly stood back to give the porters room and watched as they carefully transferred Adam from the bed to the trolley.

'How long will he be in theatre?' she managed through her tear-filled throat as they pushed him along the ward and out into the corridor past a worried-looking Danuta.

'As long as it takes.' Matron took her arm and steered her towards the swing doors. Her austere expression softened momentarily. 'I know how hard this must be, but try not to worry,' she said softly. 'He's in very capable hands, and Mr Fortescue will do his utmost to pull him through this.'

Polly stared at her, wanting to believe her, but mistakes had been made already and now Adam's life hung in the balance. But she said nothing and pushed through the doors to find Danuta restlessly pacing the corridor.

When she had answered all of Danuta's questions as well as she could, she tucked her hand round Danuta's arm and led her away from the ward. 'I need some fresh air,' she said. 'The smell of this place is getting to me for once, and the thought of having to wait while they dig about inside Adam is making me feel quite ill.'

They slowly went through the silent reception area and down the steps until they were outside. A thin line of light along the horizon heralded the dawn as birds started twittering and the gulls began to screech at one another.

Polly sank on to the bottom step and looked at the sky, wondering what this new day had in store for her. Emotionally she was drained, and lack of sleep made her feel heavy with weariness – and yet she knew she had to find the strength to face whatever came, for the people she loved most in the world depended upon her.

'You will not be going to Scotland today, I think,' said Danuta, as she lit their cigarettes and puffed smoke into the still, cool air.

Polly stared at her in horror. 'Oh my God,' she gasped. 'I'd forgotten all about Scotland.'

'It's not surprising,' said Danuta, daintily removing a wisp of tobacco from her tongue and flicking it away. 'There has been much drama this last half-hour.'

'But what kind of mother am I to forget something so important?' Polly crushed the barely smoked cigarette she hadn't really wanted underfoot. 'I must ask Matron if I can use her telephone. Perhaps Kate Jackson can arrange for me to speak to Alice, so I can explain to her why I can't come just yet.'

'It is a little early, Polly. Miss Jackson will not be in her office.'

'I've got her private number in my bag...' Realisation dawned and her spirits tumbled further. 'I left it at home,' she muttered, 'and I dare not go and fetch it in case I'm needed here.'

'I will go and find it.' Danuta stood and ruffled her hair until it stood in spikes. 'I will come back very quick,' she assured her, and then set off at a fast walk and was soon out of sight.

Polly remained on the hospital step and listened to the sounds of Cliffehaven waking up. The milk cart rattled by, pulled by the plodding dray which knew the round so well, he probably didn't need the dairyman to guide him any more. The newspaper man cycled past shortly after, his tuneful whistling sounding quite cheerful for such an early hour.

More nurses and doctors were in evidence now, ambulances were being driven out ready for emergencies, porters were hurrying back and forth, and the sky was struggling to lighten beneath a heavy pall of cloud.

Polly sighed. It appeared that fate gave with one hand and took with another – and, as life went on around her, the gloomy day only added to her misery.

Danuta was out of breath by the time she reached Beach View. She had a stitch in her side, and all the running and rushing she'd done this morning was taking its toll. As she let herself into the house, she discovered Peggy was standing in the hall as if waiting for her.

Peggy's expression was fearful. 'Why aren't you still with Polly? Has something happened to Adam? He's not...?'

Danuta was so out of breath it was a few moments before she could reply. 'He's just gone in to theatre, and I've come to get Kate Jackson's private number. Polly needs to speak to her,' she panted, holding her side where the stitch was hurting her.

'I have already done that,' said Peggy. 'She gave me her home number some time ago, so I was able to get hold of her very quickly. I've told her what has happened, and she suggested she might try to arrange for Polly to speak to Alice if they can get a line through to Scotland. Unfortunately it would be long-distance, and with so many lines down because of the bombing, it may take a while to get the connection – but I'm sure Kate will manage something so Polly can speak to Alice.'

Danuta smiled. 'That is what Polly was hoping,' she said. 'I will go and tell her.'

'Before you leave,' said Peggy, 'is there anything you wish to tell me, Danuta?'

She met Peggy's rather stern gaze and felt stabs of guilt and fear. 'I do not understand,' she hedged.

Peggy's eyes glinted determinedly and her gaze slowly travelled from Danuta's neck to the hem of her coat. 'I think you do,' she said softly.

Danuta realised she could no longer prevaricate. She lifted her chin defiantly. 'How did you find out?'

'I wondered several days ago,' said Peggy, 'but when you got dressed this morning I knew there was no mistake. How far gone are you?'

Danuta bit her lip, not quite daring to meet the older woman's eyes. 'Five months,' she replied. 'If you wish me to leave,' she rushed on, 'then I would ask you to give me time to find another billet!'

'Oh, my dear,' sighed Peggy. 'I'm not about to throw you out. I'm just disappointed that you didn't trust me enough to tell me.'

Danuta looked at her then and saw genuine sorrow in Peggy's face. 'I am sorry,' she murmured. 'I am thinking you would be ashamed of me. It is not good to have baby and no husband, and I did not want you to think I am bad person.'

Peggy gave her a sad smile as she lightly

brushed Danuta's cheek with her fingers. 'I would never think of you as bad, Danuta – and not really knowing your circumstances before you arrived here, how could I judge you?'

Danuta felt a surge of hope. 'Then you are not angry?'

'Why should I be?' Peggy looked genuinely surprised. 'These things happen – especially during wartime when the future is so uncertain.' She blushed a little and dipped her chin. 'I'll let you into a little secret,' she whispered as she drew nearer. 'I was expecting Anne before I took my marriage vows at the end of the last war – so I do understand, Danuta. Really I do.'

Danuta felt a great tide of warm affection for Peggy Reilly and only just managed to resist throwing her arms about her. 'So, I can stay here?'

'Of course. You'll need to be looked after, and once the baby arrives then I'm sure we can come to some arrangement over babysitting and such.'

'But you will soon have your own grandchild to care for.'

'The more the merrier,' said Peggy, and laughed. 'Don't look so flabbergasted, Danuta, what did you expect? For me to turn my back on you?' She shook her head and drew Danuta into a warm embrace. 'Your brother was much loved, and it's an honour to help his sister in her time of need.'

Danuta hugged her back, the baby moving between them.

Peggy slowly released her and giggled. 'Lively little chap, isn't he?'

At Danuta's shy smile, Peggy patted her cheek. 'Don't worry, I'll sort out all the paperwork for the extra rations and vitamins.' Her smile was bright, her eyes watery. 'Think of us as your family, Danuta. We will take care of you and your baby for as long as you need us.'

Danuta was close to tears as well. 'I must go to Polly,' she snuffled into a handkerchief. 'She will wonder where I have got to.'

'Do you want me to telephone the Red Cross and let them know you won't be in today?'

'Please.'

'And do you want me to register you with our doctor and arrange for the district nurse to call round?'

Danuta shook her head. 'I already have doctor, and I see midwife at clinic.' She took a hesitant step towards Peggy and quickly planted a soft kiss on her fragrant cheek. 'Thank you,' she breathed and, before she could make a complete idiot of herself by bursting into tears, Danuta fled back to the hospital.

Polly and Danuta sat in the relatives' waiting room as others came and went and the clock ticked ever more slowly through the long, anxious hours. Cups of tea had been brought by a probationer and left to grow cold, cigarettes had been smoked and mashed out into the large ashtray that sat on a low side table, and the linoleum covered floor had been paced. It felt as if they were in a cage, and Polly was as restless as a tiger.

They were sitting alone when Peggy arrived at eight-thirty with a flask and a packet of sandwiches. She shut the door firmly behind her and sat down on one of the uncomfortable chairs that lined the walls. 'You left without breakfast, and I know what the tea is like in these places,' she muttered.

As she unscrewed the lid of the flask, the heavenly aroma of real coffee drifted into the room. 'Don't ask how I got this,' she warned softly. 'Let's just say I found it at the back of the larder.'

'If I know Jim,' murmured Polly, with a wan smile, 'it more likely fell off the back of a lorry.'

'Lorries and husbands certainly have their uses,' Peggy chuckled. She tapped the side of her nose and winked before digging into her string bag for the china cups. 'I thought we'd appreciate our treat even more out of proper china,' she murmured as she began to pour the coffee.

Polly's mouth watered as the dark, milky coffee was divided between them and, as she took her first sip, she realised she couldn't remember the last time she'd had such a perfect drink. It was ambrosia, soothing and sweet – and yet sharp enough to give her the boost she'd needed so badly.

Once every drop had been drained, the sandwiches were handed round, and although Polly didn't feel in the least bit hungry, she discovered she could manage at least two of the lovely soft rounds of bread with their home-made blackberry jam filling. They made her feel like a child again, bringing back the haunting memories of that long-ago seaside holiday with her parents.

'Mrs Brown?'

They turned as one to regard the tall, grey-bearded man in the smart suit and waistcoat who stood in the doorway. A smoking pipe was clenched in the corner of his mouth, his white, curling eyebrows looked as if they'd been brushed daily, and his thumbs were dug into his waistcoat pockets where a fine gold watch and chain dangled across his broad chest.

'Yes?' Polly got to her feet fearfully. This had to be Mr Fortescue – or God himself if Matron was to be believed.

'Mrs Brown.' His voice was a deep, rich baritone, and when he smiled, his face lit up, making him appear benign and fatherly. 'I'm Mr Fortescue, and I apologise for not having spoken to you before this,' he said, as he shook her hand.

'Now, you're not to worry, Mrs Brown,' he continued as he took the pipe from his mouth and inspected its contents. 'The operation was more straightforward than I anticipated, and your husband is now being looked after in the recovery ward.'

'Was it more shrapnel? Is there any damage to his brain?'

'Ah, yes, I was forgetting. You're on the nursing staff here.' He stuck the pipe back in his mouth and puffed on it as he once again dug his thumbs into the waistcoat pockets. 'It was a blood clot, Mrs Brown. A rather nasty one, but I got it all out and stitched him up again quick smart.'

'What is your prognosis for recovery time?'

He raised a magnificent eyebrow. 'He should wake within the next hour or so, and if he does not succumb to further clots or infection, I expect to see an improvement over the next few weeks.'

'Weeks?' breathed Polly. 'But he's already been

403

here for over three months.'

He looked down at her, his expression kindly beneath those fearsome brows. 'These things can't be hurried, Mrs Brown, and although I can understand how impatient you must be to see him fit again, you must let nature run its course. He has some way to go yet to full recovery, and I wouldn't expect him to leave here until the New Year at the very earliest.'

'Oh.' Polly's spirits deflated and she found she had to sit down, for her legs simply wouldn't hold her any more. 'I was hoping we could go to Scotland for Christmas,' she murmured.

'He is certainly not fit enough to travel to Scotland,' Fortescue said firmly. 'And I doubt he will be for some time to come.' He lowered his brows and eyed her intently. 'I hope you aren't planning to leave us, Mrs Brown? Your husband's recovery depends in part on your regular visits to his bedside. The sight of a loved one perks up patients no end, and I firmly believe it speeds the healing process.'

Polly bit back the tears and swallowed the lump in her throat. 'I'll be here all the while he needs me,' she replied.

'Good, good.' He pulled out his pocket watch and checked the time. 'You may visit for five minutes in about an hour. He should be coming round from the anaesthetic by then, but I warn you, he will be groggy and not making much sense until it's worn off.'

He smiled at Polly. 'I'm needed elsewhere,' he muttered around the pipe-stem. 'Good day to you, Mrs Brown.'

It was now the middle of November. Ten days had passed since Adam's operation and, as Mr Fortescue had promised, he seemed to be making much better progress. The plaster casts had finally been removed from his leg and arm, the awful scar on his chest was fading nicely to a thin white line, and his head bandages had been reduced to a single strip of gauze which covered the cotton padding over the entry of his last operation.

Polly knew how close he'd come to death, for she'd surreptitiously read his notes. If that blood clot had moved more swiftly, it would have killed him instantly. Mr Fortescue might not be a god but, in Polly's estimation, he was damned close to being one, and she joined the ranks of his greatest admirers.

Adam's recovery could be seen every time Polly visited, and she knew he was feeling very much better when he began to complain that he was bored and restless. His physiotherapy wasn't due to start for two weeks, and although the nurses massaged the wasted muscles in his arm and leg, he was frustrated at being kept in his bed.

Polly tried to persuade him that it was too soon to be up and about, but being a man, he wouldn't listen. It wasn't until Mr Fortescue read him the riot act that he finally took notice – but he did it with little grace, and by each evening, he was morose and out of sorts. He'd always been an active man, good at sport, fit and healthy, and Polly could understand his frustration, but she did wish he wouldn't be quite so grumpy during visiting hour.

Kate Jackson finally came to Beach View with the news that there would be a special link set up between the two hospitals so that Alice could speak to both her parents. Matron had agreed to this, and Mr Fortescue had given permission for Adam to be taken to her office in a wheelchair. Polly was overjoyed, but it left her with a serious dilemma. She would now have to tell Adam why Alice was in Scotland.

It was the day before the link-up and Polly could leave it no longer. She got special permission from Matron to go on to the ward early that morning so she could tell him while he was still in a good frame of mind.

'Hello, Pol,' he said cheerfully. 'What are you doing here so early?'

Polly sat down and took a deep breath. 'Darling, there's something I have to tell you.' She saw the fear flash in his eyes and hurried to reassure him. 'It's not something bad – well, not all of it – but mostly it's wonderful.'

He winced as he dragged himself up the pillows, but his gaze was steady and questioning. 'Go on,' he murmured.

Polly gathered the tattered remnants of her courage and told him everything. From the day she'd said goodbye to them, to the miraculous day when she'd learnt that Alice was alive. She was aware of his blue eyes darkening at times with anger, saw the tears shine before he blinked them away – but his gaze never left her face as he gripped her hand.

'So, that's why Alice is in Scotland,' she finished. 'And tomorrow we'll be able to speak to her on the telephone line they've opened especially.'

'Why didn't you tell me before this?' he asked gruffly.

'Because you were too ill, and I was afraid it would make you worse. I was also frightened you would hate me for sending her away in the first place,' she admitted in a whisper. 'And I was already feeling guilty enough and couldn't have borne that.'

He studied her for a long moment, and then reached up and tenderly wound his fingers through her tangle of curls. 'My poor little Polly,' he said, his voice unsteady, his eyes suspiciously bright. 'How could I ever hate you? You're my most precious girl, my beautiful Rapunzel with hair that sparks fire and eyes that make my heart beat faster.'

Polly kissed the palm of his hand as he cupped her cheek.

'It must have been so hard for you, Polly, and I can't begin to imagine what you've been suffering after losing your family like that. I'm so sorry I wasn't able to help you get through all this.'

'You're helping me now,' she whispered against his lips. 'Get better soon, my darling, and then we can go and see our baby.'

'I promise to do my very best,' he murmured before kissing her.

The next morning found them sitting in Matron's office, Adam in the much-hated wheelchair, and Polly on the very edge of the unyielding chair. She was so keyed up that when the telephone rang she flinched.

'Cliffehaven Memorial Hospital. Matron's office,' said Matron in her very best telephone voice. 'Thank you.' She smiled at Polly and passed her the receiver before discreetly leaving the room.

'Hello, Alice?' Polly shouted through the static.

'Mummy? Is that you, Mummy?'

Her heart thudded with joy at the sound of her child's voice. 'Yes, darling, it's me, and Daddy's here too.' She put the receiver between them so Adam could say hello, and they heard Alice squeal in delight. 'Where are you?' she demanded. 'I can't see you. Are you coming to get me now?'

'We're a long, long way away,' said Polly after swallowing the lump in her throat. 'We can't come just yet, because Daddy's got a bad leg.'

'I miss you, Mummy.' The little voice was plaintive and close to tears.

'And I miss you too,' Polly managed, her arms aching to hold her, her heart drumming with painful yearning.

'How's my little pumpkin?' said Adam. 'Is she still ticklish?'

Alice giggled. 'Oh, Daddy, you are silly. 'Course I am.'

'Then you keep all those tickles for when I come and see you,' he said gruffly.

'Daddy, I want to come home.' Her piping voice wavered and stuttered. 'Why can't I come home?'

Adam had to take a deep breath before he could reply. 'It isn't time yet,' he said softly. 'Daddy has to have lots of sleeps and so do you until then.'

It broke their hearts to hear their little girl sobbing at the other end of the line, and Polly could barely speak through her own tears. 'Alice,' she said. 'Listen to me, Alice, sweetheart. Mummy and Daddy will be with you as soon as we can. We promise. But *you* have to promise to be a big strong girl and not to cry any more. Mummy and Daddy don't want you to cry, it makes us feel sad.'

'All right,' she hiccuped. 'I'll be a good girl. Grandma said I was a good girl, but she went away in the water. You won't go, will you?'

'No,' they said in unsteady unison. Polly gripped the receiver. 'Darling, we will write and send you some toys. What special thing would you like us to send you?'

'I've got lots of toys,' she said plaintively. 'I want my teddy.'

Polly closed her eyes. That teddy had been a present from Adam the day Alice had been born. It had been with her every night in her cot, and had even been squashed into her satchel when she'd started school. It must have been lost on that terrible night. 'I will send you a new teddy,' she said over the static. 'A lovely teddy you can cuddle.'

'All right.' The small voice sounded distant and very vulnerable.

A man's voice interrupted. 'I'm sorry, but you must finish now.'

'Goodbye, Alice, darling,' said Polly in a rush. 'I love you.' She blew kisses as Adam took the receiver.

'I love you lots, pumpkin, and when I see you, I'm going to hug you and kiss you until you're all gobbled up.'

Just before the pips went and they were cut off,

they heard the throaty chortle of their little girl and it broke their hearts.

It was almost the end of November, with only four weeks left to Christmas. There had been no let-up in the air raids, and most nights had been spent huddled round the paraffin heater in the Anderson shelter as they listened to the hundreds of bombers and fighter planes heading for London and the Midlands. Liverpool and Manchester had been as badly hit as London, but Coventry had almost been obliterated, and the people of Cliffe-haven counted their blessings as they remained relatively unscathed.

That was not to say it had escaped completely, and night after night, as the sirens shrieked out their warnings, Danuta and the others with the Red Cross ambulances were on stand-by to help the injured. Houses already weakened by nearby blasts crumpled into rubble, time bombs went off and incendiaries exploded over the rooftops. The fire and ambulance services were in constant demand as they worked with the wardens and did their best to rescue people and get them safely to hospital.

Cissy had received two letters from Joe Buchanan, and went about in a daze of happiness. She and Amy had been accepted into the WAAFs and proudly wore their uniform every time they came home to visit from their airbase billets, which were some miles away to the north. Life was exciting and busy, Witherspoon just a bad memory, and Danuta was delighted that her con-tribution towards his downfall had led to Cissy finding fulfilment at last.

Her own career as an ambulance driver hadn't gone so well.

Danuta had been in her element until she'd been closely questioned by the head of the ambulance service and told very firmly that she must stand down because of her pregnancy. She'd been angry and disappointed, for she'd felt well and healthy, apart from some early-morning sickness, and it was ridiculous to make her stay at home when there was so much she could have done.

The sirens had gone off at six the previous evening, just after Polly and the other three nurses had left for their night shifts at the hospital. Jim and Ron were on warden and fire-watch duty, so Danuta, Peggy and Mrs Finch spent the rest of the night in the shelter. They hadn't slept well, or comfortably, as hundreds of planes flew overhead and the Bofors guns thundered from the cliff-tops and esplanade. The whine of the little fighter planes as they engaged in dogfights, and the shrieks of some going down, had them all on edge.

The all-clear hadn't sounded until five-thirty that morning, and they'd wearily returned to the house to survey the damage of the night's raid. A bomb had gone off in one of the terraces behind them, and the vibration of it had broken two of the remaining windows and knocked most of the crockery off the shelves in the kitchen, leaving it shattered on the floor.

While Peggy rushed out to see if anyone needed help, Danuta swept up the mess and tried to find some more hardboard to cover the broken bedroom windows. The water had been cut off,

411

one of the mains had taken a direct hit, and the fire in the range had gone out, but Mrs Finch found enough water in the kettle to make tea over the primus stove.

Danuta felt very tired, and after drinking the welcome cup of tea, she went to lie down. As she lay there and watched the sky lighten through the open curtains, she rested her hands on the swell beneath her sweater.

She hadn't felt the baby move for several days now, and there seemed to be a dull, constant ache below her belly she couldn't shift. She had been warned she might get a few gentle contractions now she was approaching her sixth month, but it worried her all the same. There was an indefinable something that didn't feel quite right, and she was glad the midwife was due to visit the next day.

Deciding she was probably making too much of it – what did she know about having babies, except from medical books – she closed her eyes and drifted off to sleep.

Adam was making huge progress at last, and Polly knew it was because of that telephone call. Letters and parcels were simply not enough, and he was determined to recover sufficiently to travel to Scotland for Christmas.

Mr Fortescue and Polly chided him for pushing himself too hard, but Adam took no notice. He sweated and strained during the physiotherapy sessions on his arm and leg, and had finally thrown away the crutches. Now he leant heavily on a walking stick as he stomped about the hospital, impatience and frustration writ large in his expression.

There would be no return to his fighting regiment, for which Polly was profoundly grateful, but the army would still employ him as a much-needed mechanic once he was passed fully fit. However, his main focus remained on Alice, and the sooner he and Polly could get to her the better and if that meant every muscle in his body ached, and he was completely drained by night-time, then so be it.

Polly watched him struggle and fight and knew the reason, but it didn't stop her worrying about him. In the quiet moments when she and Mary sat over cups of tea, she voiced her concerns.

'He tried to persuade me to go up there on my own,' she said as they sat in the canteen after their night shift. 'But as much as I long to be with her, I couldn't possibly leave him to do that journey alone. It's a long way, and after what I went through to get here, I suspect it will be quite hazardous as well, and although he's coming along very well, he isn't as strong as he likes to think he is.'

'But it's the spur he needed to get him out of bed and walking again,' murmured Mary. 'He's surprised us all at how quickly he's recovering.'

Polly sighed. 'I know, and I'm hugely grateful to everyone for helping him. But I keep expecting something else to happen to stop us getting to Alice.' She gave her friend a rueful smile. 'The fates haven't been particularly kind of late, and it's a bit like waiting for the second shoe to drop.'

Mary laughed. 'I know what you mean. The

413

mother-in-law is threatening to move in, and every time we have a raid I wonder if it's the one that'll bring her house down and force her to act on her threat.' She pulled a face. 'Lord knows how long we can live together before murder is done.'

Polly giggled and finished her tea. 'These things are sent to try us,' she said cheerfully. 'But I think murder would be going a little far.' They shared a look of understanding as they smiled at one another. 'I'm off,' Polly said, grabbing her things. 'See you tomorrow.'

Danuta woke and winced as a needle of pain ran up her side. She must have been lying awkwardly, she thought, as she climbed off the bed.

She shot a glance at the sleeping Polly, who must have come home while she was taking her nap. Stretching her back, which always seemed to have an ache in it somewhere these days, she ran her hands over her tight, swollen belly. But there was no response from the child inside, no flutter of fingers or gentle undulation of its body.

'You're tired too, I expect,' she muttered through a huge yawn. 'And I don't blame you. It is very boring to do nothing all day.'

She walked across the room to fetch her hairbrush and, as she reached for it, she felt a stab of pain that took her breath away. Curling into it she began to keen, the sweat beading her forehead as a chill of fear ran down her spine.

'No,' she pleaded. 'It's too soon. It can't be.'

'Danuta!' cried Polly. 'What's wrong?'

'Pain,' she gasped. 'Terrible pain.' She gasped as

she felt something warm trickle down her thighs to pool on the floor, and focussed on it as the pain began to subside, terrified she would see blood – but it seemed she had merely wet herself. 'I am sorry, Polly. I have...'

'It's all right, Danuta,' Polly said quietly. 'I think your waters have broken. Let's get you back to bed, and I'll ring the doctor.'

'It is too soon,' Danuta moaned as Polly gently led her the short distance to her bed. 'I cannot have this baby today. It must not come.' She collapsed into the welcome softness of her bed and buried her face in the pillows as the pain returned. This time it was sharper still and deeper, more urgent. 'Polly. Polly help me.' She clutched at Polly's hand.

'I'll shout for Peggy to ring the doctor. Hold on, Danuta.'

Danuta felt her snatch away her hand and heard her race for the door. Through the mist of pain she could hear Polly's loud, urgent cries for Peggy to ring the doctor immediately. And she knew her baby was in danger.

She gasped as the pain clenched like a fist. 'Polly,' she breathed. 'Polly, help me. I am frightened for my baby.' She reached for Polly's hand, saw the fleeting look of fear in her friend's eyes and turned away in tears. 'It is my fault,' she sobbed. 'I am too careless. I work and work and did not think of my baby.'

'Hush, now,' soothed Polly, stroking back her sweat-soaked hair. 'You've done nothing wrong, Danuta. I promise. Now, let me help you get cleaned up and undressed.'

Peggy rushed in. 'The doctor's on his way. I caught him just as he was leaving on his rounds, but I can't reach the midwife – she's delivering a baby on the other side of town somewhere.'

'Then I'll just have to do my best,' said Polly, 'but it's been a long time since I worked on maternity, and I hope the doctor gets here quickly.'

'You stay with me?' Danuta pleaded as Polly slipped a clean nightdress over her friend's head.

'We'll both stay for as long as you want,' said Peggy, gathering up the discarded and soiled clothes. She shot Polly a worried look. 'I'll dump this lot in the laundry and get you a nice cold cloth to put on your forehead,' she muttered before racing out of the room and down the stairs.

The pain was coming again and Danuta gripped Polly's hand. She forgot her English and let out a stream of Polish as she tried to deal with the awful sense that she was being squeezed in half – that she'd endangered her precious child by being thoughtless and stubborn – that this pain was her punishment.

'I've left the front door open with Mrs Finch standing guard until the doctor comes,' said Peggy, rushing into the room with a clean cloth, a pile of newspapers, and a bowl of cold water.

Spreading the newspaper over the puddle by the gas fire, she wrung out the cloth in the cold water and gently bathed Danuta's face. 'How quickly are they coming?' she murmured to Polly.

'About every five minutes,' was the grim reply. 'Danuta, I'm going to need to take a look and see what's going on down there. Can you roll on to your back and lift your knees?'

As the pain eased, Danuta uncurled and did as she was asked. She was too far gone to feel any embarrassment.

'She's almost fully dilated,' murmured Polly. 'Whether we like it or not, this baby is on its way. Peggy, get hot water, clean towels, a pair of scissors and some disinfectant – barring that, alcohol would do.'

Danuta was crying now and begging Polly in Polish not to bring her baby out – to try and keep it where it belonged until it was the proper time – for it was all she had left of Jean-Luc and she'd promised to keep it safe.

But her pleas were for nothing because, of course, Polly didn't understand and Danuta was in too much pain for her overwrought brain to work in a foreign language.

'Now, now, Danuta. I'm here, my dear.' Dr Craig was rather out of breath after climbing the stairs, but his gentle voice had an immediate soothing effect on them all as he introduced himself to Peggy and asked Polly for a quick summary of events.

Danuta grabbed his hand, jabbering away in Polish, begging him to stop the baby from coming – to make everything all right.

'Let me have a look and see what's happening down there, and then I can give you a better idea of what to do about it,' he said calmly. He examined Danuta and then placed his stethoscope on her swollen belly and listened intently.

Danuta watched him fearfully, her gaze, fixed to his face, trying to read his expression and gauge his reaction to what he was hearing. She'd been a theatre nurse long enough to know when a doctor was worried about his patient – and she could see Dr Craig's frown as he moved the stethoscope over the tight drum of her swollen belly. Another deep wave of pain began to overwhelm her and she gritted her teeth and tried to fight it.

'Try and work with the pain and you will find it much easier to bear,' said Dr Craig. He took her wrist and felt her pulse, and then returned to the other end of the bed. 'When you feel the urge to push, then do so with all your might,' he said softly and calmly. 'Your baby is on its way.'

'But too soon,' she panted. 'Is he alive? Can you hear his heartbeat?'

'It was very faint,' he replied, as he washed his hands in the bowl of warm water Peggy had brought upstairs. 'He is in some distress, and must be delivered quickly if he's to have any chance of survival.' He glanced at her as he dried his hands, and the doubt in his expression served only to stoke her deepest fears.

The pain was deeper now, more demanding, and the urge to push was overwhelming. She strained and strained and then fell back against the pillows, drenched in sweat, her heart beating like a drum.

'The cord is round the neck,' said Dr Craig sharply. 'Don't push until I tell you,' he ordered Danuta. 'Pass me those scissors, Nurse Brown.'

Danuta could feel the pain returning and the unstoppable need to push her child out, but she resisted, clinging to him, knowing it was all she could do to help save him.

'Now you can push all you like.'

Danuta pushed for all she was worth, the sweat stinging her eyes, every muscle in her body working to give birth.

'That's it, well done,' said Dr Craig.

Danuta felt her child slither from her. There was no cry – no sound at all as Dr Craig wrapped it in the towel. 'Is he alive?' she asked fearfully. 'Why doesn't he cry?'

Dr Craig didn't answer as he laid the bundle on the other bed and gently cleared its mouth and nose before massaging the still chest and breathing into its mouth.

Danuta was vaguely aware of the contraction which shed the afterbirth – of Polly swiftly cleaning her up and pulling the sheet over her. Her whole focus was on the tiny bundle on the other bed, and the man who was so desperately trying to stir life into it

'I have done something wrong for this to happen?' she asked fearfully. 'I have hurt my baby?'

'It is nature's way sometimes,' he murmured sadly. 'You did nothing wrong, Danuta.'

A feeble cry broke the awful silence, and Danuta burst into tears. She reached out for her baby, every part of her yearning to hold him.

'You have a daughter, Danuta,' said Dr Craig, as he carefully placed the bundle in her arms. 'But she is too small and very weak.' There were tears in his eyes as he regarded her. 'I'm so sorry, but there is nothing I can do to save her. You must prepare yourself to say goodbye to her.'

Danuta looked down at the tiny scrap in her arms. A daughter. Jean-Luc's daughter, born of love amidst a time of fear and danger – but born too soon, already preparing to leave her. 'Her name is Katarzyna,' she managed through her tears. 'It means "Pure" in Polish.'

Danuta felt her heart drawn to her as she ran a soft finger over the dark down of her head, felt the tears prick as she saw how beautiful her eyelashes were, how sweet her tiny mouth. She was blinded by her tears as she put her finger against the palm of Katarzyna's star-like hand and felt the ache of profound love as those little fingers curled and tried to grasp.

She kissed the sweet wrinkled face, holding her close, breathing in the scent of her as she heard the fading heartbeat slow and become still. She held her baby to her heart and finally looked through her tears to the sobbing Peggy. 'Our baby is with her father now,' she whispered. 'Please, I would like some moment alone with her.'

Chapter Twenty

The death of tiny Katarzyna had affected them all, and during the following days, the people living at Beach View were faced with the reality of how tenuous the thread of life had become and vowed to do something about it.

Danuta was kept in hospital for a week. It should have been longer, but she defied everyone by discharging herself early, saying she had no business taking up a valuable bed when so many others were in greater need – and that she was determined to attend Katarzyna's funeral and to see her laid to rest beside her uncle Aleksy in the tiny village churchyard outside Cliffehaven.

Matron hadn't been happy about it, and it seemed to underline her opinion that Danuta was headstrong, and that being Polish could be the only excuse for her bad behaviour.

Danuta didn't care what the old witch thought of her. Lying in bed during those long, empty nights, she had come to a decision, and once she was back at Beach View, she began to put together her plan for the future. It would be a very different future now Katarzyna was with her father – but one that would fulfil her need to serve this new country that had sheltered her, and to play her part in its victory against Hitler.

The physical and mental challenges Danuta had faced over the past year had made her strong and determined. She and Ron spent long hours walking the hills, and bit by bit, Danuta felt her strength returning, her muscles hardening again, and knew she was ready. It was two weeks before Christmas when Ron introduced her to his colleague and, after a gruelling session of questions and tests with him, she returned to Beach View to pack.

Peggy was in the kitchen as usual, busy trying to put together some strange concoction dreamed up by the Ministry of Food. Jim was reading the evening paper by the fire, Polly and Mrs Finch were knitting, and the other girls were upstairs listening to music on the gramophone.

'Peggy, I have come to say that I will be leaving tomorrow,' said Danuta.

'But why? Where will you go? It's almost Christmas.' Peggy wiped her hands on her wraparound apron, her expression concerned. 'This is all a bit sudden, isn't it?'

'I have been offered a job at another hospital,' Danuta lied smoothly. 'It is a post as a theatre nurse. I must leave early tomorrow morning.'

'But that's marvellous,' said Polly, standing to give her a hug. 'Which hospital?'

'The St George in London,' Danuta replied, having been well briefed. 'I know it is very dangerous there, but I have waited too long for my skills to be recognised, and I must go.'

Polly grinned at her. 'I'm leaving too. Adam and I have decided to go to see Alice for Christmas,' she said. 'We had the most fearful row about it, because I don't think he's at all ready to travel, but my heart won over my head, and we leave at the weekend.'

'It seems everyone is leaving,' sighed Peggy. 'Christmas just won't be the same, what with Cissy on duty at the air base, Anne tucked away in her little cottage with Martin, who's been forced to take a long rest, and my boys down in Somerset. I have half a mind to get on a train myself and go and see them.'

'There's nothing stopping you,' muttered Jim from behind his newspaper. 'If you can get the permits to travel, then go. Da and I will look after this place.'

Danuta saw the hope dawn on Peggy's face, and understood her longing to be with her children.

'What about Mrs Finch?' Peggy was flustered

now, the hope and doubts fighting a battle within.

'To be sure, me and Da will look after her too, and I'm sure we'll survive on her cooking for a week.'

'Pies for pudding?' twittered Mrs Finch, dropping her knitting and twiddling with her hearing aid. 'What on earth are you talking about, you rogue?'

'I said I'd put up with your cooking,' he shouted.

'How very rude,' she said with a sniff. 'My cooking is excellent. And there's no need to shout, Jim Reilly. I'm not deaf, you know.'

Jim rolled his eyes and grinned before he turned his attention back to Peggy. 'I'll go to the office tomorrow and see what I can do. I'm sure they'll let you go – it's been almost a year since you've seen them.'

'Could you come too?'

He shook his head. 'I'd love to, Peg, me darlin', but I've a cinema to run, warden and fire-watch duties to see to and Mrs Finch to fight with. You go and I promise to try and get to see them soon as I can.'

Danuta watched as Peggy excitedly clapped her hands and began to write a list of things she would have to do before she left. Danuta's heart ached with the familiar longing that haunted her now – the longing to hold her baby again, and to celebrate the magic of life and hope, and the profound bond between mother and child.

She glanced at Polly, who looked radiant now she knew that she would be seeing her little Alice very soon. Leaving them to chatter and discuss their plans, Danuta went upstairs and quietly began to prepare for her own adventure.

Danuta went to say a last farewell to Katarzyna, sitting by the grassy mound of her last resting place, talking to her, telling her of her plans as the chill night closed in. When she returned to Beach View, she and Polly talked long into the night, both too excited to sleep.

As dawn finally came, Danuta silently left her bed and opened the curtains. The seagulls were already squabbling on the roof opposite, the salty scent of the sea coming through the open window as light threaded a stitch along the horizon and bronzed the clouds. It would rain before nightfall, but it didn't matter. This new day heralded the start of her new life.

Excitement churned alongside nervousness as she dressed carefully for her long journey to Berkshire. Her case was packed and stood ready by the door, and although her clothes might be second-hand, they'd been carefully laundered and pressed, and she felt she looked very smart.

Polly woke some minutes later, and they went down to breakfast together. Talk was desultory round the table – goodbyes were always hard – and Danuta didn't have the heart to let them see how excited she was about leaving.

The time came to walk to the station, and she gently declined Polly's offer to accompany her. 'I think it is best to say goodbye here,' she said, softly. 'Thank you for being my friend, Polly. I will never forget you.' She gave her a hug and turned to Peggy.

'Thank you,' she said, taking her hand. 'You have given me a home, and love and support through my dark time. Aleksy and I bless you for that.' She had tears in her eyes as she gently kissed Mrs Finch. 'Goodbye, *Babunia*. Stay well, and know that I love you.'

With a smile to Jim and Ron, she hitched the strap of her tattered canvas bag over her shoulder, picked up her case and gas-mask box, opened the door and purposefully closed it behind her. She didn't know what lay ahead, but she would face it with courage, for her time at Beach View had shown her that there was love in the world still, and that enmity could be vanquished.

Danuta looked back as she reached the corner of Camden Road. Ron was standing on the doorstep, watching her. He was the only one who knew her true destination, and the dangers she would probably have to face, but her secret was safe with him.

He lifted his hand in salute, and she waved back before she turned away and headed fearlessly into her future.

Polly missed not having Danuta to talk to, and it was only after she'd gone that she realised she'd left no forwarding address so she could write to her. Then, she reasoned, she could always send her letters to St George's; they would find her there.

She was packed and ready to leave. As she stood in the hallway to say goodbye to everyone, she felt a tug of regret. She'd suffered many heartaches, in this house, but Peggy and her family had cherished her as if she was their own, and the joys had more than compensated for the tears she'd shed with Peggy. She would miss them horribly. She would probably never return to Cliffehaven, but she would always stay in touch.

Peggy gave her a hug, and a soft kiss on the cheek. 'You must be so excited at the thought of seeing Alice,' she breathed, her eyes sparkling. 'I know I can barely sit still thinking about my boys, and what a lovely Christmas we'll have together.'

Polly nodded, too emotional for words. 'I'd better go,' she said finally when she'd kissed everyone. 'Adam will be getting impatient, and we don't want to miss our train.'

'How will you get to the station?' asked Peggy. 'The trolleybus isn't running today because the rails were blown up.'

Polly giggled. 'Mr Fortescue has insisted his driver take us in his Bentley. How's that for a stately departure?'

'I do wish you weren't going,' said Peggy. 'This house is going to feel very empty without you and Danuta.'

'I'm sure you'll find someone to take our places,' murmured Polly, who'd overheard her on the phone the day before talking to someone at the Billeting Office about her empty room.

She gathered her things and stepped outside. With a smile and a wave, she ran down the steps and headed for Camden Road and the hospital. The wind off the sea was chill, but the sun was shining and all was right in her world. Adam was well again, and soon, *soon,* she could hold her precious Alice in her arms.

She stopped and looked back at Beach View Terrace and smiled. She hadn't known what to expect when she'd arrived here those few traumatic months ago, but the love and solace Peggy and her family had provided had seen her through, and she would hold the memory of them in her heart forever.